W9-CSU-686

Jessica Rydill lives in the West Country with her collection of slightly unnerving dolls. She became obsessed with the departement of Drome after volunteering for a French workcamp in 1980, when she encountered some of the places mentioned in this book. Her interests include myth, dreams and East European music.

Find out more about Jessica Rydill and other Orbit authors by registering for the free monthly newsletter at www.orbitbooks.co.uk

Also by Jessica Rydill

Children of the Shaman

The Glass Mountain

Jessica Rydill

www.orbitbooks.co.uk

An *Orbit* Book

First published in Great Britain by Orbit 2002

Copyright © Jessica Rydill 2002

The moral right of the author has been asserted.

A CIP catalogue record for this book
is available from the British Library.

ISBN 1 84149 112 8

Typeset in Cochin by
Palimpsest Book Production Limited,
Polmont, Stirlingshire
Printed and bound in Great Britain by
Mackays of Chatham PLC, Chatham, Kent

Orbit
An imprint of
Time Warner Books UK
Brettenham House
Lancaster Place
London WC2E 7EN

To my sister, Sarah

Acknowledgements

Once more, I would like to thank my editor Tim Holman for his invaluable input. Miller Lau supported me gamely through the difficult bits, despite her own struggle with cancer. And last but not least, Sue Simmons, performance poet extraordinaire, who helped me imagine the scenes inside the Mountain (even though I did not use the lichen!).

Prologue

Outside the castle walls, the rain fell as if it would never stop. The stranger stood at the chamber window, staring out over the battered parkland with a sombre expression. Ever since he had come to this accursed country, it seemed to have been raining; and when it was not wet, the wind blew, a crazy wind with an edge to it that plucked at the brain. In his mind's eye, golden steppes unfolded under an azure sky, like the enamels of an *eikon*. He could not believe that he had left the court of the Staryetz to seek employment in this forgotten hole, where Death lay like dust on the sheeted furniture, and brooded in the alcoves.

On the parquet floor beside him stood the two suitcases that had travelled the miles from Sklava with him, and his papers – travel permits and a letter of introduction – were folded in a wallet slung from his back. For this journey, he had assumed the guise of a monk, and he observed with a cynical eye the black robes, straggling beard and long unkempt locks that decked his reflection. Only the yellow hue of his eyes that glinted at him from the glass was like a note to remind him of his true nature. The great Magus Kaschai, called the Deathless, would never have humbled himself to such a disguise; but Semyon knew he was not deathless, not yet . . .

The chamber door skreeked open, and a page with a pitiful cough announced his master: the Doyen of Ademar, Lord of the Forest, Seigneur of the lands between Yonar and Axar. Semyon struggled to keep his face straight as he listened to this long recitation. Was he not a subject of the mighty Staryetz of all Sklava, who needed no other title? And the personage that entered the room only served to increase his mirth. For a moment, he wondered if he were in the presence of a living corpse: an old man with a ghastly pale countenance, straight as a skeleton, who walked leaning upon his cane as if it were the iron stand that held up his bones. Semyon bowed.

'Greetings unto you, Semyon of Kiyev,' said the old man in a voice that creaked like the hinge. Semyon approached to bow over his outstretched ring as if the Doyen were a Biskopa or a Patriarch. He found the old man's gaze upon him, steel blue; the eyes were all that lived in the wasted carcass.

'Do you bring me greetings from my cousin, the noble Staryetz?' said the Doyen. Semyon dared not speak for fear that he would burst out laughing. True, kings and emperors might call the Staryetz 'cousin' out of courtesy; but it was absurd that this petty lord in a dark corner of a shattered realm should permit himself the familiarity. He reached into his wallet and brought out the letter of introduction that the Staryetz had dictated to his secretary, months ago, it seemed. The master of the Sklavan empire could barely sign his own name, but he was wily and astute as any high-born Boyar.

The Doyen took the letter in his bird-like grip, broke the wax seal and read. Semyon waited, watching his lips move. The letter itself was a formality, inviting the Doyen to give credence to the bearer and to use him as one of his own subjects, et cetera. It was Semyon who carried the Staryetz's instructions in his memory, perfect to the last letter. He watched the old man read with hungry eyes, eager to reach the heart of the matter – and taste its blood.

At last, the Doyen folded the letter and raised his eyes. He seemed to gaze down on Semyon from the height of scorn, as if he wondered what ragged figure the Staryetz had dispatched to deliver his news.

'It says here that you are a mighty magus, the most powerful at court,' he said. Each word was crisp, loaded with doubt. Semyon bowed. 'Do you have a tongue in your head?' said the Doyen sharply.

'It pleases my master to name me thus, Mon Seigneur,' said Semyon, rolling the foreign words round his tongue.

'I see that you have some grasp of Franj,' said the Doyen. Leaning on his stick, he limped to the campaign chair that was the sole piece of furniture in the room. He sat down, clutching the letter against his knee. His robes were rich, but his woollen cloak had been carefully darned and patched.

'Also some grasp of the Arts Magical,' said Semyon, glancing at his suitcases to make sure that the page had not touched them.

'Indeed, that was why my cousin sent you to me,' said the Doyen, turning his gaze towards that corner of the room. 'He knows of my long-cherished plan to raise up Neustria, our great lost empire. He has written me many letters assuring me of his support. But I trust he has not sent me some mountebank, a counterfeit conjuror that he thinks will satisfy an old man in his dotage.'

Semyon enjoyed the time it took him to answer. 'Do not wrong my master, *Gospodin*,' he said, using a title only he knew to be unsuitable for the Doyen's rank. 'I will be apt for all your purposes, even for the awesome task to which you intend to exalt me.'

'You have, at any rate, a courtier's tongue, in spite of your mean attire,' said the Doyen with a thin-lipped frown. Turning to the page, who had spent the last few minutes vainly trying to stifle his cough, he said, 'Leave us.' When the boy had gone, the Doyen did not speak at once but spent some moments studying Semyon, as if trying to unnerve him. But Semyon, who knew that his own master's smile could bode infinite reward or imminent execution, was not troubled by an old soldier's dour glance. He waited, his eyes modestly downcast, while the old man inspected his frayed and mended habit and the tangles in his hair and beard.

'What word does your master send to me?' said the Doyen at last.

Semyon decided that it was time for an oration. Gazing at the ceiling, he proclaimed, 'Know that my master, the mighty Staryetz of Sklava, has hearkened to your plea and approved your noble cause. He will give you all aid' – *except money* – 'in the reconquest of the lands once known as Neustria. And he has sent me, Semyon the Magus, to lay my powers at your feet and to do as you command. Above all, in the secret matter concerning your son.'

'My son,' the Doyen echoed, and his voice might have been some reverberation of the hills. Semyon sneaked a glance at his face, and saw without pity the lost look that had touched the old man's features and withered them with the frost of age and grief. He waited, in a semblance of respect, for the moment to pass, and was caught unawares when the blue gaze seized his own. For the first time, sweet fear returned and he knew the pleasure of serving a dread ruler. 'Can you bring him back for me?' said the Doyen. 'Are you the one?'

Semyon bowed, with his hand on his breast, recognising the divine madness of power. Power was a sweetmeat bestowed by the great, but it gave him joy to serve in its shadow. 'Truly, *Knyaz*, I am the one,' he said, using the word for 'Prince' as he should have done before. The Doyen noticed.

'You honour me with many outlandish titles,' he snapped. 'I pray you, call me Mon Seigneur after the manner of my vassals. These foreign terms do not sit well with me.'

Commanding one moment, petulant the next. Semyon studied his new lord sidelong. The Doyen might be a petty prince beside the greatness of the Staryetz, but he had learned all the tricks of the absolute ruler – the whims, the changes of mood, the vanities. A servant must study these foibles in order to satisfy the will of the master. Only thus would he himself grow in favour, and in power. Semyon had magic to play with like a toy under his hand, but the scent of temporal power was a more potent drug – above all, the power to manipulate one's lord by subtle means. He was eminent in court at Kiyev because he could do so much more than merely flatter his chosen liege. Let Kaschai think himself omnipotent! Those who were clever knew that these were new times, when magic alone was not enough to hold sway.

'Mon Seigneur,' he said, 'I know how to raise your son from the dead. To bring him back alive, not as a wraith or a walking corpse.'

The Doyen stared at him, breathing fast. 'I have dreamed so many times of this day, since I lost him, and of hearing those words,' he said. 'Now it seems like another dream that you stand before me, telling me that which I wish to hear above all in this world. I fear to wake.'

'Do not fear!' said Semyon, turning and striding to pick up one of the suitcases. 'I carry here the means to raise him up. Within this insignificant box, a world lies waiting at my command. With its power I shall turn death to life and tears to rejoicing.' He paused, wondering how much he should reveal at this first interview. It always irked him to explain the workings of magic to his clients; they were forever asking awkward questions, and the Doyen proved to be the same as the rest.

'You tell me that you carry a whole world within that leathern chest?' he said, raising his brows. 'You ask me to place great faith in you.'

Semyon quelled an impatient urge to open the suitcase and let the old fool see just what it contained. 'Truly, this world lies at my command,' he said, with a show of modesty. 'I shall draw upon its vital forces and use them to summon the soul of your son and knit it once more with mortal flesh. But you must understand, Mon Seigneur, that this is the most profound magic. I will have need of other elements to sustain your son in his new being.'

'You speak darkly, Magus,' said the Doyen. 'Tell me what it is you need.'

Semyon could see that it would be no use trying to mystify his patron with arcane words. Just as the Staryetz relished the aura of the occult, even though he was clever enough to see through its trappings, so the Doyen demanded plain speech and a clear explanation. Semyon bridled a little at the thought that he must eschew the pleasure of mystery.

'Mon Seigneur, I can bring your son to life – but it will be a short term, merely ninety days. To keep him in this sublunary world, I will need more than the forces that I carry with me.'

'Say on,' said the Doyen wearily. 'I take it you must perform certain rituals. That you need to observe the movements of the stars and planets.'

'The stars do not rule our destinies,' said Semyon, pausing for dramatic effect. The old man must understand that magic needed more than simple words; it cried out for embellishment, burning cressets and swirling incense. He relished for a moment the shock his next words would create. 'I must have two human souls and the heart of a thrice-powerful shaman.'

To his disappointment, the Doyen studied him, his face unmoving. 'Two human souls and the heart of a . . . shaman,' he said. 'And these will be easy for you to procure?'

The old fox was mocking him! Semyon felt chagrin redden his cheeks. He turned away, trying to contain his anger. How dare this insignificant country squire disparage his craft?

'I am a stealer of souls,' he said, staring out at the green parkland beneath the rain. 'Give me two mortal beings and I will husk them like corn. But the heart of a shaman – that is not so easy. Few bear the name thrice-powerful. I know of none in the empire of Sklava, from the west to the distant east. And I am the man who knows the name of every shaman in the land, whether insignificant or great.'

Behind him the Doyen's voice said, softly, 'I have heard of these shamans. And a shaman slew my son.'

Semyon thought it best not to divulge that he himself was a shaman, and thrice-powerful. There was no need to mention Kaschai the Deathless, who was too wily to keep his heart inside his body. He found himself hoping that the Doyen would pronounce the task impossible, and give him leave to go.

'Then you have them in this . . . country of Neustria,' he said, turning back to face the room. The Doyen had a strange look on his face, one that unnerved Semyon, though he was careful not to show it. It reminded him of a dog's animal mask before it attacked.

'Tell me what makes a thrice-powerful shaman, Magus,' he said. 'It may be that I know where one such is to be found.'

Semyon thought quickly. 'Mon Seigneur, they have all three shamanic powers,' he said. 'They can heal, they can kill, and they can travel beyond this world. And when they die . . .' He paused uneasily. 'It is not certain that they are truly dead,' he added, noticing how lame the words sounded.

The Doyen seemed to stare off into space. 'How strange it is that he should be suited to your purpose,' he said. 'I have dreamed so long of revenge that the sweet taste became bitter, and gnawed at my entrails. I do not know where he dwells, save that he is here, in Neustria, his life mocking me with every breath. He slew my son, and still lives.'

'You have someone in mind,' said Semyon, wondering for the first time about the shamans of Neustria. He had imagined that they would be few, and weak, or the country would by now have gathered its severed lands together under the guiding hand of a mighty ruler. It had not occurred to him that there might be any that warranted the description thrice-powerful, thus creating the risk that his mission – the magical part – might succeed.

'Take his heart, and bring it to me,' said the Doyen. 'His heart, and the souls of his progeny. There were two. This alone will assuage my bitter grievance and quiet my mind at last. I will have no other. I can tell you their names, and when you have brought me my son, you, Magus, will find them and use them to heal his life.'

'There must be many whose souls I could use,' said Semyon quickly. 'Why send me on an errand to find two who may be well hidden?'

'I will have no other,' the Doyen repeated.

Semyon repressed a sigh. His hope of a swift return home faded like smoke in the air. 'Tell me their names, Mon Seigneur, and I will begin the work,' he said.

'The man you seek is named Yuda Vasilyevich. I will have his heart, and the souls of his children.'

Chapter 1

The two girls stood side by side on the table, which represented their chariot as they entered Persepolis. Annat was brandishing a horse-whip, which she cracked with a ferocious sound over the heads of her captives, who crouched on the floor, their summer gowns fluffed with dust and their petticoats awry. Beside her, Eugenie stood with her hands folded demurely before her, though her cheeks were flushed with excitement. As Queen Zenocrate, she was wearing a diadem hastily coiled out of piano wire. Her porcelain beauty made a fine contrast with Annat's fiery darkness; she wore a gown of layered taffeta strewn with pink and red woven peonies, and a muslin bertha that modestly covered her shoulders and décolletage. The merest hint of white pantalets peeked out beneath the multitude of petticoats, stiffened with crinoline, that bore up her skirts. Beside her, clad in the black the law forced her to wear, Annat stood with her legs spread out. Although they were modestly hidden by white broderie pantalets, her skirt was cut short just below the knee, and the fichu that decorated her bodice was askew. Wisps of dark hair escaped from the smooth chignon on her head, and she was a picture of dishevelment that caused Mademoiselle de Clignancourt's heart to sink in dismay when she flung open the music room door to see who was making such a noise.

The mistress clapped her hands together with a sharp report, once, twice.

'*Les jeunes filles!* Annat! Mademoiselle de Bouget! Come down from there *at once!*'

The two young women stared at her. Eugenie's pretty mouth made a rounded O of horror, but the mistress saw Annat's dark brows clamp down into a mutinous frown.

'At once, I say! What is this disgraceful charade? Agnes and Therèse, you may stand up. Now, who is responsible for this? I am waiting!'

Annat sprang down from the table, a manoeuvre that revealed still more of her pantalets. She turned and offered her hand to Eugenie, helping the Princesse descend with all the gallantry proper to a man – but not to a young maiden of seventeen! Mademoiselle de Clignancourt observed this proceeding with pursed lips. Every time that girl returned from the six months spent with her father, she was nothing but trouble! And the trouble seemed to last longer with every visit.

'Well,' she said crisply, 'I am waiting for an explanation.'

The four girls faced her. Agnes and Therèse, who

were undoubtedly dupes, tried to brush the dust from their skirts as if she could not see them. Annat glared at her, holding the Princesse de Bouget's delicate fingers in her sallow grip. Mademoiselle hardly needed to ask who was to blame; it was the Vasilyevich girl, up to her usual tricks, with the Princesse abetting her, since Eugenie was all too clearly infatuated with the little pirate. Against her will, Mademoiselle felt a twinge of amusement at the incongruity of it. The de Bougets were an old Doxan family, who could trace their ancestry back to the time of the Empire; the Vasilyevichs were upstart Wanderers from Sklava, who had settled in Neustria barely a generation past. What Eugenie's mother, *Madame la Princesse* de Bouget, would say if she knew of this misalliance, heaven only knew.

'We were rehearsing a scene from *Timur the Lame*, Mademoiselle,' said Annat. There was no fear or remorse in those dark eyes, only defiance. Many girls at the school bore a dark complexion and swart eyes, but only the Wanderer had that ivory pallor that hardly darkened under the summer sky.

'So I see,' said Mademoiselle, who was not to be intimidated by some chit of a girl, even one with uncanny powers. Annat looked down. 'You two, Agnes and Thérèse, go back to class. I shall deal with you later. As for you, Mesdemoiselles Vasilyevich and de Bouget, you may wait for me outside the Principal's office. And I will take that whip!'

Arm in arm, Annat and Eugenie scurried along the carpeted corridor towards the Principal's rooms.

Eugenie had forgotten to take off her crown, and it was Annat who stopped her and hastily plucked the wire diadem from the Princesse's chestnut ringlets.

'Do you think they'll thrash us, Anne?' said Eugenie, with a mixture of curiosity and fear.

Annat blew out her cheeks. *'Pouf! Non,'* she said. 'They never thrash the seniors. And they couldn't thrash you, *Mademoiselle la Princesse*. Think of the *scandale*!'

Eugenie laughed through her fingers, and Annat longed to kiss her soft lips. She caught the Princesse by the waist and pulled her against her, as she had seen her father do with women. Eugenie struggled a little, and laid her hand against Annat's mouth.

'Someone is sure to come by!'

Annat released her, smiling. Sentimental friendships between pupils were not frowned on, but she knew that her feelings for Eugenie went beyond that. The rose-madder lips, the azure eyes, those hidden, faintly swelling breasts . . . She did not think her desire would meet with the Principal's approval.

'I want to kiss you, Eugenie de Bouget,' she said, and then they both burst out laughing and hugged each other before hurrying on to meet their doom.

The Principal's office was painted white. Heavy jacquard curtains draped the window, woven with pomegranates in red and gold. The Wheel of Doxa hung on one wall, but it was the only hint of a religious hierarchy in the school. The other panelled walls bore gilt-framed maps, and a large globe of the *orbis terrarum* stood near the window. There was a desk, and a chair in which the Principal sat. She wore a gown of slate-coloured damask, a watch pinned to her breast, and a lace collar ruffled to the throat. Her face was smooth under its powder, so smooth that Annat wondered whether she ever smiled or frowned.

'Mademoiselle de Clignancourt has been telling me . . .' she paused, as if to allow space for a sigh, 'of your latest exploits, Mademoiselle Vasilyevich.'

The two young women stood side by side before the desk. Mademoiselle de Clignancourt herself sat on a spindle-legged chair, the skirt of her blue dress spread out in heavy, sumptuous folds. She was holding the whip in one hand.

'Madame, we were rehearsing—' Annat began.

'Silence! I do not care what colour you choose to give to your mischief. All I know is that once again, you have been found as the ringleader in a scene of hoydenish behaviour not acceptable for the young ladies of this Academy.'

'But Madame—' Eugenie began.

'Mademoiselle de Bouget, one would have thought that someone of your rank and breeding would have known better than to sink to such depths. Or to let yourself be led by Mademoiselle Vasilyevich, against whose influence you have been warned. But as an agent, not a principal, in this enterprise, your punishment will be less. Your privileges are suspended for the rest of the week, and you will spend the leisure hour copying passages from the *Livre de Bon Conseil*. You may go.'

Annat felt Eugenie sigh. A thrashing might have been preferable, for they would be denied each other's company, and they both knew how dull were the nostrums of the *Livre de Bon Conseil*. She would have liked to touch her friend's hand, but she knew that Madame's gaze was fixed on them both, and she had to stand alone while Eugenie padded from the room in a rustle of petticoats. When the door had closed behind her, Madame focused on Annat alone.

'As for you, Mademoiselle Vasilyevich, what am I to do with you? Heaven knows I have suffered enough of your mischief. Need I tell you again that it was only as a favour to your aunt, one of the most respected *professeurs* in this city, that I agreed to take you on. You have privileges most of my pupils can only dream of: you are spared attendance for all the winter term and half of the spring, so that you may stay with your father; you are excused afternoon lessons and evening study, because of your attendance at the *Shkola*; and, out of respect for your aunt, I have permitted you to modify your attire in this extraordinary way, which can barely be called modest. Nevertheless, for the past two years you have abused my kindness and flouted my rules. You have been warned many times, and yet once more I find you using your influence to mislead other girls, and in particular, the Princesse de Bouget, to whom you show a most unhealthy attachment. What do you have to say for yourself?'

Annat's emotions welled up in her chest, hot and tight. She let loose a tirade in furious Franj, spilling out all the frustrations that had been building up in her since she returned to Madame Mireille's Academy for Young Ladies.

'But they are stupid rules, Madame! How can I rehearse for a play if it is not permitted to act? And why is it wrong for us to stand on the table? Nobody saw us except Mademoiselle de Clignancourt, and there was no need for her to be shocked—'

'Enough,' said the Principal in her cool voice. 'I see that, as usual, you show no remorse. I have no alternative but to send you home until I have decided whether or not to expel you. I will write to your aunt.'

She lowered her eyes as if there was nothing more to be said. Silenced for an instant, Annat stared at her in dismay. She had never imagined that the Principal would consider her expulsion. She started forward a pace, and began, 'But Madame, you cannot expel me! I have to come here to learn the Arts and Sciences which they do not teach at the *Shkola*—'

'Perhaps you should have thought of that before embarking on your latest rashness,' said Madame, gazing up at her.

'Please punish me, Madame! I'll do anything. I could write lines, or study the *Livre de Bon Conseil*, or you could whip me—'

'A senior? That would be most unseemly. You have leave to go, Mademoiselle Vasilyevich. The interview is finished.'

Annat opened her mouth to protest, but Madame had lowered her gaze once more, and picked up her pen. Mademoiselle de Clignancourt had risen to her feet and was looking at Annat with something like regret, for she liked the girl's spirit, even if she deplored her behaviour. Swallowing a sudden urge to cry, Annat bobbed a quick curtsey and fled the room. She would have liked to run up to the dormitory in search of Eugenie's consoling arms, but she did not want to get her friend into more trouble. Instead, with drooping shoulders and bent head, she walked along the marble floor that led from the Principal's office to the stairs, and slouched down towards the basement where her cape hung on its peg.

She would not go straight home to Aunt Yuste. Instead, she would go to the *Shkola* early. Though her classes did not start until after lunch, some of her friends might be there already – or she could take refuge in the library to do more work on her current assignment.

There was a book of poems by the Angliyan poet Xelle that Eugenie had given her, bulging in the hanging pocket of her cape. Annat took out the small volume and gazed at the foreign characters. The Anglitskuyi used the same writing as the Franj, but their tongue was quite different. Xelle had believed in the cause of freedom, which was why Eugenie had chosen his poetry as a gift for Annat. Inside, she had inscribed a few couplets of her own, dedicating the gift to her 'beloved friend'. Annat squeezed the book in her palm, wondering if Eugenie shared the same passionate and physical sensations as she did. Perhaps, if she were expelled, she would never find out; it was most unlikely that she would meet the Princesse de Bouget outside the Academy. She shut her eyes, feeling a prickling in her nose and beneath her lids. It would be shaming if someone found her weeping here, in the cloakroom.

To reach the *Shkola* from the Academy, Annat would have to take a tram. Outside were a spring day and a blue sky shot with grey, which made her spirits lift. The streets of the elegant *quartier* where the Academy stood were bustling with traffic. A *gendarme* rode by in his stiff uniform of blue serge, with a white feather in his kepi, and saluted Annat as he passed. There was a *boulangerie* across the road, where a small queue waited for the latest batch of fresh loaves, and next door a *boucherie chevaline*, with a plaster horse's head neighing disgustingly above the window. Outside, a nag that looked ready to be horsemeat drooped between the shafts of a small cart loaded with produce from a farm on the outskirts of the city. As Annat crossed the road, she caught the astringent scent of citrus from the piles of misshapen lemons and small, fierce oranges that grew on the south coasts.

The city had changed so much since she came here as a child, four years ago. Since the new City Council was elected, all the old rules of the Neustrian Empire governing dress had been enforced. Women had to cover their legs, and married women their hair; men could not go shirtless, and the respectable wore hats. Masalyar, the town that had once seemed so free it was almost lawless, had become a shadowed, austere place. No wonder her father had decided to leave as soon as possible after bringing her back to her aunt! Annat sighed as she walked down the street towards the tram halt. The new rules made little difference to her, since it had been much the same in her childhood home, the village of Sankt-Eglis. At least in the city no one persecuted Wanderers, or even seemed to notice the black she was obliged to wear. But the change seemed ominous to her, as if it were the beginning of something less harmless.

At this time of the morning, there was no one else waiting at the tram stop. At first, Annat took out the book of Xelle's poetry and tried to read, but her mind was too busy to concentrate on the foreign words. She put the volume away, and gazed at the business of the street, only half aware of what passed before her. A group of *nonnes* in their white sea-bird wimples and blue habits flocked past, two abreast; an elegant *citoyenne*, dressed in a plaid gown and bodice, the skirt stiff with many petticoats, swept by; bicycles bumped over the cobbles and tram rails, and manicured horses, their coats polished to a high shine, paced elegantly down the road, their riders seated high above the walkers. Annat was a lone Wanderer, unregarded, a shadowy figure standing with her back to the railings of the *Jardin des Plantes*.

Like most of the other women in the street, Annat wore a poke bonnet. Hers was made of plain straw, sheltering her face from the spring wind. She glanced up at the sky above the tall roofs of the houses opposite, to see the white clouds scudding past on their way inland from the sea. It was hard to believe, standing here in the midst of Masalyar, that she had once gone on a Journey so strange that no one would believe her if she told them of it, a Journey beyond the world. At the *Shkola*, the Teacher Sival was currently instructing them in the theory of such Journeys, and he often turned to Annat to ask her about her experience. It seemed odd, sitting cross-legged on the floor in the warm classroom, to talk about the frozen land she had visited. As if it were a dream that had happened to someone else, another Annat. The child of four years ago seemed very different to the young woman standing at the tram stop today. And yet none of her fellow students at the *Shkola*, all shamans like herself, had undertaken such a Journey, or would dare to try it until they were fully trained. After those classes, they would regard Annat with a touch of awe; but then they had all heard of her father, Yuda Vasilyevich, one of the most powerful shamans in Masalyar.

Annat folded her arms under her cloak. She wished she were with her father now, travelling to the city of Yonar in the distant north. But she had to spend six months a year living with her aunt in Masalyar and studying, the months of spring and summer, when it would have been wonderful to ride on the trains with *Tate* and follow him as his apprentice . . . Instead, she only lived with him during autumn and winter, and at those times he mostly returned to the city to live in a small house out near the marshes. The *cabane* . . . The best times there happened at the Winter Solstice, when her brother came home from university and Aunt Yuste and Sival left the *Shkola* to stay with them. They celebrated the Candle Feast together for nine days, and the snow closed them off from the outside world.

A movement overhead caught Annat's eye, startling her out of her dreams. At the same time that she heard the ringing bell of the approaching tram, she saw a flock of birds wheeling above the rooftops, like pigeons or starlings. But these birds made heavy black shapes against the sky, their crooked wings beating slowly as they circled overhead in a crowd of darkness. Crows. Annat's heart began to beat faster than it should, and she hurried to meet the tram as if she were running from a nightmare. It was only when she had collapsed on to a wooden seat, and the humming tram was speeding away from the halt, that she bent her head to peer out of the window at the sky above. They were there, on patrol above the streets of Masalyar, just as she had seen them four years ago, spying on another city far away.

Chapter 2

Annat had barely begun to master her panic when she reached her stop and descended not far from the *Shkola*, which stood near the Railway station and the docks. Her first instinct was to ask the Teacher what it meant, but he knew no more of her past than she had told him. Her father would have been the one to tell, but he was far away, out of the reach of her thoughts. She scurried up the steps into the building, unfastening the ribbons that tied her bonnet beneath her chin, and letting it slip back on her shoulders. She paused for a moment on the floor of black and white tiles, and gazed up the tall stairwell towards the apartment that she shared with her aunt and Sival. Two fears, vying with each other in her mind: would Madame Mireille have sent the letter to her aunt by hand, and would Yuste have read it already? The shadow of the crows seemed to encircle her earlier anxiety, mocking it with the pattern of its black wings.

She pushed open a swing door and stepped through into the *Shkola* itself. The usual smells, of *kava*, *tabak* and the burnt-toast scent of clumsy magic, came to meet her. The atmosphere was so different to the aseptic world of the Academy, with its faint whiff of furniture polish and dried lavender. The spices of lunch being prepared in the kitchens below hung in the air, and Annat's mouth began to water. The murmur of voices from the classrooms either side of the passage came to her as she hurried along. She was making for the students' common room on the floor below, where it shared the basement with the dining room and the kitchens.

To her regret, she found the common room deserted. Morning classes had not finished yet, and no one had so far arrived for the afternoon sessions. Most of the older students like Annat either attended another college or *école* in the morning, or worked to support their studies. Taking off her cloak, she slumped into one of the velvet-covered armchairs that filled the common room, and put her slippered feet up on a low table. There was a loud, muffled boom from upstairs, and she suppressed a smile. The younger students were learning how to control their powers, and there were always accidents at the start of term. No one had yet set light to the building, but some of the classrooms bore the scars left by students who had not mastered their fighting skills. Often she would see them over lunch, with singed hair and eyebrows, or their hands newly bandaged from power-burns.

Annat herself was taking two courses, Advanced

Healing and Travel. Because of the time she spent with her father, she had been able to skip many of the more basic studies, but both he and Sival had insisted that she follow the five-year Healing course in full. Annat found the Healing lessons hard work and often dull, but she looked forward to her weekly Travel class, when Sival might be distracted into telling them of his own Journeys, or persuaded to levitate. Sival was not himself a shaman, but he had brought with him from Ind certain skills of the saddhus or holy men of his country, and the young shamans he taught were fascinated by this magic, which had nothing to do with their heritage.

The door swung open, and Dani strode into the room, hugging files. Like Annat, he was a Wanderer, the only other one in her class, but he came from a much stricter home. He sported a black hat, side-curls or *peyes*, and the beginnings of a brown beard. He was tall for a Wanderer or a shaman; he sat down stiffly in a chair opposite Annat and greeted her without looking at her directly: 'There is One in Zyon.'

'One, and One only,' Annat responded. 'Hi, Dani. How's your *mame*?'

Dani put the files down on the floor at his feet and sat gazing at them. 'She's well, thank you, Natka,' he said. In spite of his distant manner, Dani was Annat's friend, but the Law of the Wanderers forbade him to look at women. Annat smiled secretly to herself, wondering if the Law of the Wanderers had ever stopped her father looking at women, not to mention her brother. But neither Yuda nor Malchik was particularly welcome in the *Beit*, the House of Teaching where the Wanderers of Masalyar gathered to pray. She liked Dani because he had befriended her in spite of her family's doubtful status in the community.

'Did you read the commentary of Rashim Edra Ben Shammi that I gave you?' he went on, sitting back comfortably in his chair and staring awkwardly at his lap. He was forever giving Annat passages from the Zahav, the book of Wanderer commentaries and teachings, to read. Since she was neither a man nor a scholar, this was a strange thing to do, and Annat suspected that Dani liked her a little more than he should a simple friend. She thought that he had stolen glances at her when they were sitting in class.

'I tried to read it,' she said, determined to be honest. 'But I had to spend so much time on the theory that the Teacher gave us to prepare for today.'

The thought of the Travel lesson recalled to her the crows she had seen this morning. 'Dani,' she went on, 'have you noticed anything strange in the city?'

Dani swung his head from side to side. 'I don't know. Nothing particular. But I tried a small Journey exercise last night, as Sival advised. I made some notes when I returned.'

Annat leant forward in her chair, intrigued, and Dani leant back in his. She was excused such exercises because of her Journey four years ago; today's lesson would be the first one in which she was allowed to participate fully.

'What did you see?'

She caught a glimpse of his brown eyes. Rather hesitantly, he began to use *sprechen*, which he often avoided with Annat, for much the same reasons that he shunned her gaze.

– *I met your father.*

– *My father!* Annat shrieked her thought, and saw Dani wince. There were still times when she forgot how loud her thoughts could be; it was no help that she perceived the thoughts of other shamans as writing, whereas they seemed to hear hers.

– *How did you know it was him?*

– *The most powerful shaman in Masalyar? I could hardly miss him. Also he said* – Dani paused – *'Who the f*** are you?'*

Annat covered her face with her hands and laughed. This was so typical of her father that it could not have been anyone else. No shaman would greet another in such terms if they met while Travelling in a shaman world. Formal courtesies and a wary exchange of greetings were expected; Sival had explained to them that they might encounter other Travellers during their first Journeys, and should always make their excuses and withdraw. A trained shaman on serious business would not want to be disturbed.

– *What did you say to him?* she asked.

– *What could I say?* Dani raised his eyes to heaven. – *I apologised for disturbing him. Then he told me to stay and explain what I was doing.*

– *Where were you? What were you doing?*

Dani shook his head. – *I wish I knew. I did all the things Sival advised us to do. I went into trance mode, chose a shaman gate and entered. It didn't seem very interesting. Just one of those transdimensional corridors that appears as a passageway full of boxes. When I met your father, he was looking inside the boxes.*

— But Sival told us there was never anything in the boxes!

— I think that may be one of those things they don't teach us about. To stop us interfering. Maybe they think we couldn't deal with what's inside.

— Did Tate *tell you what he was looking for?*

— He said he was trying to find a rogue shaman. He said, 'There's a rogue shaman from Sklava on the loose. I can smell him, but I can't find the b*******.'

'A rogue shaman from Sklava!' said Annat, excitedly. 'But *Tate* is hundreds of miles away, in Yonar. He never told me anything about it.'

'I guess outside this world, distances don't matter,' said Dani, embarrassed to be showing off his knowledge. 'I think it was he who brought me there. He opened a box that had my name on it.'

'"Dani Magidovich",' said Annat, trying not to laugh. 'Perhaps he thought *you* were the rogue shaman.'

The bell rang to signal the start of afternoon class. Dani stooped to pick up his files, and Annat clambered out of the chair, shaking out her skirts. 'I think you should tell the Teacher,' she said. 'I have to see him after class. I saw the crows flying over Masalyar.'

'Crows?' said Dani, unable to avoid looking at her in surprise. Annat felt an unexpected shyness of telling him what she knew.

'Come on, we don't want to be late,' she said, hurrying for the door. 'I'll explain after school!'

The classrooms of the *Shkola* were very different to the formality of the Academy. There, the pupils sat in rows behind wooden desks facing a chalkboard, and called their teachers Madame or Mam'selle. The floors were made of wooden parquet polished to a shine, and the high windows bore a framework of bars – elegantly curved, but bars nonetheless. In Sival's classroom, there were no chairs, but a shingle of comfortable cushions strewn across the carpet. In spring and summer, the windows hung open to let in the sound of the streets outside, and the walls were covered in an array of pictures and writings, some inscribed in Sival's neat italic hand, others printed in the script of his native tongue, Khafji, the language of Ind. There were clumsy, vivid drawings of Indic bazaars, people and animals, sent to him by the children of his nephews back home; delicate illuminations in which blue-faced gods addressed their love to veiled maidens; and many torn-out pieces of paper or cardboard from packets that had once housed the produce that passed through Masalyar, whether it be grapes, oranges, *tabak*, *kava*, leather, charcoal or sugar. Sival told each new class how these fragments of an alien culture entranced him with their foreign letters and stylised images. He was particularly fond of paper bags from the hundred-year-old *confiserie* Chez Celimene, with its picture of an old-fashioned lady carrying a parasol, and as they grew yellowed with age, he would stick up new ones.

Sival was waiting for them as they filed into the room; he sat cross-legged on the floor, wearing his usual attire of tunic and *dhoti*, with a small cap set neatly on his nearly bald head. His skin was dark as tobacco and marked in many places with the darker spots of age, and he had smiled many wrinkles into the skin. They called him Teacher, or sometimes *Guru-ji*, and he called them *mes enfants*, my children, in accent-less Franj. He waited until they had all found their favourite places and made themselves comfortable amongst the cushions. This was less than easy for some of the women, since the new dress codes of the City Council forced them to cover their legs to the ankle; a few, like Annat, had taken to wearing knee-length skirts over pantalets, in an attempt to regain some freedom of movement. The more conformist or fashion-conscious had to arrange their heavy skirts and petti-coats, so that at last they looked like peony blossoms spread out over the floor, settled amongst the thick satin flounces of their gowns. Some of the boys were scarcely more comfortable in stiff serge suits, and Dani in particular kept moving, trying to find a better way to sit. Sival watched them indulgently; when he was certain that they were settled, he began to speak in his softly modulated voice. It was as if he were telling them a story.

'Today, *les enfants*, we will speak again of Travel,' he said. 'I hope that, one by one, you have begun to make your own Journeys, and to learn a little of the galaxy of shaman worlds surrounding this, our outer world.' He paused, smiling to himself at the mixed metaphor. 'But before you begin to make the Great Journey, and Travel freely amongst the stars, you must learn how to protect yourselves when you go forth alone. Zelie, please take us on from Chapter Ten, page three hundred and four of Sorgay.'

There was a short, collective sigh as the students picked up the thick volume and spread it out on their laps. Annat was glad that she had remembered to mark the page last week. She wished that Sival had asked her to read instead of Zelie; the girl had a boring, singsong voice, which made it more difficult to follow the long sentences. She was tempted to *sprechen* with her friend Pashmir, but she knew that Sival would notice; he had been teaching shamans for so long that he had learned all their tricks. She glanced at Dani, thinking of his encounter with her father, and watched him writing notes in the margin with a lead pencil.

'Annat,' said Sival suddenly, 'what do you think Sorgay means when he talks of "the dark and under road"?'

It was no use pretending. Without raising her eyes, Annat said, 'I was not listening, *Guru-ji.*'

'Share your thoughts,' said Sival gently. Sometimes, when he had reason to be angry, this could become a punishment; usually, he was truly interested to know what made his students inattentive.

'Dani told me that he met Yuda on his Journey,' said Annat. Two of the younger girls giggled, and Sival gave a short sigh.

'I see that Yuda can still disrupt my lessons even when he is not here himself,' he said. 'I know that Sorgay is hard to follow, *mon enfant*, but you need to know his words. Did you read through the text last night?' Annat nodded. 'Then you can tell me of the dark and under road.'

Annat hesitated, trying to shape her thoughts, and then began, 'Some paths lie outward, to worlds beyond the stars. Others go inward, to worlds below the ground, shadow-places.'

'Very good. But why does it matter, Pashmir?'

The Sulimite girl looked up at Sival from under her long lashes and said, 'The inward worlds are more dangerous.'

Sival nodded, as if she had just told him something new. 'When you go on a Journey, *mes enfants*, you must learn how to leave a trail. That way, if you are lost, others may follow you to bring you back.'

Annat thought of her own Journey, when she had entered an underground world with her father. She did not remember him leaving a trail. She hesitated to speak her thought aloud, though she feared that some of her fellow students might have overheard it; they must be sick of hearing about her adventures. Pashmir voiced it for her.

'I understand,' she said tactfully, earning a quick smile from Annat, 'that the great shamans do not always trouble to leave a trail.'

'It is true,' said Sival. 'Iskander of Xeryx refused to lead others into danger. Some have taken trusted companions,' he added, answering Annat's thought. 'But a young shaman, a lone shaman, should always leave a trail. And I shall teach you that today. You can put Sorgay away now,' he added, chuckling to hear their groans.

Annat's attention did not wander during the next hour. At first, Sival told them stories of famous Journeys, sketching pictures in the air with his hands. Then he asked them to enter trance mode, a simple precondition for most Travel, and to make a trail from there. When they awakened, they found the classroom littered with the results of their efforts. Zelie had managed to call up most of Sival's collection of paper bags, and scatter them in a long line. Pashmir had conjured a jinni, a sullen being with yellow eyes, which refused to speak and vanished in a puff of smoke. Dani produced Ebreu letters, which danced in the air; and Annat had, to her dismay, summoned a shadowy trail of black-winged birds. A few of the others had caused objects to manifest, such as pencils, erasers and chalk; one boy materialised some sad, soggy ectoplasm; and the rest had nothing at all.

'Not bad for a first attempt,' said Sival, as someone scooped up the ectoplasm and dropped it into the wastepaper basket. The other manifestations faded. 'But it is important to leave a trail that others will understand. I want you to practise this at home. Please try not to summon ectoplasm; it leaves a stain on the carpet.'

'Why did I make crows?' said Annat.

'I don't know,' said Sival. 'I expected the paper trail from Zelie – yes, you may pick them up and re-attach them to the wall – and Dani and Pashmir both showed shapes that I would expect, belonging to their myth and religion. I was rather hoping that you would show me a train, Annat, since you made your Journey underground in that unusual vehicle. Crows are unexpected.'

'I saw them flying over the city this morning,' said Annat, suddenly cold. Sival gazed at her, unsmiling.

'We will talk after class,' he said. 'But now, *les enfants*, we must return to Sorgay to read what he says about trails. I think you may find it interesting.'

Yuste Vasilyevich sat alone in the spring twilight that filled her office in the *Shkola*. The firefly globe of an oil lamp provided insufficient light for her to read the two letters open on the desk before her, but she already knew what was in them both. A storm of shadowy emotions filled her and, as often at such times, she was reminded of the sea near her old home in Sankt-Eglis, which seemed so placid and could prove so deadly.

She knew that Annat was avoiding her. The girl had returned for afternoon lessons, sure enough, but class had long finished, and Yuste was certain that Annat was lingering in the common room with her friends, putting off the time when the trouble with Madame Mireille would have to be faced.

Yuste took off her gold-rimmed spectacles and laid them lightly on top of the desk. She only needed to wear them for reading. She massaged her temples with her fingertips, wishing it did not have to be like this all the time, one long fight. Each year, when Annat returned from her months with Yuda, it grew a little harder to keep her in check. And this year had been the worst yet. Only a few weeks since the start of term, and already Madame Mireille was threatening to expel the girl! Yuste would have laughed if she had not felt so bone-weary.

She wondered whether to send to Yuda. As twins, they shared a power that no other shaman seemed to possess; and it was the only power Yuste had left. She could reach out to her brother in her thoughts when he was far away, and he could answer. It was not like *sprechen*, the silent speech that shamans used amongst themselves, which never worked at a distance. Yuste thought of Yuda and saw the vivid, busy patterns of his mind outlined against her lids. But what would she tell him? That she was worried about Annat? That Malchik had sent her a letter?

Yuste opened her eyes and laid her right hand on the thin paper of the second letter, as if she could read it through her fingertips. At least Yuda might understand what his son had written. The jagged black handwriting, the broken phrases, all spoke to her of a disordered mind. She had received so many letters from her nephew, full of news about his college life, and always carefully written; and now this!

The door opened, and Sival came in; he had his arm round Annat's shoulders. Yuste let the letter slip from her fingers to the desk, and gazed unspeaking at her niece and the Teacher. Sival's high forehead was creased.

'Annat has something to tell you, my dear . . .'

Yuste looked at her niece's pale face. No doubt Annat thought she would escape a scolding if she brought Sival to speak for her.

'I've received a letter from Madame Mireille. Delivered by hand this afternoon. She wants to know why she should not expel you from the Academy.'

'It's so unfair!' Annat took a step forward. 'All I did was to rehearse a scene from our play, and that witch de Clignancourt reported me.'

'Annat, you know why I sent you there. It is one of the few liberal academies in Masalyar. At least it is not run by the *nonnes*, and they do not require you to sew. Or practise etiquette. You know that it is a favour for them to accept a Wanderer—'

'Is that my fault?' Annat interrupted. 'Those rules are wrong. You say so yourself!'

Sival broke in, holding up his dark hands with the soft, pale palms.

'That is not why I came with Annat to see you, Yuste.'

'What else could there be?' Yuste leant her head on her hand. 'What else has she done?'

'Nothing.' Sival sat down on the floor cross-legged, and Annat squatted beside him. He had never been fond of chairs. 'You know that we have been studying Travel.'

Yuste managed a smile. 'And I said that Annat has already done enough Travel for one lifetime.'

Sival glanced at Annat, who was looking morose, and said, 'Annat becomes impatient with the theory when she has had so much practice.'

'I still don't see why we have to leave trails. Yuda hasn't told me about it,' said Annat, pouting.

'That's because he expects us to teach you,' said Yuste. 'A couple of dry old *professeurs*, while he makes it seem as easy as magic.'

Sival folded his hands. 'It is not like you to be bitter, Yuste.'

'All she talks about is Yuda. He lets her do as she likes, and I'm the horrible old woman who has to instil some discipline.'

Sival ran his hand over his forehead, back through his thinning hair. 'Annat saw something today that troubled her. A shadow of the past.'

'The crows are flying over Masalyar,' said Annat, looking up at last, straight into Yuste's eyes. Yuste's hand reached convulsively for Malchik's letter, and she snatched it up, leaning forward to thrust it at her niece.

'Read this, Natka,' she said. 'Tell me what it means.'

As Annat took the wafer of paper in her grasp, Sival said, 'Does this mean anything to you, Yuste, this talk of crows?'

Yuste stared at the Teacher, aching for the long-lost power of *sprechen*, which would have avoided so many clumsy words. 'I do not know, *Guru-ji*,' she said. 'But Malchik writes of little else.'

Having skimmed a few lines, Annat raised her eyes and said, simply, 'Malchik is in danger.' Yuste met the strange, limpid gaze that, like so much else, the girl had inherited from her father; as always, she felt at a loss, knowing that she could once have guessed the thoughts beneath its surface. When Annat was a child, Yuste had sometimes been able to overhear her thoughts, though unable to answer; but Annat had learnt the skill of keeping them private.

'Tell us about the crows,' said Sival, as the two women stared at each other. Annat held Malchik's letter out to him.

'Ademar has risen again,' she said. 'He is coming

south. I have seen his spies over Masalyar, and Malchik saw them in Axar.'

'But Ademar – wasn't that the name of some petty warlord in the north?' said Yuste. 'He tried to stop the Railway People building a tunnel under the forest. He was dealt with, and they finished the work not long after. The Railway People would never have sent emissaries to Yonar if they thought there might be some peril at their backs.' She did not need to voice her other doubts; surely Yuda would know, would have sent word to the city, if one of the northern seigneurs was planning an attack?

'Ademar has risen again,' Annat repeated. 'We have to go to Malchik.'

Yuste gazed at her, hands clenched in her lap. She felt bewildered, cross and afraid. She wanted to catch her niece by the shoulders and shake Annat out of her inscrutability. She plucked at her hair, untidying the neat bun, and heard her own voice, hoarse and shrill, demanding, 'Annat, please explain what you mean. Neither Sival nor I have time to decipher riddles. What have Ademar and his crows got to do with you and Malchik?'

She saw at once that she had misinterpreted her niece's seeming calm. Annat seemed to shrink in on herself. 'Don't you understand?' she whispered. 'It's not just us in danger. It's the city. The south. Everything.'

'I am worried sick about Malchik,' said Yuste. 'I have never received such a letter from him before. I thought he was losing his mind. Now you tell me the crows are real, there's some threat. What can I do? I'm not a shaman, and your father is hundreds of miles away.'

Annat uncurled. 'We can't wait for Yuda,' she said. 'You and I will have to set out for Axar, as soon as possible. Just the two of us. We could get the night train.'

'I think, Annat, before you rush off anywhere, that you need to explain properly what this is about,' said Sival. 'You may know what awaits you, but Yuste is your guardian, and she needs a little more than the hints you have given. Why is the Lord of Ademar a threat to Malchik now? The young man seemed very distressed.'

Annat lowered her eyes. 'I'm not certain why Malchik is so afraid. But he always knew more of Ademar than I did. Yuda killed the old man's son and Heir, Zhan Sarl. And it was Sarl who used to summon the crows. How can they be back when he is dead? I can see no answer. No good answer.'

Yuste looked at Sival, and gained no comfort from his expression. 'Natka,' she said, using her niece's diminutive name, 'that was finished with years ago. Yuda dealt with it, and you helped him. I have heard the stories of your Journey into the world underground. But there has been peace in those parts for a long time. It will need more than a flock of crows to convince me that something has changed.'

Annat gave her grave stare. 'You saw Malchik's letter,' she said. 'He's not mad. He's seen the signs, and he knows what is happening. We have to go before it's too late.'

'I think Annat is right,' said Sival. Before Yuste could protest, he went on, 'But I do not think the two of you should leave tonight. You will need someone to help you. As you have said, Yuste, you have no powers, and Annat needs someone to guide her. In Yuda's absence, you should enlist the help of another shaman. I think you should approach Boris Grebenshikov.'

'Sival, I hope this isn't one of your jokes,' said Yuste, sitting upright. 'Who in the name of Zyon is Boris Grebenshikov? He must be a White Sklavan with a name like that, and they don't love our people.'

'Boris Andreyevich is a detective. He attended the *Shkola* a couple of years before Yuda, and your brother knows him. They know of and respect each other, but their approach is a little – different. Boris has always preferred not to use his powers if he can help it.'

'Good grief, you don't mean Bald Boris?' said Yuste. 'Of course I've heard of him. I dare say he doesn't have much in common with Yuda, though I've heard it said he sometimes works outside the law. Well, I suppose we've all done that,' she added, glancing at Annat's shortened skirt. 'But why should he help us?'

'Because I shall pay him, Yuste,' said Sival. 'No arguments, please. I take seriously what Annat has told us, her fears, and this letter. I think it concerns the safety of Masalyar itself, and the lands beyond. For that reason alone, I think Boris Grebenshikov will help you. I will contact him tonight.'

Chapter 3

The offices of Messrs Grebenshikov and Stromnak (Deceased) lay on the fourth floor of a building in a quarter that neither Annat nor Yuste had visited much. It was further away from the docks than the *Shkola*, in an area that was respectable in name, and whose tall streets had a tattered look. The structure was stiff with marble on its lower storeys, but higher up, above the tram wires, the plaster facing had crumbled, laying bare the rough-cut stone beneath. Pigeons crowded the windowsills, and left their feathers and droppings to clog the nets that failed to keep them off. A thin layer of tawny grime had made the windows almost opaque, so that they admitted daylight with a dirty tinge, like washing-up water.

As she and Yuste sat on two threadbare chairs in the waiting room, Annat found herself wondering about Stromnak, and how he had died. Yuste perched beside her, tense and silent, clutching her mighty leather reticule balanced on her lap. To Annat, her aunt looked a dowdy figure in her brown velvet costume with the Wanderers' badge pinned to the sleeve, and her bonnet pulled forward to cast her face into shadow. Annat would rather wear black at all times than endure the shame of putting on a Wanderers' badge. She could not understand why Yuste chose to bear it just so she could be free to put on brown or grey.

Annat carried no handbag, and her bonnet had slipped back on her shoulders, as usual. She occupied herself watching the secretary who sat behind a desk at the other end of the room, clacking her typewriter keys in ceaseless cacophony. The woman had a bright little face like a bird, and rouged lips that she often pursed. She wore a costume of smooth blue serge, fastened up to the neck, and patterned with a modish grey and red plaid. She showed no interest in either Annat or Yuste, pausing in her work only to put messages into cylinders that she proceeded to insert into a vacuum tube, whence they vanished upwards into the ceiling with a faint pop.

The door to the inner office swung open and a short, stocky man put his head out. The top of his head was hairless, but two furrows of brown and grey grew stubbornly above his ears, as if he had favoured an eccentric tonsure.

'Missis Vasilyevich?' he said in a flat voice. As Yuste rose, Annat observed that Grebenshikov wore grey trousers, a white shirt and braces, but no jacket. He had neither a cravat nor a necktie, and his vest showed in the open collar of his shirt.

Yuste extended a gloved hand. 'Good morning, Boris Andreyevich,' she said, speaking Sklav. Annat was startled when Grebenshikov took the outstretched hand and bestowed a dry kiss upon it. He stood aside to let Yuste enter the room, and gave Annat a nod as she followed. He avoided her gaze, rather as Dani had done.

He was a shaman, and not strong enough to hide it. His thoughts were warded, but the signature of his power gave off a coppery sheen. Annat knew at once that she was more powerful than him, but she had learnt at the *Shkola* not to flaunt her superiority. It was bad manners, and also unwise. She had no doubt that Grebenshikov would be taking her measure in a similar way, and would have noticed that Yuste had lost all but a few traces of her power.

In his office, grubby blinds were pulled down to filter out the morning sunlight. Grebenshikov sat down with his back to the window, behind a desk that seemed to rise like a slab of monumental stone. On its surface were a blotter, covered with ink blots and scrawls, a spelter inkwell and pen-tray, and a gun. With a murmur of embarrassment, Grebenshikov picked up the pistol before Annat had time to examine it, and slipped it into a leather holster that he wore over his shoulder, so that the weapon tucked under his armpit. A shaman with a gun! Annat knew many fighting shamans, and few of them deigned to arm themselves. It must mean that Grebenshikov had little confidence in his powers.

There were two armchairs placed before the desk, and Annat settled into one, drawing up her slippered feet and receiving a disapproving glance from Yuste, who sat stiffly upright on the edge of the sagging cushion. The chairs were upholstered in faded, worn leather, and they smelled deeply of *tabak*. Boris Grebenshikov sat back in his chair and looked at them. Then he leant forward, drew open a desk drawer and pulled out a cigar. He proceeded to cut off the end, stuck it in his mouth and lit it with a lucifer.

'Excuse me,' he said. 'I know that it is considered ill-mannered to smoke in the presence of ladies, but I find that it helps me to think.'

'There's no need to stand upon ceremony, Boris Andreyevich,' said Yuste. 'You know that we are not ladies. We are Wanderers, and shamans like you. Or, as you probably know, I used to be a shaman.'

Boris leant on the desk and stroked the ash from the butt of his cigar. He looked straight at Yuste, and his eyes were grey. His face had a light tan that the winter months had not wholly faded, high cheekbones and a certain broadness, as if he had Halek ancestors.

'Take off that damn badge, woman,' he said.

Yuste looked startled, opened her mouth as if to retort, and then unpinned the Wanderers' badge from her sleeve. Boris seemed to relax. He blew the smoke high, and sat back in his chair.

'Prakhash Sival sent word to me last night,' he said. 'I understand you require my services to accompany you to Axar.'

'Did he tell you what our business is?' said Yuste, putting the badge into her reticule. Boris smiled round the cigar.

'He told me it concerned a matter of civic security,' he said.

'We don't know that for certain,' Yuste responded. 'What we do know is that my nephew is in trouble. He is a student at the University of Axar, but like my niece, Annat, he has been caught up in shamans' matters in the past.'

'The Gard Ademar affair, to be precise,' said Boris, raising his eyebrows.

'You know about it?' said Yuste.

'I read your brother's report at the time. I like to keep up to date with what my peers have been doing.'

Annat did not need special senses to detect the irony in this. Unlike her father, Boris Grebenshikov did not have a reputation as one of the most powerful shamans in the city. Indeed, she had never heard of him in all the shaman gossip that circulated at the *Shkola*.

Yuste waved her hand. 'You've done more than I, Boris Andreyevich. I never read his reports. But I am neither an employee of the Railway People nor one of their external agents.' She paused. 'You are one of their agents, am I right?'

Boris drew on his cigar. 'Why would the union instruct someone like me?' he said, letting the question linger in the air like the smoke.

'I don't know,' said Yuste. 'Even after five years living in the city, there are things I am still finding out. For most of that time, I have shared a house with Sival, and I still don't fully understand his link with the Railway People. I do know that he seems to have arranged an appointment for us to see you at remarkably short notice. And who are we?'

'Yuste and Annat Vasilyevich,' said Boris. 'Besides, I know that Sival wouldn't waste my time with trivia. It may be that this trouble only concerns your nephew, but then again, it may concern the rest of us.'

He opened his desk and pulled out a sheaf of papers. Topmost was a printed page with a coloured engraving of a coat of arms. As he held it out to Yuste, Annat moved to peer at it. It showed a shield with a red ground, and four black crows' heads. A helm with an elaborate crest surmounted the shield, and its supporters were two deer, white harts. A scroll at the bottom of the page bore the words 'Seigneurs Sorel D'Ademar'. Annat found herself looking up into Boris's grey stare.

'I've been doing some research,' he said. Annat wondered whether it would be worthwhile trying *sprechen* with him, but she knew now that there were formalities to be observed.

'When?' she said.

'Last night.'

'You think these people have something to do with it?' said Yuste, studying the shield.

'I think it's likely, but I don't want to jump to conclusions. The long and the short of it are that I've decided to take on your case. I'll come with you to Axar and see whether we can discover if there's anything behind your nephew's concerns.'

'And mine,' said Annat.

'It's a little more than coincidence,' Boris agreed. 'When do you want to take the train?'

'Annat and I are packed and ready,' said Yuste, handing the page back to him.

'I'll come with you,' said Boris, rising from his chair and stretching. He put on his jacket, buttoning it at the front, and went to a concealed closet in the panelled wall, from which he took out a long trench coat, a trilby hat and a valise. Yuste stood up, and Annat imitated her, watching as Boris donned the trench coat and hat. He was still smoking the cigar.

'The next train to Axar leaves just after mid-of-the-day,' he said. 'Let me take you ladies to lunch,' and he gave Annat a mischievous wink behind Yuste's back.

It was only a few weeks since Yuste had visited the *Gare* Sankt Karl in order to say goodbye to her brother and take charge of Annat. That had been such a different occasion, almost festive, and most of the Railway People had turned out to wish the emissaries to Yonar good speed. The embassy represented the next stage in the great plan to extend the railway north, and they all wanted a piece of it. The high vaults of the station had been draped with red and yellow streamers, a brass band had been playing, and someone had decked the engine's polished brasswork with white ribbons.

Today the station was its drab and ordinary self, filled with noise, steam and soot. Passengers and loiterers crowded the concourse and members of the Railway union sauntered amongst them, resplendent in their red uniforms. Most of the trains waiting at the buffers were only due to travel short distances. The Black Train, which went all the way to the northern terminus, had already departed, the roofs of its wagons freighted with guards. Trains that travelled no further than Axar did not need such heavy-armed escorts, and it was usual for only two of the train crew to carry arms; they would stay in the caboose out of sight of the passengers.

As she, Annat and Grebenshikov studied the board to see what platform their train would depart from, Yuste felt herself assailed by unwanted emotions. Three weeks ago, she had been dressed in her best, a dove-grey gown with a white fichu, and a bonnet adorned with rose-pink ribbons. Inside the station, no one enforced the Neustrian laws, and the Railway People were quick to drive out informers or agents provocateurs who might loiter on the concourse, ready to report the unwary. Yuste had climbed up on to the footplate to kiss her brother, and he had smiled into her eyes, a smile that still had the power to make a shiver go through her. Behind him his lover, Shaka the Engineer, had waited by the controls, his broad arms folded across his chest. It had been so different to today's furtive and fearful excursion. Yuste had never taken the train out of Masalyar alone; she hurried along, keeping one hand on her drab bonnet and the other to lift her skirts out of the dirt, while her bag dangled from her arm. Annat was carrying their two light overnight bags.

Yuste thought of her brother, the person she loved – and hated – most in the world. Was it because of him that she had never married, staying faithful to their childhood bond long after he had outgrown it? Or was it simply that their fateful adolescent fight had made her barren as well as powerless? Her brother might have so many notches on his bedpost that he could scarcely count them, but she had none. After he abandoned his young wife and children, it had been Yuste who cared for Annat and Malchik as their mother retreated step by step into insanity. When Yuste had fallen ill, the *kinder* had left home to live with their father, and the next year had been a time of confusion. The doctors and shamans who removed her womb seemed to have taken out most of her insides, and she had convalesced slowly, sitting out in an invalid's chair in the *Jardin des Plantes* with only Sival for a companion. She had sometimes wondered if something would spring up between them, a quick salamander of love, but over those months she had realised that she idolised him as a teacher and respected him like a father. It was not merely the difference in their ages; the adolescent passion she had nurtured for the young man who came to teach them, she and Yuda, had faded over the years, leaving her at ease with a dear friend who could never be more.

When she was almost well, her brother had returned from his strange Journey. Since then, it seemed she had always been busy, working at the *Shkola*, and looking after Annat for six months of the year. She had sometimes longed to renew the old closeness with her brother, but the injury he had done her lay between them like an unanswered question. What more could she do to reproach him when she knew how much he had reproached himself? She wondered if he sometimes read the accusation in the depths of her mind even when she was unconscious of it. She did not feel bitter, but she could not escape the knowledge that if it were not for him she would still be a shaman, and perhaps able to conceive and bear children. Who, after all, would be interested in an old spinster with no womb?

She hoped Annat could not overhear her musings. For all of her niece's life, Annat had been the daughter that Yuste could not bear herself. Annat's mother had rejected her not many months after the birth, and it was Yuste who had nursed and reared the child for thirteen years, until the cancer came. When Annat returned from the time spent with her father, it seemed as if a distance had grown up between her and Yuste. Annat had left Yuste as a child, and returned as something much closer to a young woman. Since then, the distance seemed to have increased. Annat could *sprechen* with her father, which she could not do with Yuste; a bond had grown up between them that had everything to do with the dangers they had shared. Yuste had watched with a sense of helplessness as her niece, her child, had grown further from her and closer to the charismatic father she in so many ways resembled.

'Can I give you a hand with the bags, Missis Vasil-yevich?'

Yuste blinked. A porter with a trolley had approached her, tipping his cap. As she saw his wide smile, she recognised him; she knew many of the station staff, by sight or by name.

'Good afternoon, Mister Drazic,' she said, earning

the smile. 'We don't have much, but I would be very grateful if you could help us.'

While Annat placed the two suitcases on the trolley, and Grebenshikov quickly added his own, Drazic said, 'Going after your brother, Missis? Or is it a quick trip to the seaside?'

'We're going to Axar to visit my nephew,' said Yuste, as they set off along the platform. A porter was welcome as a bulwark to guide them through the crowds. 'He is studying there at the University.'

'It's good to have scholars in the family,' said the porter. 'We're hoping that my grandson may go to college after his Baccalaureat.'

'And how is Missis Drazic?' asked Yuste, following him as he steered the trolley deftly between the flurry of feet and wheels that blocked his way.

'Doing fine, thanks, Missis. In the summer, I'm going to join her out at the farm. We've bought a claim out in the empty lands, near Valens.'

'Rather you than me,' said Yuste, and regretted it at once. 'I'm sorry, Mister,' she added quickly. 'I lived too long in the country. I'm a city woman now.'

'I reckon the city's a little better for Wanderers, in spite of them new laws,' said Drazic reflectively. 'At least you know where you are.'

Yuste sighed. 'That's certainly true, Mister,' she said. 'But they aren't new laws. We had to obey them for years outside the city. It's the new council that has enacted them here.'

Drazic leaned towards her, confidentially. 'I needn't tell you who's behind it,' he said, and glanced over his shoulder. 'Since the dockers got the majority on the City Council, nothing's been the same. We're feeling it over here, I can tell you. Even the Front has to watch her step.'

The Front was the Railway People's elected leader, one of the most powerful people in Masalyar. Yuste found herself looking at Drazic with a sense of complicity. Even though most Railway People were Wanderer-friends, she had always been careful not to assume this. 'I don't know why it has changed,' she said. 'There's been tolerance for years, but suddenly the Franj have taken against outsiders. Not just Wanderers, but Sklavs, Moreans, Kadegins and Sulimites.'

'There's something of that, it's true,' said Drazic, looking her up and down with a kind of sadness. 'But to my thinking, it's more of a religion thing. All the Doxans together. One true faith. Whatever it is, it's changed things for the worse,' he added, glancing at the Wanderer badge that Yuste had restored to her sleeve once they left Grebenshikov's office.

They stopped near the head of the train, close behind the engine and its water tank, next to a carriage that had some free compartments. 'Will you be comfortable here?' said Drazic. 'A bit sooty for some tastes.'

Yuste chuckled. 'My brother would expect me to ride on the roof, petticoats and all,' she said. 'Annat and I can manage the bags from here.'

In spite of her protestations, Drazic insisted on carrying their bags into the compartment and settling them in the overhead luggage rack. Yuste knew he would be horrified if she offered him a tip, and was a little uneasy when Grebenshikov proceeded to do so.

'Don't worry,' he said, seeing her face as he shouldered through the narrow compartment door. 'I'm not associated with the Union. He took it from me.'

'But it's demeaning,' said Annat at once, sitting down by the window. Yuste settled herself on the leather banquette opposite.

'Annat,' she said, with a warning look.

Boris Grebenshikov did not answer at once. He took off his trench coat, folded it and put it in the overhead rack, balancing his hat on top of it. Then he sat down next to Yuste. He gazed at Annat for a few moments, before replying, 'He won't think it demeaning when it comes from me. He might have been offended if your aunt had tried to pay him. But I'm nobody, a passenger, not one of the Railway People.'

'How do you know about all that?' said Annat, staring at him. Yuste was tempted to reprimand her again, but she knew how useless it would be. In spite of her time at the Academy, Annat had learnt no sense of propriety. She was as blunt as she had ever been.

Grebenshikov sat back in his seat, stretching out his short legs. 'I make it my business to know things, Missis,' he said. 'To work as I do in this city, you need to know about all sorts and manner of people. And how to avoid offending them,' he added, glancing at Yuste, who lowered her eyes and smiled. Annat too sat back in her seat.

'I've never ridden inside before,' she said. 'I always go on top with *Tate*, or ride in the driver's cab.'

'I don't think anyone rides the roof on this train,' said Yuste. 'For one thing, it goes too fast. There's only one stop between here and Axar. It isn't like the Black Train.'

Annat looked out of the window at the platform, where more passengers were preparing to embark. 'I wish I could have gone to Yonar,' she said, wistfully. 'No one has ever been so far north.'

'That's just why Yuda didn't take you, Natka,' said Yuste. 'He knows you need to finish your training. Heaven knows you can ill afford to miss more days. But at least this way I will have time to decide what to write to Madame Mireille.'

Annat looked at Yuste, frowning. 'I don't want to leave there, Yuste,' she said. 'I have friends. Even the Doxoi.'

'I will write to Madame,' said Yuste. 'And I know that their rules are stupid and petty. But if you do not abide by them, you cannot attend the school.'

Annat reached into her cloak and drew out the volume of poetry by Xelle. 'Eugenie gave me this,' she said, holding it up but not offering it to Yuste.

'Mademoiselle de Bouget?' Yuste raised her brows. 'You must find something to give her in return. You should not be in her debt.'

'It isn't like that!' Annat cried.

Yuste drew breath, stemming her own anger. 'We are poor Wanderers, Annat,' she said. 'It would not be right for you to take gifts and give nothing in return.

Though Eugenie might not care – I'm sure she is generous – others might speak ill of you.'

Annat bent her head, her face flushed as she looked at the book in her lap. Watching her, Yuste suddenly wondered if there were more to this than met the eye. Usually, Annat would be as proud as she was. But the gift from the Doxan princesse – was it a love token? Yuste resolved not to press her niece further.

'I have heard of Xelle, but I cannot read the language,' she said, mildly.

'We're studying it,' said Annat, still staring at her lap. 'That's why I was rehearsing scenes from *Timur the Lame*.'

'I had to study that at school,' said Boris, suddenly. 'I found it more exciting than poetry.'

Annat looked up, her eyes suddenly bright. 'I love the scene where he enters Persepolis, in a chariot drawn by the captive kings of Tyre and Nineveh,' she said.

There was a jolt. The train was pulling out of the station. With a sense of panic about her heart, Yuste watched the platform gliding past, a scene of men in stovepipe hats or velvet renaissance berets and women perched like half-dolls above their heavy skirts.

'We're leaving,' she murmured, but Boris had begun to quote lines from the play.

'Holla, ye pampered jades of Asea,
What, can ye draw but twenty miles a day,
And have so proud a chariot at your heels,
And such a coachman as great Tamburlaine?'

Annat went on:

'Is it not passing brave to be a king
And ride in triumph through Persepolis?'

Boris chuckled. 'That was all I could ever remember,' he said. 'It looks as if you've learned the whole play.'

'I will play Timur,' said Annat, then she too glanced out of the window. 'If Madame Mireille will take me back,' she added.

The train pulled into Axar five hours later. Annat peered out of the window, trying to see if she could remember anything of the city that she had last visited five years ago. Then it had been dusk, and she had been riding the roof of the train, with her father and the guards. It seemed odd to be sitting in comfort inside a carriage, sipping hot *chai* from a flask that Yuste had brought along, and nibbling bread rolls and bitter oranges. She felt regret for those wild, uncertain days, when she had been travelling into a new world. Except for the anxiety of yesterday that, when she faced it, concerned nothing more sinister than a flock of birds, she might have been travelling with Yuste merely to visit Malchik at his college. The only strangeness came from the presence of Boris Grebenshikov, and he seemed so quiet and unremarkable that it was hard to feel any anticipation in his company. He might be a shaman detective, but it was clear that for him this was just another job, and one that he viewed with neither enthusiasm nor dismay.

They passed the towers of the cathedral, the Doxan Dom, and Annat wondered whether she would have a chance to look inside this time. The temples of Masalyar were encrusted with flamboyant and excessive decoration, images of saints and martyrs with doll faces, and painted tableaux showing scenes from Holy Writ. Annat still recalled her astonishment when she had realised that the Doxoi worshipped not the One, but the Mother-Goddess and God-Son together. The two were said to reign supreme in heaven, as eternal consorts. Annat had questioned Eugenie about it at length; it was the first time she had found a friend who was a strict Doxan, and the two girls had compared the tenets of their respective faiths with curiosity and some laughter.

The tall and tawny spires turned to gold at the touch of the setting sun, which flashed from the gilded wheels set atop each pinnacle. On the topmost tower, the builders of the old empire had set the crowing cock that symbolised Neustria, supreme even above the church.

'You know the temples in Sklava are a different shape,' Boris said to Annat.

'How can they be different to this?'

'The domes are shaped like an onion, and gilded or set with mosaic tiles so that they glitter in the sunlight. In Kiyev, where I was born, a forest of them rise from the roof of Sankt Vladimir.'

'My grandmother came from Kiyev,' said Annat, dreamily. 'And my grandfather came from Ades.'

'Listen to you,' said Yuste. 'It's time we were getting ready to leave the train.'

Boris sat back in his seat and gazed at the paper wrappers, orange peel and empty cups with which they had strewn the carriage. 'We'd better hurry then,' he said.

When they descended from the train, Annat blinked in the strong lights of the station that made the dusk outside look dark. They had pulled in at a different platform to the one where the Black Train had halted. She, Boris and Yuste each carried a suitcase. The crowd at Axar seemed more serene and stately, flowing from the train down towards the concourse and the Doric pillars of the station entrance. She felt both eager at the thought of seeing Malchik, and slightly wistful that their journey had to end here, so soon after it had begun. She glanced at Yuste, whose face was pale with tiredness, and wondered how her aunt could be content never to leave Masalyar, year after year. If Annat had her way, she would have spent the summer travelling the road with Yuda, and the winter at home with Yuste, taking lessons in the cold months. The thought of school summoned the image of Eugenie, and Annat felt a sharp, unexpected pain, like a stitch in her side. It must not be too long before she saw the Princesse de Bouget again; Madame Mireille must take her back, Annat would promise her anything.

They stood side by side on the steps outside the station. A wide, cobbled space separated the building from the town, and rows of gas lamps were being lit, giving off a camphorous green light. The western sky was wine-stained and apricot above, fading into a thin green. A few hackney carriages were drawn up at the foot of the steps, but the other passengers were making their way on foot across the cobbles, towards a broad street whose lights coiled into the evening.

'Perhaps we should hire a hansom cab to take us to the University,' said Yuste, looking anxiously at the small black carriages.

'No need for that,' said Boris. 'It's a short walk, and the evening is mild. I'll carry your valise, Madame,' he added, with a quick smile.

'In that case . . .' Yuste answered the smile and offered him her suitcase. They set off down the steps and Annat, cradling her valise in her arms, wished she had brought a rucksack. She strode along a little way ahead of them, following the enticing lights of the main street. With a quick pang of guilt, she realised that she was glad that she only had Yuste to watch over her. Yuda would have taken the lead, confident in everything, but here Annat was the one who led while the others followed. She glanced from side to side at the tall, shuttered houses, catching here and there a glimmer of light through the louvres, or the glint of a carved grille, or a grotesque head ornamenting a doorway.

The dusty road came to a crossroads, a *carrefour*, and Annat paused, knowing she could go no further without Boris's directions. In the centre stood a dark fountain, and water trickled from the carved snouts of dolphins, catching the light as it fell. There were tall lanterns at each corner, and they threw converging beams of smoky luminescence into the sky. Annat looked up to the place where they met, high above the top of the fountain, and caught her breath. Where the beams of light crossed each other, they left a shape of darkness above them, and to her sight it seemed to take on a distinct form: the shadow of a crow. Annat swung to look back at Yuste and Boris, wondering if they had noticed anything, but they were deep in talk. When she turned back, the shadow remained, clear and ominous, as if someone had left her a warning. She knew in her heart that the threat from Ademar was spreading; she had seen its out-riders in Masalyar, but here they were already installed. An invasion was coming that would threaten her whole world.

She was glad when they found themselves walking under the sheltering walls of the University. Its out-line was as easy to recognise as that of the Dom: pointed pinnacles vaulted from the apex of the roofs, each one studded with tight fern buds; gargoyles hung low over the street, menacing passers-by with their mouths; and the clock-tower's black bulk over-shadowed the moon. The entrance was a double-doored opening in the wall, and Boris approached it first to rap at the wood with one bronze knocker. The sound rang out like a pistol shot, and Yuste started.

'These places have rules about women,' said Boris, confidentially, as they waited. 'I'd better do the talking.'

'I'm the boy's aunt, for Zyon's sake!' said Yuste.

'Trust me,' said Boris.

A smaller opening set within the massy wooden door opened, and a man looked out. He wore a black gown over his suit, and a bowler hat; the effect was incongruous. Boris took his own hat off and said, in accentless Franj, 'Good evening. We would like to visit the student Malchik Vasilyevich. My name is Grebenshikov, and these are his aunt and his sister.'

The porter gave Annat and Yuste a disapproving glance. 'It is customary to write in advance, to request a visit,' he said.

Yuste stepped forward and fixed him with her brown stare. 'This is an emergency,' she said. 'My nephew is in trouble. There was no time to write.'

'I haven't heard of any trouble,' said the man.

'I have received a letter from Malchik,' said Yuste. 'But I do not see why I should show it to you. I am his aunt, and I insist that I be admitted. If you do not believe me, would you be so kind as to conduct me to the Master's lodgings?'

Annat felt rather than heard Boris wince. He stretched out his hand as if to prevent Yuste from lunging at the porter, and said, 'The ladies have had a long journey, and are tired. Perhaps it might be better to continue this conversation inside.'

'I don't want anyone creating a scene,' said the porter, and he plainly thought that Yuste was about to do so.

Boris took a grip on Yuste's arm, though with a gentle hand; Annat could see her aunt trying to wrest free without anyone noticing.

'We have no intention of creating a scene, as you put it,' he said. 'But it is late, we have not dined, and we would welcome the chance to sit down.'

'You'd better come in then,' said the porter, stepping back to leave the entrance free.

Boris ushered Yuste over the threshold, and then Annat; she thought that he was smiling to himself. Once inside, they found themselves in the gatehouse next to the porter's lodge, standing on massive stone flags. Beyond was a cool, dark quadrangle, with a few scattered windows lit from within. The porter took the opportunity to study them all closely, in the light cast from the windows of the gatehouse.

'Wanderers,' he said, as if this were a complaint. 'They can't stay here; no women allowed to spend the night within the University precincts.'

Before Yuste could speak, Boris said, 'I assume that there are lodgings close by for the use of female relatives?'

'They could try Madame Charbon,' said the porter, grudgingly. 'But you'll have to stay here. She doesn't take unmarried men.'

Boris turned to Yuste. Before he spoke, he gave a sigh. 'It seems we will have to split up —' he began, but she did not let him finish.

'Never mind that. Am I to see my nephew tonight, or not?'

The porter gazed at her with his small, colourless eyes. His mouth was framed with a set of sour lines, as if he had never smiled. Yuste stared back, her fingers clenched over her handbag. It was the porter who quailed first. 'You'll find him across the courtyard, on the scholars' stair,' he said. 'Second floor up. They have their names above the door.'

Chapter 4

at was a little ashamed when she saw her
nt's face pale at the mention of Cluny's name.
r!' she said. 'What do you mean, he is of
?'
the Doyen's bastard son. But he saved us all.
d us escape. And I was afraid they might have
.' Annat realised that she was holding Cluny's
hers. She looked up at him and smiled. 'If it
r Cluny, I would be dead.'
perhaps this . . . young man can tell us some-
ut where Malchik is. And what all this crow
s about,' said Yuste. Her face looked drawn
as if an eraser had taken away all its colour.
ned to perceive this more quickly than the
he stepped up behind her and took her arm.
Yuste did not shake him off. 'Monsieur,'
with his faint smile, 'these ladies have had
ney, and something of a shock. The porter

'I assume we may leave our bags here?' said Boris. The porter gave him a look, as if he was minded to remonstrate, but he seemed to have lost the will to put up any more obstacles.

'So long as you don't expect me to look after them,' he replied.

Yuste hurried out into the quadrangle without a backward glance, and Boris and Annat followed her.

'Your aunt is a strong woman, Missis,' he said.

Annat did not think before answering, 'She has to deal with that sort of stuff all the time.'

Boris did not reply, but she felt him watching her with a shaman's acuity. With the studied wariness that all shamans showed when encountering a stranger of their own kind. Annat knew, and in this respect she was conventional, that she was not expected, as a young female shaman, to take the first steps to inviting *sprechen*. Even her father observed these codes of etiquette, which had evolved to protect shamans from each other. She would have to wait for Boris Grebenshikov to send her a thought and, because of her age and sex, he was likely to take his time, even more than a *frummer* like Dani. If they had not been shamans, such restraints would have irked her, but she had already experienced a little of what a hostile mind could do. It made her feel at ease that Boris Grebenshikov was in no hurry to start sharing her thoughts.

They found Yuste hesitating outside the door to a dimly lit staircase. Hearing them approach, she swung round and demanded, 'Is this the right one?'

'It looks like it to me,' said Boris. With a small

hesitation, he added, 'Do you want me to go first? The old git said Malchik was on the second floor.'

'Thanks for your kindness, Boris Andreyevich, but I shall go first,' said Yuste. 'I have nothing to fear from Malchik.'

She strode through the door and began to mount the wooden stair, her skirts rustling about her. Even in such cumbersome clothes, she could move quickly and neatly. Annat and Boris followed her, and their feet together made a racket clattering up the wooden treads. They paused together on the second landing, where two doors faced each other. Above the left-hand door was a neat plaque, enamelled in a flowing script with Malchik's name. Yuste drew breath, stepped forward and knocked firmly at the door.

The three of them stood together in foolish silence, waiting for the sound of footsteps, the rattle of bolts, the opening of the door. Instead, they heard a stillness that slowly let in the murmurings of the building, the rumble of other feet overhead, the distant slamming of doors, voices calling and laughter. After a pause, Boris Grebenshikov said, 'Looks like he's out.'

'He can't be out,' said Yuste. Once more, she struck the door with her knuckles, and the wood resounded like a hollow box. Annat saw a frown on her aunt's brow. 'He must be in,' Yuste said. Raising her voice, she called, 'Malchik! It's *Tante* Yuste. Open the door!'

Boris thrust his hands into the pockets of his trench coat. 'Students do go out,' he said.

'Do you take me for a fool, Boris Andreyevich?'

said Yuste. 'You saw the letter. I don[...] would be out enjoying himself.'

There was a sound from behind th[...] opposite swung open. The young n[...] was tall, dark-haired, but it was h[...] caught Annat's attention. He wore [...] jacket, knee-breeches over silker[...] starched cravat and a velvet beret.[...] was so startled by this spectacle tha[...] nise the man within the clothe[...] towards her, his hands outstretc[...] gesture.

'Annat? Is that you?' he said.[...]

It was his voice that Annat rer[...] had given him greater breadth [...] was a long way from the pal[...] recalled, glimpsed in a few mo[...]

'Cluny!' she cried, and lau[...] flinging her arms round his nec[...] in a strong grasp, lifting her of[...] to see you!' she cried, muffl[...] As he set her down, Yuste ap[...] set in a frown. Even if she d[...] prieties, she wanted Annat t[...]

'Annat. Who is this youn[...]

Annat grinned at Cluny. [...] moment of pure joy. '*Ta*[...] d'Ademar,' she said, well av[...] would create. 'He saved m[...]

A[...]
'Adema[...]
Ademar[...]
'He's[...]
He help[...]
hurt hin[...]
hand in[...]
wasn't f[...]
'Then[...]
thing abo[...]
business[...]
and tired[...]
Boris see[...]
others, fo[...]
This time[...]
said Boris[...]
a long jou[...]

was none too welcoming. Is there somewhere that Madame Vasilyevich could sit down?'

Cluny drew his hand from Annat's. 'But of course! How thoughtless of me,' he said, with true concern. 'You must come into my rooms. I suppose your bags are still at the porter's lodge. I'll ask my man to have them sent up.'

Boris cleared his throat. 'The porter told us ladies were not allowed to stay within the college precincts,' he said.

Cluny laughed. 'He always says that. He thinks all women are agents of the devil. There's nothing to prevent aunts and sisters staying the night. And all sorts of women get smuggled in, some of whom could not be called ladies.'

Yuste rallied enough to say, 'I have never asked to be called a lady. I am a Wanderer, and woman is a good enough name for me.'

'I don't think Clement is fond of Wanderers either,' said Cluny, ruefully. 'But even the Master is afraid of him. You'll be most welcome to stay here.'

'But where is Malchik?' Yuste demanded.

The young man looked uneasy. 'I'm not sure,' he said. 'But we can have a talk when you are comfortable and Planchet has made us some *kava*. Or *chai*, if you would prefer it.'

'What do you mean, you're not sure?' said Yuste.

Boris intervened. 'Let's do what Monsieur d'Ademar suggests, Missis,' he said. 'I myself would welcome *kava*. Or something stronger, if you have it,' he added.

Beyond the inner baize door, Cluny's sitting room

was comfortably furnished and unexpectedly tidy. There was a velvet-upholstered chaise-longue, a couple of leather armchairs, and a bulging, overstuffed divan, piled with cushions and bolsters. Annat noticed the easel, standing near the shuttered windows, draped with canvas. In the opposite wall were two panelled doors, and Cluny opened one and called for his servant. While Boris helped Yuste to the chaise-longue, Annat approached the young man, curious to see what lay beyond the inner door. She was not quick enough, for a short, iron-haired man with the bearing of a soldier emerged. He wore a white shirt and a black waistcoat with a black cravat and a high collar; his trousers were of the same dark serge. He gave Annat a suspicious look.

'Planchet,' said Cluny, without condescension, 'I have guests. Old friends. Would you be so good as to make some *kava*? And I think the gentleman will be taking a glass of whisky.'

'Very good, Messire,' said the man. Annat wondered if he too came from the castle of Ademar, and whether he was an ally of Cluny's or someone sent by the Doyen to spy on his bastard son. As he returned into the inner room, Cluny turned to her and said, 'Planchet is an old family retainer. But he's my servant, not my father's. He's looked after me since I was a little boy, after I left my nurse. And he's always taken my part.'

Annat answered him with a smile.

'You have grown,' Cluny observed, blushing. 'How is your father?'

She stopped smiling. 'You know he killed . . . Sarl.'

'Of course.' Cluny did not avoid her gaze. 'I'm afraid it was for the best. I shouldn't say that, of course. And it destroyed my father. But I don't suppose he would have let me go if it hadn't happened.'

'I'm . . . sorry,' said Annat.

'Don't be. Strange times, eh? Look at us now. Do have a seat. You must be tired too.'

'Not me,' said Annat. 'They didn't punish you for helping us?'

As they moved to join the others, Cluny said, 'In the chaos following my brother's death, they never found out. Otherwise, I don't think I'd be alive to tell you.' He gave a brief, bleak smile. 'You know my father is not a forgiving man.'

Annat gave a little shiver. How could she forget the Doyen of Ademar, who had condemned her to be burnt at the stake? She touched Cluny's wrist and said to him, softly so the others would not hear, 'I've seen the crows again, Cluny. They're back.'

'I know,' he answered, patting her hand. 'Your brother talks of little else. The trouble is, Annat, that he's disappeared.'

She gazed at him for a while. 'You're sure?'

'I haven't seen him for two days. Yesterday, I told the Master.' He glanced at Yuste and Boris, conscious that they were listening now. 'I mean, one day doesn't seem that strange, but when I went to his room yesterday morning . . . Nothing's disturbed, he hasn't packed his bags or taken any spare clothes. He's just not there. I'm sorry,' he added, as Yuste covered her eyes with her hand.

'It's so unlike Malchik, just to leave and tell no one,' she said. 'He has always been a responsible boy – if careless, sometimes. You were his friend?'

Cluny sat down on the divan opposite, and Annat curled up in one of the leather armchairs. 'Yes, we were friends,' he said. 'I'm sure he would have told me if he was going away. I know he would.'

'But he was troubled in his mind?'

'Well, he was in a panic about the crows. More than the crows. I think you'll agree, it's unusual to see crows in such large numbers. It reminded him of the way my brother Sarl seemed to have some power over them. I expect you know that crows are the badge of our House?' Boris nodded. 'Well, Malchik seemed to think they were an omen. A warning.' He paused again, looking at his hands.

'Not very likely, you'll admit,' said Boris, leaning back in his chair. Cluny looked from him to Yuste and back.

'I think I can say that I know Malchik quite well by now,' he said. 'Although I only came here at the start of last term, it's as if we've known each other all our lives. And he's sensitive to things that other people don't notice. He's not a true . . . shaman, but he picks things up. I've never seen him so frightened.'

'He writes to me often, but he has never mentioned your name,' said Yuste. 'Unless you are the one he calls his *bon copain*.'

'That would be me,' said Cluny, looking embarrassed. 'I believe he wanted you to meet me before he told you who I was. *Les Ademar* have not been kind to

70

your family. Understatement,' he added, wringing his
hands, a gesture that reminded Annat of her brother.

'But where could Malchik have gone?' said Yuste.
'Was he troubled in his mind? He sent me a letter that
seemed close to madness.'

'He was in a terrible funk,' said Cluny. 'The odd
thing is that he seemed to have calmed down. We sat
up till late drinking and discussing what to do. The
next morning, he was gone. I think if I'd known about
the letter, I'd have advised him to tear it up and send
something a bit less . . . colourful. Now, I just don't
know. I think I'd better take you to see the Master of
the college.'

As he was speaking, Planchet returned with a
pewter tray bearing two dainty *kava* cups and two
glasses of whisky. Yuste took her *kava*, saying, 'I'd like
to see Malchik's room first. I can't understand why he
should have run away. Unless someone has abducted
him.'

'There's no sign of any struggle. And I'm sure that
I or Planchet would have heard something,' said
Cluny. 'It's rather as if he got up in the night and
walked out. Only there's nowhere he could go. The
college gates are locked after ten of the clock, and
Malchik isn't the type to climb out. Not from a second-
floor window.'

'Has the college been searched?' said Yuste, sipping
at her *kava*. Annat peered into her cup, surprised at
the darkness of the liquid within. Planchet obviously
made it strong.

Cluny nodded. 'The Master made an announcement

yesterday in Hall,' he said. 'They looked everywhere, even the cellars.'

'Everywhere?' said Boris, raising his eyebrows.

'I'll admit that there are quite a few places where someone could hide,' said Cluny. 'The Master doesn't know about all of those, but we – the students – took care to check that he wasn't hiding there.'

'But there must be ways to get in and out of the college that don't use the gate. You're students. Don't tell me you're too much in awe of Clement to break out now and then,' said Boris.

'Of course,' said Cluny. 'But they involve the sort of climbing that Malchik can't do. Believe me, he's tried. The college is built like a fortress, and most of the escape routes involve the roofs. They make him dizzy.'

'I think you'd better show us his rooms,' said Boris. 'Were they left locked or open?'

'They were open,' said Cluny. 'And Malchik only locks his door when he goes out. We all do. Unless we don't want to be disturbed,' he added, gazing at the floor.

Boris stood up, swigged his whisky and took off his coat and hat. 'It's safe to leave these here?' he asked.

'Very safe,' said Cluny. He stood up, smiled and took off his hat. 'It's good to be informal,' he said, with his shy charm. 'I'll send Planchet to fetch your bags from the gatehouse now.' He approached the chaise-longue and offered his arm to Yuste. 'Are you well enough to accompany us, Madame?'

Yuste laid her hand on his wrist and smiled, exerting

a slight pressure to lift herself from the couch. 'I am not as frail as I seem, Cluny,' she said. 'Please call me Yuste. I am not used to people addressing me as Madame – except at the baker's. Unless you plan to sell me a loaf.'

'Indeed not,' said Cluny, beaming. 'I shall be happy to call you Yuste, Madame – when I remember,' he added, hastily.

They crossed the landing with Boris in the lead, and Yuste leaning on Cluny's arm. Annat followed, trying to summon up her special senses. Like Malchik, she was sensitive to strangeness, but she could not feel any now. Boris paused on the threshold and examined the door carefully, running his fingers along the edges. When he opened it, he repeated the process with the baize door inside, while the others waited for him to finish. 'I'm looking for threads, hairs, scraps of cloth,' he said.

The room beyond was the mirror image of Cluny's in shape, but much more sparsely furnished. A leather armchair beneath the window looked as if it had been borrowed from Cluny. Next to it stood a neat desk of plain wood piled with papers and books, and a wheel-backed chair. There was a table in the middle of the floor, surrounded by a motley of cheap chairs, bearing a plate with a half-eaten and mouldy croissant. A few traces of Malchik's Wanderer faith were scattered across the table – a pair of candlesticks holding half-burned candles from last Kingsday, a tarnished silver spice box from home, and a neatly folded prayer shawl. A canvas cloth covered the floor, which was strewn with balls of screwed-up paper, and a pair of trousers dangled from one of the chairs.

'Is it always this messy?' Yuste asked Cluny.

'I'm afraid so. Malchik doesn't have a servant to take care of him, as I do. Planchet has offered to help, but he won't have it. Of course, the bedders come every day to make our beds and take our washing.'

Annat was studying the pictures pinned to the walls. Of course there was a *mizrach* on what must be the eastern side, to show Malchik where to face when saying his prayers. The others were carefully coloured prints, one of which showed an amply naked female form. One of Cluny's strange paintings hung above the fireplace, recognisable because it looked as if he had tried to produce an *eikon*, a flat study with no perspective and stylised trees. In the background, a mountain loomed over green fields where strange beasts grazed.

'Cluny, what's that?' she said.

Cluny joined her and inspected his work. 'Interesting, isn't it?' he said. 'I was rather hoping that you could tell me what it meant. Malchik has vivid dreams, and this one made a big impression on him. So I tried to paint it. I am not an art student,' he added hurriedly. 'I study the Humanities, like Malchik.'

'He's never mentioned anything like it to me,' said Annat. 'It's a beautiful picture.'

'Thank you,' said Cluny, looking down. 'Since I have been to the Museum and seen real painters, I find my work looks rather quaint. But I know no other style.'

Boris was going over the room, unfolding the balls

of rolled-up paper and reading them. Yuste stood with her hand on the door of the inner room.

'Is this Malchik's bedroom?' she asked.

'He sleeps in there,' said Cluny. 'The other room is used as a pantry – we both use it, since Planchet occupies my spare room.'

Yuste turned the handle and stepped into the inner room, which was unlit. It seemed that all the students' quarters benefited from electricity, though Cluny's apartment had been lit with oil lamps. Yuste turned the switch on the wall, and a single bulb came on in the centre of the room, hanging from the ceiling. This must mean that the college possessed its own steam-powered generator, Annat reflected; such things were unusual outside the wealthier parts of Masalyar. She blinked in the strange, artificial light, following Yuste as her aunt approached the bed. The two square pillows carried no indentations, and the sheets were firmly tucked under the mattress. The shutters had been drawn back, and there was none of the disorder of the outer room. A small dressing table stood beneath the window, set with a ewer of water, a basin and a cut-throat razor; Yuste opened the doors of the tall armoire and peered inside at the neat row of shirts, starched collars and carefully pressed trousers. Pairs of shoes were lined up on the bottom of the armoire, and a row of drawers held socks and underpants. Closing the door, Yuste sighed, and studied her reflection in the long mirror fixed to the outer door; she untied the strings of her bonnet and fiddled with her hair, while Annat stood behind her, examining her own reflection in the unkind light of the bare bulb. Yuste turned to her with a smile that showed the lines of tiredness. She touched Annat's cheek with a delicate hand.

'You have no need to worry about your looks, Natka,' she said.

Annat felt ashamed. Yuste had overheard her thoughts, and when she should have been worrying about Malchik's disappearance, she had been studying her own appearance.

'I'm sorry, *Tante*,' she said. She had grown to be a little taller than her aunt. Yuste's smile widened.

'Tell me I am not as faded as I look,' she said. 'If this is the power of electricity, I shall be happy to settle for candles and oil.'

'I ought to know where he is,' said Annat. Before Yuste could answer, Cluny put his head round the door.

'I should have mentioned that we found Malchik's pyjamas folded under the pillow,' he said. 'He must have gone out wearing the clothes he stood up in.'

'At least he was not sleepwalking,' said Yuste, brushing past Annat, who stayed gazing at her reflection. 'Has Boris found anything?'

'Only the pages of an essay,' said Cluny. 'He's examining the blotter now.'

They returned to the outer room, leaving Annat alone. She sat down on the edge of the bed, and stared at herself. Something her father had said to her echoed in her thoughts. *Shamans can choose whoever they want.* She missed, how she missed, the comfort of *sprechen*.

There were times when she would have loved to share her thoughts with Yuste and to receive an answer. The best she could hope for was that her aunt would overhear what she was thinking, or that Annat could send her something in confidence. At times like this, words spoken out loud seemed so clumsy, and yet her best friend, the woman she wanted to be her lover, could no more share Annat's thoughts than she could fly.

For some reason, she thought of Cluny's face, his dark eyes that were melancholy even when he smiled. He was the only dark one in his family; the rest, Sarl, Huldis, Casildis – even the Doyen – were fair, with pale eyes. She gave a little shiver. What if Sarl had somehow come back from the dead? The thought that he might be out there somewhere, looking for her . . . It made the harder shadows the fey light cast seem more ominous than the softer darkness of candles. Malchik had been afraid too; afraid and alone in this room, sitting on the bed as she did now, after Cluny had retired for the night, when something had happened – but what?

Annat thought of Yuda, and that thought gave her some comfort, though he was miles away. Even in Yonar, he might turn his thoughts south. If only Yuste still shared the same power as her twin, which she must once have possessed; but here Annat was the strongest shaman, stronger even than Boris Grebenshikov. Strong she might be, but Boris would know as well as she did how inexperienced she was. Alone in this room, he like Yuda might know what signs to look for, what traces Malchik might have left behind.

She closed her eyes. The mirror would remember what it had seen, like shadows traced in the glass. Her father had shown her how to question a mirror, but he had also warned her not to do it in his absence. Yuda seldom gave warnings, but when he did, they were to be heeded. She stared back into the reflection of her own dark pupils. She was here, and Yuda was not. She doubted whether Boris Grebenshikov would possess such power. He was a plain shaman, one who could claim few of the darker powers. If this was to be done, she must do it herself.

She stood up, and strode back into the outer room, where the others were studying the blotter. Boris was holding it up to the light to make out the imprints that Malchik's nib had pressed into the surface. But she did not need his skills to see the crow shapes doodled across the surface in black ink. If only she were linked to Malchik as Yuste was to Yuda! All she could tell was that her brother lived, just as she felt the faint flame of her aunt's presence and the distant glow of her father's.

Cluny came to meet her, his brow furrowed. 'This is really puzzling,' he said. 'It's just as if he vanished into thin air.'

'You don't think he stepped into one of your pictures?' Annat teased him.

'They don't have that power here.' He broke into a worried smile. 'Oh, I see. A joke. I almost wish he had done that. But then we'd see him staring out at us. Like a fish in a fish bowl.'

'He didn't say anything about . . . about the mirror in his room?'

Cluny shook his head. 'Looking-glasses are strange things,' he said. 'I remember that, when my brother – Sarl – died, they all turned black. Every single one. As if someone had painted them from inside. After he was buried, my father smashed them.'

'It must have been frightening,' said Annat.

'I've never talked to anyone else about it. Except Malchik. He came to know my father quite well in the short time he was detained at the castle. I think my father was growing fond of him. Until he escaped, and joined forces with our enemies. That's you, by the way,' he added, with a mirthless laugh.

Annat touched his sleeve. 'Does your father still want revenge?' she said.

'Oh, yes. It doesn't matter to him that you helped to bring a lost daughter back to him. All he cares about is Sarl's death. I don't like to think what kind of life my sister – Huldis – leads there. She can't leave, as I was able to. And I'm not going back,' he added, setting his mouth into a thin line.

Boris lowered the blotter and gave them an exasperated look. 'Could you discuss this some other time? I'm trying to concentrate.'

'Please excuse us,' said Cluny, smiling at Annat, who was less easily mollified.

'What we're talking about may be important, Mister Grebenshikov,' she said. Boris sighed.

'I've no doubt it is, but I'm trying to work out how much of the scribbling on this blotter is significant and how much relates to the *De Naturae* of Iolcas, a subject that seems to have caused your brother some difficulty. I need graphite powder. Has your servant brought our bags up yet, Monsieur d'Ademar?'

'Mother, I forgot to ask him,' said Cluny. 'Excuse me.'

After Planchet had been dispatched and had returned with their luggage, Boris was able to produce the graphite powder from the tool kit in his valise. He scattered it over the blotter, shook it from side to side and blew away the residue. The fine dust had settled in the indentations left by Malchik's pen, and it was now possible to decipher what he had written. Cluny craned over Boris's shoulder and said, 'That's our last week's essay. But I can see some stuff about crows too.'

'It looks like part of the letter he wrote me,' said Yuste.

'Is there anything you don't recognise, Missis?' Boris asked her. Yuste pored over the paper, her fingertip hovering over the part-obscured lines left by Malchik's letter. As she reached the bottom of the blotter, she paused.

'I don't remember this sentence,' she said. 'But the letter was very confused. I'll fetch it from my reticule to compare it.'

While Yuste was away, Annat knelt by the desk to study the lines she had pointed out.

'Did you read the letter as well?' said Boris. And then, suddenly, she caught a faint whisper of thought, as if someone had spoken softly close to her ear: *sprechen*?

Annat found herself smiling. She had to make an

effort to shape her thoughts and send them to him, a slight awkwardness that always accompanied *sprechen* with a stranger.

– *Not closely. But Yuste's right. This is something else. I don't know what it means.*

'"The Rom know something. Bottom of *Rue des Salines, Place Vergey, Ruelle Amboise . . .*"' Boris quoted. 'I can't read the rest. They look like directions. But who or what are the Rom?'

'Ah,' said Cluny. 'The Rom.'

They turned to him, expecting him to continue. Cluny rubbed his hands together as if he were massaging the knuckles, and seemed to struggle over what he should say.

'What's the problem?' said Boris.

'We're . . . students are . . . not supposed to visit the Rom,' said Cluny. 'They are *tziganes*. Traveller-gypsies. They have certain things in common with Wanderers. The second curse of Megalmayar —'

'Not more Doxan rubbish!' Yuste exclaimed, overhearing him as she returned with her bag.

'It is part of Doxan legend rather than the Rule of the Church,' said Cluny. 'The Church says that the Mother only uttered one curse, that against the Wanderers. But the story of Her second curse may have grown up to explain the nomadic nature of the *tziganes*, who —'

'Good grief, is this a lecture?' said Boris. Cluny looked so crestfallen that Annat was caught between an urge to laugh and a wish to defend him from their interruptions.

'Why was Malchik interested in the Rom, Cluny?' she asked.

He gave her a small, thankful smile and said, 'Malchik liked the *tziganes*. As a Wanderer, and also because the Rom love music. He started to visit them in secret.'

'I see. So we're to conclude that Malchik was stolen by gypsies?' said Boris.

Yuste shook her letter at him. 'What is wrong with you, Boris Andreyevich? It might explain where Malchik has gone. There may even be an innocent explanation.'

'The gypsies don't steal young men, *Zhïdova*,' said Boris, folding his arms. Annat gaped at him, unable to believe what she had heard, while Yuste turned crimson. 'What? What have I said?'

'How dare you call me that! As if it were harmless,' said Yuste.

Boris looked at her with a perplexed expression, scratching behind his ear. 'You must know that I wouldn't—' he began.

'Would you call my brother that?'

He raised his hand in a gesture of doubt and dismissal. 'You know I didn't mean it as an insult, Yuste. If you know me at all.'

('What's the matter?' Cluny asked Annat.

'He called her a *Youpin*. A Yid,' she whispered.)

'It's clear you don't know me at all, Boris Grebenshikov,' said Yuste, slapping the flimsy letter down on the desk next to the blotter. Boris straightened, looking at her thoughtfully.

'I'm sorry, Yuste,' he said. 'I wouldn't want to offend *you*.'

Yuste met his eyes with a suspicious look, as if she suspected him of laughing at her, however gently. But his face was serious.

'Perhaps we had better forget it was said,' she answered. 'But as a White Sklav, you should know well what these terms mean to us. To Wanderers.'

'That's how you think of me, eh? As a White Sklav?' said Boris, turning his back on her to survey the blotter with its black marks.

'That is what you are, Boris Grebenshikov. Please, I must sit down. I am beginning to have a headache.'

'I think,' said Cluny, intervening gently, 'it might be better if we continued in the morning. Perhaps then we could follow up this address that Malchik has left, and maybe visit the Rom themselves. I have asked Planchet to organise the sleeping arrangements in my chambers. The ladies can occupy the outer room and you, Monsieur Grebenshikov, can take my bed. I will share with Planchet.'

'You are very kind,' said Yuste, who had taken a seat on one of the chairs ranged round the table.

'There's no need to give up your bed,' said Boris. 'I can sleep on the floor.'

'I insist,' said Cluny. 'I will try not to disturb you in the morning, when I get up for my run. Planchet has heated some water for the ladies' *toilette*, and everything is ready.' He paused as Yuste and Annat started to laugh.

'Forgive us, Cluny,' said Yuste. 'You must think us

uncouth barbarians, but we do not make a *toilette*. We wash, we brush our hair, and make ready for sleep. And we say our evening prayers,' she added.

'Yes, Malchik taught me a little about that,' said Cluny. 'All those blessings or *baruchot* that you have to make. I must say, we Doxans have an easy life.'

Yuste glanced at the silent detective. 'Boris Grebenshikov, I would make my peace with you,' she said, softly.

'Not at all. I was at fault,' said Boris, and his face did not relax into a smile.

Yuste gave a little shake of the head and, gathering up her skirts, made her way back to Cluny's rooms. Annat lingered a little, looking from Cluny to Boris, the one with a sombre face, the other smiling nervously.

'I'm – ah – afraid we haven't been introduced,' said Cluny, holding out a tentative hand. Boris looked at it in surprise, then took it and shook it warmly.

'The name's Grebenshikov,' he said. 'Annat's aunt has engaged me to help look into Malchik's case. Though it seems that may be harder than we at first anticipated.'

'I hope you'll excuse me asking,' said Cluny, glancing sidelong at Annat as if he wanted her support, 'but what is a White Sklav? I know that Annat and her family are Wanderers, but since I came to Axar there seem to be so many other nuances and races I've never heard of.'

'I'm like you, Mister,' said Boris, with a grim mouth. 'I come from a pure Doxan family with no taint of Wanderer or Darkman blood. I don't imagine Yuste meant it kindly. There is small love lost between my kind and hers.'

'But you're not like that, are you?' said Cluny. 'You don't think there's any taint.'

Boris turned away. 'What I think doesn't matter. I have to watch what I say.'

Annat stepped towards him. She did not want to speak out loud, however much she trusted Cluny.

– *I know you didn't mean it*, she thought. – *But Yuste* – She broke off, unable to articulate the meaning even in her mind. – *Yuste is complicated, Yuste can be unfair, Yuste is proud*. There was too much to be said.

'Never mind,' said Boris aloud.

'Time for bed,' said Cluny cheerily, scooping up Annat's hand as if it were the most natural thing to do. She let him lead her from the room, and thought of what it would be like to kiss him on the mouth. Would it be as sweet and heady as it had been to kiss Eugenie? They halted together on the landing, and Cluny looked down at her as if he too could read her mind.

'You have no idea how good it is to see you,' he said. 'When we've solved this business with Malchik, you and I will have such a lot to talk about.'

Annat found herself smiling up at him. He put his hands on her shoulders and said, 'You are much prettier than you were four years ago. And much prettier than your father.'

Annat laughed, enjoying the compliment and its allusion to her likeness to her father, whose striking appearance was notorious. Cluny blushed and added,

'As you can tell, I'm not used to talking to girls. Of course, my father would have liked to marry me to some heiress, and that's another reason I got away as soon as possible. Your brother, on the other hand, is something of a ladies' man. Older ladies, at that.'

Annat covered her smile with her hand. 'Malchik?'

Cluny nodded. 'I think you should hesitate before sharing this information with your aunt,' he said.

'I hope we find him soon, Cluny. I think – I feel – that he is in danger.'

'Mother, I hope so too. I keep wondering whether my presence here has made things worse. Made things happen. Ademar has a long shadow,' he said, taking her hands and pressing them between his own.

Annat waited until she was certain that Yuste slept. The lights in the outer room had been extinguished, but a crack of radiance still shone from beneath Planchet's door, and she could hear him and Cluny conversing in low voices. The room Boris occupied was dark. She had made herself comfortable on the chaise-longue, giving Yuste the chance to occupy the couch, which could be transformed into a bed. Now she sat up in the gloom, thankful that her night vision allowed her to see in the blue shadow, and began to peel off her nightdress. Goose-pimpling with cold, she hurried to dress herself, struggling with the folds of the noisy petticoat that even she had to wear under her shortened skirt. She had noticed that it always took women longer than it did men to dress, though the formal attire that Cluny assumed no doubt needed some care and preparation; but men like Boris or Yuda could be ready in minutes. She paused, half-naked in the dark, and gazed at Boris's door. Odd as it seemed, she thought there had been a trace of something like affection in his calling Yuste 'Zhidova'. And Yuste was not someone who readily inspired affection. She sat listening to her aunt's even breathing, feeling a trace of sadness that they were so estranged from each other. She did not dwell on the emotion; even now, in sleep, Yuste might sense what she was doing and wake to interrupt her.

Instead of putting on her boots, she tugged on the soft leather slippers she kept for indoor use. She knew that she could have pulled on a robe over her night-clothes, but she felt that dressing was like putting on armour, to ward herself against what she might dis-cover from the mirror. When she was ready, she did not at once rise from the chaise-longue, but waited, watching her aunt's slim form lying motionless beneath the covers, except for the faint stir of Yuste's breathing. In the blue darkness, Yuste still bore the faint aura of a shaman, an echo of the powers that her brother had erased. Annat, who seldom thought about her aunt, or questioned her own feelings, could not imagine how one would survive such a loss. She thought of stroking Yuste's grey-brown hair (though she could not see its colour in the dark) where it lay unfastened on the pillow. She longed for a moment to snuggle in beneath the covers beside her aunt, as she had done when she was a child. There had been so much to fear at night in those days, after her birth-mother died: the monsters of the furniture, the strange shapes of dreams, and faces she did not know that gaped at her from the shadows.

Now Annat herself had become a creature of the night. Darkness alone was not enough to frighten her. If it hid powerful and magic forces, she too could walk amongst them unseen, her eyes aglow like a cat's. She stood up, turning away from the sleeping Yuste, and moved softly across the parquet floor towards the baize door. Her power was like something she wielded between her hands, but it was also a coil of fire that thrummed in her veins and nerves. She laid her hands on the fabric of the inner door, before drawing it open and swiftly unlocking the outer one. She slipped through the opening and pulled it close behind her, taking care not to let the lock snap shut. There was a dim light on the landing, and cool air drifted in from the open door downstairs, smelling of wood-smoke-laden mist. Annat lingered for a moment, letting her shaman's senses tingle into life, as she breathed in the scent and silence of the night. Malchik's room remained unlocked; she entered on soft feet, and turned the knob to illumine the electric light.

Everything was as they had left it: the blotter laid aside on Malchik's desk, with a dusting of graphite powder; and the pages of Malchik's discarded essay that Boris had carefully straightened and laid out on the table. Annat crossed the room, feeling the warmth of her brother's presence as if he had only just that moment left. Her hand brushed across his folded prayer shawl as she passed, and she paused to look up at Cluny's painting, glowing in its frame.

Somehow it was a little eerie to enter the deserted bedroom. She sat down on the bed, facing the mirror, and gripping the coverlet with her hands. The mirror stubbornly showed her her own reflection, stained in the wan light of the solitary bulb. Annat felt her own heart beating, and knew she was afraid. She waited, drawing in deep breaths, and trying to remember what Yuda had taught her about questioning mirrors. At last, after a few minutes had passed, she stood up and approached the glass. As she drew closer, it seemed to her imagination that her image wandered and rippled, as if the mercury had liquefied or turned to water. She laid her hands on the cold surface of the glass, and closed her eyes. The time had come to plunge down, into the dreaming darkness of her shaman mind. Like a diver on the brink, she drew a deep breath, and jumped.

Chapter 5

Yuste woke not long after dawn with a stiff back and a dry mouth. She rolled back the covers and eased herself out of bed, thinking of the carafe of water that Planchet had left standing near the window, where it would be cool. At once, she saw that the chaise-longue was empty, and too tidy to have been slept in. Cursing under her breath in Sklav, using words that Annat would have been surprised she knew, she flung open the door and burst out on to the landing. The stone chilled the soles of her bare feet, and the frosty breath of morning drifted up from the open door downstairs. Where had Annat gone? Had she strayed out into the night alone, on some errand Yuste could only guess at?

Yuste drew breath and called her niece's name. The sound of her voice echoed in the stairwell. She felt more anger than fear, but it was her fear that gave rise to the anger. She could imagine so many dangers too quickly. She reminded herself that Annat was not merely a vulnerable girl of seventeen. Annat had powers that could sear an ordinary attacker to cinders. Of course, the child must have gone out searching for Malchik. Annat would think that she knew better than the others, her foolish old aunt and some detective with limited powers. She might have gone out into the dark to make a scan, to let her mind travel through the countryside, seeking Malchik or trawling for shaman worlds.

Yuste started to shiver. Her limbs might ache, but she was no longer fatigued as she had been yesterday. Curse it, she had only forty years! And here she was, stiff in bone and sinew as an old woman, trembling in the cold of a spring dawn. No wonder Annat despised her, when she had to lean on Boris and accept Cluny's courtesy as if she were some frail and delicate flower. She strode back into the inner room, to find that her cry must have wakened the others. Planchet was standing just outside the door to his room, fully dressed, and Boris Grebenshikov had just emerged in his silk dressing gown, the dark hairs on his chest showing at the throat; there was no sign of Cluny yet. Yuste remembered that she was wearing no more than a nightgown, and snatched up her shawl from the foot of her bed, draping it round her shoulders.

'Good morning, Boris Andreyevich; Monsieur Planchet,' she said, trying to hide her confusion.

'Where's Annat?' said Boris, striding towards her.

'Does Madame require some *kava*?' said Planchet, in his grave, soft voice.

'Yes, thank you, Monsieur,' said Yuste, who was not accustomed to the presence of servants. She watched the man give a little bow and retreat into his quarters before she answered Boris. 'She's gone. Her bed's not slept in.'

'Shit,' said Boris, running his hand round the collar of his dressing gown.

'I haven't looked in Malchik's room yet,' said Yuste. She sighed. There they were again; anger and fear. She looked at Boris's unshaven face. He looked drawn; plainly he too was not someone who enjoyed an early-morning awakening. A sigh stretched her thin frame. 'She could be anywhere.'

'I doubt if she's left the college,' said Boris. 'Remember, Clement guards the door, and Annat couldn't know any other way out, unless Cluny showed her. She can't have gone far.'

Yuste was not quite listening to him, though she took in the sense of his words. 'I know that she is powerful,' she said. 'But that only draws down greater danger. And she can be reckless. She is like Yuda; she loves the smell of danger.'

'Not like us, then,' said Boris, wryly. She focused on him.

'I was never a shaman long enough to learn,' she said. 'But no matter. Annat is still young; she is a woman. Too young to know true fear, and how to master it. Yuda can teach her how to use her powers, but he cannot teach her good sense. Even if he tried, which I doubt.'

'I'll bet he did try,' said Boris. 'You do try with

young shamans, especially if they're your *kinder*. Let's look in Malchik's room.'

As they crossed the landing, Yuste found herself saying, 'You seem to know Yuda better than I was aware.'

'We've worked on a few missions together. Railway stuff,' he said dismissively. 'He knew me when Stromnak was . . . still alive.'

'Stromnak?' said Yuste, doubtfully, before recalling where she had seen the name. 'Oh – your partner.'

'That's right,' said Boris, walking into Malchik's empty room. 'My dead partner.'

The electric light was on, not yet dimmed by the dawn filtering through the unshuttered windows. Yuste found herself studying the room, and she saw at a glance two changes. The door to Malchik's bedroom stood ajar, and the light was on; and a bare space marked the place where Cluny's picture had hung on the wall. Boris was ahead of her, crossing the room in quick strides, and flinging open the bedroom door. They saw at once that the room was empty; the bedcover had been crumpled where Annat – if it were Annat – had sat on it, and Cluny's picture lay on the ground, the glass broken. There were no other signs of violence or struggle.

Boris stooped to pick up the broken picture. Yuste heard him gasp, and she too saw something like a wisp of smoke or a length of cobweb that seemed to hang between the picture and the surface of the mirror. When Boris drew the picture against his chest, the thread did not break, but seemed to draw out in length;

it vanished into the mirror like a fishing-line into a clear pool. Tiptoeing, Yuste approached the detective, until she could almost touch him, and as she did so, her eye caught something scribbled on the floor: three words in Kurillic characters, the alphabet of Sklavic. *Mountain, River, Forest*.

She looked up into Boris's face and felt her own face naked, with artifice and manners stripped away.

'Holy Mother,' he said, 'she's gone into the mirror!'

'Zyon,' said Yuste under her breath. She sat down on the bed where Annat had sat, drawing her shawl close about her. There could be little doubt that Boris was right: somehow, Annat had entered the mirror, and left them a trail to show them where she had gone.

'What does it mean?' she asked Boris. '"Mountain, River, Forest"?'

'It's the picture,' he said, turning it round so she could see the image behind the cracked glass. 'But Mother knows what it means.' He handed the frame to her, with the wisp of spider-web still adhering to it, and approached the mirror, stretching out his hands. 'I don't have the power,' he said to himself. Yuste watched him lay his hands on the surface and his forehead against it. She waited, feeling with her atrophied senses the flow of his power. Her mind was racing, thought spilling over thought, as she conjectured and dreaded what had happened to Annat.

Boris stepped back, withdrawing his hands. 'It's no good,' he said. 'Someone opened a shaman door here, but they've sealed it. And I can't tell where it led.

Look,' and he held up the end of the thread, broken off.

Yuste hugged the broken picture against her chest. 'We can't follow her into the mirror,' she said. 'But the trail may still work.'

Boris sat down beside her on the bed, taking his head in his hands. 'The boy must have gone the same way,' he said. 'By the Mother, I hope he did. Or we've lost two *kinder*.'

'Annat has left us a message, and this picture,' said Yuste.

'Woman, you'll admit it's not much to go on.'

'Annat knows how to make a trail,' she insisted. 'It will lead us to her.'

'You seem very confident,' said Boris. 'We don't know what this means. It's a riddle.'

Yuste looked down at the image in the picture. 'Think, Boris Andreyevich. Someone must have sealed the shaman door. Annat would not have done that. She would have left it open so that we could follow her. Therefore, someone was using this mirror. They used it to trap her. And I do think that Malchik went the same way.'

Boris rose to his feet. He looked at his own reflection and Yuste's in the innocent mirror. Once more, he approached the glass, and laid his hands on it. He seemed to feel the surface, letting his palms caress it as if searching for flaws. His hands left brief marks of condensation as he moved them across it, blurring the reflected room beyond. 'It's true,' he said, in a dull voice. 'The girl was here. And I can feel traces of someone else – much fainter. That would be the boy. There's nothing else, nothing to tell me where they went. But they were here.'

'Boris Andreyevich,' said Yuste, 'I have no power that could tell us that. I am all but useless.'

He swung round at her. 'I should have known! I should have checked the mirror yesterday.'

'Why?' she said, with a faint smile. 'It's not often people vanish into mirrors.'

'Your niece thought of it,' he said, roughly.

'It doesn't matter now,' she said. 'Do you think it matters to me? How easily we could all be wise after the event. You and I have to work with the powers that we possess.'

Boris sat down on the bed beside her. 'Let me see the picture,' he said. Yuste handed it to him, and he fingered the fragment of spider-web still attached like an umbilical cord to the canvas. 'I'd swear, if I had the power, that I could read this,' he said.

'What do you mean, Boris?'

'The thread may have broken, but the girl left the pattern of her journey in each fibre of it. Repeated once and again. What we need is someone who can decipher it.'

Yuste studied her companion. He could not be much older than she was, but his smooth pate gave him an air of middle-aged gravitas – an air that was misleading, she was beginning to see. Small and compact, he reminded her of the men with whom she felt most at ease, her brother and Sival. But there was an air about him of one bewildered and lost, and striving against his bewilderment with all his masculine intelligence.

'Cluny must be our starting point,' she said. 'It is his picture, and he must know what it shows.'

But once woken Cluny could tell them no more than he had confessed to Annat: that he had painted the image for Malchik after the theme of his recurring dreams. They removed the broken glass from the frame and set the picture on the table in Cluny's room. When they were all washed and dressed, they gathered round to study it once more. Cluny knelt on the floor to examine it closely, touching the piece of thread with cautious fingers.

'It's just like spider-web,' he said. 'And you say shamans can do that? Leave something for others to follow, like a paper trail?'

Yuste nodded. 'Our problem is that Annat's trail is too subtle for us to translate,' she said. 'The girl thought better of us than we deserve. Or more likely she was in a hurry.'

Cluny stood up, his eyes bright with eagerness and morning energy. 'I still think we should go to see the Rom,' he said. 'Even if Malchik was sucked into the mirror, they might be able to tell us what this picture represents. They travel everywhere. And there are shamans amongst them who might be able to read the thread.'

'I suppose it's worth a try,' said Boris. 'Just now we don't know where to begin.'

'Cluny is right,' said Yuste. 'The scene in the picture is very distinctive. There can't be many places where you will see a mountain standing by itself in the middle of a plain.'

Cluny glanced at the picture, and paused to study it. 'Now you come to mention it, it is rather remarkable,' he said. 'One sees a mountain range, but not a solitary peak. Unless it's a volcano,' he added. 'I've never seen a volcano, but I don't imagine they look like this. I assumed that as it was a dream-picture it would be like those mountains that children draw. But Malchik was quite specific.'

'A mountain standing in the middle of a plain,' said Boris. 'I've never heard of anything like that in Neustria. Unless it's in the north.'

'You'd think people would want to brag about it,' said Cluny with a nervous laugh. 'I mean, one would expect word of something like that. Everyone has heard of the Lepas Mountains and their famous peaks.'

'I've heard of the range. Not the famous peaks,' Boris snapped. At once, Cluny knew what to say to cover any embarrassment.

'My family home lies much nearer to the mountains than does Masalyar,' he said, smiling at Boris. 'Sometimes we could even see them on the eastern horizon, when the weather was clear. I suppose the point is that there aren't any singular structures.'

Yuste saw that Boris was struggling not to be charmed by Cluny's easy manners. She smiled inwardly, briefly distracted from her worries. But if Annat and Malchik had been taken beyond Neustria, where could they have gone? There might be many lands in the world that could hold such a peak, and the Rom could not know them all.

'Cluny,' she said, resting her hand on his wrist to distract him from mollifying Boris, 'you said yourself the picture represents a dream. Is it possible that this could be one of the Lepas Mountains?'

'Things would be so much easier if it were,' said Cluny, gazing down into her eyes with a hint of sadness. 'But Malchik definitely told me that the hill stood in the centre of a plain, all by itself. He said that it shone in the sun – like glass.'

Yuste withdrew her hand and gathered up the heavy reticule from the couch. 'I want to see the Rom. Now,' she said. 'Have you made a note of Malchik's directions, Boris Andreyevich?'

Before he could answer, Cluny interjected, 'I have asked Planchet to come with us. He is – was – a man-at-arms, and I think it would do no harm for him to accompany us. Also he can carry the lunch.'

'Good heavens, child, this isn't a picnic!' said Yuste, both amused and annoyed.

'Well – if I can explain – I think it might be good manners to bring gifts of food to the Rom. They are very hospitable, but they are also quite poor. I thought a few bottles from the college cellars might be just the thing.'

Yuste did not know whether to laugh or weep. In many ways, Cluny reminded her of Malchik, though she doubted her nephew knew as much about charm. 'That is an excellent idea, Cluny,' she said. 'Come, Boris. You can carry the picture, and I shall carry myself!'

Boris had noted the direction from Malchik's blotter in his pocket-book, and they set off into the town with Cluny in the lead, and Planchet bringing up the rear with a wicker hamper. Yuste could not help thinking how absurd they must look; they did indeed appear like a carefree party setting off to picnic by the river, and as it was a fine day, they were not alone; clusters of students, crow-like in their black gowns, seemed to be heading the same way. Yuste wished she had not thought of crows; she glanced up at the blue sky, but there were no watchers on patrol this morning.

They paused on a street corner while Cluny consulted with Boris on the directions. Yuste leaned against a wall in the shade, and Planchet stood stolidly at a distance. She would have liked to speak to him, but he seemed to keep himself apart, as if he did not trust familiarity. His long, blunt face was weathered, dark as leather, and she wondered whether he was accustomed to serving indoors as he did now. As Cluny led them down a narrow passageway between two tall rows of dwellings, their walls lime-washed with saffron paint, she hung back to speak to him. She spoke Franj.

'A pleasant day, is it not, Monsieur Planchet?' she said.

Planchet looked at her as if she were mad. 'I wouldn't call it pleasant when folk go missing in the night, Madame,' he said.

He was right, and Yuste felt sharply the foolishness of her easy pleasantry. She also recognised a rebuff, but she was determined not to give up. 'Is it true that you come from the Castle of Ademar, Monsieur?' she said.

Planchet did not look at her. 'I've served Monsieur *le Batard* since he was breached,' he said. 'I am his body servant. But there's no need for you to call me fancy names, Madame; I am Planchet.'

'Then you should not call me Madame, Planchet, for I do not come from the high-born gentry. I am Wanderer, and we have no titles in society.'

Planchet continued to look straight ahead, his face expressionless. 'My old master, the Doyen of Ademar, burns Wanderers,' he said. 'But Seigneur Cluny is my only master now.'

Yuste was not sure how to receive this statement, though she felt a little encouraged by it, blunt as it was. Instead she found herself thinking aloud. 'It is our good fortune that no one in Masalyar talks of burning Wanderers,' she said. 'They have brought back the old sumptuary laws, and we must observe them.'

'We all live under Neustrian law,' said Planchet, and Yuste guessed that she would get no more out of him. With a little bow, she went forward to rejoin Boris and Cluny, who were once more conferring at the end of the street.

'That was Ruelle Amboise,' Cluny was saying. 'I'm pretty sure these directions lead to the Source Vergey. It's a short walk from the water-meadows.'

'It seems a little elaborate if Malchik simply wanted to go to the river,' said Boris.

'Oh, he would have gone straight to the bridge,' said Cluny. Yuste could tell that Boris made him nervous.

'There's a track that leads from here directly to the moorings. The path to Source Vergey is on the opposite bank.'

'And you reckon we'll find the Rom near this Source Vergey?'

Cluny gave several vigorous nods. 'The town council forbids them to camp in the water-meadows. And I am breaking college rules by attempting to visit them. So did Malchik.'

'If we're right, Malchik has a little more to worry about than college rules just now,' said Boris, raising his eyebrows.

'Don't take any notice of him, Cluny,' said Yuste. 'Lead us to the moorings. If there is any trouble, Boris Andreyevich and I will vouch for you.'

With a grateful smile to her, Cluny strode off across the open, stony road that crossed the end of Ruelle Amboise. The path became a well-trodden mud track that led between some tumbledown dwellings, though by the smoke issuing from the chimneys they were not deserted. Washing hung from the bushes in the overgrown gardens, and Yuste could hear the crowing of chickens as they scratched in the yard. She gathered up her skirt to stop it trailing in the dirt, and reflected as she often did that she should have emulated Annat's more liberated dress. Buoyed up by petticoats and skirts, she felt like a ship under sail.

Cluny was hurrying down the sloping path, and she glimpsed the river's blue sheen ahead. Suddenly there was a din from the farmyard as the hens set up a crowing and cackling, as if a fox had burst in amongst them. Yuste paused, and felt a cold shadow across her heart. There was a shadow in the sky, not the shape of a passing cloud, but a great mass of dark wings and harsh voices, belling in unison.

As soon as she had stepped into the mirror, Annat heard a sound like a door slamming shut behind her. She tried to turn back, but she found herself in darkness, rushing forward, drawn by a force more powerful than a lodestone. She could see nothing, and the only sensation was one of speed. She threw her arms up in front of her face, as it to ward off an impact, for it was terrifying to hurtle through a void, without even the touch of wind against her face to give her comfort. None of the Journeys she had made into shaman worlds had begun like this; it was as if a mighty will had seized her and was dragging her to an unseen destination.

Annat struggled to call upon her powers, but they seemed frozen inside her, tiny sparks that she could not stir into a flame. Then panic cut her like a knife, for she was losing all sense of self; her body seemed to shed its boundaries, and particles of darkness streamed through her as she broke into fragments. Only wet tears on her face told her that she was still whole, a shape bounded by emptiness. She pressed her hands against her face to feel the water, and licked at her fingertips to taste the salt. Salt of the sea, her mother's grave, its burning taste on her tongue brought back her courage. She spread out her arms, bracing herself to swoop through the shadow like a bird. If she could fly, she would no longer be a victim, borne through the rushing silence against her will.

The force snapped like an India-rubber band stretched beyond its limit, and Annat was flung forwards, falling headlong to the ground. Her hands broke her fall, bruising against smooth stone, and she lay where she had dropped, with the breath driven out of her. For a few moments, she was too jarred by the impact to lift herself; there was a ringing noise in her ears, which slowly dispersed and faded into the sound of laughter.

Her hair had come loose and as she sat up, her bones sore, she pushed it out of her face. She was in a round room, smooth as a shell and dark as onyx. Opposite her stood a man-high mirror in a gilded gesso frame, and beside it the dark figure of a stocky man watched her with a smile of contempt.

Annat sat back on her heels, rubbing her palms against her skirt. She did not think it wise to use her powers; if this were a shaman, he commanded forces far stronger than any she knew. His skin was golden-dark, his eyes rich brown, the face framed with a beard and long, straggly hair. An *eikon*-face, rich as the enamelled mosaics of monkish saints in a Doxan temple; but his smile did not fit the sober dignity of their features.

'*Zdrasvuytye, Gospodina!*' he greeted her, speaking Sklavic. She recognised the native accent, subtly different to her own. Annat got slowly to her feet, straightening her skirts. He was a shaman, she was sure of it, but there was something strange about the signature of his power. He had not tried to hide it from her, and it seemed crooked, like a light caught and severed by a prism. He was certainly powerful, but with no exceptional strength that could explain the force that had drawn her here.

'Who are you, Mister?' she said, tensing on her feet. She was not sure whether her own powers would answer her summons. She flexed her fingers, and sensed the dim, strangled sparks inside her. This man had disabled her, quenching her inner fires. He must not know that she was afraid.

He looked at her, chin on his hand. 'You must be Annat Vasilyevich,' he said.

She kept her feelings closed in her fist. She could not allow him to read her, scrape out her thoughts and emotions to examine them like scraps of meat. He wanted to play a game where he made the rules.

'You brought me here, Mister,' she said. 'You know why.'

'I brought you to join your brother, little shaman. I needed a pair.'

Not long ago, Annat would have cried out her brother's name and demanded to be taken to him. The wish rose in her heart, but her father's teaching helped her to keep it in.

'I saw him in the mirror,' she said. 'He was calling to me for help.'

'I thought that would bring you here,' said the shaman. 'I let him find the mirror. Being an innocent, he did just what I wanted.'

Annat folded her arms across her chest. 'It seems a

lot of trouble to catch two *kinder*,' she said. 'You must
have wanted us badly.'

'Is that how you see yourself? As a child?' he said.
'I see a woman, and a powerful shaman. Though not
of my rank, of course. You are lucky, for my master
seeks the heart of a powerful shaman. Yours would
not be strong enough.'

'The heart of a powerful shaman. What does he
want that for?'

'He wants it, but I need it. I have been collecting
the . . . ingredients for a great magic. Follow, there is
someone I want you to meet.'

He did not try to exert his will over her, but Annat
thought it would be unwise to resist. She followed him
into the space behind the mirror, where a neatly shaped
tunnel, smooth as a worm-cast, led from the round
chamber into another, lighter room. He kept glancing
over his shoulder to check that she was following, and
his eyes twinkled with cold merriment.

The brilliance of the new chamber took her by surprise. Its crystal walls caught and diffused the light
that fell from a hole in the roof, a jagged vent cut into
the rock. Rainbows curved and shimmered on the floor,
drawing bands of colour across its leaden surface. For
a moment she was dazzled by the brightness, the
swords and shafts of light that arced and cut across
each other, dividing the shade. He turned to face her
like a magician conjuring a string of coloured scarves.

'This is the Crystal Chamber,' he said, and she heard
her brother's voice speaking her name. Shading her
eyes, she glimpsed two shadowy figures, both striped

with sunlight. Then Malchik strode out of the confusion of colours and crushed her in his arms. The strength of it surprised her; with her face pressed against his corduroy chest, she reached out to embrace him. The familiar smell of his clothes, the starch of his collar, the bittersweet tang of cologne – all these things added up to a sense of her brother, who was both weaker and stronger than she was.

'Touching,' said the stranger's voice, light and dry. As Malchik released her, she saw his face, pale and with two days' growth of the soft stubble he called a beard. If only he could *sprechen*, there was so much he could have told her already! His brown eyes behind their lenses observed her with concern. Resting his hand on her shoulder, he turned towards the stranger and said, 'You'd better tell us what you want. Now you've got us both.'

'But surely your sister will want to greet an old friend?' said the shaman, conjuring a second figure from amongst the play of light and shadow.

As Malchik gripped her more tightly, Annat tried to ward off a sudden light-headedness. Dizzy and sick, she denied to herself that the man was who he appeared to be. She leant against her brother, feeling her senses swamped by the sea-cold gaze that seemed to reach out to harm her across ice and death. He was still tall, but his great frame seemed to have shrunk on itself. His face had the pallor of rotten fish, and his eyes were sunk in sockets with a liverish stain. He did not look like a dead man, but one kept too long underground, where the sun never shone.

'Don't you recognise me, Annat?' he said, in a strange, hoarse voice, rusty with disuse.

'Sarl,' she said. Naming him did not seem enough; though she had seen him die four years ago, he was standing before her, not as a decayed corpse, but something alive. She drew breath, not so much afraid, but with her senses offended and disgusted by this unnatural event. Now she knew why the whole world had seemed awry since the day she had seen the crows flying over Masalyar. They were the long edge of Sarl's shadow, the shadow of Ademar cast like that of a gnomon across the south.

'I brought him back to life,' said the other one, in a horrible, self-satisfied voice. 'He lives, but only for ninety days. To keep him above ground will take two souls, and the heart of a powerful shaman.'

'You want our souls,' said Annat, softly. She did not feel much anger, or even suitable fear. Her mind was at work, busy with thoughts of how they might escape.

'Your souls were specified by my client. You need not fear that I want them now. The heart and the souls must be taken together, and regrettably I do not yet possess the heart. A lack which I will shortly rectify.'

'You had better keep your promise, Magus,' said Sarl. 'Or your own heart may serve the purpose.'

The man seemed to pretend he had not heard these words. 'My client, the Doyen of Ademar, has given me clear instructions,' he went on. 'I must seek out the most powerful shaman of Neustria. And your father, Yuda Vasilyevich. They happen to be the same.'

Once again, Annat pent up her cry of protest and

defiance. She glanced up at Malchik, and his brown gaze succoured her like honey. He too had grown stronger since they travelled together through a shaman land.

'I don't think you'll find my father such an easy catch,' he said.

The Magus shrugged. 'Whether it is easy or difficult, I shall catch him,' he said. 'And you will wait here until my return. I have provided for all your needs, except escape. You will find that you cannot leave this mountain. It is easy to come here, much harder to depart.'

There was nothing they could say in answer. As they watched, the Magus bowed to them – unsmiling, this time – with his hand on his breast, and beckoned Sarl to follow him from the room. Neither Malchik nor Annat made a move to prevent them, but they turned to watch them enter the passage that led to the chamber where the mirror stood. As he passed them, Sarl gave them a cheerless grin that showed most of his teeth and his livid gums. He had a shambling walk that they did not remember, as if he lacked the strength to hold his great frame upright. Somehow, this was more chilling than his former vigour, for it evoked a certain pity. They watched the tall, stooping figure following the Magus out of sight, and when it was gone, Annat gave a little shiver.

Things were not turning out entirely as Semyon had planned. True, he had raised the old man's Heir from the dead, and captured the two Wanderers with an ease that surprised him. The mirrors were working to his satisfaction, allowing him to travel without the tiresome need for horses and long journeys. He had performed feats that, when he returned to the court of the Staryetz, would surely bring him riches and renown. All that he wanted. He had planned and plotted, and the one thing he had not bargained for was the character of the Heir himself.

He could hear Sarl's noisy breathing in the close darkness of the mirror. When Semyon had raised him up, he had expected gratitude; or else a mind that, like the Doyen's, was fogged with pious delusion. However, Sarl had shown himself swiftly to be neither naïve nor biddable. Though his body had not regained its living strength, his mind and his shamanic powers were sharp and strong, and he had seen at once what Semyon needed to hide; that his own heart would serve very well to complete the magic that confirmed Sarl's presence in the world. He knew it, and seemed to enjoy reminding Semyon of it, as if he needed to confound with evidence of mortality the powerful magus who had given back his life.

His thoughts well warded, Semyon ground his teeth. This half-dead scion of a minor lord would not threaten him! In an instant, his skill could wipe the smile from the upstart's face, and send the body back to dust and the soul to hell. He had striven not to speak his mind to Sarl, trying to console himself with the inner knowledge of the forces he commanded. He had smiled and laughed at the raw threats, but the shame of it was, they made him nervous. He could not quite believe that Sarl would only utter those words, and not act upon them.

They stepped out of a mirror into the cool, leaf-filtered light of the castle. Semyon found himself sighing and relaxing, as if he had passed a trial. He hurried across the room to check that no one had tampered with his suitcases. He was not so foolish as to open them in Sarl's presence, for it was better to preserve an air of mystery, but when he touched them he could sense their contents, waiting passively until he should unleash them again.

He did not like to keep his back turned towards Sarl for long. He jerked upright with a little too much haste, to find the Heir gazing out of the green-glazed window at the world to which he had recently returned.

'In all your journeyings, have you ever visited hell, Magus?' he said, quietly.

Semyon disliked this type of question. To deny it seemed to suggest a limit to his powers, but it would be weak to lie.

'The living do not enter hell. Not even such as I,' he said, sitting down at the board with the suitcases placed either side of his chair.

'You lie,' said Sarl, turning smoothly. He had not lost assurance, though his limbs did not always answer his will. 'I saw shamans in hell.'

Curiosity overcame Semyon's need to hide his ignorance. He felt a kind of hunger to hear about the worst of all worlds. He had thought it a myth, or a place that shamans could not enter by any path he had learned of.

'Tell me of it,' he said, leaning forward.

'Why should I give you so much? Besides, it is forbidden to tell,' said Sarl, and smiled when he had spoken. Semyon itched to blast that smiling face, which seemed to jeer at him with superior knowledge. He could travel between worlds, he even kept such a world amongst his possessions, but he could not unravel the secrets of death.

'Many men swear there is no such place. And no paradise,' he said. He felt like a boy, a young boy being teased by an elder. He recalled the hot humiliation of studying under Kaschai, who mocked ignorance and success alike.

Sarl splayed his hand on the windowpane. 'I cannot answer for paradise. I saw hell,' he said, gazing across the distance as if the place had opened before his eyes.

'But I brought you back,' said Semyon, and could have bitten his tongue at the pleading the words implied.

Sarl folded his arms across his chest. 'I hope my father paid you well,' he said, without emotion.

'My reward will not be paid in coins,' said Semyon, trying to feel the sincerity he portrayed.

'Each man has his price,' said Sarl. 'It need not be money. Do not pretend you serve my father out of love, you, a stranger.'

'I do the bidding of my master the Staryetz, who ordered me to aid your father in his great cause.'

Sarl turned away to the window once more, as if uninterested in these protestations. 'My father's great cause,' he said. 'He is marching south, and I am not there to ride beside him like a man.'

'Your time is limited,' said Semyon, hoping Sarl would not notice how much pleasure he got from these words. 'We have to find this Vasilyevich and bring him back to the mountain. Then, when all is done, you will ride to join your father and his warriors, and my work will be accomplished.'

'Vasilyevich,' said Sarl, letting the word roll across his tongue as Semyon did. 'I had him at my mercy. I slew him. But he has lived, while my bones mouldered under earth.'

'Then you will have your revenge!' said Semyon. 'Just as your father wishes. You shall see him die, and his heart will give back your life.'

'You understand nothing, Magus. He is my hell,' said Sarl.

Semyon could not see how his promise failed to satisfy this monster that he had summoned with earth and spells. Moist mother earth had given up the body, and he had conjured the soul across worlds and time, knitting them together to make something like a man. A shaman who could ward his inmost thoughts from Semyon, and one who could even conceal the fact that he was a shaman. Semyon had heard of such creatures but, when he raised Sarl, he had not known that he was bringing such a one into his presence. The silence, the absence of power humming like a treadmill, unnerved him. Even the great Kaschai could not conceal his powers from his peers – though he would never have sought to try.

'Your animal spirits are low, *Gospodin*. At least you can taste the pleasures of the flesh that have been denied to you so long.'

'They give me no pleasure,' said Sarl. 'Food is dust, and wine is ditchwater. I feel no lust for any man living. My body is a shell, and my heart is rotten. If you do not fulfil your promise, Magus, I shall tear out yours and find two souls to serve my purpose where I please.'

A sudden knock at the door made Semyon start. He was sure that Sarl must have noticed. He was sweating, and he felt his hands tremble. Nothing and no one had ever roused such abject fear in him. In a high, strained voice, he bade the visitor enter, and the door opened to admit Sarl's younger sister, Huldis. Semyon felt himself relax like a sack of bones. Tall and slender, the young woman haunted the castle like the shadow of a birch tree. She seldom spoke or raised her eyes, but at the sight of her, Semyon felt his cock stirring into pleasant life. As always, lust and death were close together. He itched to slip his hand under the skirts of that long, modest dress, and to caress those smooth thighs. Licking his lips as if a rich meal presented itself after a morning's fast, he spoke her name.

'Mon Seigneur,' said Huldis. Silver-fair hair coiled round her head and flooded down her back. Semyon had not truly seen the colour of her eyes, but he suspected that they were blue, a colour that was rare in nature, and so more precious.

For an instant, he had almost forgotten Sarl. The Heir strode across the room to greet his sister, who struggled not to flinch from his touch. 'Jean,' she said in a colourless voice. 'You are back.'

Sarl reached out as if to grasp her arms, but his hands did not touch her. Semyon wondered whether this girl was his weakness, something that could be used against him later.

'Is there any word from our father?' Sarl asked. His tone in speaking to his sister was wholly different to the one he used when speaking to Semyon. The violence, the cold indifference, were withheld, as if he feared to damage that fragile form.

Semyon saw the flicker of her gaze as she looked up into her brother's face and struggled not to recoil from him. Unsurprisingly, the half-dead creature that had taken the place of a living man disgusted her. Semyon admired the delicacy with which she strove to hide her feelings. She was fastidious, and he would enjoy her flinching from him when he seized her and taught her the rough secrets of desire. He leaned on the back of a chair, watching brother and sister together.

'He has taken Mont Eldemar, and is marching south,' she said, failing to hold Sarl's gaze. 'Let me go with you, Jean. It frightens me to stay here alone. There are too many ghosts.'

Sarl touched her face, cupping it with a careful delicacy that made Semyon shiver in spite of himself. 'But can you bear to travel with this ghost, Huldis?' he said.

She tried to smile at him. Her mouth stretched into the shape of a smile, but it was awry, twisted by her other emotions. 'I want to help you, Jean. I want to see you whole again, as you once were.'

'You know what must be done to make me whole?' he said.

'I know.'

'It will take three lives,' said Sarl. 'Lives of people who helped to bring you back to us, Huldis. My father may have forgotten that, but I cannot. He chose them. I did not.'

'He wants revenge for your death,' said Huldis.

'That puzzles me,' said Sarl. 'Why does he need revenge when he will have me beside him, body and soul? A man slew me in battle. I would have taken his life. That much is quit between us.'

'Our father suffered your loss. He has spoken to me of it often, since I came back here. He thinks that justice should be meted out in double measure.'

Semyon cleared his throat. He felt he had watched enough of this touching scene. He wanted to be quickly gone to Yonar, and back with their prisoner. It amused him that Sarl seemed to have some scruples about killing the man who had destroyed him. The thought that Sarl should have any scruples was entertaining in itself.

'Bring the girl too, *Gospodin*,' he said. 'We shall not be long.'

Sarl turned his head slowly and gave him a terrible stare from those red-rimmed eyes. 'I have not finished speaking with my sister, Magus,' he said. 'Be patient, or I will cut out your tongue as well.'

With an effort, Huldis laid one of her long hands

on her brother's sleeve. 'There is no need to speak so harshly, Jean. This man is an honoured guest of our father, and an ambassador.'

Sarl's gaze, still turned on Semyon, showed exactly what he thought of him, but aloud he said, 'You must forgive me, Huldis. The passage through hell has not mended my manners. We shall accompany the Magus on this task, which I have need of, but take little joy in.'

Could the dead lie? Semyon found himself wondering. He did not know whether to believe that Sarl felt genuine regard for his sister, or whether he was merely using her to serve his interests. Sarl did not even try to hide from Semyon his hunger for a new life, despite the price it would exact; yet he continued to protest that he did not hate Vasilyevich, who had killed him. The bluntness of these foreign nobles was alien to the Magus, accustomed to the subtleties and secret knives of the Sklavan court. There, pretence was everything, and show more important than the truth it concealed; each courtier took pride in his artifice, or he would find himself relegated to his estates, a rough boyar. Semyon could not bring himself to imagine how the Staryetz would reward the plain speech of the Doyen and his son, unless the despot found it amusing. Perhaps, with his crafty soul, he would divine a hidden subtlety that Semyon failed to detect.

At least he had recovered his nerve. For an instant, he had quailed before the contempt and hatred in those pale eyes. He had forgotten who he was, and what lay at his command. He could no longer expect to dazzle these bumpkins with the brilliance of his magic, but he might still manage to remind Sarl that he was not a negligible adversary. Now that he had begun to study the Heir's weakness, he was learning that which he might use to his advantage later on.

'The mirror waits for us. Through it, we shall reach Yonar in a few moments, a journey that would else take us many days.'

'How is that possible, Magus?' said Huldis, and for a moment he caught a flash of something unfamiliar in her glance, as if she could not quite conceal an emotion, though he had no idea what it was.

'I can pass through the mirror, and travel through the space between to bring us safely out of another mirror in Yonar. I have already looked through to see the mirrors of the city, and found one suitable to our purpose. If anyone has the misfortune to disturb us, he will perish.'

He held out his hand, wondering if he dared to exert his will over her and bring her to take it. Not in Sarl's presence, he decided; but he let his gaze rest on her face until she looked away. She must be drawn to his flame, this frail moth; or a bee hypnotised by his honey. He had enjoyed scores of women, from princesses to scullery-maids, though a little force sufficed to subdue the latter. He knew that he gave them pleasure, even as they screamed and protested their virtue. But he did not wish to taint his lust for this perfect flower with conjuring. He would corrupt her, until she came to him of her own free will.

Chapter 6

Beyond the river, a well-trodden path led across the water-meadows to some low hills surrounded by woods. On either side of the track, the fields were thick with a haze of snake's-head fritillaries, their small lanterns at a distance blurring into a purple sheen. Yuste loved these rare flowers, and to see them in such abundance would have given her cause to dawdle, studying their patterns across the marshy ground; but overhead there was another pattern on the sky, the movement of the crows as they circled, beating time with each swoop like starlings before sundown. Instead of the chittering voices of starlings, the larger forms would set up a mindless cawing, one echoing the other. They seemed to fly without purpose, but their presence hung over Yuste, fraught with meaning.

Every member of the party had noticed the phenomenon. Cluny and Planchet had conferred in low voices, glancing at the sky, and Boris had touched her sleeve, saying, 'Those are the ones?' Now they were hurrying their steps, eager to reach the cover that the trees would provide, though Yuste doubted that the crows had been sent to watch them. Their presence was a message, and one whose meaning she could not yet decipher.

She tried to focus her mind upon the Rom. Some might say that they were kin to the Wanderers, but the two groups mingled very little. The Rom lived on the roads, travelling in convoys of wagons, settling for days or weeks outside towns where they were seldom welcome. The Wanderers' exile had taken a different form; they had settled within cities and villages, living as strangers amongst their neighbours. In all the lands of the old empire, Doxa was the state religion, and the Wanderers were uninvited guests; Yuste knew of no country where they were known by their true name, Ya-udi, and free to live without constraints. Yet, unlike the Rom, they were seldom persecuted, driven from their homes or murdered. They knew they were not safe, but the threat was withheld and concealed behind the false smiles of daily life. The Rom had to deal with daily hostility, words that became blows, and the enmity of civic leaders. All these things made them mistrustful of strangers, and Yuste saw no reason why they should welcome her or her friends.

They were approaching the edge of the wood. Great unfurled pavilions of deep green leaves hung still, inviting her to enter their shade and silence. Cluny paused in the sunlight, at the place where the path meandered in between the trunks. As she joined him, he whispered, 'I think we should stay closer together from now on. They will be watching us, you know.'

Yuste followed him out of the field into the sudden, cool twilight. Above her, floating canopies shut out the sky, filtering the sunlight and allowing a few fingers of light to reach down to the earth below. She could hear Boris walking behind her, his footfall heavy on twigs and dead leaves; but Planchet was almost silent, and she had to glance back to see he was there. Boris was smoking one of his cigars, and its pungent smell seemed both comforting and out of place. Yuste watched Cluny threading his way between the trees, light- and sure-footed, and thought that she and Boris were urban trespassers, blundering through the wood as if it were a street in Masalyar.

She wondered if Boris knew what a din he was making, or whether he was using his deeper senses to search the wood for danger. She could not help thinking that her brother would have been quiet and alert to both kinds of danger, and cursed herself for comparing the two men. At least Boris did not somehow treat her as a cipher because her powers were so weak. Yuda would have taken all the responsibility himself, leaving her to feel helpless and useless. Some traces of her shaman sense remained, and she could, if she concentrated, perceive things that Cluny, with all his wood-craft, would not.

'Well thought, Madame Vasilyevich,' Boris growled. Yuste gasped. No one had ever overheard her thoughts, except Yuda. She had considered herself condemned to the same inner silence as those who lacked any powers. Except for the traces of word and emotion that she used to sense in Annat, she had been alone, with no company but the voice of her twin. And he was so seldom near her, and so often unwilling to share anything with her. She hung back to walk beside Boris.

'It's not possible, Boris Andreyevich. No one can hear my thoughts.'

'I just did. Maybe you're not as damaged as you thought you were.'

'Boris, I was thirteen. That's . . .' she hesitated, 'twenty-seven years ago. Ever since I came to Masalyar, I've mixed with many shamans. None of them has ever heard me thinking.'

'Maybe they weren't listening,' said Boris, starting to grin.

Yuste could not help it. She laughed out loud, drawing an alarmed and even reproving look from Cluny. 'Do you wonder if, all this time . . . ?'

'They must have assumed they couldn't hear you. And most shamans are noisy. It's so easy for them to send thoughts, they have to learn how to be quiet. I can still remember the classroom at the *Shkola*. No one said anything out loud – but it was bloody deafening!'

'Do you think I could hear your thoughts?'

Boris gazed at her. She could tell that he was thinking before he replied, but there was nothing magical in that. 'We'll have to try,' he said at last. 'Not here. Our guide is looking impatient.'

They hurried after Cluny, while Planchet patiently

followed with his burden. The path climbed to the top of a small rise, and over the top forked smartly to right and left. Painted pebbles marked the junction, red for the right and blue for the left.

'Source Vergey is this way,' said Cluny, indicating the left-hand trail. 'The other path goes to the waterfall.'

'Sounds pleasant,' said Boris, smiling round his cigar at the young man's discomfiture. Cluny sighed. 'I suppose our arrival won't surprise them,' he said.

'You seem to know this route very well,' said Yuste, raising her eyebrows. 'Considering that it is forbidden to visit the Rom.'

'I . . . er . . . well, I might have accompanied Malchik once or twice,' said Cluny, blushing.

'What do you make of the crows, hmm?' said Boris, rubbing his palms together.

Cluny gave a small shrug. He did not look happy. 'They are something to do with Ademar. And my brother,' he said.

'This brother of yours – not a nice man, I take it? Not the sort of person one would welcome back from the dead.'

Cluny did not share Boris's humour. 'I'm sorry,' he said. 'I can't laugh it off. And you wouldn't understand unless you had met my father, or visited the castle. They are other times. More dark,' and he turned on his heel and set off down the track, tugging at a piece of twig and breaking off the leaves, as if he were a boy. Yuste and Boris followed him more slowly, watching his hunched shoulders and bent head.

'I don't think we know what we're up against, Boris,' said Yuste. She too plucked a leaf and twirled it between her fingers. 'You and I have scarcely ventured outside Masalyar. We've only heard stories of life in the wild lands.'

'You're right, Missis,' said Boris. 'I'm a city man. I've never travelled the iron road, or gone beyond the sea. The crimes that I pursue are crimes of the city. Sure, they need a shaman to solve them, and they can be dark enough – but there's none of this stuff with crows and castles.'

She smiled up at him. 'I know,' she said. 'I've sat in the common room and listened to the others talk. I'm a very good listener! Even little Annat has made Journeys that I can only imagine . . .' She broke off and fell silent. Boris patted her shoulder.

'We're on the way to going to find her,' he said. 'Vasilyevich and Grebenshikov. They were a couple of clowns, but they made good.'

Yuste could not help laughing, though she managed to stifle the sound enough to keep Cluny happy. 'I shouldn't laugh,' she said, remorsefully. 'But sometimes one has to, you understand that, don't you, Boris Andreyevich? I can hardly believe she's gone. Or Malchik either. It seems so . . . improbable that a mirror could swallow them up.'

'I guess we're on the edges of that world,' said Boris. 'The world we've heard others talk of, but never visited ourselves.'

Cluny turned towards them, pressing a finger to his lips. As he did so, Yuste saw that they were approaching a clearing, overshadowed by even taller trees. She could hear the sound of water and smell wood-smoke on the still air.

The moment they stepped into the clearing, there was a riot of barking. Dogs came bounding towards them, small terriers with stumpy legs and mangy fur, thin hounds with starveling ribs, and big half-breed wolves baring their yellow teeth. Behind them followed a scattering of children, laughing and whistling to the dogs, though whether to call them off or egg them on was unclear. Cluny, who was foremost, stood stock still, and the first dog to reach him stopped to sniff at his legs, growling and wagging its tail. As the rest of the pack approached, Cluny put his fingers in his mouth and let out a shrill whistle. The dogs paused, some barking, others milling about his feet, while the children jeered and laughed.

Afraid of the dogs, Yuste was more interested in the children. Some were naked, the little ones, but most wore rags; scraps of second-hand clothing so faded and torn that they had lost all colour and scarcely looked like garments. The naked skin that showed beneath was brown and thick with grime, smeared and streaked from playing in the water. None of the children wore shoes, and their eyes looked bright and wild, as if they had not eaten well for a long time. When Cluny shouted out some words in an unknown language, they fell to giggling and mimicking him.

'*Gaðjo ðilo!*' they shouted.

Cluny gave up his attempt to speak their tongue,

and called out to them in Franj, 'We want to see Mother Zari!'

The dogs seemed to have lost interest and were wandering away, fighting each other or scuffing at the ground. The children drew nearer, and Yuste found their stares disconcerting. They were too dark for Wanderers, but something about them, like a memory, tugged at her. She stepped out from Cluny's shadow and walked towards them. Some of them laughed, chattering like starlings, while others pointed, calling out more unfamiliar words. *'Devi Rom,'* she heard, and *'Romani rasa . . .'* Then one girl came up to her, and held out her hand cupped, in the age-old begging gesture. But she said, 'Ya-udi.'

Yuste felt a thrill of shock at hearing the words. They had recognised her, and not merely through her dress. She wondered whether it was true that some ancient bond linked Wanderers and Rom. She looked at the little girl, whose head was alive with lice, and felt a mixture of revulsion and sympathy. The little girl continued to hold out her hand, asking for money in a sing-song voice.

'I think we'd better walk into the camp,' said Cluny. 'These ones are too little to be much help.'

He set off, and the others followed, while the children danced around them, tugging at their clothes, holding up begging hands and shouting words that might be insulting or friendly.

The caravans stood grouped together near the spring, their shafts empty. There was no sign of any horses. A big bonfire burned in their midst, with a soot-stained copper kettle hanging from a metal hook. Here and there piles of rubbish were dotted, almost middens, with an attendant cloud of flies. Pungent scents met Yuste's nostrils, clouding the cool air of the forest; the wood-smoke was strong and bitter, mingled with a hint of faeces.

As they approached the wagons, women emerged from within. They were less ragged than the children, and a love of vivid colour marked their dress, whether in scarves or skirts or shawls. Some were young, others wizened by sun and grime and a lack of teeth into an uncertain agedness; they watched their visitors with curious stares that Yuste could not be certain were hostile.

Cluny led the way. He approached a caravan on the left; it had a characteristic barrel roof, a keyhole-shaped door, and was decorated with weathered blue paint. At the top of the steps stood a young girl, somewhat younger than Annat, whose clothes enhanced her pert figure. Her mouth was sullen as she watched them, smeared with bold rouge that also decked her cheeks. Cluny bowed, sweeping off his hat.

'Mademoiselle Flora,' he said. 'We have come to speak with Mother Zari.'

Biting her lip, the girl stared at him, drying her hands on her apron. 'I know you, Gadjo, but who are these others?' she said.

'Friends of Malchik, including his aunt,' said Cluny at once. The girl gave something like a shrug and turned back into the darkness of the caravan, leaving them to wait outside.

'Who is Mother Zari?' whispered Yuste.

Cluny glanced round the clearing at the other women, who still stood in the doors of their wagons, watching.

'She is the leader of the clan,' he said. 'We have to win her confidence if we are to receive any help from these Rom.'

The wait seemed long. Yuste found the various smells persistent, almost overpowering, and the buzzing of the flies in the silence distracted her. At last, the girl re-emerged, unsmiling, and said, 'Mother Zari will see you now.' She stood aside so that they had to pass her to enter the caravan. Cluny went first, bowing once more before he squeezed past her; Yuste followed, inhaling the girl's perfume and clean sweat, before she found herself in the dark interior. There were no lamps or candles, only what daylight could penetrate through the lace curtains at each window. As her eyes became accustomed to the twilight, Yuste realised that the interior was as clean and ordered as the camp seemed dirty and neglected. At the rear was a wide bed set in the wall, screened with heavy embroidered curtains; the walls were adorned with painted leaves and flowers in many colours, blue and red above all; and a narrow table stood beneath a window on the left, spread with a linen cloth on which balanced a silver teapot, china cups, and a strange-looking figurine. At once, Yuste was reminded of the old doll that Annat had taken with her on her Journey north, the doll that she had broken; this one had the same stiff painted wooden features, a dress of red silk, and a thick wig of brown hair.

A woman was sitting on the other side of the table. Sun-lines had cut deep into her face, and her eyes were set far back, like polished stones, in their sockets. Her large form was shapeless, wrapped in a crocheted shawl, and a red kerchief covered her hair. She was in her middle years, not old like the crones Yuste had seen outdoors, and she smiled with a fine set of white teeth, one at the front capped with gold.

'Welcome, friends of Malchik,' she said in a voice husky with tobacco. 'Which of you is his aunt?'

Yuste stepped forward, extending her hand, and Mother Zari took it in both her own, their soft wrinkles and hard rings brushing against her skin. 'Sit,' she said, and Yuste lowered herself on to the small stool on the opposite side of the table. The woman's breath smelled of cloves. 'Sit you also, men,' Zari added. Cluny stepped forward and began, 'We have brought gifts of—' but she interrupted him.

'Gifts can wait,' she said. She turned her smile back to Yuste. 'A little Wanderer,' she said, patting Yuste's hand between her own. 'Our old kin.'

Yuste glanced at the doll. She was feeling strange, overpowered by the scents, the warm hands touching hers, a dizzy sense of the past rushing towards her. 'Is it true that the Rom are kin to the Wanderers?' she found herself saying.

Zari took a deep, raucous breath. 'Megalmayar, the great Queen, the great Mother, cursed us both,' she said. 'She laid a curse on the Wanderers because they betrayed her Son. So she said. And she cursed the mothers of the Rom because they disobeyed her, after the rising of her Son. She drove them out of Zyon, and they came across the sea, to Masalyar, before it had such a name. She was an angry woman, the Mother,' and she gave a short laugh, like a bark.

Yuste smiled. 'People say it is only a legend,' she said.

Zari shrugged. 'What do they know?' she said. 'A curse has power, even when it was an unjust curse. The Wanderers live in exile, and the Rom travel endlessly, with no land or town for a home. You wear a Wanderer's badge, my sister,' and she touched the piece of fabric pinned to the sleeve of Yuste's costume.

'Did Malchik come here?' said Yuste.

'Many times. He loved our music. He was not so bad, for a Gadjo,' and she gave Yuste a cheeky, gap-toothed smile. Yuste found herself warming to the woman.

'Malchik is lost,' she found herself saying. 'He has been taken from us by . . . sorcery . . .' She hesitated over the word. 'And my dau— my niece, Annat, went after him. She is a shaman, and she left us a trail.'

'Why should you tell this to Mother Zari, a stranger?' said Zari, no longer smiling.

Yuste found the words coming out in a rush. 'You – the Rom – have shamans amongst you. And you travel long distances. We thought you might be able to tell us what the trail means. We cannot understand it.'

'Show me,' said Mother Zari.

Yuste unfastened her reticule and took out the

broken picture with the wisp of thread attached to it. 'Do you recognise the scene in this picture?' she said. 'Do you know where it is?'

Zari took the picture from her and studied it. She passed the thread between her fingers. 'I am not a shaman,' she said. 'And I do not know this mountain. But I have travelled all my life within Franj, passing up and down the great river. There are a few amongst our clan who have come from outside, from east of the Lepas Mountains. One of these is Andras. When the men return from horse-trading, I will summon him.' She laid the picture on the table, face up. 'While we are waiting, you will sit with me,' she said. 'Share our food. It is not often that Gadji come amongst the Rom. Share our drink. Andras will come!'

The Crystal Chamber was open to the elements, and Annat caught a fugitive scent that drifted down with the cold air from outside. It was the sweet, fresh smell of grasslands. She sat down in the chair that Sarl had vacated, and her brother sat beside her. She noticed for the first time that he was wearing strange clothes: trousers of sand-coloured corduroy, a red waistcoat, and a white shirt with a high collar and cravat. His brogues were polished to a dazzling shine. Annat blinked, realising in the midst of her dismay that she had never seen a Wanderer man dressed in such garments before; the colours alone broke all the rules. She resolved to question him about it later.

'Do you know where we are, Malchku?' she said.

'He – Semyon – referred to it as the mountain.'

'I saw that in the mirror. It looked strange – not like stone.'

'I've been alone most of the time. That was why I tried to call you from the mirror. I've been pretty stupid, don't you think?'

'I don't think you could have done anything else.'

'Someone – or something – brings food for me. I suppose that should have alerted me, but I never thought that he wanted us both.'

'Well,' said Annat, helping herself to a handful of rice and fish, 'it won't help us to sit here and figure out who's to blame. We have to try and escape. And if we can't do that, we need to work out how we can stop the Magus from stealing our souls. At the very least, we must delay him until help arrives. We have to stop him performing this magic to make Sarl a living man.'

'Nobody knows where we are, Natka. I don't think anyone will come to rescue us.'

Annat smiled at him, her mouth full. When she had finished chewing, she said, 'I left a trail when I went into the mirror. It wasn't a very good one, but I think it may lead Yuste to us. I used the picture of the mountain that Cluny painted for you.'

Malchik folded his arms across his chest. 'Natka, we don't know where the mountain is. Nor will Yuste.'

Annat picked up a few grains of sticky rice with her fingertips. 'It doesn't matter. The trail should lead them to us. But we can't worry about that. We have to leave it to Yuste.'

'I suppose anything would be better than sitting here

waiting to be plucked like a pair of geese. I have to say, Natka, I am glad that you came through. It was bad enough being here alone, until that man brought Sarl. You saw him.'

Annat wiped her mouth on her hand, only to find that there were napkins lying beside each plate. Linen napkins, neatly folded and pressed. A carafe of water stood in the centre of the table, with three silver beakers. She was careful to choose one that had not been touched; she did not want to drink from the one that Sarl had used.

'I wish there was some way we could warn Yuda,' she said. 'He might be able to get a message back to the city. He might be able to stop them.'

'He's in Yonar, isn't he? It may take them a while to reach him.'

'Not if they use the mirrors.'

They fell silent. It was not as terrifying to them to find themselves in such a strange place and such circumstances as it might have been to someone who had not shared their previous experiences. They had travelled together through the realm of La Souterraine, and faced the wrath of a deadly goddess. But that very experience had taught them to recognise how much danger they faced now. Fear was in their minds rather than their hearts. Malchik drummed his fingers on the table.

'It was only after Cluny came to the college that I realised the Doyen might still be interested in revenge. And then the crows came . . .'

'I thought that, after Huldis was returned to him,

he had given up his grievance against us. We all thought so . . .'

'Except Yuda,' said Malchik, completing her sentence.

Annat stood up. 'I want to start, Malchku. I need to move. I don't want to be sitting here when they return.'

He looked up at her, blinking against the sunlight. 'Where do we start?' he said.

She found it funny, and a little frustrating, that he looked to her for a lead, though he was the elder. Though Malchik had traces of shamanic ability, all they did was to render him vulnerable. When confronted with magic, he was lost, and turned to Annat or his father for directions. She folded her arms. 'Why don't we return to the chamber with the mirror? If there is no other way from there, then we are trapped indeed.'

Malchik followed her obediently, like a dog on the heels of its owner. His presence, evinced by the sound of his footsteps behind her, was reassuring, and Annat found that she needed comfort. Her thoughts kept returning to Sarl's face, and the knowledge that he had gone to find her father. She was afraid too that they would find the other chamber sealed, with no way out but the mirror it held. Semyon would have made sure that they could not escape through there.

The round chamber was warm, even stuffy, and Annat did not like the traces she could sense of Sarl's presence and the cold heart of the Magus. She circled the mirror, whose surface was black, reflecting nothing.

The glass was tepid to the touch. Except for the opening from which they had emerged, the chamber walls were smooth, like the inside of a scraped-out melon. With her hand touching the mirror frame, she turned to gaze at Malchik. There was something odd about his expression, a hidden watchfulness, as if he were not at ease with her. Annat wanted to question him, but she knew it would have to wait.

'Malchik?' she said, and he started, as if he had been far off in reverie.

'It looks as if we're stuck,' he said, with a strange lack of emotion. Annat moved away from the mirror and approached the rock wall, letting her fingertips glide across it. Though the stone was opaque, it had a depth to it, as if it were made of cloudy crystal. Slowly, she walked the circumference of the chamber, drawing her hand across the surface. It was as if she were looking for a pulse or a heartbeat, anything that would let her know that the chamber was not sealed and lifeless.

'What are you doing?' said Malchik, moving restively. A shaman would have let the question fall softly into her mind, like drops of water. She found it odd to hear her brother's voice. She had never heard inner speech from him, and she wondered what it would sound like. Sometimes, words spoken aloud seemed so clumsy, compared with the smoothness of *sprechen*. She paused to smile at him.

'I was hoping there might be a hidden door,' she said. Malchik, who was leaning against the stone jamb of the entrance, shook his head.

'The Crystal Chamber seems more likely,' he said. 'That's where the food appears.'

With a sense of futility, Annat followed him back to the dazzling room with its tantalising scents of fresh air. All the walls were thick with crystals that seemed to have burst from the rock. She stroked her hands over their hard edges, seeing with her inner eye the crystalline structures bedding deep into the body of the mountain. Semyon had chosen a prison that would defeat the strongest shaman. She forced herself to move slowly, exploring every cranny from the ground to the highest she could reach. Malchik followed her with a listless gait, his chin sunk to his chest. Now and again, Annat would glance back to the table with its empty chairs and dishes of food. She wondered how long it would be before Semyon and Sarl returned, bringing Yuda back a prisoner.

There was a grain of hope. Yonar was a large town, and they might not find Yuda at once. When they did find him, her father had powers that equalled Semyon's. He could draw on forces she did not understand. He would be less easy to capture than a simple shaman, or an inexperienced one like herself. And he was cunning. When he knew how the land lay, he might let them take him, to find the means of freeing Malchik and herself.

Annat closed her eyes. She was not concentrating. Somewhere here there must be a door, a portal that gave way to the deep workings of the mountain. In this room, they were at the summit, and she could sense the tunnels spiralling below. The peak was riddled with worm-casts, long burrowings that crawled down from the apex to its foundations. One of them had to lead up to this eyrie, from which Semyon could oversee his domain. She let herself relax against the crystalline wall, sinking against its sharp points as if she could melt into their surface. They were cool and still, taking her into their confidence. Hundreds of thousands of years were stored up in their structures, glass made out of stone.

'Annat?' said her brother.

'Shut up, Malchku!' she shouted, from the depths of her trance. Her surface mind lay like a meniscus over the deep water into which she was sinking. She would become one with the mountain, which in all its stones held no love for the magus who was its suzerain. Annat sank towards the bottom, where the dark strands of rock were melded into the earth, rising like fossilised waves from the busy ocean. Her head ached, and her mouth was dry. She wondered if she would turn to stone and become a crystal figure welded to the wall against which she lay.

Something rushed up to meet her, like a slap in the face. There was a hollow, a cavity, close by; a shaft that delved beneath her feet, mocking her with its emptiness. She surfaced, gasping, and ran her hands through her hair.

'May I speak now?' said Malchik.

'What?' she said. Her eyelids were heavy with dreaming. Feeling a little drunk, she turned to face him, leaning back against the studded wall. Malchik looked so concerned that she had to smile. 'There's a passage near here. But it goes straight down,' she said.

'You know how I feel about heights,' said Malchik.

Annat straightened, rubbing her palms together. 'Let's find it first,' she said.

This time, she could skim across the surface of the wall until she found the entrance to the shaft. She fondled the crystals with an erotic attention, as if they were Eugenie's flesh. At last she found one that was too symmetrical, a glass knob that turned under her hand. She started back as a panel in the wall swung inwards, revealing what looked like a small cupboard, lined with mirrors. But there was an updraught that licked her face, and she guessed at once what faced her. She burst into free, joyous laughter.

'Malchik, it's a lift! You don't need to worry about the height.'

'What do you mean?' His face was twisted with bewilderment.

'An elevator. Inside the mountain. Like those ones in the city, in the Railway Union building.'

Malchik came to join her, and inspected the mirror-panelled cupboard with slow deliberation. From below, they could hear the grinding of its steam-powered workings. 'So Semyon doesn't just rely on magic,' he said, raising his eyebrows at her.

'It would take a lot of magic to power a lift,' she said. She took a bold step into the cupboard, and stood facing her brother, grinning at him. 'Come on.'

'We don't know where it goes,' said Malchik.

'Down,' she said, stretching out her arms to him.

She took a firm grip on his sleeves and drew him towards her. As soon as he had crossed the threshold, the massive door swung shut behind them, and they were caught in the glow-worm light of naphtha lamps set into the floor. Malchik took hold of Annat's arms in his turn.

'I'm afraid, Annat,' he said. She looked up into his face, wishing she could send him her thoughts of eagerness and excitement, but instead she felt a little shock as the elevator cabin gave a jolt and plunged down into the core of the mountain.

Semyon surfaced from the mirror gasping for air as if he had been about to drown. A glimpse had told him that the room beyond was deserted. He stumbled over the gessoed frame and found himself in a chamber with whitewashed walls and a wooden bed above which hung the sign of the Wheel. As Semyon bent double, grasping his knees beneath his robe and swallowing breaths of air, Sarl stepped out of the darkened glass as if he had just been for a country stroll. Huldis followed him with careful grace. The moment her feet touched the floor, the surface of the glass crazed over and the mirror cracked, fragmenting into pieces of silvery mosaic. Huldis took a step back, and Sarl turned his head in surprise.

Semyon stared at the broken glass in horror. Pushing past Sarl, he rushed to the frame, seizing it and staring into his own disfigured reflection.

'What is this, Magus?' said Sarl. 'What does it mean?'

Semyon ignored him, running his right hand over the face of the mirror and taking care not to dislodge any of the pieces.

'Tchernobog!' he said. It was somewhere between an oath and a plea for help to his dark god. If he told Sarl the truth, the Heir was likely to gut him on the spot like a fish. As he turned, he tried to compose his features into a calm smile.

'Why did the mirror break?' said Sarl.

'It has never happened before,' said Semyon, aware that this was not an answer.

Sarl laid his hands on Semyon's shoulders. It would have seemed a friendly gesture if his grip had not been so tight.

'Tell me what it means, Magus.'

Semyon quailed before the stare of those pale eyes, ice-blue, sunken in their sockets. He felt that Sarl was pinning his soul to a board, like a preserved insect. Only rage at his own weakness kept him from collapse. He moistened his lips with his tongue.

'We cannot go back. Not that way.'

'No doubt there are other mirrors in the town,' said Sarl. Semyon could not answer him at once. 'Well?' said the Heir.

'Not so, Mon Seigneur. The link has been broken. To return to Ademar, we must travel by land, like other men. It is a longer journey to reach the mountain.'

'That was careless of you, Magus. You know my time is short.'

'I don't know how it happened!' said Semyon, giving way to panic.

'You are the great magus from the court of the all powerful Staryetz. So my father told me. And you will find a way to convey us back to the mountain where your captives wait, once we have found Vasilyevich.'

He released Semyon, who grovelled on the ground, scrabbling at the fastening of the one suitcase he had chosen to bring. It held a whole shaman world, and its power had brought Sarl back to life. Semyon had captured the world months ago, with Kaschai's help. He knew he had learnt only a few of its powers. The suitcase fell open, and a draught of warm air, sweet and wholesome, touched Semyon's face: the smell of the steppe in summer. The suitcase appeared empty, except for a few rags of clothing, but Semyon could sense the trapped world quivering under his fingers, awaiting his command.

'Have no fear, Mon Seigneur, I will find a way,' he said, running his fingers through the empty space. He could almost feel the wild grasses stirring under his fingers. He would find a way, for if he did not, he knew all too well what Sarl would do. His mind worked rapidly. There must be a reason why the mirror had cracked this time, when it had never done so before. Perhaps there was some hostile magic working against him. He snapped the case shut and rose, able to look his unwelcome companions in the face. 'I will find a way,' he repeated, hugging the valise against his chest.

'I hope that this is indeed Yonar,' said Sarl.

Without answering him, Semyon strode to the door and opened it. The passage outside was deserted. He

the smells of food and wine and the well-
trodden carpet underfoot that this was an inn. An inn
where they could lodge, perhaps. It should not take
him long to find this Vasilyevich. All shamans had a
signature, a trace that other shamans could read, like
dogs nosing each other's scent. He made for the stair-
head that he could see at the end of the corridor, letting the others follow in his wake. He was careful not
to look over his shoulder as if he were anxious that
they might not follow.

Sounds rose from the stairwell, the shouting and
clash of plates from the kitchens and the hubbub of
voices from the bar. Semyon plunged into the mêlée
of foreign voices with relief; Sarl would hardly murder
him before witnesses. There was an entrance hall at
the foot of the stair, paved with ashlars, and wood-
panelled walls adorned with stuffed stags' heads. The
smell promised rich sauces and palatable wines.
Semyon stepped through the open door into the throng
of voices, and met a brief silence as the guests took in
the newcomer. He was glad that he had chosen the
robes of a Doxan priest as his disguise, for the pause
did not last. Even when Sarl and Huldis joined him,
their tall and richly clad figures making them stand
out amongst the russets and blues of artisans and
merchants, there was only a murmur of curiosity and
perhaps enough movement to clear a space around
them.

Sarl laid his hand on Semyon's shoulder. 'Let me
talk, Magus,' he said. 'You sound like a stranger.'

They managed to find the innkeeper and, in spite

of his appearance, Sarl charmed the man with his manners. The innkeeper became voluble with regret. They must surely know that the city was *en fête*, full of visitors who had come to see the strangers from Masalyar. Sarl shook his head. They were strangers themselves, he said. The innkeeper had known that they looked like quality. But he had no beds, and they were like to find other inns in the same predicament. Sarl smiled, and gave the man a coin. They would chance their luck elsewhere, and sleep in the stables if they must. The innkeeper protested; stables were no place for a young lady. There was a house of nuns where she could find refuge, he was sure.

With a sigh, Semyon stepped out into the cobbled street, taking leave of the wine and rich sauces that had made his stomach tighten. The sun glistened off the setts and glowed on the rich earthy pinks of the roof tiles. He thought with longing of the marble-faced mansions of Kiyev and the golden spires of the great temples. Then Sarl clapped him on the shoulder. 'We may not need a place to sleep, my friend. Not if we finish our business before nightfall.'

'He is here, somewhere,' said Semyon, looking past Sarl at his pretty sister. The thought of her should have comforted him. Her wan face watched him without expression, frozen and demure.

'No doubt we will find him with the strangers from Masalyar,' said Sarl. Semyon wondered if the Heir understood what a city was, with its myriad streets and cellars and rooftops. You could not hunt a man down like a stag in open country; you had to search amongst the confusion of scents and sounds, of shaman minds and those with no powers. He gazed up at the skyline, where towers and façades and the spires of temples were jumbled together. Sarl grinned at him. He had read Semyon's thought, and it amused him.

'You will find me a good hound, Magus,' he said. 'I know the scent of our quarry.'

Chapter 7

When Andras returned from the horse fair with the other men, even Yuste could tell he was a shaman. He stepped into the interior of the caravan, smiling, and she took in the signature of his power, a warm, glossy amber like the sap from a tree. He glanced towards her and Boris with slight surprise that barely showed on his features, registering them both, the whole and the maimed shaman. His eyes were narrow, berry brown, and his skin had a pale copper hue. His rust-coloured hair was neither long nor short, and combed back from his face.

'You sent for me, Mother Zari,' he said, speaking French so the strangers would understand. Yuste was startled at the clarity of his thought. Boris, like most shamans, kept his thoughts warded. Andras seemed to hold his out on an open palm. She had no doubt that there were secret places and inner recesses in his mind, but if so, he chose to hide them in plain sight. She found herself smiling up at him. He was young, with an energy that had not been staled by years or trouble.

'Welcome, Andras,' said Mother Zari, beckoning him with ringed fingers. She gestured towards Yuste. 'My sister is a Wanderer.'

Andras studied Yuste. He did not return her smile, but he seemed to regard her with curiosity, as if trying to understand the way in which her powers were blunted. She looked down with a sense of shyness, unwilling to let this young man know too much of her so soon. Andras listened as Mother Zari explained the reasons for their visit, and all the time he did not speak; he barely moved the muscles of his face until Mother Zari had finished, when he said, 'Let me see the picture.'

Yuste felt a complicated emotion, between envy and desire. How she had longed to be like this, in the full flight of her powers, young and strong! She had given up pining for the lost chances a long time ago, and meeting Boris had stirred only the beginnings of regret. She held the picture out to Andras without speaking, and thought she saw a moment of compassion in his face. There was a fine difference between compassion and pity, for the latter carried with it a hint of scorn. She discerned that Andras saw her as a veteran, one wounded and scarred by many fights. He did not view her as a victim, who had succumbed both to violence and to self-pity. When he took the picture from her, their fingers touched, and Yuste wondered whether Boris too perceived all the fine details of this inter-action, which he would be able to hear without too much effort.

Andras pulled up a stool and sat down at the table between her and Boris. Planchet and Cluny, who had latterly been sitting on the bed, leaned forward. Andras fingered the piece of spider thread that Annat had left, and studied the image in the frame. He had not looked at it for long when recognition showed in his eyes, and he began to smile.

'This is a place in Sklava,' he said. 'I have not travelled there, but I have heard the tales. It is called the Glass Mountain, or the Warlock's Mountain. It lies across the Lepas Mountains, many miles to the east.'

'In Sklava?' said Boris, and Yuste leant forward to peer at the picture. If Annat were there, how would they reach her? Such a journey might take minutes for someone swept through an enchanted mirror, and weeks for someone who had to travel there overland.

Andras turned his smile to Boris. 'The mountain is famous because it stands alone in the middle of the steppe. As if it had fallen from the sky. Are you a man of Sklava, Gadjo? I hear it in your voice.'

'I come from Kiyev, not the steppe,' said Boris. He gave a short sigh, and ran his fingers through the few hairs on top of his skull. 'It's been a long time since I was there, and I would not have chosen to go back.'

'Is Annat there? Can you tell?' said Yuste, fixing the young man with her stare.

'She is there,' said Andras, putting the picture down on the table, face up, and letting his fingers feel the thread. 'She left us this trail to follow her.'

'Is she in danger?' Yuste felt hungry for anything that he could tell her; she wanted to devour every scrap. Andras gazed at her, thinking, his thoughts more opaque. It was not as if he had shuttered his mind, but rather that he had retreated from her, as if he were wary of her intensity. Yuste drew back with her body, sitting up straight in her chair. Her fingers moved to adjust the strings of her bonnet.

'I do not think she is amongst friends,' said Andras, taking time to choose his words.

Yuste glanced at Boris, who made a face at her. It was wry, but it reassured her. They had both known, or guessed, that Annat's disappearance was sinister.

Cluny stood up. His head touched the low ceiling of the caravan. 'If it is in Sklava, at least it is not my father. Or my brother,' he added.

'This one is the son of Ademar. The good son,' said Mother Zari, with emphasis.

'We heard at the horse fair that the old man is marching south, with a big army,' said Andras, not looking at Cluny. 'He has taken Mont Eldemar, and cannot be many days' march from Axar.'

Cluny stepped forward. 'The Doyen?' he said. 'Is this true?'

'He came up with one of our clans, and they died. His troops slaughtered them.' He added a few words in Romani to Mother Zari, who shook her head and lifted her hand to her face in a gesture of mourning.

'My father does not like the Rom,' said Cluny. 'But he does not like many, save those he considers true-born Franj.' He stopped short, and Yuste saw the look of pain in his face. 'My mother was Rom,' he said, suddenly.

Everyone but Mother Zari looked startled. 'You are Rom?' said Andras.

'There is a tribe of Rom that settled in the forest,' Cluny said. 'My father took their queen as his wife, and after she left him, my mother became his concubine. She was young, and my father was a handsome man. It is in his age that he has become hard-set in his mind. When he was young, he only hated the Wanderers.'

Yuste gave a start. Mother Zari had reached out to touch her hand.

'If Ademar is marching south, then we must leave this place,' she said. 'And you too, my sister. You must travel east, to seek the Glass Mountain.'

At first, Yuste simply stared at her. Thoughts rushed through her brain: the meaning of the crows; the need to warn Masalyar of the coming invasion; the danger to Annat and Malchik. She had not needed to make plans beyond this point, as if finding someone who could read the picture would solve all her problems.

'I don't know what to do,' she said, suddenly aware that Mother Zari, though she seemed warm and friendly, came from an alien culture, one that Yuste knew little of and did not understand. She wanted friends to advise her, and all the people who surrounded her were of recent acquaintance, even Boris Grebenshikov. In some ways, he felt like an old friend, someone she had known for a long time, but they lacked the experience of the past that she shared with Sival, or even Yuda. She must remember that she was paying Boris for his services, as well; she was the one who had to make a decision and give instructions.

'You must go east,' repeated Mother Zari. Yuste saw in her mind's eye the stickle-backs of the Lepas Mountains, the range that ran like a spine between Neustria and Sklava, down to the Middle Sea. The task seemed too vast for her to imagine. She must travel to the mountains and then cross them; beyond that lay a further journey to reach the Glass Mountain, where she might face an unknown adversary. She felt the first sensations of panic, the moisture on her palms, the pulse throbbing in her wrist.

'I don't know where to begin,' she said, in a voice that sounded cold and calm to her. As if her childlike emotions were locked inside, apparent to no one but herself. If she was to lead an expedition, now was not the time to reveal her weakness. She gazed into the eyes of Mother Zari, envying and admiring this woman who commanded and shepherded her tribe, even the men. The woman seemed to be waiting for Yuste to speak; or perhaps she wanted them to go, for the Rom would need to strike camp if they were to leave the area before the Doyen arrived with his army.

'What will happen to you? Where will you go?' she said, suddenly ashamed of the selfishness of her fears.

Mother Zari gave a little shrug. 'We will go with you,' she said. 'Or you can travel with us. There is a place, a town, just west of the Lepas Mountains, where you will find the means to cross. East is a good way for us too. Out of the way of the accursed Ademar.'

'But what if we bring danger after us?'

Mother Zari did not answer, staring back at her with unsmiling eyes. 'We will go with you,' said Yuste.

'Wait a moment,' said Boris. 'I think we need to be clearer about where we're headed. I'm as keen as anyone to get out of the path of this Doyen of Ademar, given what I've heard about him. But if we think Annat and Malchik are trapped, or held, in this Glass Mountain, I for one want to study a map to see where it is. And how we can get there.'

Mother Zari's lips moved a little, as if she were beginning to smile. 'Listen to me, Gadjo,' she said. 'We will travel to the feet of the Lepas Mountains, to the town of Dieulevaut. And from there you will fly into Sklava on the wings of the wind, as if you were angels sent by the Mother.'

Yuste's hands closed on her reticule. 'Right,' she said. The fear had changed to a kind of energy, one that would sweep her up and drive her on. 'We must fetch our belongings. Boris, go back to our lodgings with Monsieur Planchet and fetch what is necessary. You will come with us, Cluny, of course.' She was frightened for a moment to think that she was telling him not asking him, giving orders as if she were a war-leader. But Cluny swept an impeccable bow, and Planchet stood up and saluted, as if he understood himself to be at her command. Her hands trembling, Yuste waited for Boris to disagree. Instead he stood up, thrusting his hands into the pockets of his trench coat.

'This is what you want, Yuste,' he said. He spoke it like a statement, not a question.

'I want to find Annat and Malchik. I don't want to go alone. Will your contract stretch that far?'

Boris nodded. 'But I think I'll be sending a wire to Masalyar,' he said.

After he and Planchet had left, Yuste felt the beginnings of regret. She was tempted to run after them, to tell Boris that he was free to return to his city if he wished, where he would be needed to organise its defence. She wished that she had not been the one to take the decision away from him. But in the midst of her doubts, she remembered the swarming crows that had clouded the sky today, and the terrified words of Malchik's letter. It gave her strength of purpose, but it was no consolation; she suspected that there must be a connection between the Doyen's southward march and the disappearance of her wards.

The elevator plummeted with unexpected speed, and Malchik caught Annat's hand. They were in darkness, and the only sounds were the rushing of the air and the grinding of the lift machinery. Annat felt more eagerness than fear, and she willed her strength into her brother's hand. She knew that he was no coward; he had more fears to face than she did.

The lift cabin began to slow, and settled on its springs with a rocking jolt. They could hear the steam-powered motor that moved it churning its pistons and flywheels until it slowed to a steady beat. The doors glided open and, leading her brother by the hand, Annat stepped forward. She and Malchik were standing in a tall gallery, whose roof was hidden in darkness hundreds of feet above their heads. Deep shafts carved into the wall let in long shafts of light, which formed the only source of illumination; she stood still, watching the sparkling motes that drifted through the threads of sunlight. Straight ahead of them was a blank, sheer cliff, which curved away to right and left out of their sight.

Malchik drew his hand from hers, and laid it on her shoulder. 'Mother,' he breathed.

'We must keep moving, Malchku.'

Annat chose the path that curved to the left. With Malchik at her side, she walked between the fingers of daylight, which sometimes illuminated her brother's sleeve or his hair, showing her a moment of colour. The gallery seemed to take the form of a ring, but soon it became clear that they were following a spiral path, for the rock beneath their feet sloped gently downwards, and they reached a place where they entered a high tunnel, no longer walking in the shadow of the tall cliff. Still the pinholes drilled into the rock let in spines of brightness, and Malchik and Annat walked through them as if traversing the threads of a spider-web, which touched their faces but left no sensation.

'Do you think this is the best thing to do?' said Malchik. 'To head downwards?'

'We have no choice. The Crystal Chamber lay at the summit of the mountain.'

'I wonder who hollowed this out. Semyon can't have done it alone, even if he is a magus.'

Annat let her fingers graze the rock. It had a smooth, crystalline texture, and where the sunlight touched it, it reflected dull gleams of light. Black crystal. Obsidian.

'Perhaps the whole mountain is made of crystal,' she said.

'I wonder what it looks like from the outside.'

She smiled. 'Let's hope we're going to find out!'

The spiral path seemed to be widening its sweeps little by little as they moved downwards. The ground sloped so little that at times it was hard to believe they were descending at all. Annat began to feel tired; she had passed the night without sleep, and it was starting to tell on her.

'How long have we been walking?' she said.

'I've no idea. The sun seems to have moved, but it's hard to tell when we keep travelling in circles.'

There was a movement in the darkness ahead of them, and something jumped at them in a flurry of rags and feathers. Malchik threw up his arms to shield his face, and Annat dropped down on one knee, letting power flow from her upraised hand. She was careful not to use too much, both to manage her resources and because she was not sure what they faced. The blue fire sprang from her fingers, and there was a shriek, a smell of singed feathers and hair. The shape fell back from them, and Annat heard a soft thud as it hit the ground, and the sound of muttered curses. She glimpsed Malchik's eyes, wide behind his spectacles.

'The crows . . .' he said.

'I don't think so,' said Annat, picking herself up. The voice was speaking to itself in Sklavan. She approached the shape sprawled in a heap on the ground. Here and there the needles of light showed her pieces of faded black cloth, a shoe, a wisp of grey hair. As she drew close, the figure jerked away from her, shrieking. Annat made out a long, thin form, wrapped in layers of cloth, fur and feathers, with sturdy boots at the end of its bony legs. She kept her hands in defensive position, and spoke to it in Sklavan.

'Who are you? What do you want with us?'

'Baba Yaga, Baba Yaga,' mumbled the figure.

'Is it human?' said Malchik over Annat's shoulder.

Annat crouched down by the person on the ground. She made out a glistening, frightened eye.

'Keep away from me,' said the voice, clearer this time, and Annat recognised that the speaker was an old woman. 'Tell your master I mean him no harm. What harm can I do when he's taken all my powers?'

'Who are you, grandmother?' said Malchik, stooping over.

'Baba Yaga,' the old woman repeated.

'Is that her name, do you think?' he asked Annat.

'Not a name. It means "grandmother witch". Like in the stories.'

The old woman was now sitting upright, rubbing her shins. They could see that her long grey hair was held in place by many pins, each with an ornately carved piece at the end. Snags and locks were escaping on all sides, and she proceeded to put them back in place one by one.

'Who are you, then, if the Master didn't send you?' she said. 'And why did you jump on me like that?'

'You jumped on us,' said Malchik.

Jessica Rydill

'We are prisoners of Semyon the Magus,' said Annat.

'You too, eh?' Baba Yaga's speech was muffled by a hairpin that she was holding between her teeth. 'Can't see what he'd want with the likes of you.'

'He wants to take our souls, actually,' said Malchik. 'We are sorry if we hurt you, but you startled us.'

'You startled me, young man. No one comes down here, no one – unless it's the Master himself or his servants.'

'We were trying to escape,' said Malchik.

The old woman threw back her head and laughed. 'Escape? From the Glass Mountain?' she said, when she had finished. 'I suppose someone will do it one day.'

'Are you a witch?' said Annat.

'Of course I am. Why else would he keep me alive, down here in the dark? I'm not *the* Baba Yaga – there's never just one. Many of us, many witch-sisters, but we all have the same name. That's what you do when you become a witch. You give up your name and you are Baba Yaga.'

'Can you help us?' said Malchik.

'Help you escape?' she said, looking from one to the other. 'Why should I do that, supposing I could?'

'You could escape with us,' said Malchik.

The witch began to laugh again. It was not a pleasant sound, but it seemed to be genuine merriment. 'The Master's spells bind me here, young man,' she said. 'Even if I could find a way out, I couldn't leave. It's as simple as that.'

Malchik turned to Annat. 'Do you think . . . ?' he said. She could not see his face, but she understood his tone of voice.

'Semyon doesn't need spells to keep us here, Malchku.'

She crouched down beside Baba Yaga, offering the witch her hand. 'If you help us, we will help you.'

'And what makes you think you can help me?' The old woman stared at Annat's outstretched fingers. 'I have no friends. No human friends. People stay clear of witches. There's no reason you should do anything for me.'

'We will, if you help us,' said Annat. The witch seized her hand in strong claws and sprang to her feet without any sign of infirmity. She dragged Annat with her, and the girl flinched; the old woman smelled of dust and mouldy leaves. Baba Yaga took Annat's face in her grasp, and turned it towards the light.

'What are you, anyway?' she said. 'You have power, but you're no witch.'

Annat looked up into the gleaming eyes, dark as rock-crystal. 'I am a shaman,' she said.

Baba Yaga looked from her to Malchik. 'Not him,' she said. 'Two children, alone and lost inside the Bald Mountain. You'd better come with me,' and she took a firm grip on Annat's shoulder, hauling her down into the darkness that lay ahead.

The inn where Sarl had bribed the innkeeper to give them rooms sat on the narrow island where the two great rivers met, the Kron and the Zahan. Huldis had refused to be packed off to any walled convent. She had almost kissed the innkeeper's hands when he found her a tiny room under the eaves, with a door that locked. Did Semyon suppose her too innocent to understand his lecherous glances and the way that his eyes traced the curves of her form? She lay fully dressed on the narrow bed with its straw-filled mattress, her hands clenched by her sides. She was waiting for the house to fall silent.

Since the time she had spent as a prisoner of the Cold Goddess, at the heart of the world called La Souterraine, Huldis had found it difficult to sleep. In that place she had been caught between life and death; it was as if she had been asleep for twenty-three years. When the goddess took her, Huldis had been thirteen; she had awoken to find everything changed, while she herself was only three years older. Now she was twenty, but inside she felt both old and young, a child and a woman.

It was her sister, one of her rescuers, who had taken her to refuge in the forest, amongst the women of the Rom. At night, Huldis had strayed from their underground home to visit the spring dedicated to the goddesses they worshipped, or to wander through the sacred grove. With her sister's help, she had recreated her memory, and begun to understand the years that had passed; but all that had ceased when her sister grew big with child – children – and left to rejoin her husband. At the same time, Huldis had returned to the Castle of Ademar, to live with her father.

Huldis sometimes wondered whether her sister had

any idea what this would do to her. It was not the Doyen's age or the isolation of the castle that made daily life so close to being unbearable; it was the living memories of the life she had lost, and her father's refusal to cease from mourning the death of his Heir, his only legitimate son. The old man could sleep no more than she, so he insisted that she sit up with him during the night, reading aloud from the holy books of Doxa. She obeyed without argument, but her heart and mind were elsewhere; either caught in the pain of her past, or dreaming of the forest outside, where she could wander free, like a shadow.

No one, not even Sarl, suspected that she might have shamanic powers. Like her brother, she had the gift of being able to hide her nature from others. Semyon himself could not have divined what she was. Huldis had learnt to be secretive during her early years in Ademar, and she was glad that she had perfected the skill since her return from captivity. Only Aude, her maid, had known the secret of the Doyen's eldest daughter, a secret that Huldis had bestowed on her friend like a talisman. In those days, they had been like twins, nourished by the same wet-nurse – Aude's mother – and never out of each other's company. But in the end, their friendship had not kept them safe from the Cold One, that hungry goddess who dwelt beneath the forest. She had stolen Huldis and kept the girl in her icy realm, while Aude, bereft, had aged and moved away, married, borne children, and died.

Huldis often thought of her friend. It remained hard for her to accept that so much time had passed in her absence. She still grieved for Aude. She felt maimed, as if someone had cut off one of her limbs and left her to struggle on. It did not surprise her to learn that *'la belle* Aude' had gone on to take her own life. Sometimes Huldis wondered if she should do the same, but she feared that she might find herself once more caught in La Souterraine, this time for good.

Semyon and Sarl should be asleep by now – if Sarl ever slept. She imagined her brother lying motionless like a corpse on a stone plinth, staring open-eyed into the night. Much as she loathed Semyon, she pitied him having to share a room with such a companion. Once Sarl returned from the dead, she no longer found her wakeful nights a peaceful time; she would lie afraid in the dark, clenching her fists.

Huldis rose from her bed and took down from behind the door the hooded cloak that she wore out-doors. In this early spring, the nights were chill and there was sometimes a frost. The cloak was woven from fine homespun wool dyed a dark midnight blue, and the women of the Rom had given it to her while she lived amongst them. Blue and green were favourite colours of the Doxoi: blue the colour of the Mother's robe and green the symbol of the Son's resurrection. Huldis fingered the fine wool as she clasped the cloak at her throat and drew the hood forward to shadow her face. The women of the Rom did not worship the Son or His Mother, God-Son and Mother-Goddess; they venerated the twin powers of the forest, Dark and Light, Cold and Warm. Huldis now shared their faith.

She did not feel sleepy, and she was not afraid.

While the guests of the hostelry slept, and while her brother and the Magus were closed up, she had her own business to attend to. Yonar was a city of secret alleys and passages between the houses, which the citizens called *traboules*. Someone who wanted to avoid the streets could follow these to cross the city undetected. Though Huldis had a rough idea of the direction she needed to take, she did not know what dangers might await a solitary woman walking the city at night. She carried a knife under her cloak and she was warded by the cincture of her powers, which no one else, not even other shamans, could perceive.

Having descended to the ground floor of the inn, she let herself out of the front door, to find the entrance to a *traboule* next door. It looked like a passageway leading into a courtyard where more entrances might be found. There were no windows, and it was roofed in from the night, but the clue to its nature came from the flickering oil lamps set above the doorways, which dwindled out of sight up ahead. Drawing her cloak about her, Huldis set off into the dark. She darted between blocks of shadow, shunning the light, and pausing often to wait with her back to the stone wall, listening for footsteps.

At this time of night, even the long alleyways were deserted. The townspeople used them, not criminals, though they would have made a perfect hideout for bravos or knifemen. With a strange sense of freedom, Huldis let her sixth sense probe the gloom ahead. It was so odd to be alone, with no one watching her. Her soft-shod shoes made hardly any sound on the cobbles, and she might have passed as a wraith, a ghost summoned from the city's past. She knew that the Kadagoi had built a city of their ancient empire on the crossing of the rivers Kron and Zahan. Beneath her feet lay the foundations they had laid, fragments of ancient wall lining the cellars, or ornate capitals set into the corner of a street.

Up ahead, through the night, the light she was looking for shone like a beacon. There were many shamans in this city, and she had sorted through them, the bright and the dim, the colourful and the dull, searching for a signature that she recognised. To her eyes, Sarl's power seemed blue as a lump of ice hewn from a glacier, but the ice was tinged with flame. Semyon gave off a rich, oily brown odour, musky as the glands of a civet cat. Huldis suppressed a laugh, wondering if other shamans could read and perceive these differences, or whether she alone could do so. Like Sarl's power, the one she sought was silver-blue, but it was shot with twists of gold and amber. She followed it like a hound bent to a scent, ignoring signposts and taking only entrances that seemed to bring her closer. She had not yet decided what she would do when she found him.

Yuda had married Aude. This was one of the few facts Huldis had learned before her sister took her to sanctuary in the forest. She remembered the time just after her return as a confusion of brightness, noise and sensations. It was like being born, yet with thoughts and feelings developed enough to describe the new world in which she found herself. Very different from the tranquillity that followed, when she lived amongst the women of the Rom. Sounds, smells, tastes, all had been bright and new. She had lived only for the moment, shutting out the memories pressing down upon her, and enjoying the company of her unexpected friends. And they had been unexpected; her younger sister grown into a tall woman with masses of hair, her sister's blackamoor husband, and the little Wanderers, so small and dark and quick.

Huldis let these recollections surface in her mind like jewels as she navigated her way across the city, using Yuda's power as a lighthouse. They had served as a store of hope when she returned to the castle, to live under the thrall of despair. She saved them and hoarded them, using them only when her heart turned her thoughts to suicide. Outside her new prison, she knew that a world of noise and colour existed, one that might some day break in upon her again, to bring her back to freedom.

The house she was seeking lay in the oldest part of the city, under the lee of a steep cliff on which stood a basilica of the Mother. Raising her head, Huldis saw torches burning against the sky, a guiding light for pilgrims at any time of day. She walked down the cobbled street, past shuttered windows and doors barred with ornate grilles. Slowing her pace, she paused from time to time to study the glass above that reflected only darkness, or the chinks of light that still showed between certain louvres. Her heart beat like a drum as she came to a stop before a tall building, four storeys high, which bore wrought-iron balconies beneath each window. The street door had been freshly painted, and its brass knocker was shaped like a hand clasping a ball. Huldis did not knock.

She stepped back a pace. The windows were not only shuttered but curtained with panels of crocheted lace. Breathing slowly, she sent out her own thoughts, flying into the air, and called out the shaman's name in silence. As she waited, repeating the call from time to time, she began to feel exposed and unsafe in the empty street, as if her call echoed loudly from the closed-up houses. She took a firm grip on the handle of her knife, and willed Yuda to answer her. It was not possible that she had come to the wrong place; there was no mistaking such a signature of power, she had encountered none like it.

Suddenly, she saw a light from a first-floor window as the shutters were thrown back. The curtains twitched, and a moment later the casement opened and a man looked out. He called out to her in a strange language, and his voice sounded angry. All her uncertainty kept Huldis from answering. She could not see the man's face, and she did not know how Yuda might have changed in four years. There was a pause as he waited for her to answer, before he spoke again, in Franj this time.

'Who the hell are you?'

She recognised the timbre of his voice, deep and a little harsh, and the trace of accent when he spoke her tongue. Instead of answering aloud, she sent the thought of her name in answer. He seemed to hesitate before replying, 'You'd better come in.'

The window was closed, and Huldis waited. She saw shadows moving before the glass, outlined against the yellow light within, and heard the murmur of voices. A little later, quick footsteps sounded on the stair, and a steady tread crossed the hall. Clasping her cloak and her knife together, Huldis watched as the door opened, and felt a shock of fright, surprise and amusement when a slight man stepped over the threshold. She had forgotten that, just as her family were tall and stately, Yuda and his daughter were small and compact. After the light she had followed across the dark city, it was absurd to face a small shadow.

'Did you come here to tell me I was short?' said Yuda. Huldis gasped. It was so strange to relax the vigilance that kept her powers hidden that she had made no attempt to ward her thoughts.

'I – I'm sorry, Monsieur.'

'I take it there's some other reason why you have come all this way to wake me in the middle of the night?'

Huldis did not know what to say. She let the cloak slip back so he could see the knife. Yuda cocked his head. 'We can discuss this in the street if you want, or you can come upstairs,' he said.

Huldis bethought herself of the impropriety this entailed. She should not visit a man who was not of her family alone, without a chaperone. Yuda shook his head. 'I'm sharing a room,' he said. 'Two men and two girls. No chance to threaten anyone's virtue,' and she saw his grin. There had been so much she wanted to say, and now she found herself in his presence, she was tongue-tied. She nodded, and he ushered her into the house, closing the door behind them.

'You've grown,' said Yuda, looking up at her. Huldis stared at him, remembering his face, pale skin and dark features, and eyes so intense you did not look at them for long. She let her gaze fall, as she should in the presence of an elder. 'It's up the stairs,' Yuda said, and Huldis observed the stone floor with its carpet of raspberry wool, and the stair-runner held in place by brass rods, each finished with a fleur-de-lis. The walls were of dark panelled wood, and a number of doors led off the entrance hall, each closed on its secrets. She began to mount the stair, slipping her knife into its sheath at her belt, and gathering up her long skirts with her hand.

'How is Casildis, my sister?' she said over her shoulder, and thought that her voice sounded cold and formal.

'Very busy. You know she has five children now?'

Huldis gave a little shiver. The tall woman with the golden hair, who had once been her little sister. 'Is she well?' she asked, using that same, cool tone.

'I think so.' He paused. 'I go there sometimes, to see my daughter.'

Huldis stopped, leaning on the polished banister, and turned to look at him. 'Your daughter?' she said, not understanding.

'One of the twins is mine,' he said. 'Casildis was carrying the children of two men. Unusual.' As Huldis continued to stare at him, her mouth open, he added, 'If the wind changes, you may get stuck like that.'

'But her husband . . .'

'It's old business, Missis. We are friends. Strange friends.'

Huldis went on climbing up to the second landing, her thoughts rushing through her mind. Once again she had returned to the world of violent, vivid colour, where rules seemed to be broken and no one spoke in a whisper. Suddenly, she laughed.

'You seem to find my affairs amusing, Mademoiselle.'

Huldis found she could speak, and the words rushed out. 'Oh no, Monsieur Vasilyevich, but I have been pent up for so long in my father's castle, where one can neither shout nor run, and every day is the same, that I had forgotten how it was to be with you and your people. I have been thinking that I was back in La Souterraine, trapped under a new spell.'

'So we didn't do the right thing, sending you back there.'

It was not a question. Huldis, after her laughter, felt tears fill her eyes. 'You did not know. And it was not so bad when Cluny was there, but he left, and then I was alone with my father. And then Sarl came back . . .'

'What?' said Yuda, in a loud voice, and then swore in his own tongue. A sallow-skinned woman with long eyes appeared on the landing above, and said, '*Kak sovut, Vasye?*' Yuda ignored her. He leaned against the wall of the stairwell and gazed at Huldis with his alarming eyes.

'I thought I killed him,' he said. Huldis sat down on a carpeted step, and found the words pouring from her mouth.

Jessica Rydill

'My father could not give him up. He summoned a magus from the court of the Staryetz, who used his magics to conjure my brother from the dead. And they are here in this city, hunting you.'

Yuda ran his hand through his long hair. Jet black, it carried a few threads and filaments of grey. 'I just didn't need to hear that,' he said.

The woman spoke again, in Franj this time. 'Vasye, bring the girl into our room. She looks dead beat. Lukacs is making some *chai*.'

Yuda gave a little shrug. 'I don't suppose the others will thank us if we wake them up too. Come, Huldis. You can sit in comfort in our luxurious apartments and tell us the whole story.'

Chapter 8

The journey east from Axar to Dieulevaut customarily took three days. They set out from the spring before sunset, travelling at a steady pace. Andras, who lived alone, had agreed to carry Yuste and her friends in his wagon. Harnessed to two horses, it was less richly decorated than Mother Zari's, as if he had owned it only for a short time. From Cluny's story and from a few shared words with Mother Zari, Yuste had discovered that the Rom were matrilineal. Though the men had daily power, the clan head was a woman, and Andras owed loyalty to his mother's family.

The Rom had packed up their belongings, harnessed their horses and made ready to travel with speed. Yuste and Boris kept out of the way, sitting in their quarters with Cluny and Planchet. The manservant had changed his uniform for a green tunic, leggings and a leather jacket of *cuir-bouilli*, a process of hardening leather that Cluny explained to Yuste while they were waiting. Cluny had not put on his traditional attire for travelling, but had donned a corduroy jacket and his favoured velvet hat. He had however produced a short sword in a plain scabbard, which he showed to Yuste and Boris.

Yuste found herself viewing Cluny with new eyes. Soft-spoken, charming, courteous, he still carried a piece of steel that suited a medieval warrior. She tried to imagine his past life, which he had given up only months ago, to come and live in her world of steam and iron. Planchet seemed a little embarrassed by the curiosity that his garb provoked. They persuaded him to produce a weapon, and Boris admired the morning-star, a mallet adorned with murderous spikes. Planchet hefted it in his hand, and they saw the muscles bulging under his tunic. Yuste took care not to ask him what he thought of the orders Cluny had given him to flee the Doyen's troops. She thought the conflict between his loyalties must pain him, even though he had chosen Cluny to be his master.

As the wagon jolted across the unmade road out of Axar, the four of them had a good view out of the rear window. The spires and towers of the old city stood in silhouette against the pale western sky, and jutting clouds with edges of saturated rose and flame moved slowly south, like the harbingers of battle. Yuste imagined them as the Doyen's banners flaring across the sky, and she was not surprised to see the black wings beating overhead as the crows closed on Axar. She sobbed, and Boris squeezed her wrist.

'I sent a message to the Railway People,' he said.

'But what am I doing, Boris Andreyevich? What do I think I'm doing? It should be my brother heading east, not me.'

'Your brother is in Yonar, Missis.'

Yuste sent him her thoughts. She was afraid for the people in towns further north, which had already fallen under the Doyen's sway. What about those who might not meet with his approval? She could scarcely believe that an old warrior out of the past had raised an army to fall upon Masalyar and all its hopes.

— It's hard to imagine. But you've seen the sword and the morningstar. Real weapons.

The thought was something familiar, like an old coat. Yuste did not look at him.

— It's us, Boris. We're running away. We should be going to defend our city.

— Hasn't it taken everyone by surprise?

She had to smile at him. She found Cluny looking at her, waiting for her to speak, and she said, 'I'm sorry. Boris and I can communicate like shamans. But it is a little rude.'

'Not at all. It must be handy to share your thoughts so quickly.' He sighed. 'I was wondering what it means to run from my father. To declare myself a traitor.'

'You're not a traitor, Cluny. You're leaving to help your friends.'

He raised his eyes to hers. 'Don't you think, Yuste, that there must be some link between the disappearance of Annat and Malchik and my father's expedition? If it is a coincidence, it seems rather neat.'

Before Yuste could answer, Boris said, 'He's right. I don't know why, and I can't figure out the connection, but there has to be one.'

'Does it matter?' said Yuste. 'We will find them, and rescue them. That's all.'

Boris wrinkled his forehead. 'The Doyen might want to stop us rescuing them, if he finds out that's what we intend. Just a thought.'

'And where is my brother? Where is Sarl?' said Cluny.

Yuste sat back, leaning against the wooden wall of the caravan. 'We don't know anything,' she said, 'but it might not help us to know. All we have to do is reach the mountain, and then —'

'They are *inside* the mountain.' Yuste started. Andras's voice came softly from the front of the wagon where he sat to drive the horses. She had not realised he could hear them talking.

The western sky was blue as steel. Yuste watched it through the window. At first, she could make out the shapes of cypress trees, so much blacker than the sky. But as time passed, there was nothing but a deep, velvet blue, intensified by the lanterns they had lighted inside the caravan. They made a supper of bread and cheese and tinned meat, which Planchet had provided from the college buttery. The bread was made with sourdough, and Yuste found its bitter taste comforting with the salty butter. The others watched and waited as she said the blessings over her food in *Ebreu*, a language they could not understand.

'Do you think they will follow us?' Boris asked

Cluny when they had finished their meal. Planchet cleared away the plates and put them in the bowl for washing crockery that Andras had shown him. Like the Wanderers, the Rom had strict rules as to what was clean and unclean.

Cluny placed the sword in its scabbard on the table. 'I don't know. I wish I knew what was in my father's mind when he set forth.'

Boris grunted. 'I'm a bit like Yuste,' he said. 'I can't believe this is happening. Neither of us has spent much time out of Masalyar, let alone in the northern wilds. I can remember things from my childhood in Kiyev, of course. Swords, for instance. I've watched the *Druzhina* of the Staryetz ride by in their silver mail.'

'What is *Druzhina*?' said Cluny.

'Bodyguard,' said Yuste. 'All the Sklavan nobles – the boyars – have such a following.'

'We are your *Druzhina*, Yuste,' said Boris.

'Very funny, Boris Andreyevich. A Wanderer with a *Druzhina*? My people are forbidden to bear arms in Sklava.'

Boris seemed infected by enthusiasm. 'Not here. Not yet,' he said, fishing in his pockets for cigars and lighter. Planchet set one of the bottles of wine on the table and produced some glasses.

'It is cold,' said Yuste, shivering.

'I'm sure the wine will warm our bodies and our spirits,' said Cluny. 'Mine could do with warming.'

The caravan travelled throughout the night. Planchet rolled himself in his cloak and went to sleep on the floor, while Cluny occupied one of the banquettes against the wall, his hat tipped over his eyes and the sword close to his hand. By mutual agreement, they had offered Yuste the bed, though it was big enough to hold several people. But she could not sleep, and Boris sat up with her by the yellow light of the swinging lanterns. He produced a bottle of slivovitz from his bag, and they sipped from the clear liquor, passing a glass out to Andras.

'Yonar lies north of Ademar,' said Boris after a silence. 'I doubt if the Doyen can field an army on two fronts.'

'We don't know,' said Yuste. She had taken off her bonnet and placed it on the table, but she still wore her coat for warmth. 'Did you learn anything at the Railway station?'

Boris shrugged. 'No trains travelling north of Axar. Refugees heading south. The place was in an uproar. I had to show my official pass to get near the telegraph operator.'

'Did they know how close the Doyen's army was?'

'It seems he took Mont Eldemar first to guard his back. Left a garrison there and headed south. Between there and Axar there's few towns of any size, apart from Taraskou. The rumour was that Taraskou surrendered yesterday. He could already be on the outskirts of Axar.'

'Zyon,' said Yuste. Though not sleepy, she felt very weary. 'I have to let my brother know somehow.'

'I don't see how. I doubt if there's a telegraph between Dieulevaut and Yonar.'

Yuste gazed at him, rubbing her eyes. 'The fact is,

Boris Andreyevich, I can use *sprechen*. Yuda and I can share thoughts at a distance.'

'Good grief.' He downed the remains of his glass. '*Nazdravye*. Is that because you are twins?'

'I suppose so. Sival hasn't yet found any other shaman twins in this country.' She sighed. 'I don't know of anyone who could get a message to Yonar, especially if the trains are stopping at Axar.'

'There may be no trains from Axar tomorrow,' said Boris, with a grim face.

'We are on our own, aren't we?'

'Afraid so, Yuste. No back-up if anything goes wrong. But I'm used to that.'

'Not me, Boris Andreyevich. I'm a teacher, not a special agent.'

Boris refilled her glass and his own. 'So how does it work, this long-distance *sprechen*? Can I listen in?'

Yuste laughed in spite of herself. 'I can't stop you. Be my guest. The only remarkable thing is the distance.'

She rested her elbows on the table and hid her face in her hands to aid her concentration. At first, she could hear the rattling of the wagon, the thud of the horses' hooves, and the regular breathing of the sleepers. When she used *sprechen* with Boris, it was on a shallow level, as easy as her conscious thoughts. To reach Yuda's mind she had to sink deeper, moving towards the realm of sleep. The external sounds dimmed and she became conscious of her pulse and the blood singing in her ears. She felt Boris's mind putting out feelers, following her with a certain unease. He seemed to feel that he was trespassing in some private world. Yuste offered him a hand of thought, and brought him after her, down to the place where her own mind and her brother's seemed to run close together, like lodes in a rock.

Yuda's mind was noisy and awake, a world of little lights. Yuste let herself reach out to touch him, a cautious movement that must not startle him. She sensed his moment of confusion before he was there with her. If she opened her eyes, she imagined that he would be sitting beside her, as they rode together on a coal train through a mine.

— *What is it?*
— *Are you still in Yonar?*
Instead of answering, her brother noticed Boris.
— *What's he doing in here?*
— *A friend.*
— *No way. This is for us, not visitors. Tell him to piss off.*
Yuste felt Boris withdrawing from her mind with no further prompting. Now it was just she and Yuda together, in the strange light of their shared consciousness.

— *You've been using* sprechen.
— *I can. I didn't know I could.*
— *What's the matter? I can't stop long.*
Yuste let the knowledge flood between their thoughts, telling him how Annat and Malchik had disappeared, and about the Doyen's southward march. She felt him listening without sharing his emotions; he had an air of impatience.

— *We're in deep trouble, Yuste. Not just us — everyone. Sarl's back.*

— The crows . . .

— You keep going east. Head for the mountain. I've got stuff to do here. I'll let you know . . .

— Take care, Yuda, she cried into the silence, but he was gone, leaving her alone in the dark.

Baba Yaga lived in a cave hollowed out in the rock, like a wormhole in an apple. At first sight, Annat was surprised to find it a cosy place, for it held a traditional Sklavan stove, with a sleeping shelf above it loaded with colourful blankets. The floor was lined with animal skins, and a warm yellow glow allowed her to see the witch a little better. Baba Yaga was tall, as Annat had guessed, a woman past middle age but not yet old. Her face had a weathered look, even after her time underground, and her nose was sharp as a hook. She made Annat sit down on the wooden bench that was the only furniture the cave held, apart from a gnarled table. Malchik had to stand. The witch was still studying Annat's face, as if she were reading a book. Annat was breathless from the speed of their journey to the cave, but she took care to return the woman's glance, and not to seem afraid.

'I need an apprentice,' said the witch. 'I never had one of my own. With your powers and my skills, we could defeat the Master.'

'We want to defeat him,' said Annat. 'But most of all, we want to escape.' She did not wish to disagree too openly, but she knew it was important to remind Baba Yaga of their true intentions. The old woman glanced at Malchik, as if she had forgotten him.

'Who's we?' she said. 'Oh yes, your brother. A fine-looking young man.'

She stood up and went to the stove, opening the oven door where she started to poke at the coals inside. Malchik hastened to Annat's side and whispered, 'I don't like this.'

'Trust me, Malchku,' she said. She did not dare say any more, for the witch had straightened and fixed them with her stare.

'What does the Master need two souls for?' she said.

'He raised a man from the dead. And he needs two souls to keep him alive,' said Annat.

Baba Yaga closed the stove door. 'It's not easy to steal souls from the living. Not even for the Master,' she said. 'A soul can't be cut out and put in a bottle. He should have come to me.' She wiped her hands on her apron, shaking her head.

'We want to keep our souls,' said Malchik.

'Of course you do, young man. What good is a body without a soul? The eyes are open and the heart beats on, but nothing is left inside.' She wiped the soot from her hands on her apron. 'I've made up my mind. Baba Yaga will help you.'

Annat looked at Malchik. What if he trusted her judgement, and she was wrong?

'What are you going to do?' she said.

'The Master taps me for my power. But he cannot cut out the core of me, the witch part. I can still do spells, and I'm going to do one for you. It will spirit you away from here. Far away. Somewhere he can't reach you.'

'You can do that for us, and you can't escape your-self?' said Malchik, creasing his forehead.

'He has special chains of enchantment to keep me here. But as for you, there's no reason to suppose you could escape any other way. The mountain is sealed. There are ways in, but no way out. Remember it was Baba Yaga who told you that.'

Malchik laid his hand on Annat's shoulder. 'Why should we trust you?'

'Your sister knows,' said the witch.

Annat found her brother's gaze on her once more, seeking her assurance. She was the shaman, who must know all there was of magic. Once again, she found herself crippled by the lack of a way to send him her thoughts. She wanted him to know the true complexity of their situation: she did not wholly trust the witch, but she saw good reasons why the woman should help them. Pride kept her from admitting that she might be as lost as he was. Yuda had trained her, she was seven-teen and a powerful shaman; she dared not let her brother know she had any doubts. Malchik squeezed her shoulder.

'If you're happy, Annat,' he said.

Cold in the pit of her stomach, she nodded. She was gambling her life and his, when it might be best to leave the witch and continue their journey into the heart of the mountain. If she spoke now, he would follow her, perhaps a little disappointed. Annat made herself smile. She was like her father; she must be certain.

'What do you want us to do?' she said.

The witch nodded. 'Sit you down, boy, opposite

your sister,' she said. She cleared a space in the centre
of the table between them, and made them lay their
hands palm downwards on the tabletop, with the
fingertips outspread. Annat smiled at her brother, but
he did not return the smile. He watched Baba Yaga
as she moved around the room, sweeping up glass
bottles, candles, herbs and powders. Annat touched
his finger so that he turned back to her.

'Don't you trust me, Malchku?' she whispered.

'It's her I don't trust. But you know best,' he said,
forcing a smile.

Baba Yaga came to the table and let the things she
had gathered fall from her apron in a heap. She worked
quickly, sprinkling herbs and powders over Malchik
and Annat's joined hands. She mouthed words in a
soft language, lighted candles and waved them overhead, before blowing them out. Annat had never witnessed anyone casting a spell, and was surprised by
both the deliberation and the haste.

A mixture of substances, some smooth, others
scratchy, was piled over her hands. A streak of lapis
lazuli wound amongst the dried leaves and the crushed
cinnamon. Baba Yaga took twelve red candles and lit
them one by one, spilling drops of the hot wax on the
table and Annat's skin. The woman hardly seemed
aware of Annat and Malchik as she worked. From time
to time, she would pause to consult a book, as if she
were baking a cake and needed to check the recipe.
Annat saw Malchik move restively in his chair. They
were not in an uncomfortable position, but as the magic
began to build in the air, she felt the same restlessness.

The heat from the stove seemed to spread, filling the room with lazy warmth. She blinked, conscious of the beginnings of drowsiness.

Baba Yaga pinched her shoulder. 'You must not fall asleep, girl,' she said. Annat looked across at Malchik, to see that his eyelids were fluttering. The witch had lighted several cones of incense, and their pungent smell, the odours of sandalwood and frankincense, made it still harder to keep awake. Annat yawned. The witch strode across to Malchik and nudged him awake. 'Face each other,' she said, 'look at each other.'

Annat gazed at her brother, his brown eyes pale behind their polished glass lenses. He had changed since she had seen him last. The softness had gone from his face, and he was a man. She tried to analyse what changes had made this difference. It was something to do with the prominence of the bones in his face, the slight shadow of unshaven blond beard. She felt a little regret for the soft, vulnerable boy that she had grown accustomed to. It was as if he had finally made the decision that took him over the border into manhood, closing a door behind him. Annat remained on the other side of that door. She wondered what it was like, that other life across the border, so close and yet so separate, and she thought of Cluny . . .

'You must keep very still,' said Baba Yaga's voice. 'Concentrate.'

The witch took a black, iridescent feather to waft the smoke from the candles, spreading it into every corner of the room. She took careful paces each time she did so, as if she were measuring out the steps of a dance. Watching her, Annat thought that she looked graceful. She was not at all the same as the person who had shrunk from them in the corridor, like a bundle of rags.

Annat thought that the feather was leaving trails in the air that were more than just patterns in the smoke. They looked to her like words or runes; they even reminded her of the *Ebreu* script she had once seen written in the depths of a ring that her father wore. She wondered whether they were the same, or whether this magic used something similar. As she watched, they seemed to leap and fade, leaving an emptiness behind them.

Baba Yaga pushed her cheek, not roughly, so that she was facing Malchik. 'You must concentrate,' she said. Malchik looked at Annat with an expression she could not interpret, and once more she wished she could share *sprechen* with him. She felt that he was thinking intensely and trying to will his thought towards her, but she could hear nothing.

Baba Yaga stood beside the table, letting her gaze travel over the items that she had assembled, as if to search for something that was missing. She picked up a new candle, its wax black as mud, and lit it from one of the red candles. She opened the oven and took out a small cake, which she placed on the table. She let the molten wax from the black candle drip on to the cake, and then took a bite out of it, eating wax and cake together. Then she handed the cake to Annat, saying, 'Eat.' Annat took a cautious mouthful; the cake tasted of salt, flour and the slight bitterness of the wax.

She chewed a few times, gagging on the bitter taste, and made herself swallow. The witch carried the cake over to Malchik, and told him to take a bite, which he did. When he had swallowed the morsel, Baba Yaga placed the remnant of cake on top of the pile of herbs and powders, and set light to it. It burst into flame and Annat was tempted to jump to her feet, pulling her hands clear, but she could not move. Instead, she saw the ingredients dissolving into a blue flame that burnt without heat.

The flames played over her fingers and those of Malchik. They did not seem to dwindle or be consumed, but instead to spread. They gave off neither scent nor smoke. Baba Yaga stepped away from the table and crouched down. Once again, she was muttering to herself, and Annat thought that she was speaking to the flame, invoking it. Malchik moved his fingers just a fraction so that his index finger covered hers, as if to offer comfort. His touch did console her; she had seldom felt so uncertain or alone.

The witch rose to her feet and began to dance backwards round the table. She was singing a song in Sklavan, but it was an ancient chant whose words Annat could hardly recognise. She no longer felt sleepy, but alert and curious. She saw Malchik open his mouth to speak – then everything went black. She could neither see nor hear, and she could not breathe; she no longer had any sense of her body with the pulse of her blood and the warm sensations of touch, taste and smell. Blinded and silent, she had been transformed into something like an amoeba, a helpless blob of pure spirit without form. She felt Malchik's presence beside her, crying out without words, and she knew she had failed him; the witch had taken their souls.

The room into which Yuda ushered Huldis was small, and crowded with two bunk beds. In those on the left, a young blackamoor lay awake under the covers, his hand supporting his head. The bunk below was empty, the covers neatly folded back, and the long-eyed woman sat down on it. Both bunks on the right-hand side were empty, and the occupant of the upper berth had left sheets, blankets and covers dangling over the edge. Yuda flung them up on to the mattress with an irritable gesture.

'Who's the girl, Vasye?' said the blackamoor.

Yuda turned to look at Huldis, who lowered her eyes. She felt shy and a little afraid to stand in a room where no one else seemed to be Franj.

'Old, past business, Niko,' said Yuda. 'This is Huldis. She comes from a culture that's even more . . . traditional than Yonar.'

'More traditional than Yonar?' The young man gave a whistle, but his eyes smiled at Huldis. 'Has she ever seen a Darkman before?' he added.

'Huldis knows Sergey Govorin,' said Yuda. 'But if she was like me, she probably thought he was the only one.'

Niko grinned, showing white teeth. 'That's so neat,' he said.

'Don't mock the girl, Niko,' said the woman on the lower bunk.

'Me? I'm pleased to meet her. Very pleased.' He swung his legs over the edge of the bed and dropped to the floor, standing before Huldis in strange garments, a buttoned tunic and trews tied at the waist with a cord. He held out his hand, and she stared at it. The palm was a delicate pink, like a shell. Yuda slapped him on the shoulder.

'These people don't shake hands, Niko,' he said. 'They either kiss you or kill you.'

The woman shook her head. 'Hallo, Huldis,' she said. 'My name is Su Lin, and I was born in Cine. A very long way from here. All of us are ambassadors from the city of Masalyar to the people of Yonar, or Lon as it is called in your tongue. Sit down beside me, as we have no chairs in our spacious room.'

They all sat, Huldis beside Su Lin and Niko and Yuda on the lower bunk opposite. Huldis took off her cloak, for it was warm in the little room, and found them all staring at her long green gown, which hung to her ankles. Her head was covered with a light cambric veil, held in place by a simple circlet.

'Very traditional,' said Niko, shaking his head. 'Where's Lukacs got to with the *chai*? Is he brewing his own piss?'

Su Lin gave a snort, and Yuda suppressed a smile. 'So you're a shaman, Huldis,' he said. 'But you can hide it.'

She nodded. She felt a little dizzy in the room with its warmth and its strange people, as if she had tasted liquor after abstaining for many years. She realised that Yuda was watching her with close attention, and touching her thoughts with a light touch, just enough to search out the truth of what she said. Now that she had lowered her defences, she was not sure how to raise them again. And she need not be afraid of Yuda; she had to trust him, for there was no one else.

'Tell me what you are doing in Yonar, Missis,' he said. 'And why you came to find me.'

Huldis found her tongue heavy and her thoughts dull. As she struggled to find her words, Yuda suddenly sat up straight, muttered a curse and clapped his hands over his ears. The others looked at him in surprise.

'What's the matter, Vasye?'

He screwed his eyes shut and mouthed two words at her. Su Lin shrugged. 'It's like this with shamans,' she whispered to Huldis. 'Things happen, and you just have to be patient.'

Huldis smiled at her, and found that she could not avoid staring at the woman's face with its smooth, golden skin.

'Poor kid, she's exhausted,' Su Lin said to Niko. 'Listen, Huldis, we can find a bed for you here if you want. Then you can go back tomorrow morning. We do sometimes sleep in this house.'

As she spoke, the door opened and a man with short brown hair came in backwards, carrying two beakers of steaming liquid.

'Here's the *chai*—' he began, only to be interrupted by Su Lin, who held a finger to her lips.

'What's the matter? Chief getting a telegraph?' he

said, setting one of the mugs down on a table against the wall.

Yuda surfaced, rubbing his eyes and blinking. 'Is that *chai* I can smell?' he said.

'Sure, Chief. Who's the girl?'

'Huldis, meet Lukacs. Lukacs, meet Huldis. I hope one of those is for me.'

'I left yours in the kitchen with mine,' said Lukacs. He was the oldest person there, his face graven with lines of humour and tobacco. His eyes were a light hazel and he gave Huldis a wink as he spoke.

'Was that Yuste?' said Niko, accepting a beaker from Lukacs.

'That was Yuste,' said Yuda. He stared at the floor. 'I'll have to see the ambassador.'

'Why? What?' said Su Lin.

'Zyon,' said Yuda, ruffling up his hair. 'Do you want the bad news first, or . . . the other bad news?'

'I'll get the *chai*,' said Lukacs, pushing the door open.

'I don't suppose Yuste would bother you if it was good news,' said Su Lin. She picked up her beaker and blew on it. 'I hope this is green *chai* and not that foul Sklavan stuff.'

'Yuste says someone has kidnapped the *kinder*. One. Two, she says the Doyen of Ademar . . .' he glanced at Huldis, '. . . has decided to march south with a large army. Heading for Masalyar. The first they knew was crows over the city – flocks of crows.'

'Who or what is the Doyen of Ademar?' said Niko, all but dropping his *chai*.

Yuda was staring at Huldis so hard that she was

almost afraid. 'Your turn, Missis,' he said. 'I want to hear what you know.'

This time, the words spilled out. She told him – them – about Semyon's coming to the castle, and the raising of Sarl. She told of the plot to steal two souls – the souls of Yuda's children – and to capture him and take his heart. At the end, she remembered her father's vainglorious words about his plans to reconquer Neustria. Starting with the godless city of Masalyar. When she finished, there was silence. Then Niko said, 'Wow,' in a quiet voice. Su Lin reached forward to give Huldis a pat on the knee. Yuda lay back on the bed and pulled the pillow over his face.

Lukacs returned with two more cups to find them all thus disposed. 'I missed something, huh?' he said, in a tone of apparent uninterest.

Yuda surfaced, throwing the pillow on the floor. 'I should have known!' he shouted. 'Everything was quiet. I swore I'd pull that place down stone by stone, and that's what I should have done. Never listen to women. Least of all the mother of your child.'

'Thanks, Yuda,' said Su Lin dryly. 'Do you want that minuted for the record?'

Lukacs stood in the doorway, holding the two beakers of *chai*. 'Do you want this or not, Vasye?'

'Fuck the *chai*!' said Yuda. He stood up and began to pace the room. After a moment, he flung himself on the bed and pulled something out from under his mattress. Huldis watched as, with shaking hands, he lit a cigarette.

'Someone's kidnapped Annat and Malchik,' said

Niko. 'Sounds like a mean Mother. Oh, and Yuda's best buddy is in town. Someone he only killed four years ago. Plus there's going to be a war. The dead guy is planning to conquer Neustria.'

'Sit down, Vasye,' said Lukacs. He did not seem offended to have been sworn at. 'Drink your *chai*. And tell Mamma Lukacs what all this is about.'

Yuda glared at him. 'You're a cheeky fucker, you know that?' he said. But he took the beaker of *chai* from Lukacs, and they sat down side by side on the lower bunk. Yuda asked Huldis to repeat her story and, when she had finished, he added the news he had received from Yuste.

'The ambassador is going to love being wakened from her beauty sleep,' said Lukacs, rolling up his eyes.

'She's got to know, Lukacs,' said Su Lin. 'This means we're cut off, on the wrong side of an invasion.'

'She's got to release me,' said Yuda.

'I don't see her doing that, Vasye,' said Niko.

'They aren't her *kinder*. And someone has to stop this magus giving Sarl back his life, or we're all screwed.'

Su Lin looked straight across at Huldis. 'What are you going to do, girl?' she said. 'Doesn't look like there'll be much sleeping here tonight.'

Huldis stood up, gathering the folds of her cloak. 'I'll have to go back,' she said. 'I don't want them to know I've gone. And they mustn't find out I'm a shaman.'

'Wait.' Yuda stretched out his hand, swigging a mouthful of *chai*. 'I'm coming with you.'

'Are you nuts?' said Niko.

'That doesn't sound like such a good idea,' said Lukacs.

'Seeing as they plan to cut out your heart,' added Su Lin.

Yuda stood up, offering her his beaker of *chai*. 'They won't do that,' he said.

'He's mad,' said Niko. 'Should we overpower him?'

'You heard the girl. No filleting until they get me back to the mountain where the *kinder* are. And they can't get back the way they came. It'll give me time to think of something.'

'What are we going to tell the ambassador?' said Su Lin.

'Face it, Su. There are twenty-eight of us. Not enough to kick the Doyen up the arse. She doesn't need me here. This is more important. She doesn't know what Sarl could do if he got his life back.'

'She may not see it that way,' said Su Lin.

'She'll have to. I'm not sending Huldis back alone.'

His hand closed on Huldis's wrist and she gave a jump, as if she had received a tingling shock like the ones she sometimes experienced when brushing out her hair. Yuda smiled at her. He seemed calm now, as if he had made up his mind and foresaw no obstacles. She had to talk to him.

'They're right, Monsieur. You ought to get away from here while you can. That was why I came to warn you. The Magus is a dangerous man. And my brother is . . . terrible.'

'He wasn't that great when he was alive,' said Yuda. Seeing her face, he added, 'I'm sorry. You knew him before he was corrupted. But I don't underestimate him; I know what he can do.' Releasing her hand, he rolled up his sleeve to show her a series of dark scars, almost black, on his forearm. 'He left me with some mementoes of our meeting. And that's not all . . .' He shook his head. 'No arguments, Missis. If it was just me and my family, I might think twice. But if someone like Sarl got his hands on a whole country . . .' He gave a shudder.

'You don't seem surprised that he is here. Alive,' she said.

'Surprised? Not very. My sort tend to meet the dead more often than you'd think.'

Lukacs sidled up to them, hands in his trouser pockets. 'The others and I have been having a word, Chief,' he said. 'We want to come with you to see the ambassador.'

'What, so she can shout at you as well?'

'It's just that we agree with you. We'd do the same. Though we think it's crazy,' he added, showing his teeth in a smile. Yuda grinned up at him.

'I suppose if we go mob-handed she won't know who to carpet first,' he said.

'No carpet in her bedroom, Chief.'

'And what were you doing in the ambassador's bedroom, Mister?'

They slipped into their own tongue, and Huldis stood by, wondering how they could laugh and joke when things were so desperate. And she knew they understood how desperate; she had sensed Yuda's urgency in his touch. Su Lin came up beside her.

'I hope you know what you're going to say to your brother and his magus, girl,' she said.

Huldis shook her head. She felt numb, incapable of ordering her thoughts.

'Don't leave it all to Yuda,' said Su Lin. 'He's cunning enough, but you're a woman. Think of a good lie, and stick to it.'

'Shall I minute that for the records?' said Niko over her shoulder, and she gave him a light punch in the arm.

The ambassador received them in her suite of rooms on the next floor up. She was sitting up, propped on pillows, in her canopy bed, dressed in a pale pink négligée. Huldis, who was accustomed to the threadbare magnificence of her father's chateau, took in with astonishment the linen sheets, crisp pillow-shams and embroidered eiderdown. The ambassador was a small woman with chestnut hair pinned into a chignon at the back of her head; she wore a pair of horn-rimmed spectacles that gave her a severe appearance. Like Yuda, she was smoking a stick of *tabak*, but hers was fixed in a long ivory holder; she flicked the ash into a silver dish on the pot cupboard beside the bed.

'How little sleep do you plan to allow me tonight, Vasilyevich?' she said. Lukacs muttered something in the Sklavan tongue to Niko, who stifled a laugh. The ambassador glared at them.

'It's war, Madame Ambassador,' said Yuda, who stood with his arms folded. 'The Doyen of Ademar is marching on the city, and we're cut off to the rear of his forces.'

She gave a sigh. 'Splendid. Just when the negotiations reach their most delicate point – and I needn't tell you how delicate it is – we are left without instructions. Perhaps without a state to represent. Are the lines of communication cut?'

'I don't know,' said Yuda. 'I got a message from my sister. She was fleeing from Axar.'

'Has the Doyen invested our base at Mont Eldemar?'

'I don't know . . .'

'What is the use of coming to me with such half-baked information? Return to me in the morning with a full report. Good night.'

She extinguished her cigarette in the silver dish and was about to turn over when Yuda said, 'Madame Ambassador . . .'

'I said good night, Vasilyevich.'

'Madame Ambassador, I want you to release me. On indefinite leave.'

The ambassador sat up in the bed, drawing up her knees in a less ladylike pose, and stared at him. Huldis recognised that she was young, perhaps younger than Yuda.

'You'd better have a damn good reason for asking, Vasilyevich,' she said. The tiredness in her face made her look almost childlike, though her little hands, linked on the coverlet, were the hands of an older woman, with rings and red nails. Yuda smiled at her, and it was not an ingratiating smile, but one of trust.

'You're not going to believe this, Missis,' he said dropping the formal mode of address he had been using until now, 'but the old bastard has had my children kidnapped.'

The ambassador passed her hand over her brow. 'They're at college now, aren't they?' she said. 'And you think the Doyen is involved?'

Yuda turned to Huldis, and beckoned her to stand beside him. 'This is his daughter. One of his daughters,' he said. 'It's dark magic. A shaman thing.'

The ambassador looked up at Huldis. Her eyes were cold. 'Then we could use her for bargaining,' she said.

Yuda put his hand on Huldis's shoulder. 'I don't think so, Ambassador,' he said. 'This girl came here of her own will. She is in the city with Jean Sorel d'Ademar and Semyon, Magus of Sklava. I think he's the one I've been searching for. The rogue shaman. I doubt that, if we followed your plan, we could hold the girl against him. He draws on forces that are unknown to me. He has brought Jean Sorel back from the dead, and he means to keep him here. To rule over Neustria, starting with our city.'

'Come here, girl,' said the ambassador. Yuda gave Huldis a gentle push, and she approached the bed. The ambassador took Huldis's hand in her dry fingers.

'You are very young, Mademoiselle,' she said.

'Not as young as I seem,' said Huldis. 'I am but twenty in mortal years, but my true age is thirty-nine.'

'Then you have the advantage of me,' said the ambassador, with a thin smile. She released Huldis's hand, and looked up at Yuda. 'I am minded to give you leave to go, Vasilyevich,' she said. 'Not because it concerns your offspring – the girl alone should be able to take care of them both – but because I can see how nearly this affects our cause. Jean Sorel was – is – the old man's Heir. There is nothing we can do to halt the Doyen's advance on Masalyar, but with this we may fight our own action on the rearguard. Behind enemy lines, as it were.'

'You understand, then, Missis. Sarl and this magus are more than just a threat to my *kinder*; they bring darkness.'

'I hope you know what you're doing, Vasilyevich. This release doesn't mean that I trust you out of my sight. Get you gone before I change my mind.'

Yuda gave her a short bow, smiling as if she had not reproached him.

Chapter 9

A t length, even Boris confessed to sleepiness. Yuste
told him to take her place on the covered bed,
and clambered out through the opening to sit beside
Andras. For a long time, they sat in silence, watching
the horses' foreshortened bodies as they trotted
through the night, and the dim shape of the next wagon
jolting ahead. Yuste felt tired, but calm. She let her
brother's thoughts roll through her mind, savouring
the sharpness and flavour of each one. At such times,
how keenly she missed their former intimacy, when
every thought had been shared and there had been no
one to keep them apart.

The rivalry had begun when Aude's family came to
the village. Yuste could still remember Aude as they
had first seen her, standing barefoot amongst the rocks
beneath the cliffs with her skirt kilted up over her
knees. Her hair had been wisps of amber light and her
skin had been liquid pale, with a hint of rose. They

had both thought her a spirit from the sea, taking flesh on their shore. They had not dared to approach her, as they stood amongst the coarse grass of the dunes spying on her beauty. Then the girl gave a shout and jumped into the water, splashing and laughing. The sun glinted off her amber head as she swam through the waves, which coiled over her pink arms and buoyed up her garments. She was a clumsy swimmer, but all they saw was the vividness of this wonderful stranger from the sea. Each had seen her, and felt they loved her.

Aude was forbidden to speak to them. She came of a high Doxan family and they were Wanderers, outcasts who lived outside the village in an eyrie perched on the cliffs. Their first meetings had happened by stealth, and it had been Yuste who dared to approach the other child, to swim out until her dark head bobbed like a seal's a few feet from Aude's own. It was so strange to think of their first words and Aude's seeming scorn on meeting a Wanderer. But they were children, and it did not take them long to abandon adult rules. When they walked side by side along the sand, Aude had begun to tell Yuste of her lost friend, Huldis. The clouds scudded overhead, the colour of seagulls, and Yuste had listened to a story she did not understand; all that came to her was the pain of loss, which she too might feel if Yuda was taken from her. She had stretched out her arms to console the weeping girl, and kissed her on the cheek . . .

Yuste pursed her lips. The memories were too strong and too sweet, even now. She should not revisit that time, when all it could do was conjure bitter thoughts, pain that had not healed, and years of loss. She should dwell in the present that had been handed to her, not luxuriate in sensual regret. But she could not forget the grains of sand on Aude's cheek, and the taste of salt.

She realised that she was not even trying to ward her thoughts from Andras; she did not know how. She glanced across at him, and he said, 'I have never seen the sea. But I have heard its voice in shells.'

'Aude used to give me shells,' said Yuste. 'Those tiny pink ones, like a baby's fingernail. I kept them for a long time after she died, but in the end I tipped them back into the sea.'

'What about your brother?' he said, staring straight ahead.

'She lost interest in me. It wasn't cruelty; she grew up, grew out of my love. But it wasn't so for me. Yuda and I quarrelled, and we fought as shamans fight. Neither of us knew till then how powerful we were. We had been trained, but not for that. Yuda nearly killed me.'

'And you hated him?'

'I did then. He destroyed my powers and made me barren. But now I don't know. Do you think it possible for one's powers to grow back, Andras?'

He shrugged. 'I don't know, lady. In your place, I would hate my brother. I would want to kill him.'

'I did,' said Yuste. She paused. 'But in the end, he gave me something that made us quits. He gave me Annat . . . and Malchik.'

'These are your brother's children.'

'It's a long story, Andras. Aude failed. She lost her mind. She was too frail to have children – frail in her soul, not her body. I think Doxa is a cruel religion. When Yuda made her pregnant, her parents forced them to marry. They cast her out. I think . . . so many things . . . she blamed herself, she blamed Yuda, she remembered the curse of the Mother against the Wanderers.' She clenched her hands together. 'We failed her. But by then, the love and the hate were all twisted up together. Yuda and Aude, I loved and hated them both. I was young, passionate and full of anger. I said, did, terrible things.'

'But she is dead.'

'At peace, I hope. Yuda ran away to the city and she lingered for a few years, dwindling. I think she took her own life, but I cannot be sure. She never cared for Annat, not from a baby, and so I had my own daughter to foster. I forgave Aude, but perhaps I killed her.'

'You cannot know,' said Andras.

'That's the hard thing. Not to know. Sometimes I wonder if there is a punishment waiting for me somewhere. I know Yuda has had to shoulder his guilt. He is a strange man. Sometimes I think he is looking for death.'

Andras flicked the whip lightly over the horses' backs, more as a caress than a harsh blow.

'It is the way with shamans. They walk with death as a friend. They travel the dark and under road.'

Yuste found herself laughing. 'Not me, Andras,' she

said. 'I'm firmly pent in this sublunary world. I have to listen to travellers' tales and read the postcards they send back.'

Andras turned his head to smile at her. 'Until now?' he said.

Slowly the light changed and softened, and dawn welled up above the mountains in the east. The Lepas Mountains. Yuste straightened and stretched in her seat. She had not slept all night, and she wondered when she would feel the after-effects. She was so used to being an invalid, having to rest in the afternoons before class, drinking herbal tea. She wondered whether she had reserves of strength that she had never tried to tap over the long years since Yuda injured her.

Certainly Andras did not show any signs of tiredness. But when the sun had risen over the mountains, the Rom made camp, choosing a place where they could tether their horses beside water. Boris stepped down from the rear of the caravan, feeling his unshaven chin, and shortly after, Cluny and Planchet followed him. By that time, Yuste had gone down to the stream to draw a pail of water, and Andras was sitting beside the camp fire that he had made and lighted with the skill of long travelling.

'Hoya, Gadji,' he shouted to them. 'Did you sleep like babies?'

Yuste smiled to herself as she came up from the river, following the women of the Rom. The heavy pail slopped water over her skirts, and she did not bring as much back to the camp as she would have liked.

Andras took it from her with a smile, and poured some of it into a billy-can that he set to boil, hanging from a iron hook over the fire. Boris hunkered down by the flames.

'Do you think it's safe to stop here, Andras?' he said.

Andras gave a shrug. He was chewing on a stick, which he used to clean his teeth. 'The horses need to rest,' he said. 'They have walked all night. And men need to rest also.'

Boris stood up, feeling in his pocket. 'I wonder about this Doyen. Will he keep his troops outside Axar, or might he send a detachment after us?'

Andras did not answer him at once; he was thinking. At length, he looked from one to the other of them. 'I do not think he will follow us,' he said. 'But I will be easier when we have made Dieulevaut.'

Boris started to pace up and down. 'We could fight,' he said. 'If they have followed us. We have two shamans – that's you and me, Andras. They wouldn't be expecting it.'

'I don't fight,' said Andras.

Boris paused, and looked from him to Yuste. She had made herself comfortable by the fire, sitting on the ground; it was not easy with her skirts and stiff petticoats, which soared around her like swollen sails.

'What do you mean?' said Boris.

Yuste answered for Andras. She realised that she had enough power to sense the general shape of his thoughts, if not the particular words. It was like hearing a hidden and long-lost music. 'He doesn't use his powers to fight, Boris Andreyevich,' she said. 'Only for healing.'

'Shit,' said Boris, turning away.

'I can understand that,' said Cluny. 'I've been trained to kill, but I wouldn't do it by choice. Planchet and I are like dogs; well trained, but not born savage.'

'And will he say that if the Doyen comes?' said Planchet, folding his arms across his chest. His voice was gruff, but pleasant to the ear.

Andras smiled faintly. 'I will fight, but not with magic,' he said.

Boris gave a snort; he was still standing facing towards the river, away from the camp fire.

'I don't call it magic,' he said. 'My powers aren't magic; I was born with them.'

'But I have heard that you don't use your powers to fight either,' said Yuste, who was not inclined to let the matter rest.

Boris swung round. 'That's different,' he said. 'I can use my powers if I have to; I just happen to think it's a waste, when I have a gun.'

Yuste smiled at him. She guessed that she had found a sore place, and was tempted, with an impulse that reminded her of Annat, to probe it. Instead, Boris challenged her. 'Would you do it, then? If you still had powers like Yuda's, would you be fighting alongside him?'

Last night's conversation still fresh in her thoughts, Yuste shook her head. 'I never did any good with my powers when I had them. And I'm not like Yuda; I couldn't kill.'

Boris strode towards her, stabbing the air with his finger. 'Exactly. You think it's any different because we're men and you're a woman? You think it's natural for men to kill?'

Yuste bent back her head to look at him. The rising sun was behind him, casting his shadow across the fire. 'You've chosen an odd profession if you don't like killing, Boris Andreyevich.'

'I'm a detective, woman. I carry a gun for self-defence. I'm meant to solve murders, not perpetrate them.'

Andras threw a handful of dried leaves into the pot, and began to stir them. He no longer seemed to be listening to their argument. Yuste watched his young face, distracted for a moment by its freshness. He was not a youth like Cluny or Malchik, but everything about him still looked bright and new. She glanced back at Boris with his worn, lined face and bald pate, and smiled. 'I'm sorry, Boris. It's easy to be wise when one has never been tested.'

'I'll say so,' said Boris. He squatted beside her, then sat down on the ground with a wince.

'We have posted lookouts,' said Andras, without turning his head.

'They should be looking out for crows,' said Boris, giving a shrug that became a shiver. 'Uncanny that.' He looked up at Cluny. 'This was your brother?' he said.

Cluny sat down cross-legged on the other side of the fire. He balanced his sword across his knees. 'My brother dabbled in dark magic,' he said. 'He gave himself up to an evil goddess.'

'There aren't too many evil goddesses where I come from,' said Boris. Cluny looked as if he were about to protest, but the detective held up his hand. 'I know; I've heard the stories,' he said. 'I am a shaman, remember? But I don't dabble in that stuff.'

'The dark and under road,' said Andras.

Boris rubbed his fingers over his eyelids. 'I'm about to get mixed up in it, though. I could never stand all that mystical stuff when I was studying at the *Shkola*. Astral travelling. It sounds too much like mediums faking ectoplasm from under their armpits and making tables float with their knees. Unlike your family,' he added, glowering at Yuste. She laughed. In spite of her sleepless night, she felt fine. Nonetheless, she was glad when Andras lifted the billy-can from the fire and pronounced the *chai* ready for drinking. He made it a strange way, with milk and sugar boiled up in the mix, straining out the leaves last of all. Cluny peered suspiciously into the beaker that Andras gave him.

'Is this some sort of potion?' he said.

'Bloody hell, I hope not,' said Boris, who had already swallowed a mouthful of the steaming liquid.

Baba Yaga stood for a while looking at the two bodies, one slumped in each chair. They still breathed, their hearts still beat, but they were mindless, empty, blind. Over the burning embers in the centre of the table bobbed the two souls, tiny lights that only she could see. She took a small, blue-painted box from a shelf beside the stove, and reached out to catch the souls in her hand. They were soft to the touch and slightly slippery. She placed them in the box and latched it shut.

It had almost been too easy. She had been tempted to let them go, but the thought that she might have something with which she could bribe the Master had been too strong. She was not sure that, powerful as he was, he had learnt the way to steal the soul out of the body.

Baba Yaga knew what Semyon kept in his one of his suitcases. He had a world captive, and he drew on its power to do magic. He thought he was a great magus like Kaschai, but his skill was crude and unshaped, the raw power of a novice. He had raised a man from the dead, but he needed this bloody and unwieldy spell to keep him alive. Two souls and a heart; she could have taught him how to work the same magic less expensively. But he was a man, a magus, and he wanted to show his dominion over the mortal world.

The witch weighed the box in her hand. No doubt he would have killed the two, the young man and the girl, and caught their souls in transit between this world and the next. As if there were only two worlds, the earth world and the afterlife. He would cut the thread of life and draw out the souls. This way was better. Their bodies lived, and they might be used for other purposes, other homeless spirits.

It was time to go. She must be ready for the Master when he returned. Perhaps, after all these years, he might agree to release her. Baba Yaga made up her mind to take the swift way, rather than skulking through the tunnels. She knew well that there were other ways to reach the Crystal Chamber; she had studied them, when there was still hope in her that she might catch the Magus unawares.

She left the chamber where she had made her dwelling and set off in the opposite direction to the one in which she had brought Annat and Malchik. She took long strides, her grey hair whispering behind her as if it were alive. She had tied the small box at her belt, and it banged against her thigh as she walked. Very far off, she thought she could hear the souls whispering to each other. It gave her a moment, an impulse of pity, but she did not stop; when she chose to cast the spell freeing them from their living bodies, she had made her decision.

This path was narrower and more rough-hewn than the one that Annat and Malchik had been using when they found her. She knew that the Miners had made it. Baba Yaga had heard of the Miners, but she had never seen them. They had bored far deeper than the level where Semyon kept her. From time to time, she thought she heard the echo of their hammers in the deep; once or twice, when she searched the winding corridors, looking for a way out, she had seen distant lights, twinkling like earthbound stars. But she took care never to go any closer. She reflected that, if she had sent the two on their way, they would soon have encountered the Miners and, perhaps, a death that would be worse than anything that Semyon could offer them.

The path rose steeply. There was no light here, not even that from shafts cut into the side of the mountain to enable daylight to penetrate. But Baba Yaga had gone this way many times without light. She kept her fingertips tracing the wall to her left, and walked with quick steps. Somewhere along this track, in a place she had often passed, a deep ravine opened on one side of the path. She would feel the breath from its depths against her cheek. She began to move more swiftly, for something about that void inspired fear in her. She counted her steps, and sure enough, felt the draught of air that told her she was approaching the precipice. Warm air.

The witch hurried. Her fingers scraped against the rough-hewn stone. She had lived such a long time in darkness, she should have learned not to fear it, but always at this place in the tunnels, her heart beat rapidly as if she were a young girl. She began to run, gasping with fright, her feet striking the firm path as if it might vanish from under her. She found herself blundering from one wall to the other; suddenly the drop was there under her footsteps. She sheered away from it, and threw herself against the far wall, the safe wall, crawling like a spider against its surface. She felt the cold of granite grinding into her cheek, and sobbed with relief. She wondered if the Magus had placed a spell here as a defence against incursion into his private apartments high in the peak of the mountain.

Baba Yaga stretched out her arms in front of her and began to walk forward, one pace at a time, like a sleepwalker. She did not notice that, in her panic, she had fallen hard against the wall and jerked the box from her belt. It had fallen over the edge of the ravine, breaking open, and the two captive souls now bobbed below her in the darkness, free and lost.

The streets of Yonar were still dark, but overhead the lid of the sky had been lifted, to reveal the pale dawn. Drawing her cloak about her, Huldis counted her way back through the streets and *traboules* that had brought her to the house of the embassy. She could barely hear Yuda's soft-footed tread following her. It was like having a cat for a companion; from time to time, she would glance back to assure herself that he was still there. Like a cat's, his eyes glowed in certain kinds of light, and she found him a troubling as well as a comforting presence. She could catch the tide of his thoughts, louder than the sound of his breathing.

They had made their plan in a few scattered minutes after the interview with the ambassador ended. Huldis remembered the bitter taste of the *chai*, still clinging to her tongue, and the change when Lukacs sweetened it for her with grains of sugar. The taste that lingered in her mouth mingled with the salty flavour of fear. Her own thoughts were as busy and restless as Yuda's. What would happen to her – to them both – if Sarl and the Magus were not deceived? Semyon might make the connection between the broken mirror and the girl he had overlooked, when she suddenly proved to be a cloaked shaman.

Yuda had instructed her in what to say, and she repeated the words to herself like a charm. *He lured me to the house . . . he took me hostage . . .* It was hard to believe what she was thinking, even though the ambassador had spoken of using her as a prisoner for bargaining. The foreign scent of Yuda's thought intruded in her mind. It was black and clear as ink.

– *They'll be only too glad to see me. They won't think about you.*

– *The Magus is subtle. And my brother is no fool.*

– *I've never taken him for a fool. That's not his problem.*

– *What do you mean?*

– *He loved me, but in a twisted way. A man like that can't bear to love another man. So he needed to destroy me.*

– *He says that he has been in hell.*

Yuda found this amusing. – *He is hell*, was all he thought.

Huldis hung back, to fall into step beside him. She pondered this, together with what she had told the ambassador concerning her true age. If she had not lost twenty-three years trapped in La Souterraine, she would be little younger than Yuda. But she was still a young woman, not much older than his only daughter. She wondered whether the lost years, when she had been trapped in stasis, had left any mark on her. Would she die before her time, old at the age she should have been old?

– *We don't know. We don't know what the consequences of your imprisonment will be.*

– *I still dream of it. Sometimes the dreams are more real than this place.*

– *I wonder whether we did the right thing, returning you to Ademar. It doesn't seem to have mitigated the Doyen's desire for revenge.*

Huldis stopped. 'I wish you would not come back with me,' she said.

Yuda touched her cheek, smiling in the dusk. 'Then you shouldn't have told me anything. I have no choice. It's not just the *kinder*. I told the ambassador the truth. It's as important to tackle Sarl and the Magus as it is to join battle with the Doyen's forces at the front. You know the plans; if your brother gets back his life – which I sincerely hope he doesn't – he will lead out another army. The Masalyans may be able to drive back the Doyen, but two armies would vanquish them.'

They walked slowly down the narrow passage between the overhanging houses, where the shapes of chimneys loomed against the sky. Huldis glimpsed a stork's nest high up, with the great bird sitting majestically enthroned, its wings folded against the dawn, the outline of its beak like a drawn sword. Shivering in the chill, she pointed it out to Yuda. It seemed like a moment of freedom with which to fight the sleepy power of her dreams, and the entanglements she would face when she returned to the inn.

They hurried past the shuttered courtyard of a house into a passageway lined with doors. Some of the oil lamps had burnt out; one or two still guttered in their niches high on the walls. Yuda was leading the way; he no longer needed Huldis to guide him, for he could navigate by the twin lights of Sarl and Semyon, their shaman power glowing through the darkness like dull stars. The ice-crystals on the ground crunched under Huldis's feet; she hurried to keep pace with

Yuda, wishing she could calm the shivering that had entered her bones, even her very spirit.

The entrance straight ahead brought them out into the glistening street, facing the timbered walls of the inn. Its windows were shuttered upstairs, but already lamps had been lighted in the chambers on the ground floor, and sounds of preparation issued from the kitchens. Yuda paused, hugging his coat about him. The dim light of the dawn glinted off his hair and his eyes, and his pale breath was smoke. Huldis stopped behind him, catching the edges of his fear. They could still decide to turn back, to hurry through the streets to the warmth of the embassy hostel. Behind the shutters, death was asleep, dreaming of blood and bones.

Yuda turned to Huldis and took her hand. His fingers were icy. 'Courage,' he said, and 'Are you ready?'

She nodded. She could not hide the shuddering that shook her as if she were an aspen. Yuda swept a stray lock of hair back from her forehead and kissed her on the brow. 'You act good, Missis,' he said, grinning.

Huldis took a pace back from him. She drew the cold air into her lungs, feeling it chill the core of her blood. Then, from the depths of her body, she let out a piercing, piteous cry, calling her brother's name, and Yuda struck her across the face, sending her reeling across the street, to fall on her back, true tears spurting from her eyes.

Still half in a sleep, Semyon stumbled out of bed, clawing his shirt from the chair beneath the window.

As he struggled with the latch to the shutters, he glimpsed Sarl's form rising fully clad from the mattress where he had not slept, like a corpse rising stark out of a coffin. Grimacing, the Magus flung open the shutters and squinnied out into the street beyond. That cursed innkeeper had given them a room high up, almost under the eaves, but not so high that he could sneak to the girl's room unnoticed.

He had not been dreaming. The scream echoed again, fresh and sharp as a vixen's bark in the night. Swearing to himself, Semyon rubbed his eyes and saw the two figures in the street below before Sarl pushed him aside. The shock of the third shaman's power was like a salt-water drenching; he saw Sarl flinch, and took secret satisfaction in knowing that even his imperturbable enemy was startled. How could it be that someone so strong had shared the same city with them undetected? They should have begun the search last night, instead of yielding to the blandishments of sleep and food. He forced himself into the gap between Sarl and the window-frame, however much he hated to touch the dead man.

'Jean Sorel,' cried the girl, more weakly this time. She was lying sprawled on the cobbles, bleeding from her nose, a sight that gave Semyon unexpected pleasure; someone else had taught her not to be so haughty! Standing over her was a small figure in a black gabardine coat, his long hair uncovered in the morning cold. Semyon searched the street for a glimpse of the shaman whose power had startled him awake, but there was no one else to be seen; only the girl lying on the ground, and the little man. Sarl was gripping the windowledge, his knuckles white.

'Yes, come out, Jean Sorel,' called the man from the street below. 'Come and see what I've brought you,' and he gave the girl's prone body a kick. Sarl took a pace back from the window, shading his eyes as if he had seen a blinding light.

'Is that him?' said Semyon, unable to hide his incredulity. Sarl did not answer him, but flung open the door and started down the corridor towards the stairs. Struggling to pull on his trews, Semyon hurried after him in bare feet. It was not to their advantage that the disturbance had wakened other guests at the inn; some were out on the landing in their night-clothes, while he had seen others leaning out of their windows. There might be a crowd by the time he reached the street, and that was bad.

He bumped into the innkeeper in the hall, and shoved past him, determined to keep up with Sarl. He must take charge, or Tchernobog knew what would happen. Sarl might kill the other man before Semyon had a chance to take him prisoner, and that would ruin their chances of completing the spell; if that happened, Semyon knew his own vitals would be in demand for the purpose.

He found Sarl standing on the doorstep, unmoving. Across the street from him, the small man stood astride the girl's form. His features stood out like black ink on parchment: he could only be a Wanderer. Semyon felt his gorge rise. He was no Doxan, but he had been chrismated, as all good Sklavans should be, and the thought of one of that race striking down a Doxan maiden disgusted him. He no longer felt the pleasure of Huldis's fall; he was tempted to run to her side and work a quick spell to take the pain out of her bruised face.

As he feared, the scene had drawn onlookers; they had formed a circle, blocking off the streets on either side, but no one had moved to intervene. Semyon stood beside Sarl, tucking his shirt into his trews, conscious of his lack of dignity.

'Good people,' he said to the crowd, aware too of his foreign accent when speaking Franj, 'this is a matter between shamans. A private matter.'

The people moved and muttered to each other, but showed no sign of going away. Of course not; a man had assaulted a young woman in the public street.

'Vasilyevich,' said Sarl, stretching out his hand; it was shaking.

The small man folded his arms across his chest, smiling. 'No need to explain, Sarl,' he said. 'Your sister has told me everything. With a little persuasion.'

Semyon saw Sarl's hand become a fist. 'You . . .' he said.

The man stepped away from Huldis. He was breathing heavily, as if he had run a race. 'A loyal little follower,' he said, his features twisting in scorn. 'A true daughter of Ademar. I tell you what, Sarl; I'll trade her with you. For my life.'

Semyon glanced at Sarl, whose livid face showed too plainly what he was, even in daylight. He could see from the little movements that the two men made that they were squaring up to each other like dogs about to fight. That must not be allowed to happen; but to prevent it, he might have to show his powers, here in the open. He thought of the suitcase, tucked under the bed in his room upstairs. At so short a distance, he should be able to draw on its forces, and disable even such a shaman as the one who faced him seemed to be. He still found it hard to credit that someone so mean and scrawny could cast such a giant shadow, or overpower a young woman as tall and strong as Huldis, who must overtop him by several inches. Semyon ran his fingers through his hair. An audience of gaping outlanders did not compare with the denizens of the Staryetz's court. It would be shameful to reveal his true measure before such a crowd.

Sarl turned to him. 'Leave this to me,' he said.

Semyon looked up at the gaunt face stooping over him, and quelled his fear. He must be the master, and this was his chance to show it. He rolled up his sleeves. 'No,' he said. When Sarl grabbed him by the shirt, he did not shrink away.

'What's the matter, Sarl? Can't control your tame magician?' said Vasilyevich.

Semyon, fighting his distaste, sent his thoughts towards Sarl. He could not bring himself to touch the other man's mind, but he reached out, ordering him to be calm. There would be other chances to repay such provocation. Now they were in the midst of onlookers, and needed the matter to be speedily concluded.

He saw Sarl's face, which had been twisted with rage, relax into the dull, expressionless mask that it usually was. The Heir released him, and Semyon, sighing inwardly, thought of a spell – nothing too dramatic, for this was not an occasion for display. In his mind's eye, he rummaged in the depths of the suitcase, and was nearly wrongfooted when Vasilyevich launched a branching stroke of power across the street at them. It was golden.

Stifling his surprise, Semyon threw Sarl to the ground with the weight of his body. From one capable of such cruelty, he would have expected something soiled and dirty, smudged with petty evil. There was no time to think; the spell had reached boiling point inside his skull, and if he did not release it, it would empty his brains out of his mouth. He opened his gullet wide and roared like a lion, or a carving of the north wind. The spell leapt from his tongue, its words unfurling like unpacked stars, growing into huge and shimmering shapes as they found their freedom.

The crowd scattered. Semyon struggled to his feet and caught the edge of the spell before it could diffuse and rush away across the rooftops. He played it like a fisherman with his line, and felt a moment of satisfaction as he let it fall on the dark-haired shaman, who looked up at it in confusion and fear. Even at such a moment, Semyon admired the beauty and force of the spell that his power had given shape, melded with the energy from within his valise. He saw it stoop over the enemy, uncoiling from itself like a whirlwind; he watched the crowd shrink back, hiding their eyes from the faces that they saw, shouting voicelessly out of the cloud; then it spun down and engulfed

Vasilyevich, stifling and extinguishing the power in his hands, and flinging him to the ground.

Semyon turned to Sarl and let the Heir see his smile. A little reminder of the might he could wield, if he chose to. It was sweeter than all the cumbersome conjurings of witches and petty magicians, who put their spells together from words and powders and magic herbs. Semyon had passed beyond that; he straddled his own secret mountain, as if he were Kaschai the Deathless.

Sarl looked from the Magus to the spell that had borne the unsuspecting shaman to the ground. He nodded, as if pleased with a good piece of work. It might irk him to show any admiration, but he was not petty enough to ignore how neatly Semyon had solved their problem. Semyon waited for the spell to work out its course. There was no chance that it would drain such a shaman of power, as it had done a hedge-witch like Baba Yaga; but it should be enough to render him no threat for the duration of their journey. Semyon wished he could be more certain how long that would be. Barefoot on the cold cobbles, he walked across the street and looked down at the Wanderer, who lay on the ground like an insect wound in spider-thread. Huldis had risen to her knees, and was wiping the blood from under her nose; her eyes were red-rimmed with unshed tears. She gave a sob.

'He said . . . he said he would destroy you,' she said. 'He wanted to hold me hostage.'

Semyon held out his hand. She must feel some gratitude, however hesitant; perhaps that would bring a change to her haughty attitude towards him. He was pleased when she took his hand and let him lift her to her feet. Gently. Mere force or seduction would not be sufficient to win this beauty; she had wit and courage as well. She might be young, but she was wiser than she looked. She glanced down at the paralysed shaman with a mixture of pity and disgust. Semyon squeezed her hand, a gesture of friendship rather than lust.

'Don't waste your pity on him, Mademoiselle,' he said. 'He is dead meat.'

The wisps of cloud were diffusing, drifting away like last night's mist. Semyon felt the shaman's black, bottomless eyes watching him, and turned away. In his way, the little man was just as unnerving as Sarl. In spite of the spell that bound him, he was smiling. Golden power! Semyon had not seen anything like it, not even at the court of the Staryetz, where shamans and magicians and magi gathered in great profusion. He thought he had taken the measure of them all, and yet here was power of a type that he had never encountered. He wondered how much chance he would have to study it before Sarl insisted on his rite of butchery. Semyon wrinkled his nose. He did not need to pretend that such spells gave him pleasure; they would take a price from him, and Sarl might not find that his new-found life gave him the rewards he expected.

'What are you going to do with him?' said Huldis.

'He returns to the mountain with us. And then . . .' Semyon sliced his hand across his throat. 'You will have your brother back alive again.'

He had been careful to release her hand some time ago. He watched her cross to where Sarl was standing, and observed once more the delicacy that kept her from flinching from her brother. Sarl took a kerchief from his pocket and dabbed the blood from her face, with the gentleness of a mother cleaning food from a grubby child. Semyon sighed and looked down at the shaman.

'I can't say I hope that doesn't hurt,' he said. 'But the numbness will wear off after a while. Then you'll be able to walk.'

The man's lips formed a word, in Sklavan. Semyon recognised it, and was startled. He had assumed that this quarry Sarl sought must be Franj. In spite of himself, the pleasure of hearing his native tongue, however insultingly, made him squat down beside his victim.

'You Sklav?' he said, unable to hide his surprise.

'Fuck off,' said the shaman. Semyon stayed beside him, on his haunches. 'Why have I never heard of you?' he said, speaking to himself. 'I thought I knew them all. And here you are in the middle of this god-forsaken country, speaking Sklavan like a native.' He rubbed his hand across his forehead. 'You must be an émigré. I've heard that there are others like you in the godless city of Masalyar. I thought it was a mere tale. No one willingly leaves the lands of the Staryetz.'

'I've been looking for you,' said the shaman, stirring and wincing. His voice was little more than a mutter.

'You?' said Semyon.

'My chiefs wanted to know what a rogue shaman from Sklava was doing in their territory.'

'That had not occurred to me. I have been most careless. I did not imagine there could be anyone in this wretched place who might be my equal. I see I was wrong.' He straightened, and stood looking down at the figure at his feet. 'Do not imagine from that that we can be friends. You are a Wanderer.' He was tempted to spit, but thought it boorish. No courtier would stoop to such bucolic contempt.

The shaman stared up at him. His powers might have been drained, but he could still ward his thoughts. Semyon had yet to find the spell that could strip away this most elementary of skills. 'I can't tell what you're thinking,' he said, making an irritable movement away from his captive. 'But at least you speak the Mother tongue, not this hideous jargon they call Franj.'

The crowd had dispersed. Shivering without his warm robe and cloak, Semyon looked up to see the Heir and his sister approaching. He wondered whether they would thank him for the trouble he had saved them. He doubted it. He folded his arms across his chest, and said, 'What is your will, *Knyaz*? Your prisoner awaits your command.'

Without answering, Sarl bent down, picked up the prone body and slung it over his shoulder. He might as well have been lifting a bag of sugar.

'You are lucky, *Magus*,' he said. 'You have brought me what I want. There will be no need to tear out your heart. Now bring us back to the Glass Mountain, where this business can quickly be finished.'

'The journey back will not be so simple, Mon Seigneur,' said Semyon. 'Remember, the mirror broke. We must travel like ordinary folk.'

Sarl turned to face him, and his cold eyes brought a chill to Semyon's marrow. 'I have seen what you can do when you call on that world of yours, Magus,' he said. 'I'm sure you have other tricks up your sleeve. We need to travel fast, remember; my days are numbered.'

Semyon saw an echo of that coldness in the eyes of the girl who stood beside her brother.

'Do it, Magus,' she said, and her voice was soft as silk. 'My brother must be saved.'

Chapter 10

The Rom and their companions spent most of the day sleeping, though Yuste and Boris took their turn keeping watch. The sky shone like a newly minted coin, and patterns of birds flew overhead, but never any crows, apart from the occasional solitary. Yuste spent some of the time gazing east, towards the mountains, wishing that there were some way they could hurry their progress. She was eager to cross to the other side so that she could learn what she had to face.

Sklava had been a coloured shape on the map in her old schoolroom, and a place conjured by the stories her mother and father told her. Her father had lived near Ades, by the inland sea they called the Black Pearl; her mother came from Kiyev, the land of true snow, in the principality of Maskovi. But the lands across the Lepas Mountains were not truly Sklavan; they were part of the empire of the Staryetz, which grew every year, as he conquered another kingdom or annexed a city-state.

Yuste thought it odd that she called herself a Sklav, when she had been born in Franj. Though her parents had spoken no other language at home, Yuste and Yuda had been compelled to speak only Franj at school. It was not the language of their thoughts, and when they used *sprechen* together, Sklavan had been their only medium. But with their friends, with Aude and her brothers, who had condescended to know them in time, they had lived inside the argot of their local village.

'Second-generation Sklavs,' said Boris, offering her the flask of brandy from his coat pocket. Yuste took a swig, gasped and laughed.

'I was born here, Boris Andreyevich. This is my country, not Sklava. I am not a subject of the Staryetz.'

The detective looked grim. 'Nor am I,' he said, lifting the flask to his mouth.

Yuste turned, looking west, back the way they had come. 'In my village, everyone called me the stranger, or the Wanderer. Or the witch.'

Boris chuckled, almost choking on his brandy. 'That's how it is, *Zhidova*. Unless you grow up in a city such as Masalyar or Kiyev. Any shaman must be a witch – or a warlock – because the village wise-woman always was a shaman. In the old days, before the word got its second meaning, all tribal shamans were shamans, if you see what I mean.'

Yuste was smiling at him. A queer feeling welled inside her. Once more he had called her *Zhidova*, a Yid, but now she knew he meant no harm by it. When Boris used it to address her, the word was an endearment, not abuse. She gave a small sigh, wondering whether she should even mention that she had noticed. Boris raised his eyebrows at her.

'This is good,' he said. 'You're learning how to ward your thoughts.'

'Don't talk nonsense, Boris Andreyevich.'

They shared a silence, turning away from each other. Yuste thought of the danger behind them as they travelled across the map. The Doyen would have his sights set on Masalyar; surely he would not let a band of Rom distract him from his purpose.

'The more distance we put between ourselves and Axar, the happier I'll be,' Boris answered her. 'We're still a little too close. Have you ever encountered an army on the march? They can spread out over a large area, and send scouts and foraging parties off in all directions. Of course, we don't know the size of the Doyen's army, but I'm willing to bet it isn't a small one. Not if he's planning to attack a city the size of Masalyar.'

'I wish we could move on,' she said.

'Nice spot for an encampment,' said Boris, glancing down towards the caravans picketed near the river.

'I feel so vulnerable.'

'You're probably right. We are vulnerable. We're near the route from Axar to Masalyar. We may be heading east, but the road they have to take goes same way before it heads south. Unless they want to cross some small but significant mountains. I reckon they could be close behind us, if they managed to take

Axar last night. It's not a walled city, and I expect the citizens surrendered. If they had any sense.'

'I would be so much happier if I knew. Where the army was, and what it was doing.'

'We'd need our own scouts and spies for that. A job that you and I could perform, if we weren't keeping watch.'

'Speak for yourself, Boris Andreyevich. I have no skill at scouting or spying.'

Boris lit one of his large cigars. He gestured with it in his hand. 'The thing is . . .' Yuste waited for him to finish. 'This Doyen doesn't like shamans. I doubt if he has any with him in his army.'

'I suppose it is unlikely. Why?'

Boris began to pace up and down. 'I've gotten so used to not using my powers that I've overlooked the simplest trick of all. We don't need to creep up on the army; we could scan it.'

'You could.'

'You can help me. It's better with two.'

'I don't think our hosts would be amused if an attack was launched while we were practising a scan.'

'I'm not that useless, Missis!' Boris stopped pacing and gave her an accusing look.

Yuste shook out her skirts and sat down on a rock. 'Very well,' she said. 'But you must show me what to do.'

Boris ran his hand over his scanty hair. 'It's some time since I did this,' he said. 'Basic shaman stuff, but I've always found it imprecise. Too . . . magical.'

Yuste looked up at him and smiled. 'Sival never

showed us how to do it when we were children,' she said. 'I expect it's one of the things you learn at college.'

'A bit like using a torch to read a map,' said Boris. 'Now you sit still and relax, and I'll do the work.' He stubbed out his cigar and stood behind the boulder where Yuste was sitting, laying his hands on her shoulders. At first, he seemed tense, but she heard his breathing become more slow and regular. He raised his hands so that his fingers lay against her temples, and said, 'It helps if you shut your eyes.'

Yuste obeyed. With her eyes closed, she was strongly aware of Boris's touch against her face, and it stirred memories in her, thoughts that she had stored away and repressed. What it was like when someone kissed you on the lips. The surprise, shock even, at the myriad sensations that set your nerves tingling, making sense of the desire that you had only read about in books. It had been so emphatically different to what she felt for her twin, who had been too close yet always just out of reach. Boris gripped her more tightly.

'Steady on,' he said. 'All I'm getting at the moment are your thoughts. And I'm trying to ignore them.'

Yuste felt herself blush, but it was not with the horrible shame she remembered from adolescence. She set the memories aside, and made herself concentrate on the neural pathways settled like moths against her face, leading back as fine filaments into the hive of life that was the man behind her. She cleared her thoughts, and at once images rushed into view; she saw the Doyen's army.

With a cry, she was on her feet. Boris staggered back, swearing and shaking his hands. 'Damn you, woman, what's the matter?' he said.

'I saw the soldiers. Their faces were close – I could see the sun on their mail . . .'

'You can't just break the link like that,' said Boris, rubbing his hands on his trench coat. 'You could hurt us both.'

'I was afraid they could see me . . .'

'They can't. It's like looking into a camera obscura. I'm not trying to scan below the surface; that can be dangerous and I don't think it would be wise when you haven't been trained.'

'I have read the theory.'

Boris rolled up his eyes. 'Do you want to try again?' he said, with little effort to hide his exasperation.

Yuste hugged herself. 'I'm sorry, Boris Andreyevich,' she said. 'I was not expecting it to be so vivid – or so close.'

Boris smudged the ground with his foot, grinding the remains of his cigar into the earth. 'Nor was I,' he said.

'What do you mean?'

'It's as if I was drawing power from you. But from what you've told me, that should not be possible.'

'I have some low residues of power,' said Yuste, trailing her fingers across the stone where she had been sitting. Boris shrugged.

'Let's give it another go,' he said. 'But please keep still. Whatever you see. Remember that they are only pictures.'

Yuste resumed her seat on the boulder. Once more, Boris laid his hands against her face. She knew that he was more nervous this time. She shut her eyes and saw again the threads of light that travelled inwards from his fingertips. She followed them eagerly, as if she had dived into a golden current, and was swept away from herself on a happy tide. It was so much easier this time; she let go of herself and slipped into the darkness, without waiting to see whether Boris was with her.

Once more she saw the army of the Franj. It was its shape that had shocked her; she had seen the brigades and the militias parading through the streets of Masalyar, and they had looked nothing like this. The tall nobles on horseback, with helms like domed steel gourds; the high painted wooden saddles in which they sat; the dull gleam of their chain mail and the glitter of their spurs. It appalled her because it showed the raw truth of the medieval armies that she had only seen depicted in books. This was a medieval army on the march; the swords were bright, not caked with rust, and the long lances were forged for killing.

Yuste recognised the landscape second. The army was on the same road they had followed last night. It was approaching them, though she did not know from how many miles distant. She would have to leave it to Boris to make sense of the unshaped images she saw. She looked around for him and was surprised that he did not seem to be with her. Once more, she dived like an eel for the web of neurons, and sank into the dark. She felt safe and confident; she could swim as if she were in the sea. She headed in deep, only dimly conscious that someone was calling her name. Something glittered below her in the dark, and she knew she must go deeper in to see what it was. She was freer than she had ever been in her life: free of her cramped body with its maimed powers. Down there in the depths was gold.

The two souls hovered like candle-flames in the darkness. They were blind and deaf, simple structures like one-celled creatures that were barely alive. But each soul was a mind, and the mind had its own shape; they were Annat and Malchik. If a shaman, or a witch, had been standing near the precipice, they would have heard the souls whispering to each other. It would have been difficult to tell them apart without faces to give them shape, but someone who knew them would have been able to distinguish between them; a shaman mind might even have perceived them as different colours.

–*Which way?* said the Malchik soul.

They had little sense of direction or distance, but the warmth of their still-living bodies called out to them.

– *This way*, said the Annat soul. They began to move, bobbing in the gloom like fireflies. They were not afraid, because the whole substance in which they moved was undiluted fear. Their bodies might experience the sensations of dread and panic, but the souls were a cold essence, lost in a night which they knew they had to escape.

It was difficult for them to travel in any direction.

They did not know how long it would be before the witch discovered her loss and returned to recapture them. But they were beginning to forget the witch already. Memory was inscribed in their forsaken bodies. All they knew was that they should not be free and alone, where any breath of air might dissipate them into silvery atoms. They moved at a slow pace, pausing to hover over the hard surfaces, before passing through them as if the stone had no substance.

Shut inside a tiny globe of brightness, all Annat could see was the writing inscribed on everything. Huge letters trailed about her, while others, infinitesimally small, circled her, dancing past like motes on the breeze. She was aware of someone who had been her brother, following her, and the warmth of his light. There was so much to see, in the great height above her and the unimaginable depths beneath. Though she had left fear in her body, she understood that this state of being was wrong. She should not be out here, free in the infinite circling of the words. There was something that she needed to do.

– *Annat*. Her brother's thought penetrated the soft shell of her. – *We mustn't forget. Forget ourselves*.

An image of her brother's likeness flashed across the starlike nerves of her disembodied mind. She turned – something turned – but there was only an essence, a brightness without shape. Now, at last, she could speak to him unhindered, thought to thought. She fluttered against him, seeking unity.

– *Annat*. The echo of his voice was insistent. – *We must return to our bodies*.

Disappointed, the fragments of Annat floated away. Tiny particles, held together by words, threads of things she had spoken, fragments of song. Behind her – or above her – Malchik remembered the shape of music. He thought of his harp and its vibrating chords. His body had a voice, and from a distance Malchik evoked the thought of song, his one true power.

Fascinated, Annat paused, caught inside the music. There was more to the place that surrounded her than its words. She listened as the song gave her shape and definition, calling her back to the place where she belonged. This was not her brother's human voice but something ethereal, stretched across the deep like the strings of a harp. Annat turned towards it, rapt by its elemental beauty, and followed it, letting it draw her through the darkness.

Nothing moved, and she did not move, but she travelled beyond the place where the witch's wooden box had broken. Somewhere, time existed, and her body lay breathing in a deep, mindless sleep. Annat remembered the shape and pleasure of her form, and wondered where it was.

A song intermingled with the threads of Malchik's voice. The sound came from inside a mortal body, but it sang to Annat's spirit. It sang her into being. It summoned her mindless body from its trance, and guided it towards the fire. Annat knew she must search for the fire. She felt Malchik beside her.

Annat was walking alone through a forest. The trees were somewhere between green and silver; they were the northern trees that she remembered from the Forest of Ademar. Scattered amongst them stood the birches, with their thin leaves, their trunks wrapped in a pale skin. Annat walked slowly, weaving a path in between the trees. From time to time, the red of the camp fire flashed, turning the surrounding air dark. It was cold, and mist hung in the air; but she could not smell the smoke. The only sensations were sight and sound, and the sound was an after-echo. Annat paused, waiting for it to come again.

A long-drawn-out cry. It was a keening sound, remote and inhuman. The voice of a wolf. Annat was not afraid. She waited, counting the time, until the small body slipped out from amongst the tree-trunks and stood facing her. It raised its muzzle and cast up the weird, eerie sound.

Annat crouched down and held out her hand, as she might have done to a dog. But this was not a dog, bred to live amongst humans. It did not know what she was. It was not like the wolves in the storybooks; its fur was a medley of colours, some smoky and dark, others light and pale. Its eyes were black-rimmed, but the irises were yellow.

'Likan,' said Annat. The wolf approached her, lowering its head submissively. Annat waited until it was close enough for her to touch its muzzle. She looked into its eyes, and felt something stir inside her. The wolf did not move; they stared at each other, and Annat felt its wildness go into her, and a little of herself enter the wolf. Now the wolf would have a human name; it would be Likan.

Its red tongue strayed out to brush her hand. It was not her dog, and she would never own it, but it was her wolf, and she was its girl. She did not know how she had found it, or who had brought them together.

A voice spoke in her ear. It was an old voice, and tired, but

it said, 'Now you are a true shaman. Now you can call your-
self a shaman.'

Annat straightened and turned round, but there was no one
behind her. When she looked back, the wolf was gone. She stood
alone, amongst the birches, wondering what it meant. Once
again, the red lights of the fire appeared amongst the trees,
further down the hill. She had to return to the camp. She began
to walk, slowly, kicking up the pine needles underfoot with her
bare feet.

They procured three horses from an inn a few doors
from the one where they had spent the night. As Huldis
swung herself into the saddle, she noticed Semyon
struggling to mount his nag, and smiled to herself. She
was not unaware that he had trimmed his beard, and
changed his monk's vile habit for the bright padded
tunic and hose of a Sklavan courtier, all trimmed with
gold braid and fur; he wore a hat of red and gold brocade, rakishly adorned with a thick band of dark mink.
Nor was she ignorant of the reason for this transfor-
mation; rather than just leering at her, the Magus had
shown the courage to reveal his vanity and to woo her.
Huldis could not help feeling less cold and disgusted
at him. Once he was in the saddle, he managed to
guide his horse to walk beside hers. Neither of them
wanted to accompany Sarl, who bestrode a tall destrier
fitting for his height, with their captive slung across
the saddle-bow like a sack of potatoes.

Semyon had salved her bruised eye and put a
healing charm on her nose. Huldis was grateful to him
for this, if only because it saved her from her brother's

ministrations. At least, in the saddle, she had captured an illusion of freedom. They had purchased a hardy mare for her, a middle-aged nag with a bright eye and a glistening coat. Huldis had never quite outgrown her childish love of horses, and though this was nothing like the choice of splendid mounts that she could call upon at the castle, she liked nothing better than the pleasure of making friends with a good, simple horse. Semyon was riding a young gelding, which seemed docile enough, and well trained to carry an inexperienced rider without demur. Huldis did not need to worry about her brother; he was a seasoned horseman, and loved horses, like other beasts, more than he seemed to care for humans.

She had been very careful not to leave her brother alone with the prisoner for more than a few minutes. A tight, dry dread under her heart warned her that Sarl had not forgotten the violence Vasilyevich had subjected her to. She would have liked to send her thoughts to the shaman, but she did not dare risk lowering the protective wall that kept her powers hidden from the Magus and her brother. Her only comfort was that the spell Semyon had cast over Vasilyevich seemed to have stunned him; though he was certainly alive, he had flopped over the horse's neck like a rag-doll.

Their journey was to follow the River Kron east of Yonar to its source in the Lepas Mountains, and there to cross over into Sklavan territory. The Glass Mountain itself lay to the south-east, at the beginning of the Great Plains, or *puszta*, as Semyon had told her the locals called it. It was a long ride, and she knew that the Magus was using all his spare time searching and studying the contents of his valise for a spell that would speed their travel. Unless they were to purchase fresh horses at every way-stop, they could not manage much above a hundred miles a day. Their mounts would need to be fed and watered, and above all to rest, if they were planning to ride them at a gallop much of the way. Huldis knew that however much her brother needed to hurry, he would never ride a horse to death. A knight and his mount were one; woe betide the servant who neglected to take sufficient care of his master's steed.

They had no servants with them on this ride. They must wash and dress themselves, and care for their own beasts. This was no hardship to her; there had been few servants to look after her at the castle, and after Aude's loss, she could not bear to choose another waiting-woman; in the same way, she had never been content to hand her horses over to the care of an ostler at the end of a day's riding. She and Aude had often been reprimanded by the Girls' Warden when they returned from the stables with mud on their shoes, straw on their gowns and smelling 'for all the world like a besmuttered farmyard!'. Huldis smiled to herself. No one but the Girls' Warden had ever used such language in her hearing; the woman spoke like an old book of prose romances.

'You are smiling, lady,' said Semyon. They were following a stony track, the one that passed for the eastern road out of Yonar. It climbed a steep hill, the first of many they would have to cross before they reached the mountains. The Kron river snaked in a valley out of sight to their left; here they were alone amongst rock and scrub, with the first doubtful flowers making their appearance amongst the stones.

'It is a fair spring day, Mon Seigneur,' said Huldis, who had been trained in the art of making courtly pleasantries. Semyon glanced overhead to where a buzzard wheeled on an unseen updraught, and made a face.

'Fair to you, my lady, but not to me. I long to return to my country, rather than wander through this wilderness.'

Huldis looked ahead to her brother's tall form, higher up the hill, sitting bolt upright in his saddle. Since Vasilyevich was unconscious, she would have to learn to use her wits. She knew the Magus did not like her brother; in fact, he must detest him.

'You were not raised to love the trackless wastes, as we were,' she said.

Semyon grunted. 'I have an estate in the countryside,' he said. 'A river runs beside it, and there are many birch trees. A pleasant place, and it lacks only one thing; a mistress to govern it.'

Huldis almost fell off her horse. Semyon had just made something like a proposal of marriage to her! She thought of her father's fury that some lowborn wizard should dare to court his only daughter – or at least the only daughter he now acknowledged.

'There must be many maidens of great beauty at the court of the Staryetz,' she said.

Semyon stared ahead, unseeing. 'None more beautiful than the Staryetzna herself,' he said. 'Her skin is like pure ivory untouched by the knife, her eyes are as sloes, and yet the pearls of her head-dress are not more radiant. Lady, you would not believe me if I told you of the brilliance of the Imperial Palace: the robes of gold brocade, the silks and tussores; the boyars decked out in long coats of fur, with beards in which you could hide an army of wrens; the handsome guardsmen of the Staryetz's private bodyguard. And the old man himself is a dirty peasant who scarcely deigns to wipe his nose or his arse.'

Huldis gasped. She had never heard Semyon speak anything but praise of his master.

'I'm sorry . . . I have shocked you,' said the Magus. 'Believe me, the old man has more wit and power than all the heads under tiara and jewelled crown across this continent of Yevropa. Most of them have become his vassals. Most of them kneel before his throne, not daring to pinch their noses at the stench reeking from their overlord. His empire stretches from Yevropa in the west, far across the globe to the great sea that borders the world – or so they say. And yet he was weaned on mare's milk in the tents of the Halekkai. They say he cut the throat of the old Staryetz and drank his blood.'

'Are you happy to serve such a master?' said Huldis, reaching forward to pat her horse's neck.

'Happy?' Semyon looked at her direct, as if he had never seen her before. 'What does it matter if I am happy? I am a powerful magus, and I serve the Lord of the World.' But he sounded as if he were repeating a lesson learned by rote.

'I have often wondered why he sent you here, to Franj, to my father's court,' she said. 'My father was an old and forgotten seigneur, sleeping in his grief. And the Staryetz sent the most powerful magus of his court to succour him.'

Semyon sighed. He wore velvet gloves, and outside of them, a signet ring set with a cameo. He studied it before he answered her. 'Since we are speaking plainly, I tell you, my lady, that my master plans to annex Franj, and all of old Neustria. Your father will reconquer the lands for him, and perhaps be named its king. You may find yourself enthroned in Priyar, joint heiress to one of the great kingdoms of the west.'

Huldis laughed. 'My father, King of Franj and Neustria? He might dream such dreams, but he is best on his own lands, amongst his own people. He is no mighty lord.'

'Why does my lady think he is marching on Masalyar? And why have I raised your brother from the dead? Sarl is the one who will rule, in his father's name. The Staryetz could do business with such a man.'

Huldis stared back at him. With his hair trimmed and his beard cut short, Semyon had revealed what he was: a young man, an upstart who commanded great powers and was wielding them in a game of statecraft beyond his capabilities. He understood, and what he understood was the kind of piece he must be in this game of chess; a pawn, easily dispensed with.

'But you must stop him!' she said.

It was Semyon's turn to laugh, without joy. 'My lady, I take orders. I do not give them. Who am I to overturn the schemes of princes?'

'I cannot understand it. You have such powers; you yourself could be lord of Neustria – even Lord of the World. Isn't the Staryetz afraid of you?'

'Once I was no more than a village shaman. Then I became a pupil of Kaschai, called the Deathless, and he trained me in the secrets and ways of magic. But I am no more than you see, lady. If I could have commanded you to my bed, I would have done it. Although I can perform more than the pretty illusions of mere magicians, and have mighty spells at my command, they are but a few. Or I would have conjured a wind out of the heavens and transported us all back to the mountain before this time.'

Though this knowledge gave Huldis some comfort, she realised that she was sorry for him. She reminded herself that he had just confessed his own plan to seduce her. But he was her only companion, and he seemed at least human, unlike the simulacrum of her brother riding ahead of them.

'Then you agree that my brother should be King of Neustria?' she said.

'He will not remain as he is now. Once we have completed the spell, he will be a living man again. Immortal and invulnerable.'

'It is the price that troubles me, Magus. The price

for all of us,' said Huldis, and she urged her mare into a canter, leaving Semyon behind and overtaking her brother on the narrow track.

Semyon watched her ride away, her veil and her silver-fair hair dancing out behind her in the breeze. She had shown a wisdom beyond her years, and he had blurted out his knowledge like a lovesick youth. She seemed ever further from him. He had given up hope of mastering her, or bending her to his will like some serving-wench. Her face and body might be lovely, but she had shown a cool mind and a will sharp as a knife. To enjoy her, his only satisfaction would be to make her his wife, and for her to choose him freely above other men. He gnawed his lip. That did not stop the stirring in his loins at the sight of her, riding astride the horse immodestly as if she were a man – or a goddess.

His troubles seemed to be increasing. Not only was there the Heir of Ademar himself, who seemed cordially to loathe Semyon; and the Doyen, who merely despised him; but now there was their strange prisoner, unconscious beneath Semyon's spell, with his golden power. Not all Semyon's rummagings in the depths of the suitcase had been for the purpose of seeking a solution to their travel plans; he had also been searching through the hidden words, the imprisoned texts, for a clue to tell him where such power might come from. He had met many shamans, and each one had his – or her – signature: some silver-blue, some crimson, some a deep glow like iron in the smelting oven; others stained and soiled with years of

horse have its head, trusting in its sense to carry him safely up to the pass. To think that these were mere hills, and that the true mountains lay before them! He almost envied the unconscious prisoner, happy in his dreams no doubt, while others faced the danger and made decisions for him.

Yuda was unconscious, but it did not trouble him much. The spell might have stunned his body and the powers under command of his conscious mind, but the thoughts beneath roamed free, steering a way amongst dreams like a small boat on a wild stream. There was no time to worry about what Sarl might be planning to do to him; he was pretty sure that Huldis would make sure he was left unharmed, and Semyon doubtless wanted his captive kept reasonably whole. Yuda did not try to fight the spell that bound him. He had spent a little time studying it at the beginning, and he had learnt that it was rooted in the valise the Magus carried strapped to his horse. A whole world in a suitcase! Yuda would have liked to find his way inside and explore, but he did not want to send his thoughts too far from his body.

Instead, he relaxed and listened to the singing of the wolves. It did not surprise him that there were wolves this close to the mountains. There would be forests on the lower slopes, and wolves would hunt there. No need to fear them unless there was a harsh winter like those of the Great Cold. Then wolves might turn to human prey. He let his mind drift until it settled amongst the wolf-pack. They were running. They hunted together; they had shed their pale winter coats and were like shadows, slipping between the trees.

Yuda caught the rank wolf smell on the wind. He paused and let them flow away from him. He crouched down amongst the leaf mould where no one could see him. Naked, less substantial than a thought, he felt the mist rising out of the hollows. There was something behind him. He turned too late, and its bulk knocked him down, its claws raking his chest and face. He yelled, and the wolf yelled back at him. Its spittle dripped on to his face. He lay still, waiting for it to tear out his throat, but the wolf straddled him, breathing breath that smelled of dead meat. It was black.

Yuda stared up at it. It seemed to him bigger than the other wolves. Its fur was like his hair, a coal colour that was unusual in wolves – and humans. He sat up, trying to shrink away from it, blood running down his wrists. The wolf's claws had scratched him, but the scratches were not much deeper than the wounds a cat might make with its paws. He stared up its narrow muzzle, and its amber gaze consumed him. A feeling like madness and the loss of self seized him. The wolf was not going to kill him, but it had devoured him. It had torn out his entrails and woven them with its own. Yuda threw back his head and yelled again, and then laughed, as the wolf lifted its muzzle in a long howl.

Chapter 11

Yuste did not ask any questions about the place in which she found herself. She accepted it, as she would have accepted a dream. She was not aware of the strangeness, or of the fact that moments before she had been helping Boris to make a scan. Nor did she consider whether she might be in danger.

She was standing in a wood at twilight, but she did not know whether it was dawn or dusk. There was a chill in the air that reminded her of autumn or early spring. All around her stood the figures of tall, shadowy pines, reaching up to a sky that was out of sight. Scattered amongst them grew slight birch trees, which seemed to glow faintly in the gloom. Just at the furthest reach of her vision, so that it seemed to change place when she moved her head, a small fire burned amongst the trees. She could smell its smoke.

Yuste took a pace in the direction of the fire and stopped, feeling a chill against her spine. All around

her, near and far, the wolves were keening. Their mourn
ful voices seemed to echo, answering each other. Yuste
did not know much about wolves, except that they
were wild and shy and kept away from human
dwellings. She had heard that they lived in the deep
northern woods where game was plentiful and people
scarce. She began to walk towards the fire, noticing
with slight surprise that she was naked, free of her
confining clothes, yet little troubled by the cold. The
fire beckoned her because she knew she would meet
someone there, not because she needed its warmth.

Her path took her into a small glade, where the sil
very birches grew thick, like a forest of wands. Yuste
slipped between them like a shadow, her bare feet
making no sound on the soft ground. She wondered
if it felt like this to be a wolf, moving through the wood
as it went hunting. It would have a much keener sense
of smell, and its eyes would see no colours, only silver
and grey. She closed her eyes and sniffed the night air,
and the scents did seem more vivid than she expected.
A deer had passed this way, leaving its light spoor in
the leaf mould. Someone spoke her name.

Yuste opened her eyes. Her brother was standing on
the other side of the clearing, leaning against a tree and
watching her. Yuste approached him, feeling oddly shy,
not because they were both naked, but because she was
now aware what a strange meeting this was. She could
see Yuda's eyes glittering under the shadow of his hair.
In the muted light, he looked much younger than his
true age. Yuste folded her arms across her chest, more
from a sense of vulnerability than from modesty.

'Did you see the wolf?' said Yuda, when she was
lose. There was black blood on his face, chest and
rms.

'You're hurt,' said Yuste, reaching out to touch him
nd withdrawing her hand.

'Nah. Not much.' He shifted his position, folding
is arms as if mimicking her stance.

'I don't know whether I should be here,' said Yuste,
owering her eyes to stare at the ground between them.

'Why not?'

'I don't know that I belong here.'

Yuda leant forward so that their faces almost
ouched. 'Look at me,' he said. Yuste raised her eyes
nd found him smiling at her. 'It's all right,' he said. 'I
von't eat you.'

Yuste tried to return his smile. 'We've followed such
lifferent paths, Yudeleh,' she said. 'We are man and
voman now, and I'm not even a shaman.'

Yuda leant back against the tree, studying her. She
ould not tell what he was thinking. 'Give me your
iand,' he said at last.

'My hand?' Yuste held it out, and almost withdrew
t when Yuda seized it in his cold, strong fingers. He
hook his head, frowning.

'You don't even like to touch me,' he said.

'I don't know, Yuda. You took everything – just
verything – from me. I'm a husk, a shell.'

'I used to think that,' he said. 'But the power is still
here. It must be, or we couldn't *sprechen*. You couldn't
e here, with the wolves.'

'What do you mean?'

247

'You are a shaman. And from now on, you'll be a true shaman. You remember Sarl and his crows? He knew the secret all along.'

'I don't understand you,' said Yuste, pulling her hand free and turning away. Yuda gripped her thin shoulders and spun her round to face him. He held her at a distance, studying her face with thoughtful affection.

'I never knew that I could heal you,' he said. 'I didn't think of it. But the power has been there inside me ever since I returned from La Souterraine. I can share it with you.'

'Even if you can – if you could – do that, why should I want it? I know who I am, Yuda; I don't need any more. Don't want it.'

'Swear that to me and I'll let you go. It's your choice. But you can't go on blaming me for ruining your life. If I know you'll be happy, I'll leave you alone.'

Yuste found herself weeping. She raised her hand to her face and smudged the tears. 'You left me far behind, Yuda, long ago. Whatever you do, you can't alter that. You chose Aude over me, and then you left us both.'

'You're so wrong,' said Yuda, relaxing his hold. 'I've never left you. But you're my sister.' He gave a painful laugh. 'We couldn't stay as we were, cocooned together like sexless children.'

'I loved her too,' said Yuste.

'That was why we fought. I haven't forgotten.'

Yuste sat down on the ground and hugged her knees with her arms. 'You see, I am still bitter,' she said. 'A sour old spinster.'

Yuda knelt down beside her. 'I've never seen that,' he said. 'I know you are angry. But it's always been lean, sharp anger, not like bitterness.'

She looked at him. 'I know that I'm envious of you,' he said. 'You were always stronger than me. I can see so much of you in Annat.'

'And you can't bear to be second best, so you'd rather have nothing?'

'I didn't say that.'

'I think you'd do anything rather than be in debt to me.'

They fell silent, looking away from each other. Yuste became aware that the wolves were circling the clearing, loping between the trees. For a moment, she forgot the quarrel, and watched the dim light making patterns on the animals' grey fur. Dropping forward on to her hands and knees, she moved away from Yuda and crawled to the edge of the glade. At once, the wolf pack surged round her, sniffing her and touching her with their rasping tongues. They were she-wolves, some in cub, others with lean flanks, old or young. Yuste touched them, feeling the harsh hair of their hackles, the soft down under their throats. She laughed, half smothered by a live coat of warm pelts. The wolves seemed to think that she was one of them; from time to time one or other would give her a nip with their strong teeth, but never drawing blood.

'Yuda!' she called. 'Come and look at this!'

Yuda walked out of the trees. He moved with the same grace and self-possession as a wolf. Yuste sat still and watched him, her arms full of nuzzling, wriggling,

fur-clad bodies. She remembered a time when she too
had shared some of that utter confidence. She had been
a wild creature, elemental, filled with the power of
storms. She might never become what her brother was,
but that had been impossible from the start. It did not
mean she was worthless as a shaman.

She stood up, shaking off the wolves, and went to
meet him.

'Well?' he said.

Yuste took his face in her hands. She knew that in
a way, she was saying goodbye to him, and many other
things that she had clutched to her heart like rags of
memory.

'I think you know my answer,' she said. Yuda took
her by the wrists and lifted her hands away from his
face.

'Are you sure?' he said. 'Sure it's what you want?'

'There's only one way to find out.'

Annat hesitated. She felt her body close about her like
a warm garment of flesh. But she had not returned to
the Glass Mountain. She found herself in a wood,
where the trees reached out of sight on every side, and
the cold scent of pine touched her nostrils. The chill
about her was tangible, but it did not seem to reach
her skin. It was as if her naked body was itself a cloak
of fur, which wrapped her against the touch of winter.

Annat crouched down and let her fingers skim over
the dry fronds underfoot. She had never felt so wild,
nor her senses so acute. Each leaf in this weird twilight seemed to stand out in silhouette, and the grey

undergrowth flashed into cold life when she turned her glance towards it. The night was alive with creatures, scurrying under the leaves on secret errands. Annat waited, listening, to the swift fear that was the breathing of a mouse and to the foragings of badgers. She understood a predator's hunger. There was so much to hunt and eat, with hot blood as piquant as wild mushrooms.

Annat laughed. She had heard of shamans who could share their thoughts with an animal; she had never considered that it might happen to her. Then the old shaman spoke to her from beyond the firelight.

'Look behind you.'

Annat turned and glimpsed the mask of a badger, lifted and silver.

'You see?' he said. 'You could never be wholly a shaman, living in the cities with their stone floors.'

'Is that why you brought me here?' said Annat. It seemed a little absurd addressing the badger.

'There used to be a shaman for every tribe, every village. And they knew – we knew – the name of our animal spirit. Mine was Badger.'

Annat bent forward, holding out her hand to the unmoving beast, but it did not approach her.

'Do I have an animal spirit?' she said.

The old shaman chuckled. 'You have to find it yourself. I cannot give it to you like a gift.'

Annat straightened, looking around her. The trees seemed to throb with the pulse of her blood. She was hungry. And when she hungered, she must go hunting.

'What's happening to me?' she whispered. 'I don't like it.'

He did not answer. She was alone, and she could no longer see the fire or smell its smoke. The colour of the trees was blue, but behind its curtain the red blood flowed, full of life and savour. Annat had felt nothing like the rapture of this hunger. It stretched her senses to the tautness of a skin drum, it was stronger than desire and smoother than love. She laughed suddenly, no longer afraid of this intoxication of the mind. She turned on her heel and began to run. At home, in the city, she could move fast, but her clothes always held her back. Clad in naked fur, she could move with such ease, and everything feared her. All the small, soft creatures of the darkness were her prey, and she felt them skimming away from her, squirrelling into the trees or burrowing under the soft mould, leaving spoor and fumets and a draught of rank scent.

And there was the pack. Her sisters. Annat had never had a female sibling, but here she found herself woven into the stream of running she-wolves, absorbed into their clan. She had not shared such pure pleasure and exuberance before. It was like being drunk – but not too drunk; like kissing Eugenie and tasting the burning sweetness of her lips. Annat no longer knew whether she was a wolf or a woman, but she did not care. Head bent low, she was running behind the leaders, the senior wolves, free from the constraints wolves knew in their animal societies.

The quarry was a deer. Its smell hit her between

the eyes: wine and venison and earth and shit. The scent of its fear sharpened her hunger.

The wolf pack circled the clearing. It made a dance, and Annat lifted her head, recognising the taste, the very dark stain of her own kin. She found herself in the flurry of wolves that fawned on Yuste, and she was one of them, kissing her aunt's strange smooth skin and nibbling at her flesh. As the skein of wolves streamed away, Annat lingered, caught between her new clan and her own folk. She hid behind the trees, slinking between the pieces of moonlight, the joy of the hunt forgotten.

She watched her aunt and her father together. She could no longer understand their words and she could not hear their thoughts; but she understood what passed between them. Human shame came back to her; she should not be watching or listening, but she could not tear herself away. Instead, she crouched low to the ground, and slowly, with leaves in her hair, became once more the shape of Annat, with the taste of salt in her mouth, her stomach knotted with the wolfish hunger she had just renounced.

Yuste and Yuda knelt down in the clearing, facing each other. The silver radiance seemed to glow off their pale skin. They were so small, and the trees so tall, that they could have been two glow-worms in the empty dusk. Annat lay on her front, edging forwards, with loam under her fingernails. She wanted to call out to them, but was afraid to break the silence. For the first time, she wondered where Malchik was, and if he too was watching somewhere, called upon to witness.

Yuste stretched out her hands, and Yuda took hold of them. They gazed at each other and so much seemed to be passing between them that Annat could not trace their quick-firing thoughts. She wondered what it was like to be a twin; she had never shared such closeness with Malchik, and she had not thought of her father and her aunt in these terms; they had seemed so unlike each other. Even to look at, their faces were different, in colour and in shape of feature. Yuda was like his father, very dark and very pale, while Yuste was nut-brown.

It happened suddenly. Annat had once witnessed the great engines that powered the trams. She remembered seeing the spark of electric fire that jumped from the electrode to the transformer, the crack of thunder and the smell of tin in the hot air. Instead of two small figures crouching in a wood, she saw Yuda change, to become a glowing man of golden power. Again, she saw the interwoven letters that were the fabric of life; Yuda was made of words. The sparks crackled from his hair and his hands; Yuste shrank back, but in a single jolt, the full force of her brother's charge emptied itself into her outstretched hands. The shock threw her across the clearing, and the air reverberated, twanging like a drum.

Annat sprang to her feet and was running before a thought could form in her mind. She found Yuda crouching over Yuste's still body, steam coiling off his flesh. There were dark soot stains on Yuste's fingers, and her face looked burnt.

'Yuste,' said Yuda; he was breathing fast, running his hands over Yuste's skin.

'You've killed her,' said Annat, who was breathless herself. Her father looked up at her, and she saw the plain fear in his face; he did not need to speak. He bent over his sister, stroking her face.

'Zyon,' he said. 'I didn't know I was so strong.'

Annat squatted down beside her aunt's body and took one of the lifeless hands. The skin was cracked to the touch. She felt for the pulse at the wrist, and it was silent.

Yuda sat back on his haunches. 'Help me, Annat,' he said. 'I don't know what to do.'

'Why did you do it, Yuda?' she said. Anger rose in her throat, choking back the words.

'I thought I could give back her powers.'

Annat bent over Yuste, whose eyes had rolled up, so that only whites showed beneath the lids. Annat forced her anger down, though she wanted to yell at her father, cursing him for his stupidity and arrogance. Instead, she let her hand caress Yuste's hair.

'Yuste,' she said. Pain was growing under her ribs. She wanted to lift her head and howl to the sky. She shut Yuda out of her mind. It was not possible to heal or bring back the dead. She had once brought her father back from the edge of death, but she feared that Yuste had gone beyond. Her aunt's body seemed empty and lifeless, like something that had never lived.

Yuda lunged past her and snatched Yuste's form up in his arms, hugging her against his breast. It was possible to overlook the strength of him and see beyond to a thin boy, crying alone on a stretch of empty sand. Annat caught the memory from him and her rage was jolted aside. She had never had any rival, or anyone so close, when she was a child. But she wished Malchik would come and tell them what to do. They were two of the most powerful creatures the wood held for many miles, and they were helpless.

'Call her back. Go after her,' she said.

'What do you think I'm trying to do?' Yuda shouted.

Yuste stirred in his arms, raising her hand as if to push something away from her face. Annat sat back on her heels, utterly surprised. Yuda cupped his hand against his sister's hair, but said nothing. Yuste touched his chest.

'Did it work?' she said, speaking through cracked lips with difficulty.

'I don't know,' he said. 'I thought I'd finished you off this time.'

'Not so easy . . . to get rid of me,' said Yuste, lifting her head and smiling up at him. Yuda bent and kissed her on the forehead. She slipped gently out of his arms, and sat back on her haunches, holding up her blackened hands.

'Power burn,' she said. 'It hurts as much as ever it did.'

Yuda licked his thumb and smeared the soot on her face. Yuste shied away from him, but Annat could see that the blackened crust was no more than that, a thick layer of carbon. Only her lips were burnt.

'I don't know where it came from,' he said. 'I was like a leaf on the wind. It flowed through me.'

'Heal my hands, Yuda,' she said.

'Annat,' said Yuda.

Annat stood up. She had forgotten her nakedness and any feelings of shame. Besides, she was scratched and smeared with earth and leaf mould; there were broken-off twigs in her hair. Yuste turned to smile up at her; it was as if the woman's face had been painted black so that only the whites of her eyes and her teeth showed through the veil of soot. Annat found herself blinking back tears. She could not move, not even to lift her arms to call up a simple healing. Sometimes, however close they were, there were thoughts and emotions she could not express, or share with her family. She clenched her fists.

'What's the matter, Annat?' said Yuda.

Annat stuck her fists into her eyes and bawled like a child. Sadness poured out of her. It was in part the after-shock of thinking that Yuste was dead, but there was more; she had realised that a time would come when neither Yuda nor Yuste would be there, and no one would stand between her and death.

Yuste stood up and took Annat in her embrace, holding her burnt hands out to either side. Their breasts crushed against each other, getting in the way. And Annat sensed what she had suspected, and what had brought her sorrow to the surface; Yuste too was full of the golden power, a column of liquid fire that burned inside her. She leant her face against her aunt's bare, warm shoulder and cried, letting her tears flow over Yuste's skin.

They made camp in the woods at the edge of the mountains. Sarl had chosen the place, though to Huldis it looked no more comfortable than many of the other hollows that gathered under the roots of great trees. She stood watching, holding the bridle of her horse, while Sarl lifted the prisoner down from the back of his mount and rolled him over on the ground. Then she saw the blood.

'What have you done!' she said, letting go the bridle and running to where the prisoner lay. There was dried blood on Yuda's face and the front of his shirt.

'What?' said Sarl, who had already started to unsaddle his steed.

Semyon came to stand beside Huldis, who had taken out her kerchief to dab at the blood on Yuda's face. The Magus said, 'Something has been tampering with our captive. Or someone.'

Sarl strode across to where they had gathered and looked down at Yuda's motionless form. 'By the Mother!' he said. 'I have not touched him, not a hair of his head.'

'I cannot hear you call on the Mother, Zhan Sarl,' said Huldis. She lifted Yuda's head and used her thumb to roll back one of his eyelids, but there was no response.

'He is far away,' said Semyon. 'The spell has sent him out of his body.'

'Huldis, I swear I have not harmed him,' said Sarl. 'You have had me in sight all this while.'

Huldis looked up at her brother's ravaged face. For an instant, she pitied him. She shook off the feeling as if it were a loose shawl, and found herself giving commands. 'You, Magus, make a fire. Sarl, you can deal with the horses. I shall look to the prisoner. He is no good to us dead.'

'At your command, my lady,' said Semyon, with only a touch of irony. He began to gather up firewood, fallen twigs, pine cones and a few broken branches, heaping them together to make a fire.

Huldis tried to run her hands through her hair, then tore off her veil. The material would be good for making bandages, if she needed them. It was difficult to remove Yuda's jacket and shirt; his body was like a rag-doll's filled with wet sand. Huldis, as she struggled with him, was reminded of the frustration of dressing and undressing her childhood dolls. That brought back the thought of Aude. She paused, one arm half out of its sleeve, and saw a frown pass over Yuda's face. Perhaps he had not gone so far off as Semyon seemed to think.

There were long rows of parallel scratches on his chest and arms, as if he had fought with an animal. The scratches had bled profusely, but they were neither deep nor dangerous. Huldis tore up her veil with pleasure, and used it to clean off as much blood as she could, using the water from her water-bottle. It was an oddly peaceful moment; her brother was at a distance, making pickets for the horses amongst the trees, and talking to them in a low voice as he took off their heavy saddles and rubbed them down. Sarl would never be cruel to a steed; though he used spurs, the rowels were kept blunt. He had often preferred to ride bareback through the Forest of Ademar.

Huldis sat back on her heels, with pieces of bloody

rag strewn over her lap. Though the blood had stained Yuda's shirt, there were no tears in the cloth. And his leather jacket was unmarked. She found Semyon looking at her. He was crouching beside his pile of wood, chanting up a spell to light the fire.

'It wasn't Sarl, was it?' he said.

'No,' she said. 'I don't know what it was.'

'He may yet wish he was dead,' said the Magus. Huldis bit her lip. She knew Semyon could not hear her thoughts, but she feared what her face might give away, even in the twilight. She rolled up Yuda's jacket and slid it under his head. Then she unpinned her cloak from under her chin and spread it over him.

'You'll be needing that later on,' said Semyon. 'Unless you want to share mine.'

'I think my brother might have something to say on that subject, Magus.'

'I'm sure he would.' She saw the Sklav's features contort into a look of hate, which he made no attempt to hide from her. Huldis crawled across to the fire on hands and knees, and began to help him build up the cone of firewood. No one managed these wild forests, and there was plenty of tinder, pine cones dry and grey with age. She wondered how often travellers passed this way.

'Not much, through this godforsaken wilderness,' said Semyon.

Huldis shrank back from him. He had heard her thought! The Magus glanced at her, and then his eyes widened. 'You?' he said.

Huldis swayed with fear. He must not discover the

true extent of her power! Semyon's dark eyes studied her face, and she feared that he would read everything before she could re-establish her defences. 'A little shaman,' said the Magus. 'Does the Heir know?' and he nodded towards Sarl. Huldis shook her head.

'Well, I'm damned,' said Semyon. 'I knew that he used to be one. I didn't realise it ran through the whole family. You kept it very quiet.'

'My father does not hold with it. He burns shamans.'

'He seemed happy enough to employ me to do his dirty work.'

'You come from the court of the Staryetz. He can overlook that you are a shaman, because you are called magus.'

'So he would burn his own daughter?'

'I don't know. I have always kept it secret. I have little power, so it has been easy. I only told my best friend.'

'How charming,' said Semyon. 'Perhaps you'd like to start this fire going, then.'

Huldis laughed freely. 'I could never do anything like that,' she said.

'Perhaps we could try rubbing two sticks together. Or you and I could make the beast with two backs.'

Huldis felt herself flush, but his desire had ceased to frighten or disgust her. 'Are your spells too weak, Magus?' she said.

Semyon sat back on his haunches. 'It is wasteful to use spells on lighting fires,' he said. He snapped his fingers and ignited a small flame from his thumb, which he held to the pile of sticks.

They felt rather than saw that Sarl had come to stand over them. It was as if he cast a shadow of cold. He watched as the flame took hold amongst the dry twigs, curling along the edge of one stick and turning its skin black.

'The fire purifies and reduces to ash,' he said, as if he were the only one there, talking to himself.

Semyon made a face at Huldis, who was not inclined to laugh. 'Have you tended to the horses, Zhan?' she asked.

Sarl squatted down beside the fire and poked at the wood with a long finger. 'I see things in the fire,' he said. 'Faces.'

Semyon sighed quietly, and took a pipe and a tin of *tabak* from the pouch at his belt. Huldis watched him as he opened the tin, took out a morsel of *tabak* and crumbled it into the bowl of the pipe. Then he lifted a long ember from the fire and drew steadily on the pipe's stem, until the wad of *tabak* had been kindled.

'I suppose it would be too much to hope for supper?' he said, giving Huldis a sidelong grin. She hardly heard him. She too was staring into the magical nest of flames.

'I see them too, Zhan,' she said. 'The faces of the long dead.'

'I should not have left you in the power of the Cold One,' he said. 'But I was in her thrall.'

'It does not matter, Zhan. I did not suffer, those many years. All time was the same to me. It is Aude I think of, and you could not have helped her. Father chose to banish her.'

Sarl sat down, drawing up his knees and resting his

hands upon them. In stillness, he was like a folded puppet. 'I sometimes thought of you when I was in hell,' he said.

Huldis did not know whether to be frightened or touched by his candour. There was so much she would have liked to ask him – for who would not be curious about the places beyond death? – but she hesitated to disturb him by asking too direct a question.

'The Doxan Fathers have written much on the subject of hell,' she said. 'I am sure they would long to interrogate you.'

'On the rack,' said Sarl, and his eyes gleamed as he glanced towards her. 'I am an unclean thing, Huldis; a man raised from the dead by sorcery.'

'He's right,' said Semyon. 'In this land of priests and sackcloth, we would all be for the stake.'

Huldis gave a little shrug. They had chosen those words, not her; she did not know enough of the world beyond Ademar, where her father ruled supreme. She looked into the flames and mused that hell would not be a place of fire; although fire burned, it also consumed, and that was the end.

'If there is hell, there must have been a judgement,' she said. She thought of the Son, angry in His heaven, His face too bright to behold. Under the Mother's looming cape of stars.

'I'd like to comfort you, Huldis. To say there is heaven above and hell below, with the green earth in between. I only know what I saw, and that I was alone.'

'No demons?' said Semyon, drawing on his pipe.

'Not as you would imagine, Magus.'

'I have conjured demons in my time. There are many species. An infinite number, perhaps.'

'Are you a true Doxan, Magus?' said Huldis.

His bright eyes held her gaze. 'I have been anointed with the chrism of the Church. But I honour older gods.'

'The Devil.'

'The old Sklav gods, that we worshipped before the Apostles of Doxa came to our lands.'

Yuda stirred in his sleep and said a word, too muffled for them to make out.

'How long will that spell hold him, Magus?' said Sarl, glancing over his shoulder.

'It should have worn off hours ago, Mon Seigneur. He's gone wandering.'

'Bring him back.'

'I cannot do that, Mon Seigneur. But he will return – he has to return.'

'I want him alive and awake when we cut out his heart.'

Huldis shivered, and thought of her cloak. She did not want to consider what she had just heard her brother say. Semyon hawked and spat into the fire.

'If you want to have his heart intact, better to keep him asleep,' he said.

Sarl stood up and walked away from the fire. 'I want him awake,' he said.

They watched him go, the tall figure loping away from the hollow where they sat to the place he had tethered the horses.

'By Tchernobog, I shall be glad when this is over,' said Semyon.

Huldis did not reply. Gathering up her skirts, she crawled back to the sleeping shaman, seeing only that the cloak rose and fell as he breathed. It was a good, thick piece of cloth and she would have liked to crawl underneath it, to curl up beside him, but modesty forbade it.

'Go on,' said Semyon. 'He doesn't care. And I'll let you know if your brother comes back. I think he prefers horseflesh to humankind.'

Huldis found herself smiling at him. She sat down, lifted up the cloak and crawled in beneath it, turning her back on the unconscious shaman. It was certainly warmer, though the ground was hard, even with its layer of dry fronds. She rested her face on the crook of her arm and lay awake, watching the fire and the Magus sitting beside it. The light picked out the dark hairs growing on his upper lip, and the colours of his tawny skin. Huldis thought of her brother, alone in the darkness beyond the firelight, and closed her eyes.

The wolves were closing in. She lay very still, not daring to move her limbs or open her eyes; but she could not stop the sighing of her breath or the warmth of her blood, and that was what drew them. She lay alone under the vast sky, and the circle drew tight around her as the grey shapes moved over the plain. Their movement was like the stirrings of grubs in a jar of flour, but they all made in one direction; the moon cast their shadows as they padded towards her, their heads bent low to pick up the scent.

The black wolf stood over her, its paws pressing down on

her chest. Spittle dropped from its jaws, splashing on her face. In a moment, less than a second, she would feel its teeth close on her throat, and the first tearing of blood and pain . . .

Huldis screamed. She threw up her arms to shield her face, but the great brute bore down on her, smothering her, its breath rank in her face. She writhed and struggled, trying to push it off her, and all she could see was the black mask, too close, and the yellow eyes. She felt its claws pressing on her body, piercing through the fabric of her clothes.

The heat and pressure was suddenly gone. She felt a wailing wind pass over her, and sank back, weakened from her struggle. She lay like a heavy weight on the hard ground, her clothes torn, her legs smeared with blood.

The blood of the moon. Huldis sat up and found its red stream trickling between her thighs, sinking into the earth. She needed rags to staunch the flow and clouts to keep it from staining. She thought of the strips of cloth she had packed in her saddlebags; but the horses were far away, across the clearing, and Sarl was there. She did not want to stand up and walk across the dark, while the blood ran down her legs. The pain of the wolf's claws was still there, deep inside.

Yuda turned over and touched the small of her back. His hand traced the length of her spine, stopping just short of the base. Huldis felt the warmth seeping from his fingers, sliding through her and uncoiling the taut muscles of her womb. She bent forwards, her chin almost touching her knees.

— *Did it hurt you?*

— *What?*

— *My wolf. Did it hurt you?*

– *Your wolf?*

– *In a way, yes.*

– *I don't know*. Huldis had only a confused memory of her dream; of pressure and fear and death.

– *It hurt me for sure*, he thought, sitting up to examine the scratches on his chest and arms.

It seemed they were the only ones awake. Semyon was bundled up in his cloak, snoring beside the fire, and Sarl was not in sight. Huldis caught Yuda's arm.

– *You must go. Run away while you can.*

His eyes smiled at her. Black and strange, they were nothing like the eyes of the wolf.

– *Remember why I came? I have to stop Sarl. Running away won't finish that.*

He glanced down at her hand gripping his bare arm, and Huldis withdrew it. Here she was, sitting in the midst of a wood, her hair uncovered, next to a half-naked man. She was too sharply conscious of the light the fire cast on his arms and shoulders.

'It is too dangerous,' she said in a whisper. 'I did not know how much my brother hated you. He said he would . . . cut out your heart while you were alive.'

Yuda had turned away from her, wrapping his arms round his knees. 'I'm sure he means it,' he said. 'He doesn't know how to deal with me in any other way. Maybe you weren't aware of that, but I was. I don't intend for him to kill me.'

'What about the spell?' she said.

He shrugged. 'I can't use my powers yet. Not in this world. But now there are the wolves.'

'The wolves are real?'

'I don't know yet. Mine made real scratches. He's a big bastard. I think he had to make his mark on me somehow. I suppose it could have been worse – he might have pissed on me.'

'Yuda . . .' said Huldis, turning towards him.

'Yes?'

'Kiss me.'

Yuda turned his face towards her. He stretched out his hand, and touched her cheek. 'I don't think that would be a good idea, do you?' he said.

Huldis flushed at his touch. She felt reckless, unchained from the reasons that would have bound her in the daytime. She saw him smile. 'When you kiss someone, it changes things,' he said. 'What would happen if you and I became lovers? It would be your first time, I'm thinking, and maybe – just maybe – I'm not the right man.'

Huldis leaned closer. She curled her arm round his head. She could feel his breath on her face. Yuda took her face in his hands and moved back so that he could get a good look at her. 'I'm . . . flattered,' he said. 'More than flattered that someone as young and fine and beautiful should think of me. But I don't think we should bring desire into this. I owe you a duty. I should be looking out for you, not lying with you.'

Huldis shrank back from him, and drew herself up into a ball. She could feel the steady trickle of blood between her legs, as if her womb were weeping. Yuda sighed. 'Men of my faith don't lie with women when they have their monthlies,' he said. 'Some would refuse to touch you. But it's not just that, Huldis. There are

many reasons. I don't make a habit of deflowering
irgins. And – listen to me, girl – I slept with your
ude. She was my wife. She bore me children. I think
'd be betraying so many people – and you too – if I
id what you want.'

Huldis began to cry, in silence. She covered her face
ith her hands, but the sobs shook her whole body.
uda sat beside her for a while, not saying anything.
hen he stretched out and wrapped his arms around
er, drawing her against him. Not in the way that she
ad wanted, but somehow she felt only relief and
afety. She could not hear Yuda's thoughts, or see his
ice; but he was staring out into the dark with a
aunted look, as if he had seen something that fright-
ned him.

Chapter 12

The cradle was swinging. Its gentle motion rocke
Yuste awake, and she opened her eyes. Over he
head was the curved and painted roof of the caravar
hung with velvet and tasselled drapes. She sat up, t
find herself in the wide bed set into the wall of th
wagon. Over her knees a mohair shawl was spreac
and beneath it layers of thick blankets. Someone ha
undressed her, and she wore nothing but her chemis
and petticoats. The rocking motion that had seeme
so gentle was agitated, as if the cart were moving at
speed for which it had not been built.

Yuste snatched up the shawl, and crawled acros
the bed until she could look out from between the cur
tains into the room beyond. It was dark and the o
lamps were lit; on either side of the table sat Cluny
Planchet and Boris Grebenshikov. Cluny was holdin
on to a drawn sword, to stop it from sliding to and fr
across the table; Planchet gripped a mace, and Bori

as playing with his gun, checking the charge chamber
or ammunition.

Yuste slipped out from between the curtains and
ne three men looked up at the soft thud of her bare
eet on the floor. Cluny started to his feet and Boris
vas not far behind, pushing the gun back into its
olster.

'By the Mother, Yuste! Are you awake?' said the
haman detective.

'Where are my clothes, Boris Grebenshikov?' said
uste, striding towards him.

'We had to cut them off you,' said Boris. 'To get rid
f the corsets. You stopped breathing.'

'You cut off my corsets?' said Yuste. She heard her-
elf and laughed.

'You've been unconscious for nearly ten hours.
During which time we broke camp and set off for
Dieulevaut at all speed.'

'My father's army is behind us,' said Cluny.

Yuste stretched. 'I remember. I saw them, before
. . .' She paused. 'Something has happened to me.'
Clutching the shawl under her chin, she stretched out
er arm and looked at her hand. Boris stepped towards
er and touched her wrist.

'By the Mother!' he said. 'You're a shaman.'

Yuste sat down in the free chair, trying to think
hrough the shock. 'I remember . . . I saw Yuda. Yuda
ealed me. He gave me back my powers.'

Boris sat heavily down on the chair beside her. 'Yuda
id what?' he said.

'We thought you were dead,' said Cluny.

'I think that perhaps, in a way, I did die,' said Yuste
'What have you done with my clothes?'

Boris shook his head. 'You won't be wearing thos
again, Missis. The Rom will find something for you t
wear, when we stop.'

'That dress cost me a month's wages, Boris Andre
yevich.'

'Mother, woman, can you do nothing but talk abou
clothes? Tell me what has happened to you.'

Yuste rubbed her hand along her thin arm, whic
was goose-pimpling. She felt caught between laughte
and distress, and a little ashamed that she cared s
much about the destruction of her gown. She had le
Axar in such a hurry that she had only packed change
of underwear; she could not spend the journey in he
petticoats and chemise.

'Perhaps Madame could wear something of Messir
Cluny's,' said Planchet. 'She might find those mor
suitable for a journey as well as for modesty.'

'I am not putting on a shirt, collar and pantaloons
said Yuste.

Boris ran his hand back over his head, fluffing u
his scanty hair. 'I think you may find that Cluny's spar
clothes favour the medieval style,' he said. He slappe
the table with his palm. 'I can't believe we're havin
this conversation!'

'Monsieur is correct,' said Planchet. 'I did not mea
to offer Madame Messire Cluny's modern attire.'

'For Zyon's sake, Planchet, you must call me Yuste
Be so good as to fetch me whatever garments you thin
fit. So long as they're warm.' She drew the shawl tigh

272

cross her shoulders. 'Boris Andreyevich, I am at your
isposal.'

'I lost you,' he said. 'You let go my hand.'

'I'm sorry,' said Yuste. 'I went on a Journey. A long
Journey. And my brother was there.' She paused,
ware of the inadequacy of what she was saying. She
was not sure that she knew how to describe what had
appened to her. 'It was in a forest. There were wolves.'
She looked at Boris. 'I don't imagine I'm making much
ense.'

'All I know is that when you and I set out to make
he scan, you had only traces of vestigial power. Now
ou've got the works. You're as powerful as I am.'

'I know,' said Yuste, touching her temples. 'My head
urts.'

Cluny resumed his seat, balancing the drawn sword
n his lap. 'It sounds like a miracle,' he said.

'So Yuda's doing miracles now, is he?' said Boris.

'He frightened me,' said Yuste. She gave a little shrug.
He drew on a new source of power. Not his own. It
early killed me.'

'But all this was in a shaman world. Just the two
f you.'

'I suppose it was a shaman world. It seemed very
eal. The trees, the wolves – and Annat was there.'

'Annat?' said Cluny.

'I never saw Malchik, which is strange now that I
hink of it.'

Planchet approached the table and gave a discreet
ow. Yuste turned to see that he was holding out an
ssortment of silks and wool, in an indiscreet blue. She

smiled up at him. 'Does your master have nothin
black, grey or brown, Planchet?' she said.

'Only amongst his modern garments, Madame.'

'I am very grateful,' said Yuste, taking the armful
of cloth from him. There was a long tunic, legging
and a fine cloak of delicate grey yarn. She draped ther
over her lap. 'You say I have been gone ten hours
Does the Doyen know we are ahead of him?'

'We're not sure,' said Boris. 'We struck camp a
soon as I brought back the news. The roads divide
about three hours back, and the Doyen's army shoul
have taken the southern fork. But Cluny is suspicious

'It's hard to be certain with all the noise the wagon
make at this speed,' said Cluny. 'But I'd swear I'v
seen torches and light glancing off steel. My fathe
would have passed our camp.'

Yuste stood up. 'Show me,' she said. 'As soon as
have made myself decent.'

Cluny's garments fitted her, except in length. Hidde
behind the bed-curtains, Yuste was overcome wit
laughter as she struggled to make the long leggings cove
her small, thin legs. She fashioned herself a pair c
rudimentary garters to hold them up. Keeping her ow
chemise and drawers underneath, she pulled on th
tunic, which reached almost to her ankles. It was modes
enough to satisfy her requirements, and yet it woul
make for much greater ease of movement than the layer
of heavy fabric and stiffened petticoats she was used t
wearing. She flung the cloak round her shoulders an
crawled out into the light of the wagon, aware that he
hair had come loose and was drifting into her face.

'By the Mother!' said Boris. 'Now you do look like your brother.'

Cluny blinked, and smiled.

'I'm not sure I should go about the streets of Dieulevaut dressed like a hoyden,' said Yuste. She was conscious of the rudimentary fastenings that kept the hose from falling about her ankles. There was a needle and thread in her bags; when she had time, she must improvise something more secure. She smiled at Planchet, who gave a nod of approval.

Cluny led her to the back of the caravan, and opened the door. The two of them crouched in the doorway, holding on to the door-jambs as the wagon jolted from side to side over the uneven road. At the sight of the darkness, Yuste felt her new senses come to life, reaching out into the night. She was almost overwhelmed by the strength and richness of the sensations that flooded in upon her, as she had been when she was with the wolves. Cluny put a steadying hand on her arm.

'How is it with you?' he said.

'Very well, Cluny. But I am like a newborn; everything in this world is strange.'

'You must feel as Annat does. See as she sees.'

'Annat has been a powerful shaman since the day she learnt to toddle her first steps. I lost my powers when I was fourteen, and have lived without them ever since. I know the theory of using them, and I can sense their raw power; I'm not sure how to bring the two together.'

They fell silent and crouched side by side, watching

the road, and listening. Yuste saw the stars weaving to and fro, making silver skid-marks on the sky; from time to time, a shooting star leapt down in a bright puff of smoke. The shapes against the horizon were those of southern trees: long, columnar cypresses and tall, swelling cork-oaks, casting up a web of twigs. Yuste watched Cluny, who was studying the road behind intently. Once again, she let her senses lick over the surface of the dark, trailing out far from her like smoke dancing in the air.

The night was alive. Just as the stars speckled the horizon, grouping together in patterns that might seem to have a meaning, so Yuste saw with her inner sight many small, glowing lights that revealed the nocturnal life of animals, the sleep of humans, and scattered less frequently, the brilliance of a shaman. She stood on the verge of a great abyss in which life glowed in tiny, scattered sparks, dwarfed by the void that held them. She felt a surge of envy that Yuda and Annat had known this all their lives, while she had been denied it for so long. She could not remember what it had been like when she was a young girl.

Cluny touched her arm. 'Look,' he said, softly.

The thing was so fleeting that she almost missed it, but one of the shapes that formed the shadows on the skyline seemed to move, and she caught the outline of a horse and rider.

'I thought I saw . . .' She trailed off.

Cluny drew his chin against his chest. 'I think they have wind of us,' he said. 'I fear that my father has sent men to fetch me back. Or worse.'

'You think they are hunting the Rom.'

'I don't know what to think, Yuste.' He slid to the floor, wedging himself between the wall and the corner. 'Is it possible that my father could have learned what we are planning to do?'

'I don't see how. Only we four know where we are bound, and the Rom. There has been no chance for treachery, even if I thought it plausible.'

Cluny pulled the door shut, closing off the night. Boris came lurching across the tilting floor to stand near them. 'See anything?' he said.

Yuste answered his question with another question. 'If someone were following us, do you think you and I could stop them, Boris?'

Boris shrugged his shoulders inside his trench coat. 'I'm not that confident you could use your powers to fight,' he said.

'I have been taught. The rudiments. Zyon, Boris, I'm a teacher!'

'There's a big difference between theory and practice, Yuste.' He spread his arms wide. 'We don't know what sort of shaman you are.'

Planchet stepped up beside him. 'Let Madame fight if she wishes,' he said gruffly. 'The best fighting is learnt in the field.'

'So you always told me, Planchet,' said Cluny. 'And I've never been tested in battle.'

'Whatever happens, we ought to warn the Rom,' said Boris. 'They will have to stop soon. They can't drive the horses like this for much longer. And when they stop, whoever is following will catch up.'

'Maybe that's the best thing,' said Yuste, musing aloud. 'Unless the whole army is pursuing us, we might do better to stop and face them. And I do not think that was an army we saw on the road behind us.'

Cluny looked to Planchet, who was listening with his head cocked to one side. 'Madame is right,' he said. 'The old man is marching on Masalyar. He would not send his whole force chasing a ragtag of gypsies. But he might send trusted men to bring back his errant son.'

Cluny bent his head. 'Maybe we should give ourselves up, Planchet and I,' he said. 'You would do better without us, and the Rom could get away scot-free.'

'No!' said Yuste. The three men looked startled at the loudness and strength of her voice. 'We can do better than that. We can draw these riders away from the Rom.'

'I don't think you understand, Yuste,' said Cluny. 'These are knights. Chevaliers. They could outride us, and then—'

'My master speaks the truth,' said Planchet. 'Do not underestimate these men because they carry swords and spears. You know nothing of our world and its rules. Even its language would be strange to you. There is no grey or half-colours in that world, only pure white or staring black.'

Yuste was surprised to hear him speak so many words, with such passion. She clasped her knees under her new, soft robe, and considered that she might have to relearn how to be afraid. Just now, she felt invincible, as if nothing could pierce her skin.

She looked to Boris, wondering what he was thinking.

The detective drew his gun and cocked it. 'Yuste's right,' he said. 'You're both right, but her advice is still sound. She's become a shaman, you see, and we have instincts. In some ways we're more animal than human. We should let the Rom go on without us, and wait for these . . . knights.' He glanced at Yuste and added, 'Are you afraid?'

'No,' she said, under her breath. 'It scares me that I'm not afraid.'

'You will be,' said Boris.

Annat opened her eyes. She lay on hard stone, but there was a rough pillow beneath her head. The dreams, and their reality, made her mind cloudy. She did not try to move, but lay staring up at the rocks overhead, which glittered dully in a restless amber light. She let her outspread fingertips touch the cold stone, giving herself time to understand that this was a physical world, different to the forest that had seemed so vivid and true. Her thoughts were full of coin-sharp images. The golden light that had flowed from Yuda to Yuste, striking through her like lightning earthing itself in a tree. Her aunt's face under its mask of soot, as calm as death. Yuda weeping, returned to the lonely boy on the seashore who had done his sister mortal harm. And the moment when Yuste stirred, as if a stone had come to life. Annat had seen the almost visible line between life and death, between a body that was lifeless and one that breathed. Yuste suddenly taking breath in her brother's arms.

These things were hard to understand. Annat hoped that if she lay quite still, she would not be forced to wake and consider them. It was strange to have seen her aunt and her father in their nakedness, and to understand that they were separate beings, whose lives had not been shaped around hers.

'Are you awake, Annat?' said a voice like the scattering of fine gravel.

Annat sat up slowly, curling up from the floor in a single movement, recognising as she did so that her own body seemed stiff and strange. She was not surprised to see Malchik's prone body nearby, or the fire, but the face beyond it was unknown. An old man's face, shaped by wrinkles. The sun had left a dark, leather hue on his skin, and his long eyes were narrow, black and small. She considered the tawny face. He was not a Darkman; she had never seen such faces in Masalyar, and its strangeness fascinated her.

'I am Derzu,' he said.

'Derzu,' Annat repeated. She returned his smile. She knew with all her senses that there was no cause for fear. She was not in a hurry to ask questions, though she was beginning to be curious. She wanted to pause and linger in the pleasure of feeling her body, her skin wrapping her own shape.

'You are the old shaman. The badger,' she said, taking her time to let her mouth shape the words.

'You followed the light of my fire,' said Derzu.

Annat wrapped her arms round her knees. 'Am I a true shaman now?' she said.

'You have named your wolf. Likan.'

Annat yawned, stretching her face wide open. 'But Likan is in the forest and I am in the mountain,' she said.

Derzu leaned forward, nearer to the fire. He was grinning, and there were wide gaps between his white teeth. 'Your father is not inside the mountain,' he said. 'Your aunt is not inside the mountain.'

'Do they know where I am?'

Derzu sat back, shutting his mouth in a steady smile. He wore a cap of skins, but the wisps of hair beneath were grey, streaked with white. Annat crawled closer to the fire. It was cold in the cave, but luxurious warmth issued from the small flames and the glowing coals.

'We are at the heart of the mountain here,' said Derzu. 'Only the Miners are deeper.'

'How did he trap you, Derzu? The Master – the Magus?'

'He did not trap me. He is young. It was Kaschai, his teacher, who shut me up in the dark. But he could not shut up my spirit. I have travelled into many worlds. More worlds than you know about.'

'Then you can't help us escape,' said Annat, sitting cross-legged.

'The Magus wants your souls, hmm?' said Derzu. 'And you have seen how easily a soul can slip out of the body.'

'I always thought soul and body were one.'

'The body would die without the spirit. And the spirit would dissipate without the body.'

'But he brought Sarl back to life. How could he do

that? Sarl has been dead for four years. His spirit should have dissolved long ago.'

'You are a young shaman, and have not yet been initiated into the worlds of the dead,' said Derzu.

'What do you mean, Derzu?'

'You have travelled in shaman worlds. But there are also the places where only the dead can dwell.'

'I think I may have been to a place like that,' said Annat. 'It was called La Souterraine.'

Derzu stroked his beard, considering what she had said. 'I do not know the name,' he said. 'How did you enter it?'

'I went myself. In this body,' said Annat, laying her hand on her breast. Slowly Derzu moved his head, nodding.

'It is possible,' he said. 'There are so many such worlds, great and small. And the Magus has caught one, and keeps it trapped in a leather case.'

'Then if I die – if my body dies – what happens to me?'

'A change,' said Derzu. 'The thing that is left when your body dies is not the same as your living spirit. Semyon wants to use your living soul. And if he uses it, you will be utterly destroyed.'

'What about Sarl?' she said.

Derzu gave a small shrug. 'The magic needs two souls, and a beating heart. Semyon learnt the spell from his teacher, Kaschai the Deathless. And why does Kaschai have that name? On the verge of death, he made the same magic. He devoured two souls and hid the heart in a safe place. As long as it remains hidden, Kaschai will live. He cannot die.'

'Semyon's going to do that for Sarl. Using us.'

Derzu was no longer smiling. He did not answer her directly, but took a twig from the fire and began to draw on the ground. Annat crawled round the fire to squat beside him. 'You cannot escape from the mountain,' said the old shaman. 'But you may be able to save yourselves. And others who come after you. Semyon is a great magus, but he relies too much on the strength of his trapped world. The secret is to set it free.'

'But if my father is coming to rescue us, and my aunt . . . we are all powerful.'

Derzu met her glance. 'You are shamans, not sorcerers. I was powerful. But Kaschai still trapped me and shut me in the mountain. I saw your father's power. Like Semyon, he can draw upon something much greater than himself, and it is changing him. You see these symbols?'

Annat bent forward to study them, and felt surprised. 'It's *Ebreu*,' she said. 'The old, sacred language of the Wanderers.'

'Can you read them?'

Annat tried, but it was like trying to count all the birds in a flock. The letters kept eluding her.

'I know a little *Ebreu*, but I can't make out these words,' she said.

'You will never be able to read all of them together,' said Derzu. 'I have them by heart, but I cannot read, and so I can write them all. These letters are buried in the ring your father wears.'

'I used it to heal him once. When he was dying,' said Annat.

'I have learned from the Wanderers. Their sages say that the letters form the word the One spoke at creation.'

'But are you not a Wanderer, Derzu?' she said.

'I am not a Wanderer. All I know is that there are many worlds, above and below. Who is to say which is the ultimate and which god will speak the final word? Your father's ring carries an amber stone. Caught in the amber are the words of formation.'

Using his fingertips, he smudged the letters he had written in the dust. Annat felt choked, as if her throat were full. 'I don't understand,' she said. 'Yuda must be stronger than Semyon if that is true.'

Derzu did not answer. He folded his hands and stared into the flames, as if waiting for a particular pattern to form. Annat stayed beside him, though she knew that she would see different shapes in the fire to the ones he saw. At last, Derzu gave a long, slow breath, like a sigh.

'Your father is stronger than the Magus,' he said. 'But he cannot draw on the spirits of a whole world.'

Annat picked at the threads of her skirt. 'Yuste was dead,' she said. 'I'm sure she was. She was dead for a few minutes, and then she came back to life. I was watching, and I saw it happen.'

'It is possible,' said Derzu. 'The force of the amber stone flowed through your father and struck her down. It also contained the seeds that would bring her back to life.'

'He took a chance. It could have killed her. He thought she was dead too.'

'Has your father studied the power he wields?'

'He spent a long time with the man who gave him the ring, the Rashim of Chorazin. He's never told me what they talked about. We are often in each other's company, but he never talks about the ring. Since he has worn it, the signature of his power has changed from silver to gold. Mine is silver.'

Derzu nodded as he listened. 'The thing you call a signature changes as you age. Amongst my people we called it *ᴅurmat*, the essence. If a shaman does evil, the *ᴅurmat* will tarnish. In most shamans, however, it acquires a patina. An old man as I am holds up a bronze shield with many notches. The Magus is young, but the *ᴅurmat* he bears carries dark blots that weaken its purity.'

'But it shouldn't change colour. That would be like having . . . blue strawberries.'

Derzu smiled. 'You have just told me how your father's *ᴅurmat* changed.'

'I know. I want to know what it means.'

'The ring changed him when you used it to heal him. And it may be the ring that brought your aunt back to life. Then she too will have a golden *ᴅurmat*.'

'She'll have powers?'

'That was your father's purpose.'

Annat stood up. She glanced at Malchik's prone body. 'I wonder if they know,' she said. 'So much power. It could burn them up.'

As she spoke, all light in the cave went out. The

fire was extinguished, and a cold wind swirled through the cavern, throwing up sparks and ashes. Baba Yaga came screaming out of the darkness, lighting her way with a skull torch whose eyes burned with a lurid yellow flame. Annat heard Derzu exclaim and she pressed herself against the wall as the witch bore down on her, whirling the torch about her head.

When Semyon woke, he ached in every limb. He rolled over to look at the embers of the fire, and groaned. His dreams had been nightmares, full of grey wolves that circled just on the edges of the glade. Sitting up, he took his head in his hands.

'Tchernobog,' he said, wishing for a moment that the dark god would burst through the clouds and blast him to smithereens.

'Does your head hurt, Magus?' said Huldis. She was stooping over the fire, adding fresh wood to the flames, with a full billy-can of water propped beside her.

'Did you have a pleasant night?' Semyon snapped. Huldis gave him a look, and did not deign to answer. Stumbling to his feet, cursing, Semyon remembered the shaman. It would have been too easy for the villain to sneak off when he, Semyon, should have been keeping watch. He found the small man sitting nearer to the fire, wrapped in a cloak. The spell still held him, but he was awake. He looked up at Semyon and smiled.

'You are not to look at me,' Semyon shouted. His nerves were on edge after the night's dreams. The man gave a shrug and turned to look at Huldis instead, watching her as she bent over the fire, balancing the billy-can amongst the heaped twigs. Semyon strode towards him and shoved the man with his foot. 'You are not to look at her either, dog,' he said.

The man raised his eyes to Semyon's face. 'I'd like to see you stop me, Magus,' he said, in the Sklavan tongue. Semyon gave in. His head was hurting too much to keep on shouting. He sat down on the earth beside the small man and said, 'So what province did your parents come from?'

'My mother came from Kiyev and my father from the city of Ades.'

'My brother is returning,' said Huldis from across the fire.

Semyon stood up in a hurry, brushing dry leaves from his robe. He saw the tall, ungainly figure striding like a scarecrow that moved, making towards them from the place where he had tethered the horses. Semyon went to meet him. He repressed a shudder at the sight of the red-rimmed eyes, the livid face. Was it possible that Sarl's appearance was getting worse?

'I trust you had a comfortable night, Mon Seigneur,' he said with false joviality.

'I did not sleep,' said Sarl, looking beyond him to Huldis. And the shaman, Vasilyevich, who had risen to his feet. He might not be tall, but there was something very noticeable about him, Semyon reflected. He moved away from Sarl, and saw the expression on his face. He could not help thinking that Sarl was looking at Vasilyevich as a dog looks at a bone.

'Zhan Sarl,' said the shaman. 'This is . . . unexpected. I thought I'd killed you.'

Sarl stalked a few paces closer. 'That makes us quits, Vasilyevich,' he said. 'I gave you a mortal wound. How is it you are alive, while I am . . . this?' He plucked at his clothes, as if they were part of his body.

The shaman wiped his nose on the back of his hand. 'You backed the wrong goddess,' he said.

Sarl was closing with him, and Semyon started to hurry after, afraid that he might lose his valuable prisoner if Sarl forgot why they had captured him.

'You struck my sister, the Lady Huldis,' said Sarl. Yuda glanced at the young woman, who was crouching by the fire.

'It seems she has a more forgiving nature than you, Zhan Sarl,' he said.

Sarl stopped. He was a few paces down the slope, so that they stood almost eye to eye.

'What do you mean?'

Vasilyevich let the cloak he was wrapped in slip to the ground, revealing the scratches Huldis had bathed the previous night. 'She tended my wounds,' he said. 'At least, I'm guessing it was her. Unless you or the Magus are being unusually gentle to your captives.'

'I never laid a finger on you!' said Sarl.

'It was a wolf,' said Yuda. 'Given the choice, I'd take the wolf every time.' He stooped to pick up the blanket, and wrapped it once more about his shoulders. Sarl staggered a few more paces until the two men were within touching distance, and dropped down on his knees. Semyon found himself gaping at Huldis, and saw her mouth rounded into the same O.

'Forgive me,' said Sarl. 'You've got to forgive me. You're the only one that can do it.'

Vasilyevich looked down at him. 'I think you've got the wrong man,' he said.

Sarl jabbed a finger at him. 'You're the one,' he said.

'It doesn't matter an arse what I think,' said the shaman. 'And you're planning to cut out my heart. I don't feel very forgiving about that.'

'Not you. It needn't be you. That was my father's wish. We can take the Magus. And your children can go free.'

Vasilyevich looked towards Semyon. 'What do you say to that, Magus?' he said. 'It seems Sarl wants you to take my place. He's in a generous mood.'

'He lies. He cannot complete the magic without my help,' said Semyon, hoping his voice did not tremble as he spoke.

'You hear that, Sarl?' said Vasilyevich. 'The Magus isn't impressed. I think you should listen to him. He's the one who knows the spell.'

'I am offering you your freedom,' said Sarl.

'Just so I'll forgive you? It's that important?'

'Say it!'

'I've never hated you, Sarl. You're the one who took against me. I don't hate you now. You're beneath it. There's only one way you could save yourself, and that would be to die. Give up the spell and go back underground.'

'I am afraid. I cannot return there,' said Sarl.

'Then what makes you think I can help you?' said Vasilyevich.

Sarl reached out and gripped his arm. 'I did you great wrong,' he said.

'And I killed you,' said the shaman. 'Like I said, we're quits. The rest is up to you.'

'I cannot do it. I must live,' said Sarl.

Vasilyevich looked down at him, and shook off his hand. 'There's nothing I can do for you,' he said. 'You don't need me to tell you what to do; you know it as well as I do. I can't give you empty words.'

Semyon felt that he needed to intervene, to re-establish control. He stepped forward, coming close to the two men, and jumped back as if he had been stung. It was as if he had dipped his hand into an alchemical spark chamber. He stared at them, seeing nothing, not even an interchange of power; but the air around them was charged.

'Stop this play-acting,' he said, feeling anger tighten his chest. For a moment of vertigo, he believed that he faced something beyond his experience, which he had no words to describe.

Sarl sprang up, stretching his long frame to its full height. He grasped the front of Semyon's tunic, lifting him off his feet.

'Play-acting?' He almost spat the words in Semyon's face. 'What do you know of men's matters, boy? You are fit for nothing but to rut, lust and fill your belly.'

'He could do worse, Sarl,' said the shaman. He had an odd voice, harsh and deep. 'He could be like you.'

Sarl cursed and let Semyon drop to the ground.

'Don't forget, Vasilyevich,' he said. 'I hold your life in the palm of my hand.'

Huldis approached her brother. She stopped to look at Semyon, who was still sprawled on the ground where Sarl had let him fall.

'I think you have forgotten our journey, Zhan Sarl,' she said. 'We should be leaving this place. We do not want another night to find us in the forest. You must make peace with one of these men, for you cannot kill them both.'

Semyon heard the shaman laugh. He stood up, brushing pieces of dry leaf from his robe. 'Your father sent me with you for one purpose, Mon Seigneur,' he said. 'To find the heart of a powerful shaman and use it to keep you alive. Time is passing. If you want to disobey your father, tell me now, and I will cease from wasting my time with you. If you wish to die, all you need do is wait. Kill me, and you will not wait long.'

'Are you threatening me, Magus?' said Sarl.

'No, Mon Seigneur. I am stating the facts. Your father is paying me well. I would not have made this journey if I thought it would cost my life, and come to nothing.'

Sarl looked from Semyon to Vasilyevich. His face had become expressionless, like a mask. A grotesque mask that a *Skomorokh*, a village clown, might wear to frighten the unwary, thought Semyon.

'Very well,' Sarl said. 'We shall ride on. You have made your choice, Wanderer; remember that I offered you your freedom.'

'It was you who made the choice, Zhan Sarl, not I,' said the shaman.

Chapter 13

The Rom gave them two horses, because neither Yuste nor Boris knew how to ride. Cluny lifted Yuste on to the back of his steed, while Boris climbed up behind Planchet, almost spilling over the other side in his haste. As Yuste balanced precariously on the back of an animal that moved disconcertingly beneath her, as if she were sitting astride a sofa that had come to life, Cluny swung up behind her and took a grip on the reins with his arms on either side of her.

'Hold on tight,' he said, his face brushing against hers in the dark. Yuste felt a little queasy as she watched the wagons of the Rom rocking away into the night. She could just see them only because of their lanterns, which were already beginning to fade. Then Cluny dug in his heels and the horse sprang into movement. Yuste seized handfuls of loose mane and clung on as tight as she could, gripping the animal's hard sides with her knees. She could feel Cluny rising and falling in the saddle, moving against the rhythm of his mount; she was jolted uncomfortably not just up and down, but from side to side. She thought she could hear Boris swearing behind them.

'The Rom are good judges of horseflesh,' said Cluny, just loud enough for her to hear. 'This is a good beast.'

Yuste did not answer him; she was unwilling to speak in case she bit on her tongue. She could not understand the pleasure that some people seemed to take in riding; her back was aching and her pelvis felt bruised. At any time she was sure that she would lose her grip and slip over the side, where the horse's hooves might strike her a fatal blow. Cluny must have perceived her misery, for he kept hold of the reins with one hand, and put the other round her waist.

'I am a modestly competent horseman, even though I say so myself,' he said.

'Thank you, Cluny,' said Yuste, reflecting how her timidity contrasted with the boundless strength and freedom she had felt amongst the wolves. Though she was still shaken and jarred from head to foot every time the horse moved, she felt much more secure settled against Cluny's chest, with his arm gripping her waist. She even dared to glance round at the countryside through which they were passing. They had left the road and were moving across the open fields. It was hard to tell in the gloom, but the land looked uncultivated, wild and rocky, and strewn with many small, thorny bushes. It reminded her of the wild hillscapes that surrounded Masalyar, where it was too dry for trees to grow, and the stony pastures were littered with box bushes and fragrant herbs.

'Do you know where we are going?' she said.

'East,' said Cluny. 'Apart from that, Planchet and I are searching for a good place to mount an ambush. I should say that Planchet is looking; I have no expertise in such matters.'

'I am sorry, Cluny,' said Yuste. 'You would be welcome to leave Boris and me somewhere, and to return to your father.'

She heard Cluny give a snort of amusement. 'Return to my father, Yuste?' he said. 'You have so little idea what that means. Remember he is the man who nearly killed Annat and Yuda. He is a good man, by his own lights, a devout Doxan and a patriot of the Franj. But he has no time for heretics, apostates or infidels. Most people he meets, in fact.'

Yuste wished she could say something to comfort him. 'I think he would be willing to receive you, Cluny,' she said.

'I am the one who doesn't want to go back. I don't want any part in his wars. I'd be happy never to see him again. He took me away from my natural mother when I was nine years old. I've lived in his household ever since . . .' He broke off.

'What happened to your mother?' asked Yuste.

'She died in childbirth not long after I left. I never saw her again.'

'Why weren't there any shamans to help her?'

'Think, Yuste. She lived in my father's *domaine*; no shamans would willingly go there.'

'But you must have relatives.'

She felt Cluny sigh. 'They wouldn't welcome me. They loathe the Doyen as much as I do. And I'm his son.'

'You don't know that they would hate you—' Yuste began, but she was cut short by an exclamation from Planchet. Cluny reined in his horse.

'Looks like he's found somewhere he likes,' he said. He dismounted with ease, and lifted Yuste from the horse's back, setting her down on the ground.

'Thanks,' said Yuste. She felt disoriented, as if she had lost all the markers that defined her place in the world; she could see very little except the crooked shapes of trees, but to her inner eye the dark was alive with busy lights, flashing and vanishing like shooting stars.

Boris slid down from the saddle and landed awkwardly, cursing under his breath. Yuste thought she heard Planchet chuckle. The servant urged his horse a few more paces until it stood beside Cluny's, and dismounted.

'We can wait here, Messire Cluny,' he said. 'There's plenty of cover from the trees.'

'Are you sure about this, Planchet?' said Cluny. 'If my father's men capture us, I risk a flogging, but you could be put to death.'

'I serve you, Messire Cluny, and no one else.'

'Isn't it a little late to be having this discussion?' said Boris. He staggered over to a tree and leaned against it. Yuste heard him sigh, then she saw the small flicker of flame as he lit a cigar. A few moments later, she could smell the musky smoke. She felt her way across to the place where he stood, and sensed his eyes on her.

'Boris . . .' she began. He said nothing to fill up the pause, and Yuste plunged into *sprechen* with a clumsy, embarrassed lurch.

– What am I going to do? Can I do anything?

It did not feel comfortable, like their last conversation before they performed the scan. It was not slick and easy, like talking to her brother. She realised too late that Boris could perceive these thoughts, even though she had not sent them to him. When he spoke aloud, she could tell from his voice that he was smiling, and she was relieved.

'There's no time to discuss this, Yuste. Do what you can. Your new powers are starting to blossom; you may be surprised.'

The conversation ended there, and Yuste could not hear his thoughts. She stood, her hands shaking, watching as Planchet led the horses down the hill and tethered them out of sight. She could not see them but she could hear the jinking of bridle and harness, and the rough breath of the beasts. Cluny stood opposite the place where she sheltered with Boris, and he too had taken refuge behind the gnarled trunk of a short, barren tree. His shape was confused by the shadow of its branches, but she could make out his drawn sword and the light on the paler areas that were his face and hands. Planchet returned, moving noiselessly up the slope, and took his place beside Cluny. Little by little, it began to be quiet, so that Yuste started to hear the sounds of the night.

It was too early for the chirruping of frogs, and this place would have been too dry. There was no breeze, and instead she listened to the stillness, in which all she could hear was Boris when he changed his stance or cleared his throat, and the faint sound of the tethered horses pawing the ground, or shaking their heads in a low whinny. She did not try to see with her inner sight, but gazed into the dark, letting her senses focus on vision and hearing. She became aware of the sweep of stars that unfurled across the sky, their faint pinpricks of light altering and flickering when she stared at them. Though they seemed to change, she felt a true sense of their remoteness, not as bright dust sprinkled across the firmament, but as the distillation of light from something vast and far away. The spaces between looked like a sweep of dark cloth unevenly dyed, picking up spillages of paler hues and layered with gauze.

Yuste hugged herself, cold in her borrowed clothes. She felt naked and vulnerable; she was so used to the armour of corset and stiffened petticoats. There was nothing between her and the night but a few layers of fine woven fabric. She was like a wolf that had been released from captivity without having learned the skills it needed to survive. She glanced at Boris, wondering if his composure hid fear or excitement. All that she knew was that she would shortly face an unknown danger, and be called upon to fight, as she had not done since she was thirteen. She thought of Yuda. There must have been a first time, when he waited to use his powers, knowing himself untested. He must have faced the same waiting that she did now – but he would have been able to rely on his training, all the years with Sival and later at the *Shkola*.

'Damn you, Yuda,' she said, under her breath. She was shivering. Like an aspen tree, trembling when there was no wind. It was true that she felt glad to see Boris standing close by; he was steady, and his form almost seemed to blend with the tree he was leaning against. She rubbed her cold hands together, wondering whether she was simply cold, or afraid, or both. The night seemed full of symbols that she could not translate, great unwieldy words that mocked her because she had not learned how to read. She could feel her powers, surging inside her; she recognised the golden tinge that she had seen in her brother. He had truly shared with her whatever it was that flowed through him, the golden current that came from an unseen source and bore them both up, pouring through their veins and their nerves. All she had to do was to reach inside, to draw up water from the well.

– *Can you see anything?* She threw another jagged thought in the direction of Boris.

– *No.*

He closed the conversation so easily with a single word. Yuste wanted to shout at him, but she was afraid to violate the silence. Even her thought had seemed too loud, as if it would echo across the rocky hillside. She glanced across at Cluny and Planchet, but both men had blended with the trees, and she could no longer make out their individual shapes.

They were all facing in the same direction, watching

the path they had followed. Studying the skyline for the motion of darker shapes against the blackness, and straining for the sound of hooves. Perhaps the horsemen had turned back; perhaps they had followed the wagons of the Rom. Suddenly, her mind was too busy, shaping her fears as scenes that had already happened: the wagons overturned and burning, and their occupants dead on the ground. Yuste tried to make herself stare at the horizon, but she kept seeing vivid colours with her inner eye; colours that would not have been visible in the dark. She realised that she did not like the open spaces of the countryside. She had become used to the enclosing walls of Masalyar. Though she had grown up living in an isolated farmhouse, the emptiness that surrounded it at night had always seemed ominous, as if when the inhabitants of the house were asleep, spirits crowded up to the shutters of the building, and the wide fields were filled with unseen activity.

She tried to imagine what the attack would look like when it came. There would be horses, and men riding them. The riders would look something like Cluny and Planchet. They would be moving fast, and the hooves of their mounts would beat a loud tattoo on the stones. They would not be expecting anyone to be waiting for them. She wondered what sort of thoughts such men might have. Would they be tired, as she was, longing for their beds? Or would they be thinking of the task that had been assigned to them, and what they must do to complete it? Or was it possible that they took pleasure in what they were doing, like hunters? Yuste could not bring her mind close enough to this last idea. She knew that Boris would at times fight, when his work required it. Yuda enjoyed fighting, or he would not have worked for so many years as a guard on the northern trains, where there was always some sort of trouble. But her brother was a strange creature; they had been so close as children, but once he became an adolescent, growing into manhood, she had ceased to understand him.

Boris shifted his position, and she heard him wince. He too had suffered from being obliged to ride a horse. They were city people, used to the dangers and routines of life amongst tall houses, where many people lived close together. Darkness did not exist in Masalyar; its streets glittered with smoky lamps, and it was possible to avoid unlit alleys. But here they had both been abandoned in the wild, where the rules were different, and the enemy would come riding out of the empty night, his mind one that could not be understood.

'Boris, I'm scared,' she said in a low voice.

He took a while to answer. 'Me too. Always am. It gets better with experience – for some.'

'Thank you, Boris Andreyevich—'

'Ssh.'

His hand reached out to stop her. Yuste stiffened, seeing him cock his head like a retriever, though he was listening, not casting for a scent.

'What is it?'

'Listen,' he said, and she too strained to unravel the silence, to search for new sounds amongst the tiny

stirrings that formed the pattern of the night. Boris
squeezed her arm.

'There.'

It was not the sound she expected to hear; something throbbed with a rhythmic pulse, like an engine.
She turned her face up to Boris.

'What is it?'

'I don't know. I think I've been hearing it for some
time. It's . . . unexpected.'

As he spoke, they both discerned another noise,
clearer and more defined than the subtle throb of a
motor. It rebounded off the rocks, and they knew that
their pursuers had ridden on to the hard ground, and
were moving fast; at last, they could hear the complex
beat of the galloping horses, striking the stone with
their iron-shod hooves.

'Damn,' said Boris. 'Why do there have to be two
things?'

'I can't do this, Boris.'

'No time to panic, Missis.' He reached for his gun,
and turned it over, checking that it was loaded. His
hands shook too.

Yuste stared at the dark like a frightened rabbit,
one that had lost the will to run from its predator. As
she feared, she could see shapes moving within the
greater shadow of the unlit ground. They moved
together in a body, and she could only just make out
individual members, the swift-moving feet of the animals, the wind-tossed cloaks of the riders. She
squeezed her hands together, and they were cold and
damp. The fire in her seemed to have gone out; it had

shrunk deep inside her, dwindling to a small, lost spark.

Then there was someone beside her. Not Boris, though she turned round to look at him. She felt the presence of her brother standing behind her, just like her shadow.

– *Yuda?*

– *I'd aim for the horses. But you have to wait.*

– *I can't do it!*

– *Bollocks. Of course you can. I'll guide your hand.*

– *You're not here.*

– *I'm in your head.* She felt him grin. – *This is interesting. Don't think about me. Forget I'm here. Or wherever I am.*

Yuste made herself look outwards. Ahead of her, the riders had resolved into shapes, dim but clear. She could see the places where their faces showed as white ovals, rimmed by their mail hoods. The strangeness of them horrified her; she felt her stomach clench. It did not help that her twin was looking out of her eyes, his separate mind using her senses. He recognised the garb of the horsemen, and she felt his cold hate. To her they were simply frightening, confusing figures, wearing a second skin of silver links that made them look like reptiles in human form. They did not belong in her century, with their primitive weapons.

'Get ready,' said Boris.

She was dizzy and weak with fear and the double vision that muddled her mind. She wished Yuda would leave her. She saw Boris balance his gun in his hand, preparing to step from the shelter of the trees.

– *Time to move*, thought her brother.

Yuste found herself impelled by his will and her own, crouching and moving away from safety towards the open ground. The riders were so near that she could feel their hoofbeats in the ground and in her bones. She bent low to the ground, remembering – but was it her thought? – that she must not allow herself to be outlined against the horizon.

– *Wait for Boris*, thought Yuda.

She watched the shaman in his dull-coloured trench coat turning towards the riders. He seemed to move so slowly that she could see every detail. He stood sideways, raising his arm with a deliberate movement, and cocking his gun. The horsemen took shape, and for the first time she felt the air stirred by their approach, and caught the scent of their horses, a whiff of straw and shit. She saw Boris squeeze the trigger with his finger, there was a flash, and the night exploded.

For a few instants, Annat was reminded of an ancient actor's mask, with gaping eyes and twisted mouth. During that time, she could not move, while fear and her imagination held her back. Then instinct and training returned, and she raised her arms, hearing the joyous ringing in her ears as the power surged up from its unknown depths and flowed out of her hands.

When she was younger, Annat had not learned how to control the forces inside her. She could use them, but seldom to much effect, and they burnt her hands. But for four years she had been studying under Sival and her father, who had taught her how to understand and wield the strength she had been born with. The witch, too, had shamanic powers, but she was also versed in the elusive science of magic. She would have been a fatal opponent for Annat if in command of her full armoury; but since Semyon had sapped her strength, she could only call on magic by elaborate spells like the one she had used to steal the souls of Annat and Malchik. She dashed the skull torch at Annat's head, but the quick blast from Annat's hands burned it from her grasp, and seared her fingers.

Annat was ready now, balancing on the balls of her feet. As the stream of power surged up inside her for a second time, she let it course through her arms and arc out of the palms of her hands. It looked like small lightning, silver and quick. Baba Yaga swung her arm in an arc and threw up a shield of burnished bronze. She had revealed her *durmat*, and it was weaker than Annat's. The silver sparks cut through the shield and stung her in the upper body, throwing her back.

Annat felt the air crackling against her palms. Her mind buzzed and sang in an ecstasy that was close to the pleasure of sex. But there was a chill of thought that kept her from going in for the kill. She had never fought a woman before, and she did not like it. The witch had harmed her and frightened her, but she was a defeated woman, aged and ruined. Annat straightened, rubbing her hands together to ease the tingling sensation that felt like stinging gnats, and waited to see what the witch would do.

Derzu stepped forward, holding a wooden staff in

his hand. He drew a shape in the air, which left an after-image on the eye. The witch staggered away from the wall where Annat's blast had thrown her, straightening her hair.

'They are mine, Derzu. I called out their souls.'

'I called them back,' said the old shaman.

'The Master will set me free when I give him the souls.'

'They were your guests, Baba Yaga. You have broken the sacred laws of hospitality.'

'Is that all you can say? After so many years trapped in the dark? Give them to me, or I will summon up the Miners to destroy us all.'

Annat heard Malchik's voice. She glanced over her shoulder to see her brother standing silhouetted against the red glow of the fire. 'My sister is stronger than you, Baba Yaga,' he said. 'She could have killed you.'

'I am already buried alive, boy,' said the witch. 'The Master has taken everything from me.'

Malchik took a pace forward. The light glinted off his spectacles. 'Then why not join us and fight him?' he said.

She gave a short, choked guffaw. 'Fight him? The four of us – a broken witch, an old shaman and two half-grown youngsters? He has the power of a world at his command. A world that he has caught and caged in a leather box. There is no hope.'

'I cannot give you the souls of these young people, and I will not,' said Derzu. 'Go back to your prison and wait, as I do. Your mind is not caged.'

'My wits are not wandering, old shapeshifter. What

good can you do, down here in the dark? I have nothing to lose. Let me take their souls, or I will call out the Miners.'

'Then you will have to call them,' said Derzu. 'Fear will not persuade me to do a wicked thing.'

Annat did not wait to see what the witch would do. With a cold, terrible certainty, she brought up her hands and released a flame that travelled as fast as light, earthing itself in the woman's back as she turned to face the wall. There was a loud crack, and the witch's body stiffened; she was lifted off her feet and hurled against the rock.

'By the Mother,' said Malchik; his voice sounded loud in the after-silence.

The witch's body slid to the ground, where it lay motionless, once more like a pile of rags. Annat shivered and wrapped her arms round herself.

'You have killed her, but it is too late,' said Derzu.

'I had to do it. She was going to summon the Miners,' said Annat. The old man turned and walked back to the ashes of his fire, leaning on his staff. Annat found her brother staring at her. She found time to wonder why he had called on the Mother. Derzu settled himself on the ground by the fire, his head bowed.

'She has already summoned them,' he said. Annat hurried across to sit down beside him.

'I had to do it, don't you see?'

Malchik followed, and she felt his hand squeeze her shoulder.

'I understand the reason,' said Derzu. 'But I do not know whether it was a good enough reason to kill.'

'The wolves kill,' she said, impassioned and desperate.

'Wolves are wolves. They act according to their nature. They kill what they need to eat. You are a shaman. You should not take life so easily.'

'I think Annat acted to save us, Derzu,' said Malchik.

'I do not like it,' said the old man.

Malchik sat down cross-legged beside Annat. Cold inside, as if all the fire had died out in her, she said, 'Why did you call on the Mother?'

'What?' Her brother blinked, confused by this unexpected question. 'We don't have time for that now, Natka. We need to work out what to do next. What to do about the Miners.'

Annat curled her hands together in her lap. She felt off-balance, as if all her strings were out of tune. She knew that what Malchik said was good sense, but between her pain at Derzu's displeasure and her own guilt, she needed to lash out, to find a sore place and worry at it.

'Wanderers don't call on the Mother,' she said.

Malchik gazed at her, a sad look but without shame. 'I'm not a Wanderer now, Annat,' he said. 'I've taken the chrism again. I am a Doxan.'

The chill within Annat soaked through all her veins. When her brother was a baby, their mother had taken him to a priest for anointing, but he had been reared as a Wanderer. He knew as well as she did what it meant to desert their ancient faith to be received into the congregation of their persecutors. After the cold she experienced physical pain, as if someone had punched her beneath the ribs. Malchik's own people would cast him out; their grandfather would mourn him as though he were already dead.

'Malchku,' she said. When the priest drew the Wheel on Malchik's brow with holy oil, he would have given him a new name. For the Doxoi, this symbolised his initiation into New Life; it meant that he was no longer subject to the curse of Megalmayar, which had condemned the Wanderers to eternal restlessness. All thought of their present danger was driven from Annat's mind; she could only think how her brother, dear and absurd, had become a stranger.

He seemed quite calm. 'I've been meaning to tell you,' he said. 'But there hasn't been time.'

'How could you?' said Annat, in a whisper. Somehow her own crime, the killing of the witch, seemed to dwindle in comparison.

'Someone asked it of me. A dear friend. My mistress.'

'What are you talking about?'

'I have been paying court to someone. But she refused to receive me unless I became a follower of the True Church. She made me see things differently. That was why I asked to be anointed a second time. To let her know that I did believe.'

Annat wiped her hand across her eyes. She thought of Eugenie, but the Princesse de Bouget had never asked her to renounce her faith.

'Is that true then, do you believe in Doxa?' she said.

Malchik hesitated before answering. 'Yes,' he said.

'After we encountered the twin goddesses in La Souterraine, Cluny told me much more about them; who they are and what part they played in the *storia* of the Mother and the Son. I knew *they* were real. In the same way, I know that the Mother is real. I don't reject the One, but I worship the Mother, like all Doxoi.'

'I know the Mother is real too,' said Annat. 'Her curse still binds the Wanderers. But it was an unjust curse. She set herself up in place of the One. She may be a great goddess, but she is false.'

'Not to me, Natka. I love it, the beauty of it all. The sadness of Her Son's betrayal and death. The joy of His return. It's all much more important than words written on dusty old scrolls. When I took my first Sharing with her – my friend – when the priest, Father Anadolou, blessed the round bread and we divided it between us, I thought I had been received into heaven. Just the two of us, and the priest, and the unseen choir that sings behind the altar screen. I never felt that when I went to the *Beit*.'

'But have you thought of what this will do to Yuda? And Yuste?'

'I have thought about it. I prayed. I know I've done the right thing. I love her, Annat; we go to the Gathering together, we share the Blessed Bread with her friends – six of us, including Cluny. He paints *eikons* for the Church.'

Annat took her head in her hands. 'It doesn't matter what I think – but *Tate*? You know he would die rather than deny that he is a Wanderer.'

'That doesn't stop him sleeping with Doxan women!'

The sharpness with which Malchik answered told her that she had touched him at last. She was not glad.

'He has loved many Doxoi, but he has not become one,' she said.

'I am not Yuda,' said Malchik. 'I want her, and she wants me. We will live in Doxa together.'

'Are you going to marry her?'

'I can't. She already has a husband. They live apart.'

'Children,' said Derzu. They had almost forgotten him, caught up in the passion of their argument. Forgotten their danger. 'The Miners are here.'

Around the edges of the cave flickered soft yellow lights, like the banks of candles Annat had seen in a Doxan temple. The flames were near to the ground, and it was with a shock that she saw the figures they illuminated. She was not sure what she had expected the Miners to be, but it had not been this. They were small, about sixteen inches high, like dolls shaped to resemble children. They had sad, wise faces with a beauty and wistful symmetry; their skins were pale, almost as white as bisque porcelain, and their eyes were dark holes, with only the faintest hint of whites, like the eyes of apes. Annat rose slowly to her feet, gazing down at the crowd of tiny people, who held the slender torches grasped in their delicate hands. It was hard to tell the females from the males; they all wore similar garments, close-fitting tunics in pale hues, the colours of smoke, dust and sky. Some carried spears, but those at the front had drawn bows, and the bodkin-like arrows were aimed at Annat, Malchik and Derzu.

Annat hesitated to harm them in any way. She felt a slight horror at their paleness, which reminded her of the skin of dead fish. But it was the only unwholesome thing about their appearance; their drawn, sad faces evoked more pity than fear. She took a step forward, and at once a hundred small shafts were released like minnows into the light. Annat ducked, but one buried itself in her hand, and she doubled up, crying out as a fierce, excruciating pain twisted up her arm. She lashed out with her powers, but nothing came; her numbed hand throbbed, and she felt as if a net woven of thousands of fine threads bound her, beneath the skin, and staunched her power at its source.

A figure in long robes the colour of moths' wings stepped to the fore of the crowd. As she moved, the archers nocked new arrows to the strings of their bows. Racked with pain, tears streaming down her face, Annat lay on her side. The small visage was close to her own: expressionless, with neither pity nor rage. The woman had long, straight hair, dark as a mole's pelt. Annat felt her brother's hand squeeze her arm, as he bent over her.

'You are our prisoners,' said the woman. 'You will be taken to the place that has become our prison, and our realm. There we will decide your fate.'

They rode through the mist in silence. They had been in the saddle all day, and the paths grew ever steeper, and the trees crowded in. Huldis had watched the strip of sky overhead slowly dull and darken, only to vanish as the mist came down. They must be approaching the edge of the tree-line, where they would find themselves on the naked mountainside, but there was no sign of the forest thinning out. Instead, the horses moved up the track in single file, their harness ringing with a muffled echo like the sound of goat-bells on the high slopes.

Sarl rode at the head, astride his destrier, sitting upright and motionless in the saddle. Yuda had been bound hand and foot, and slung across the back. Behind them, Huldis rode in something of a daze, revisiting in her mind the scenes and events of the past hours. She could hear Semyon following at a distance behind her; sometimes his horse would stumble and she would hear him curse. She did not look back.

She hoped that they would make camp while they were still within the cover of the trees, rather than waiting until they had emerged into the open pastures. At least here firewood was plentiful and there was shelter. She had lost track of the time, but it was after dusk; they had been in the saddle all day, not pausing to eat, but only when one of them needed to answer the call of nature. Huldis longed to dismount, to stretch her limbs, and to change the clouts that she used to soak up her menstrual blood. Several times today she had suffered from cramps, and had remembered with longing the heat from Yuda's hand that had eased them last night. She thought with a touch of bitterness that women were like bitches, all heats and fluids and difficulty. No man suffered such troubles; though she had to admit, with a moment of humour, that Semyon seemed less hardy than others she had known. He had fallen from the saddle twice today, and she had been forced to rescue him from the undergrowth while Sarl sat astride his horse, watching with lordly indifference.

Yuda had been silent all day. He must ache in every joint, but Huldis thought he had absented himself, letting his mind wander freely though his body was bound. Certainly he lay as limp as a sack of grain across the shoulders of Sarl's steed, as if he had lost consciousness again. When they finally stopped for the night, Sarl lifted him down and slung him on the ground, where he lay motionless, his face like a shuttered window.

'All right for some,' Semyon grumbled, sliding down from his saddle and finishing with a groan. Like an ostler, Sarl took the bridles of the three horses and led them off into the mist, vanishing after a few paces. Semyon and Huldis looked at each other.

'We'd better light a fire,' she said.

He put the leather suitcase on the ground at his feet. He seemed to be pondering a reply, then he knelt down, snapped open the fastenings and reached inside. Huldis saw him lift out what looked like a handful of light. He lifted it carefully, spoke a few words and threw it to the ground, where at once it became a well-established fire, set on piles of good dry tinder and surrounded by stones. He pressed the case shut and left it where it lay, hurrying to warm his hands at the fire. Huldis was amused when he lifted the tail of his robe and offered his rear end to the heat of the flames. She followed him and sat down close to the embers.

'Don't forget our prisoner,' she said. Semyon made a face at her, but he went to the place where Sarl had dropped Vasilyevich and seized him by the feet, dragging him the few yards across the forest floor to let him get close to the fire.

'Does the spell still hold?' asked Huldis.

'He wouldn't be here if it didn't. He's one of the most powerful shamans I've come across. I don't know what he can't do. Well, presumably he can't fly.'

Huldis suppressed a laugh. Semyon gave her a look. 'Kaschai can fly. Kaschai the Deathless. And if we cross the pass tomorrow, we will be within his lands.'

'A flying wizard,' said Huldis. 'Somehow I think that's the least of our troubles.'

'The Staryetz will be expecting a report from me on the progress of my mission. I have no idea what to tell him.'

'Don't expect my sympathy, Magus. You chose to serve a mighty and exacting lord.'

'What a fool I was,' said Semyon, rubbing his hands together. 'I had such faith in my own abilities. It would be much simpler if it weren't for that . . . brother of yours.'

Huldis rested her chin on her hand. 'He has not killed you yet,' she said.

'There's a thing! I suppose one should be grateful for small mercies.'

Huldis laughed out loud, and a startled pigeon roosting in the branches overhead took flight with a flurry and clatter of wings. Semyon glanced at Yuda, who did not stir.

'What has he got that I haven't got?' he said, with feeling.

'What?'

'I've seen how you look at him. I'm not wholly ignorant of the ways of women.'

Huldis had no wish to share her private thoughts with him. She hoped that in the firelight he would not see her blush.

'You couldn't begin to imagine, Magus,' she said.

Semyon shrugged. 'I thought that we had an understanding. That we might at least be friends.'

'I prefer your company to that of my brother. At least you are alive, and human.'

'Thank you. That is indeed a tribute to my powers of seduction.'

Huldis smiled at him. 'My marriage is within my father's gift; he would never bestow it on you, far less an accursed Wanderer. My sister made her own choice; my father will not permit me the same luxury.'

'It's the same at the court of the Staryetz,' said the Magus. 'And doubtless I shall marry to improve my position, not for love.'

'But you will be permitted to love *par amours*, Magus; I must be a chaste and loyal wife.'

'Certainly whoever gets you for a spouse will be a fortunate fellow. The curse is that your noble father will doubtless marry you to some clod who is rich only in titles and lands.'

'I shall not wax rich on your pity, Magus. I was

raised to this life, and know what is expected of me.'

He leaned towards her and spoke in a low voice. 'But it doesn't have to be like that. You do have a choice; you could be any man's mistress. You have wit, beauty and intelligence; you are accomplished in many arts; and you would find no lack of suitors.'

'If I bade farewell to my honour, Magus.' She thought of the previous night, and sighed. 'Remember that I am only here because my brother is a chaperone; when you restore his life, he will take me back to Ademar with him.'

'I cannot believe that you are resigned to your fate. That there is not a spark within you that longs to rebel.'

'Look at the shaman, Magus. He goes to meet his fate unprotesting; who can say what are his innermost thoughts?'

Semyon settled back, and threw a twig on to the flames. Watching it catch fire and begin to shrivel, he said, 'Tonight would be our last chance. Once we cross into the empire of the Staryetz, we will be watched. There will be no escape for you or me – or the shaman.'

'How would we escape?' said Huldis. 'The mist goes barely an arm's length from our faces. You cannot ride, I cannot run and the shaman is unconscious. We would never escape my brother; and I do not wish to face his anger.'

'No indeed. But if there were a chance to run, it will slip away with every hour towards dawn.'

Huldis scarcely heard him. 'He is decaying, Magus,' she said. 'There is a place on his hand where the bone has broken through the skin.'

'That is not encouraging,' said Semyon. 'Once we cross the pass, it will be weeks before we reach the Glass Mountain. So we can anticipate the company of a slow-rotting corpse.' Seeing her face, he reached out to touch her hand. 'I am sorry. It was the fool talking. Perhaps I may yet think of a way to speed us there.'

Huldis smiled at him. 'You and I must fend for ourselves as best we can, Magus,' she said. 'As for the shaman, remember that he could have sacrificed your life to save his own, but he chose not to. That must count for something.'

Semyon withdrew his hand. 'More fool him,' he said.

A sound from beyond the firelight disturbed Huldis, making the hairs lift along the back of her neck. She held up her hand to require silence, and heard the same sound. It sounded as if someone had drawn a long note from a flute, or perhaps like a bird-call; but it was not a bird.

'What's that?'

'Wolf,' said Semyon.

Huldis recalled her dream. She glanced at Yuda, but he lay still, though his eyes twitched beneath their closed lids, as if he were dreaming. She stood up, shaking out her skirts.

'There's nothing to worry about,' said Semyon. 'Wolves don't attack humans.'

'I have to go *faire le pi-pi*,' said Huldis. She hurried away from the firelight; she did not have to go far before the fog had all but shut out its tawny colour. She squatted down behind a tree, and quickly put on

317

clean clouts; the stained ones she buried under leaves and earth.

The wolf sound came again. Still it made her skin-hairs prickle; she straightened and was startled to hear another wolf, answering from a different direction. The cry was eerie, because it had an almost human sound; not the mimicry of seagulls, but a noise like despair, or thwarted hunger. She hurried back to the fire, and by the time she reached it, wolves were calling from the trees on every side. Semyon stood up to meet her.

'Not the most cheerful noise,' he said.

It was difficult to talk or think against the background of the wolf-song. Sometimes there would be a gap, and Huldis would believe that they had finished their harmony; then one would howl again, and the others would answer in turn. In the mist, it was difficult to tell how close they were. The low-throated notes sounded much closer than those that were high and piercing. She hesitated to sit down; she stood with her back to the fire, staring out at the surrounding sheets of mist, and the shapes that they took as they slowly unfolded and drifted upwards.

'I don't think I shall sleep,' she said.

'It won't go on all night,' said Semyon. He strode to the place where he had left his suitcase and brought it back, placing it close to the fire and patting its side as if it were a tame animal.

Suddenly, Huldis saw a grey shape running between the trees. She tried to fix on it, but the mist had swallowed it up. It had been small, smaller than some of her father's hounds; moving like a fox with its head down. She wanted to turn back to the fire, but she dared not take her gaze away from the mist. If there were wolves that close, she wanted to see them; she did not like to think of them circling the fire while her back was turned.

In the same place, a gap between the pines, she saw another wolf. She saw the yellow flare of its eyes, like a cat's catching the light. Chill sank from her throat to her heart. The wolf did not glance, it paused and stared at her. Huldis knew that wild creatures were shy, shunning the presence of man and his dwellings. She had encountered creatures in the Forest of Ademar, and except for the raging wild boar, they would never stand their ground. She watched the wolf move out of the firelight, loping slowly. It was impossible to attribute emotion to such an animal; it had not snarled at her, but it had gazed at her with its close-set eyes, black-rimmed.

Huldis felt that the singing of the pack surrounded them, closing in as a ring of music. As she watched, she began to see a succession of bounding shapes, that circled the fire like the figures on a zoetrope. She and Semyon were at the centre of a spinning top rimmed by wolves.

'Magus,' she said; her voice sounded hoarse.

'What's the matter?'

She pointed to the edge of the small clearing, so that he too should see the ribbon of grey pelts, the lowered heads, the swift-moving clawed feet. Semyon watched by her side, and she heard him draw breath.

'Magus, what of my brother? He has no fire!'

'Let's look to ourselves,' said Semyon. He lifted a branch from the fire and hefted it in his hand as if it were a torch. 'They will not approach the flames.'

'Perhaps we should not wait to test that. Open your suitcase, Magus; use your magic.'

Her heart missed a beat and she pressed her hand to her breast. Amongst the grey fur, had she seen one that was black, and bigger than the rest? A beast darker than shadow, the colour of coal, which stood out from the others like a white crow amongst a swart flock.

'I should not use its powers lightly. Every spell that issues from there drains life from the world within. And I may need all its force to restore your brother.'

'By the Mother,' said Huldis, brushing a stray hair back from her face with a trembling hand. She found herself repeating childhood prayers in her thoughts, to Megalmayar and Her Son; and those other, forbidden incantations that called upon the twin goddesses, preservers of the Women.

'They will not trouble us,' said Semyon.

'Then what are they doing?'

As she spoke, the first of the wolves left the shelter of the trees and began to run within the ring, just where the firelight blushed into the mist. The others followed it, and soon they were all there, touched with gold, amongst them the single black male. By instinct, Huldis and Semyon drew close together as the beasts spiralled in towards them. Semyon put his arm round Huldis's shoulders, and she did not shake him off.

The black wolf paused, raised his long muzzle and

howled. The rest of the pack echoed him. It was as if he had given a signal; the wolves turned towards Huldis and Semyon and mobbed them. Some nipped at their legs, others jumped up and tugged at their clothing, trying to pull them down. Huldis could not stop herself from screaming. Semyon swung the torch, and where it came too close, it sent the wolves yelping away, snapping with their jaws; but others would take their place. Huldis scarcely noticed at first that they did not touch Yuda, though he lay prone on the ground.

'They are trying to pull us down. To reach our throats,' gasped Semyon. As he spoke, the black wolf threw itself against him. The torch was knocked from his hand, and he almost lost his footing.

'Yuda!' Huldis shouted. 'Wake up and help us!'

Semyon staggered upright and managed to push the black wolf off him. His hands were scratched and bleeding. The torch had rolled away and was out of his reach, smouldering on the ground. With wolves pawing at her, snapping at her ankles, Huldis dragged herself towards the place where Yuda lay. The black wolf was his wolf; it had come to his aid, and she had to wake him. He had rolled on to his side and seemed quite unconscious of the events taking place around him. As she reached him, the black animal barred her way. It bestrode Yuda, pulling back its lips to snarl at her. Its grey fellows buffeted her, and she found herself falling, and their feet trampling her as she fell.

There was a burst of brilliant light. Before she hit the ground, Huldis heard the sound of a thousand wings. The mist was shedding black feathers, a storm of crows, which beat down out of the sky, flurrying around the wolves. Huldis rolled over on to her face, covering her throat with her hands. Above her, she could hear the shrieking of the birds, and the roar of their beating wings. It was as if she lay on the deck of a ship caught in a gale; she felt as if the ground rocked beneath her. The feet of the wolves thudded against her back, but she dared not lift her face to see what they were doing. She could hear Semyon shouting, and she thought he was saying her brother's name. She struggled to lift herself, but she lay underneath a struggling mass, wolves fighting crows, the black blurred into the grey, like a thundercloud stirred with lightning.

A hand touched the small of her back. A human hand. Huldis turned on her belly, and glimpsed Yuda, half seen amidst the rain of birds. He reached out to her and snatched her hands, dragging to her feet. He was shouting, but he might as well have been mute. Then his words resounded inside her head.

– *The suitcase!*

– *What?*

Yuda pulled her after him. All around her were the beating wings, so thick overhead that they shut out the mist. The fire was trampled, and she saw the bodies of wolves on the ground, torn with wounds, their eyes pecked out. Yuda's hand closed on her wrist. She saw the suitcase lying on the ground, burst open, and the light pouring out of it.

– *What are you doing?*

– *Getting out of here!*

Huldis was not sure what happened next. Yuda put his arms round her and jumped. His grip was tight and not amorous; he almost crushed the breath out of her. Huldis found herself for a moment falling over the suitcase, and then she was standing inside it; but it had no bottom, and she was falling. Her hair swirled upwards as she plummeted into empty space. She yelled with all the force of her lungs, and she heard Yuda yelling beside her; they fell together, and there seemed to be no end to the descent.

Chapter 14

Yuste felt the shock of Boris's shot in her face and teeth. She saw a man fling up his arms and fall from the saddle of his rearing steed. Cluny and Planchet burst from their hiding place and made for the other riders, who were trying to calm their mounts. The horses screamed, shied, kicking the air, huge and wild.

— *Now*, thought Yuda. She ducked out into the open, and the metal hooves beat the sky above her, and she sensed the weight of the animals as they leapt and struck the ground, turning and colliding. There was a cry as a man's leg was crushed between two massive bodies. Yuste held her ground; Yuda held her. Dizzy with the smells and sounds, she found her arm creeping out, reaching for a handful of air. Suddenly the golden power began to uncoil inside her. Just as when someone blows on a fading fire with a bellows, and the flames spring to life out of the wood, so she felt from a dead furnace the cold suddenly kindled, and its heat warming and steadying her. Her arm became a weapon, like Boris's gun, and she felt its deadly strength as she took aim with her hand, and released the power that was pent up in her.

Lightning cracked, and a yellow flame tore the night open. A vivid, hot pain stung Yuste's fingers as the fire jumped from them; she recognised the joy and rage of letting it loose, and straightened, seeing it rip a jagged path between her and one of the wretched horses. The animal leapt and plunged, throwing its rider, and fell to the ground, collapsing like the wreck of a stone house, rolling on the ground and breaking its back. Tears stung Yuste's eyes, and she felt a rush of pity and anguish. The horse had brought down its rider, smashing him beneath its weight like matchwood. She knew that the others were fighting, but all she could see were the deaths she had caused, the animal and the human; their death agonies racked her, and she felt the spirits torn free and scattered into the night.

– *Zyon.* Yuda embraced her. Unseen, she still felt his wonder at her grief. – *It used to be like that for me. But you learn to shut it out.*

The surviving horsemen had ridden their steeds free of the chaos. She heard them shouting in Franj, confused orders.

'They have a shaman!'

Boris's gun cracked again, but this time its report seemed diminished, like a snapping twig.

'You deal with him, René.'

– *Careful. He means you,* Yuda muttered in her ear.

A man was urging his horse towards Yuste. She saw the silver rowels prick the horse's sides, striking out flecks of blood. Her brother, invisible, seemed to peer over her shoulder. Yuste reached back to touch his hand, but there was nothing there. Once again, the horse seemed to move slowly, leaping like a wave over the distance between them. The man was holding a sword, and Yuste studied the way it gleamed as the starlight quivered along the blade.

– Very pretty, but he's going to cut your head off.

Yuste crouched low, making herself small, like a plant or a rock. She balanced on the balls of her feet, and the horse reared high like a breaker surging for the beach. Just like this, she had waited on the sand, the sea caressing her bare feet, waiting for the surf to shatter over her head, plunging her deep in blue and boiling water. She looked up at the sky, but all she could see was the shadow of the prancing animal, black as anthracite. The man's paler face rose high above, like the moon. Yuste aimed for the space between the eyes. Her arm quivered as the power flowed down it, issuing from her fingers as stabbing fire. She saw the lightning branch from her fingertips and leap the space between, earthing itself in the rider's forehead. The horse reared at the report, and the man fell back, his skin blackened, his eyes burnt dry. Yuste shook to the core as the horse bounded past her, galloping into the night dragging a smouldering corpse from its stirrups.

She staggered to her feet. Planchet had pulled a man from his steed and split his skull; Cluny was parrying a sword with his own blade. The sound burst in her, the smash of metal like pots and pans being smacked together, the shouting, cursing, the horses' screaming. But though she had killed two men, and another had been hurt by the horses, there seemed to be more, riding in from the dark, fresh men, beasts that had not been frightened in the first attack, but were trained to endure the terror of battle.

– *There's a lot of 'em*, thought Yuda.

Yuste looked for Boris, but she could not see him. This time, instinct made her fire on the foremost horseman; there was none of the luxury of slowness in which time was divided into many parts. She was sucked into the midst of the whirlwind, and there were tall beasts all round her, and weapons cutting the air. There was no room to draw back and aim her powers; she was small, dwarfed by the curvetting steeds. A leather-shod foot kicked her arm, and the rump of an animal nudged her, knocking her down. Yuda took charge, making her roll over out of the reach of the stamping hooves, bringing up her arms to shield her head. She scrambled under the belly of a horse, turned and pointed her hand up at the startled rider.

The sword swung. Yuste felt something part in her shoulder, a sudden inrush of cold air, a warm ooze on her skin.

– *Fuck. We're wounded*, thought her brother. In the same moment, her unhurt arm came out and the lightning burst free, lifting her off her feet. She was like an angel, taking flight in a mandorla of glory; she poured golden fire into the dark, and the man in the saddle burst into flames like a straw dummy, fire and smoke pouring from the crown of his skull.

– *Steady on*, thought Yuda, but between the pain and the joy, Yuste had broken free. She felt no fear, only the exhilaration as the power travelled through her. She let it surge into the shadows that took the shapes of knight and charger; she obliterated them from her sight beneath a veil of burning gold. She could smell the charcoal and soot as the ground caught fire, the scent of roasting meat and melting fat. Still she let the sap pour out of her veins, an infinite stream that bore her up as if she were a flake of ash or an ember carried into the sky by the rising air.

Yuda brought her down. She could almost see his face, the black brows carved into a frown.

– *That's too much. Stop, Yustka; do you hear me?*

Yuste smiled hazily into the outlines of his features that she could make out, shadowy behind the rain of fiery particles.

– *We are gods, Yuda. We have the power of gods.*

She felt his anger in her throat, but before he could answer, she drifted to the ground, shutting him out, and everything else beyond; instead, the round pebble shapes of blackness floated in, covering her sight as they merged together.

Boris Grebenshikov had hardly been aware of Yuste since the fight began. He had been busy at the edges of the fray, running from place to place until he found a spot where he could stand and reload his gun. Then he would choose a target, take aim and fire, only to move again. He knew that he was no match for a knight in mail astride a destrier; he let Cluny and Planchet come to close quarters, for they had the right weapons and the training.

He first noticed what was happening when Yuste set the man on fire. She blasted him, and he stayed in the saddle, burning like a torched pine, while his steed bucked and reared, struggling to be free of the horror on its back. Distracted, Boris turned and saw, to his astonishment, not one but two figures; one that seemed all radiance, the other all shadow. As he watched, the shining shape spread out its arms and drenched the night with fire, so that the dry trees caught alight and the rock underfoot grew hot and cracked. Boris flung himself to the ground. He had seen this happen with untrained shamans; a kind of madness took hold, as they discovered what they were capable of. He had done it himself.

He felt the fire roar past, singeing the hairs on the back of his head. His trench coat caught fire and he rolled over, cursing, trying to douse the flames. Some of the horses galloped into the dark, too terrified for their riders to steady them; others rode for safety, outpacing the wall of fire as it diminished and began to diffuse. Boris sat up, beating out the small fires that had started in his clothes. The air was thick with smoke and its haze thickened overhead, clouding the starry sky; but he saw the two figures on the edge of this hell, the shadow that was Yuda and the fiery form that must be Yuste. As he watched, the shadow vanished, and the shining shape slowly grew dim, crumpling to the ground as if it had burnt up in the heat and turned to ash. Boris leapt up and ran across the smouldering ground to the place where Yuste had fallen. She lay on her side, curled up, and there were no marks on her, not even a trace of soot; but a rent in her tunic showed the new dark wound in her shoulder with its freight of blood. Boris bent down and gathered her into his arms; she was hot to the touch, and he saw the sweat beginning to form on her forehead. If he did not do what was needed, she would burn up in a massive fever brought on by the after-shock of her excesses.

The blood was pulsing in his head; he could hear a roaring in his ears. He saw Cluny staggering towards him, shouting something, but Boris was deafened by the sound inside him. He could see that the flames had marked the young man; there were soot stains on his face and his surcoat. Boris strode towards him, lifting Yuste, but Cluny stayed where he was and pointed at the sky.

Boris glanced upwards. At first he had no idea what he was looking at; he could make out what looked like the hull of a ship, but woven from wicker; a rope that dangled from the heavens, a thick rope like a hawser; and above it something huge that glowed, as if the moon had sunk low to float near the ground, a moon with an axis of fire. Then Boris understood that the roaring sound was not in his own ears; what he could hear was the engine of the ship overhead. A flying ship: the round moon overhead was its envelope, filled with air, and he was near deafened by the throb of its engines.

He gaped at Cluny. The dirigible was hovering above them, and its occupants had let down a rope, inviting them to ascend. The captain must have seen the fires on the ground below. Boris did not linger to consider whether its crew might be friendly; he seized the dangling rope and began to climb, clutching Yuste against him with one arm. Cluny caught the end of the rope and held it steady, making it easier for him to keep a hold on the plaited cable. Boris, with only one hand free, used his feet to grip the rope. Sweat began to pour from his forehead. Yuste was a light burden, but it was all he could do to move upwards without losing his hold.

Glancing down, he saw the uplifted faces of Cluny and Planchet, who had come to join his master. He could see their fear; to them this must seem like an infernal engine descended from the heavens. Beneath their feet, the ground had turned black; he saw the charred skeletons of men and horses sprawled where they had fallen. He could feel the heat that radiated from Yuste's form, and he clenched his teeth and tried to move more quickly, though there was always a moment when he had to let go the rope to reach higher, anchored only by his feet.

Someone was leaning over the side of the ship. Boris could see the man's lips moving, but he could not hear a word. He went on climbing, the palm of his hand abraded by the rope. If only Yuste were awake, she might cling on to him, and then he could climb hand over hand! Even though Cluny was holding the end of the rope, it still swung to and fro. At last he reached the side of the gondola, and the hardest part was the last. He nearly lost his hold and fell when the man in the dirigible leaned over the edge to take Yuste from him. As the stranger lifted her over the edge, Boris seized the rope in both hands and hauled himself up the last few feet, using his feet to fend off the side of the ship. He slumped over the edge without waiting to see whether Cluny and Planchet had started to follow him.

Yuste was lying slumped on the planking floor. Boris realised as he crawled towards her that there was only one person on board the craft, the man who had tried to help him climb. He was again leaning over the side, shouting encouragement that was drowned out by the noise of the engine. Boris paused and blinked. He had never seen such a small steam engine; four tubular tanks about the size of oil drums surrounded it. He had no idea what sort of metal had been used to build it, but few of the parts looked like steel, apart from the boiler. Boris could see the pistons working urgently, but the gears had been disengaged; they were not turning the crankshaft that spun the screw at the rear of the ship.

Boris glanced up at the envelope. He could not tell whether it was filled with gas, or simply heated air. The floor was moving underneath him, a disconcerting sensation, but he bent over Yuste and lifted her up.

Somebody bellowed in his ear. Boris started and found himself looking into the owner's face. The young man had a fine, dark handlebar moustache, brown eyes and a pale face with rosy cheeks.

'Good day to you,' he shouted. 'Ignatius Brunelleschi, captain of the *Arabian Bird*, at your service. I see you've got a shaman there. Looks like she's burnt out.'

'I'm going to heal her,' Boris replied, though he could hardly hear his own voice.

'Are those your fellows on the ground? I hope so, they've started to climb up.'

'They are my fellows,' said Boris. 'But they've never seen an airship before. Be gentle with them.'

'I say, are you a shaman too? I've never seen two before.'

'Not a very powerful shaman,' said Boris. He cupped his hands under Yuste's chin, feeling the heat in her throat. He did not like healing, any more than he liked using his other powers; they always seemed too showy.

The man squatted down beside him. He seemed to be leaving Cluny and Planchet to make the climb as best they could.

'We only have one shaman in Dieulevaut,' he said. 'Le Docteur Ashmedai, and he's quite mad. Harmless, though. He's a Wanderer.'

Boris was beginning to feel irritated. He wished the man would leave him in peace; he did not want to perform a healing with an audience. 'Do you have a problem with that?' he snapped.

'Not at all,' said Ignatius. 'Although I have to say that Ashmedai has gone over to the enemy.'

'You mean he's become a Doxan?' said Boris. He searched inside himself for his dormant powers, and thought of cold. He would have to draw some of the heat from Yuste into his own body; that would help to diffuse it.

'No, he's made a pact with the Devil. So he says. Quite mad, but he's the only shaman we have, so we have to put up with his little quirks.'

There was a thud, and the gondola rocked as Cluny jumped over the side. He stared at the engine and pressed himself back against the side, then turned to peer over the edge.

'How did you see us?'

'I couldn't miss the fire. I was on my way home, so I decided to stop and investigate. You're not far from Dieulevaut, you know. You looked as though you could use some help. Who were all those men on horseback?'

'Soldiers that were chasing us. I think she finished with them,' he added, jerking his head towards Yuste.

'You mean all that was her? She's very small,' said Ignatius.

'Shamans tend to be small.' Boris wiped his forehead on his sleeve. He was starting to feel hot. He tried to think of ice floes, of chilled water and the depths of the sea. Yuste's pulse was racing and he could see the drops of perspiration running down her face. 'Have you got any water on this barge?' he said.

'Not much, I regret to say. We travel light.'

'Bring me what you've got. It'll have to do.'

Ignatius snapped off a salute, and sprang to his feet. Boris glimpsed him pausing to exchange a few words with Cluny, who gave him a sickly grin.

'Come on, Yuste,' Boris muttered. Her head was resting on his knees, and he could feel the sweat from her soaking into his trousers. The power of a shaman tended to be heat-based, and it was not easy to use it for cooling. He remembered the training as a kind of mathematical formula, which had to be written out inside his head. Now that Ignatius had left him for a while, it was easier to concentrate. He realised that the tips of his fingers had gone numb, and his hands were white. The cold had begun to take effect. Boris shut his eyes and visualised it slipping from the ends of his fingers, coiling down through Yuste's skin to cool her overheated blood.

Fever. It travelled up his arms, a burning heat that threatened to overwhelm him. He must remember to keep himself cold. His mouth was dry, and he licked his lips. He was nearly pleased to see Ignatius when the captain returned with a small pewter flask. Boris took it from him without thanks, unscrewed the cap, and held the neck of the flask to Yuste's lips. He had to squeeze her mouth open to pour in a few drops; then he tossed back his head and drank the rest.

Planchet was clambering over the side. He landed square on his feet and looked about him with a suspicious air. He seemed less frightened than Cluny; perhaps he understood too little of modern technology to be troubled by it. Ignatius gestured towards them.

'If that's everyone, I shall head back for Dieulevaut, Monsieur.'

'Whatever you want,' said Boris, who was not listening. Ignatius did not seem offended; he nodded and took his place at the tiller, where he put the motor into gear with a long, slender lever. The engine took on a new note, and the ship juddered and began to move. Boris glimpsed Cluny sliding down the side to sit on the floor; Planchet busied himself hauling in the rope. In his coat of mail, he looked as outlandish as the steam-powered flying vessel must seem to him.

Boris forced himself to concentrate. He drew his hand across Yuste's sticky forehead, and wondered why it would hurt him so much if she slipped away, leaving an empty husk. Her skin was smooth, but he could feel the lines that age and worry had made on her brow. Her hair was damp to the touch. Boris called to her, as he had done when they were making their scan and he had lost her. He felt the same sense of helplessness; every time it would be Yuda, her marvellous brother, who healed her or rescued her or brought her back. But Yuda was not here; he had vanished just when he should have been able to hold Yuste back; he had failed. Boris was shocked to realise how much this pleased him. He stared at the woman's sallow face; in the light from the smoke-box it looked pinched and unattractive. He cupped her head in his hands, trying to steady the flow of cold into her skull. It seemed to him that she might be a little cooler.

Suddenly Cluny was crouching beside him. He looked almost as pale as Yuste; the rocking motion of the craft must be making him sick.

'How is she, Boris?' he said.

Boris grimaced at him. Not sure what to tell the young man, he said, 'We could still lose her. I haven't dealt with this kind of problem before; only suffered from it myself.'

'You?' Cluny raised his eyebrows.

'It can happen to inexperienced shamans. And . . . have you ever wondered why you so seldom meet an old shaman?'

'I've met so few . . .' Cluny trailed off.

'We burn out. The human body hasn't evolved far enough to contain these powers.'

'What does evolved mean?'

Boris stared at Yuste's face once more. 'It's like growing up,' he said. He lifted Yuste up and felt her wrists, then laid her on the deck and bent down to listen to her heart. 'I don't think I can do much more,' he said. 'We'll just have to wait and see.'

'Then she could die?'

Boris nodded. 'The trouble is, her brother opened her up to powers like his own. He's had time to grow used to them. She hasn't. Stuff like that – it beats any high you can imagine, Ganasha, wine, sex . . . but when you use those powers to kill, there's a price. Always. It's not like picking up a gun – or a sword – to kill a man. It comes from inside you, and inside is where it hurts.'

Cluny hugged himself, and pulled his cloak round him. The air was much colder up here; Boris felt it as he stood up, still burning with the remnants of Yuste's fever. He sneezed.

'Bless you,' said Ignatius. Cluny glanced at him circumspectly.

'Where will this . . . ship take us?' he said to Boris.

'I think we're heading for Dieulevaut.'

'"God wills it". That's a strange name for a town,' said Cluny.

Boris sucked a good lungful of air into his chest. He felt well; if killing had a bad aftermath, healing was often rejuvenating.

'She'd better get well,' he said. 'Now we've got just the thing to carry us to the Glass Mountain.'

The Miners bound Annat and Malchik with ropes that were as slender as cotton, but strong as hawsers. Annat imagined how a fly must feel when a spider injects it with poison and wraps it in silk. Within, the nets of magic bound her powers, while outwardly her arms and legs were pinioned, bound to her sides so that she resembled a baby in swaddling clothes.

The Miners worked swiftly and steadily; they never looked at her face or tried to meet her eyes. They dealt with her as a butcher handles a great carcass, uninterested that it had ever been alive. Annat lay still, bovine and passive, watching the flutter of their tiny hands. The people were about the same size as a newborn baby, but they were completely adult and perfect. Their voices were not high-pitched, but whispering like the wind on an uneasy day when it stirs the cracks in a wooden house.

When they had bound her to their satisfaction, a team of workmen hoisted Annat on to their shoulders and set off at a trot. She could tell that they were used to manhandling large objects designed for this world in which they were the size of easy prey to everything from a weasel to an owl. They carried her from Derzu's chamber into a tunnel like the ones that she and Malchik had traversed; she did not see what became of the old shaman. She was lying on her back, staring up at the ceiling, but the light from the Miners' torches did not reach high enough, and she received only a dim impression of black vaults.

It took a team of about thirty men to shift her. Annat was impressed at the speed and sureness with which they kept moving; if they had let her go, her weight could easily have crushed them. She wondered how Malchik was faring; she could not lift her head to see who was following. The whole tunnel reverberated with whispers and the patter of the Miners' steel-shod boots. Sometimes she would glimpse figures running alongside her, either the soldiers hefting their slender spears and bodkin arrows, or women in rustling robes who came to peer at her, their black eyes rounded with awe.

Annat wished, as she often did, that she could *sprechen* with Malchik. She knew that they were bringing him after her; it took a much larger team to handle his tall frame. She could not keep her thoughts from straying, unable to dwell on their present plight. She did not know where the Miners were taking her, or what they planned to do to her. Instead, her mind was busy turning over what Malchik had just told her: that he had a lover, and had chosen Doxa to please her.

Annat was unsure which fact troubled her more. She had grown accustomed to Malchik's familiar, slightly shambling presence; she could not imagine him sharing the feelings of passion that shook her when she was with Eugenie. After all, she was the one who had inherited a portion of Yuda's looks and temperament. Malchik had always favoured their mother or Yuste, who had never lain with either man or woman. In spite of their immediate dangers, it was the ordinary future that seemed to have caved in like a ruined city whose familiar skyline had lost its landmarks. She had assumed that Malchik would stay the same; she had envisaged him living in Masalyar, sharing a house with her and their aunt, as part of the same cosy family in which she had grown up.

The absurdity of her thoughts was suddenly borne in upon her. Here she was, deep inside the mountain, being carried to an unknown destination by her small but grim captors. She forced herself to relax, and it was easy to do so within the cocoon of threads they had woven about her. Only her head and feet emerged from either end of the bundle, and her hair trailed on the ground beneath.

While she was thinking, they had left the tunnels built to accommodate those of human height, and entered a much smaller warren. The roof of the passageway hung a few inches above Annat's face, and from time to time she feared that she would graze the tip of her nose on the ceiling. Still the Miners did not slow their pace; she noticed that the tunnel had begun to slope downwards, so that often her feet were higher than her head. To her surprise, the band of men who carried her began to sing a work song; it had a warlike note, as if they were celebrating the outcome of a successful raid. Their voices were like the notes of a flute or a reed pipe; they echoed in the rounded tunnel, mingling with the patter of their footsteps and the continual susurrus of voices.

Suddenly, shrill trumpets rang out. A draught of warm air coursed over Annat's face and her ears popped as she emerged from the tunnel, borne into the midst of a vast, cavernous space that she could not imagine the Miners constructing without centuries of effort. The vaults overhead rose in tiers of crystalline splendour, catching the light like a waterfall; the light itself came from a bank of shafts set into one wall, where they had quarried deep into the mountainside to make portholes to the outer air. From each shaft, a beam of sunlight pierced the darkness, cutting across it to strike the walls of frozen crystal. Annat gazed at this sight as she was carried into the midst of the hall, almost oblivious to the crowds that swirled round her, pointing and whispering in their reed-like voices.

She was set down on the ground at the foot of a shallow dais, and Malchik was placed beside her. As he turned his head towards her, the woman who had ordered them to be brought here mounted the dais, holding up a lump of quartz that caught the light, fragmenting it and sending it spinning in many directions. 'Behold the Prism,' she said in a soft, clear voice, and a torrent of words echoed hers. She turned to approach a throne set at the rear of the dais, but she did not sit down upon it; instead, she placed the crystal on the seat and genuflected to it, as if it were an altar. Then she returned to the edge of the dais and addressed the unseen crowd whose presence Annat could only sense through her hearing.

'Beloved, we have won a victory,' she said. 'At last, we have captured two of the monsters who ventured too deep into the mountain. It is time to prepare for our journey home!'

'What have they done with Derzu?' Annat whispered, but a series of sharp pinpricks reminded her of her guards. She could not see her brother's expression; the light reflected from the lenses of his spectacles obscured his eyes.

The woman, who must be the Miners' queen, was gazing down at them. Her features suggested feelings of repugnance and fascination. 'Beloved,' she said, 'these monsters look like us, though they are greater in size than is natural. The Prism has told me how we can use them to free our world and return there, to live again amongst our friends and families.'

Annat heard something like a sigh from the people assembled in the hall. It was difficult to think of them as anything other than human, especially when she could not see them. She was unnerved when the Queen stepped down from the dais and moved to stand beside her head, close to her left eye.

'To save our world, we must restore the power that has been taken from it, wasted by impure magic,' said the Queen. It was almost as if she were confiding in Annat. Her expression seemed to suggest something like compassion. She held out her hand, and one of the guards put a sword into it; it glinted like a needle.

'Our lives are small, tiny lights, and it takes many

of us to make one spell, draining us of life and happiness,' said the Queen. 'But these great creatures have souls as big as continents. If we can draw them out, we will use the Prism to convey us back into the light.'

Then, before Annat could blink, she drove the needle into her left eye, and there was nothing in the world but pain, darkness and blood.

Though they seemed to have fallen for miles, there was only a slight impact as they landed on a small, hard world. Still Huldis felt that she had shattered every bone in her body. The breath had been smacked out of her and she lay on her back gasping, staring up at the unexpected sky. It was curved, and she wondered whether it felt like this to inhabit a fishbowl.

'Zyon,' said Yuda, and was seized with a fit of coughing. Huldis was afraid to move. She did not know where they were, except that they had fallen through the suitcase and arrived in a place that was not the one they had left. She could see the horizon without raising her head; it was much nearer.

'Where are we, Yuda?' she asked.

He sat up, and groaned. Then he said, 'What unexpectedly small trees.'

Huldis had to raise herself. She saw what he meant at once. They seemed to have landed in an ornamental garden, but one in which the trees – if they were trees – seemed to be about two feet high. They had trunks, and spreading branches, and leaves; but the leaves were dark, almost red. Yuda stretched out his hand, picked one and sniffed it.

'They could be bushes,' she said.

'Look at the trunks.' He lifted up a handful of branches, and Huldis saw what he meant; the bole of the tree he had revealed was thick with knots, stout with age. A miniature tree that had been there hundreds of years, like an oak. She let her fingers trail across the green sward, and the grass was a soft nap, barely distinguishable to the pads of her fingertips. Surrounding the garden was a wall, made from pieces of stone piled up and mortared together; it was about a span high.

'Small world,' said Yuda, grinning. As he spoke, a flock of birds passed between their faces: blue-feathered creatures no larger than bees. Yuda caught one in his palm and showed it to her, careful not to harm its delicate wings; it beat against his fingers and he quickly released it, watching it spiral after its fellows.

'Is this what Semyon keeps in his suitcase?' she asked, aware that this sounded absurd.

'He draws on it for his magic.' Yuda reached up to touch a cloud. 'I wonder whether this planet has any moons?'

'But Yuda – we are giants!'

'Not me. Not in any world.' He stood up and the upper part of his body disappeared above the cloud layer; Huldis heard him chuckle. She rose slowly to her feet, passing through the thick vapour, which proceeded to rain on her dress. Above the clouds was deeper blue, but they shut out the prospect of the world below.

'What will happen to Semyon – and my brother?'

'They'll follow us, no doubt.'

'Your wolves attacked us while you were asleep.'

'Sorry,' said Yuda. He looked around. 'I hesitate to leave this place in case we break something. But I do wonder how we get out of here.'

They both stooped and sat down again on the lawn, where their falling bodies had made an impression in the ground. They had smashed an ornamental fountain to dust, and a few flowerbeds looked like coloured pigments ground into the soil.

'Yuda, what did Sarl do to you?'

Yuda looked at his hand, where he had held the bird. 'He tortured me. And . . . things.'

'What do you mean?'

'Maybe there are some things it's better you don't know.'

'Tell me! We are friends.'

'I'll remember to punch more people in the nose.' He smiled. 'Your brother is a man who loves only men, but he can't admit it. It's against his faith, his training, his pride. More particularly, he desired me. But he couldn't have what he wanted, so instead he needed to hurt me. I don't think it has made him very happy.'

'I don't understand. My brother had a wife.'

'He's a shaman. All shamans love men and women, though most prefer one kind to the other. I think your brother saw me – saw my freedom – and envied it. But also, it gives him pleasure to cause pain. He used to beat his wife.'

'He was never like that when I knew him.'

'Maybe not. But he called on the Cold Goddess, and she found him fertile ground. She takes what is already inside you and makes it grow. Sarl had a harsh upbringing from your father; you only need to visit Ademar to see that.'

'But he asked you to forgive him!'

Yuda prodded the remains of the fountain. 'He's still caught up in it. Maybe I am too; maybe we were made for each other. I wanted someone to hurt me.'

'That's horrible!'

Yuda took her hand. 'You're still young, and you don't have darkness inside you,' he said. 'Remember Aude? You were friends. Then the Cold One stole you away, and Aude never recovered. So she came to me.'

Huldis hid her face in her hands. 'It was all my fault,' she said.

Yuda took her chin in his hand and lifted her head. 'Why?' he said. 'You can't blame yourself for what goddesses do. They're not like us. Whatever happened, it hasn't marked you. Or you wouldn't have tried to help me. Now we've got to make sure Sarl doesn't get his life back. We've got to try.'

'Perhaps if he and Semyon can't follow us . . .'

Yuda glanced up at the sky, with such a look of mock terror that she had to laugh.

'Zyon, I hope they don't fall on us.'

'Perhaps we should move.'

'I don't think we should go anywhere. This world is inhabited; somebody made this garden and planted these trees. I think we'd better wait for them to find us.'

They did not have to wait. Almost as soon as Yuda had spoken, they heard a hunting horn being winded, shrill and clear. Then, with yelping not much deeper than the squeaking of mice, a pack of hounds bounded into the garden and ran round Yuda and Huldis, leaping up and snapping at them with tiny jaws. Behind them came the hunters, a group of men astride miniature horses. The horses were caparisoned in yellow and red, and the men wore doublets of bright fabrics and particoloured hose. In their bonnets were set the feathers of the blue birds. The foremost was a tall, thickset fellow with long yellow hair, astride a white stallion; Huldis could have knocked them flying with her hand.

An older man, a brown-robed counsellor on a dun mare, urged his mount forwards to rein in beside the leader.

'What think you of this enterprise we have in hand, Your Majesty?' he said.

'Meseemeth these are the two giants that we saw falling out of the sky,' said the King. Yuda and Huldis both lay down on their stomachs so that they could look the riders in the eye. The King stared back fearlessly. 'What chance has brought you to venture upon our world, strange ones? Do you mean us weal or woe?'

Yuda stretched out the tip of his finger so that the hounds could sniff it. 'Your world is too small for us to live in, sire,' he said. 'We are seeking a way to return to our own world, and one place in particular: the Glass Mountain.'

Huldis could tell at once from the silence that followed that Yuda had said the wrong thing. The King's face was grim. He turned to his counsellor.

'What say you, Stanislaus? Shall we slay these monsters?'

Yuda's reaction was not what Huldis expected. He started to smile, and then began to speak in a language that Huldis did not understand, though it sounded not unlike the Sklavan he had used when addressing Semyon. The King gazed up at him in astonishment.

'By my faith,' he said in the Franj that, until now, she had not been surprised to hear him speak. 'Is it possible that on the world of the giants there are others bound into the service of the Emperor? What is your name, fellow?'

'Vasilyevich,' said Yuda, and a shocked pause was followed by ringing laughter.

'Behold a wonder, sire,' said the counsellor. 'I believe this enterprise will bring you good sport, and perhaps great joy. Is it not an omen that not only do these creatures seek the Glass Mountain, but that also one of them shares your royal name?'

The King edged his horse nearer to Yuda's face, though it danced uneasily and laid back its ears. 'I can tell by your accents that you are from Byela Rossiyar, and not from our lands, stranger,' he said. 'But you know our tongue as if you had learnt it from your cradle – though it must have been a monstrous nurse that dandled you! And with you, you bring this fair giantess, in shape and form most like a goddess. Is she your beloved spouse?'

Yuda glanced at Huldis, and they shared a smile. 'No, sire, but she is my companion in this adventure,' said Yuda. 'And I must admit that I too am surprised to find your world so similar to ours. The land you call Byela Rossiyar, we call Sklava, but the difference is not so great that I cannot tell what you mean. And you must be the King of the Cesky.'

The royal horseman doffed his hat. 'I am Yaroslav, third of that name,' he said, proudly. 'But you must know that we and our world are prisoners, and a great evil has befallen us, greater than any the empire could permit.'

'I know all about that,' said Yuda. 'For my friend and I came here by entering the very . . . receptacle in which you are trapped. And we may yet be followed by the magus to whom it belongs, and who has used it for his magics.'

'Are you fleeing from this magus, giant? Is he also your enemy?'

'He is planning a great spell that will draw the last drop of power from this world, and leave it barren.'

The King restored his bonnet to his head. 'Then you must come with us to our summer residence, the Palace of Zlonice,' he said. 'There we will entertain you as well as creatures little as ourselves are able. And we will discuss how it may be that the Magus can be resisted, and his spells reversed.'

Chapter 15

Yuste opened her eyes. She felt queasy and light-headed, and the ground seemed to shift beneath her. When she tried to sit up, her head swam, and she sank back, shutting her eyes once more. There was a loud noise close by, a complex beat that reminded her of a steam locomotive. She put her hands to her temples, wondering whether she had drunk too much *schnapps*.

Another hand, whose touch was not her own, came to rest on her forehead. Yuste let her arms drop to her sides, as the delicious cool of healing slid into her skull, soothing the taut veins. Deep inside, her new power coiled like a golden snake, replete from its first meal.

Yuste sat bolt upright, pushing the hand aside. 'Zyon! What have I done?'

Boris was sitting beside her. His face was stained with soot, and his trench coat was singed. 'You tried to sear the world, Missis,' he said.

Yuste seized his sleeve. 'Those men — what became of them?'

'They burned right up. Most of them. I imagine some got away.'

'Boris, I killed them. I destroyed them.'

He took her hand in his. 'Now you know why I only use my gun,' he said. 'I did the same thing once. Ever since, I've tried to keep my powers on a short leash. I know how seductive they can be. Too much of even the sweetest wine can leave a bitter aftertaste. But to look at it another way, you saved our lives. We were well outnumbered.'

'Yuda was with me, guiding me,' said Yuste. 'But I lost him. He disappeared.'

'I think you blew him out,' said Boris. 'You set up a firestorm, and not even Yuda could have stopped you. It's my fault; I should have realised what would happen.'

Yuste narrowed her mouth. 'Why blame yourself, Boris Andreyevich?' she said. 'I must take responsibility for this, and deal with it myself. Later. First, you must tell me where we are, and what this . . . extraordinary conveyance is.'

Boris stood up. 'Welcome aboard,' he said, stretching out his arms. 'This is the *Arabian Bird*, and we're about half an hour out from Dieulevaut.'

Yuste picked herself up slowly. She still felt a little dizzy. She looked up at the envelope overhead, which swung to and fro in the breeze. It was shaped like a giant teardrop, but what startled her was its beauty; like a Mardi Gras lantern, it glowed orange and golden against the night sky. Around it, like folded wings, great sails hung limp.

'Is this a dirigible?' she said, heading towards the side. Boris pulled her back.

'It's not a good idea to look over when you've been suffering from vertigo,' he said.

'Where are Cluny and Planchet?'

Boris led her fore, gripping her hand in his. There was something proprietorial about his grasp, and Yuste did not try to withdraw her fingers. They found Cluny and Planchet sheltering in the lee of the forecastle, where they could watch the approaching mountain range.

'Are those the Lepas Mountains?' said Yuste.

The range stretched before them, looking like folds of crumpled leather. Above it, the eastern sky had begun to change; the stars were dissolving as it grew in brightness. Cluny stood up, took her free hand and bent to kiss it.

'I am heartily glad to see my lady restored to health,' he said, and broke into a laugh at his own formality.

Planchet rose stiffly, rubbing his knees. 'I never dreamed to see anything like that, Madame,' he said.

'I hope you never see it again, Planchet,' said Yuste. She drew her hand from Boris's and walked to the prow. 'I think I see Dieulevaut,' she said.

The sky had turned a salty green. Under its light, the mountains began to flare up, catching fire along their peaks. Out of the mist, a city took shape, which seemed to rise on a cloud of steam, throwing bright towers into the air. Around its base, airships were tethered in flocks, bobbing together like boats moored round a harbour. The pale globes of their envelopes cast a rim of bubbles around the stone roots of the city where it clung to the mountainside.

Cluny and Boris came to stand beside her, and Boris lit a cigar. They could feel how cold the air was against their faces, but it was a vital cold, awakening rather than chilling their senses. Boris put his arm around Yuste's shoulders, and she renounced the moment of anger she felt at his presumption, and leaned against him, wondering what had changed between them. Something important had altered; it would take more time than she possessed to work out what it was.

'I'm glad you're awake to see this,' said Boris. 'It'd be a shame to miss it.'

The green of the sky had lightened to a pale and brilliant yellow. The walls of the city too changed colour, and grew in definition as the ship approached. Before, the towers had been a sober twilight grey, their roofs a dull red. As the sun cleared the mountaintops, it pushed back the shadows. The highest pinnacles changed first: light glanced from the golden weather-vanes, and the clay tiles began to glow in shades of red ochre, burnt umber, terracotta and pink. As the shadow crept down the walls, it uncovered blocks of sandstone that had weathered from a pale fawn to a rich, opaque honey colour. The glass in many long and narrow windows flashed, and the light revealed the different hues of the drawn shutters on the lower storeys.

As the *Arabian Bird* turned and moved slowly alongside the rows of moored dirigibles, Yuste could see that each was made fast to its own jetty, a sturdy platform suspended over the void. The captain steered the craft past these smaller vessels until he brought it broadside on to a wider mooring. The ship's engine changed its note as they bobbed slowly in, nudging against the side of the wooden platform. At once, two men emerged from a door in the wall of the city and came running down to the end of the jetty. One leapt aboard and seized a rope from the deck, which he cast to the other who had remained on the landward side. The second man made the rope fast to a stanchion, and at a signal, the captain turned off the engine, with a grinding of levers and a rush of steam.

'Looks like we've arrived,' said Boris, sucking on his cigar. They watched Captain Ignatius describing their arrival to the newcomer, using theatrical gestures. He showed no sign of tiredness, though he must have been up all night. When he noticed them watching, he beckoned them, grinning beneath his moustache. Still shaky on her feet, Yuste was glad to lean on Boris as they crossed the unstable deck.

The second man was a dark-skinned Franj. He gave them a bow from the waist, announcing '*Bienvenue à Dieulevaut,*' as they arrived.

'You must come back to my house,' said Ignatius. 'Though there are plenty of inns and hostels and so forth, I'm longing to hear your story, and my household is accustomed to providing for unexpected guests – though I imagine they may be rather fed up with me bringing strangers home all the time. But if I may boast, we do make the best breakfast west of the mountains. The Franj know nothing about breakfast, and the Sklavs hardly seem to bother.'

'We have no money,' said Yuste. 'We lost all our belongings in the attack. And it is not right that we should impose on your hospitality.'

'I don't want your money,' said Ignatius. 'I would be honoured to share your company, if only for a short time.'

'As it happens, I do have some cash about my person,' said Boris.

'And Planchet carries my purse,' said Cluny. 'We must pay our way.'

'I am very glad to hear it,' said Ignatius. 'But as Monsieur Crespin here will testify, I am a wealthy man and one who has many acquaintances.'

Crespin lifted his hands in a gesture that signified humorous despair, and raised his eyes to heaven. 'You must believe Monsieur,' he said. 'His hospitality is famous amongst travellers who pass through Dieu-levaut. Many return for the sole purpose of visiting him and enjoying the services of his chef. You may find yourselves disinclined to travel further.'

After some further argument, Yuste was persuaded to accept the offer of at least the chance to breakfast with Ignatius. They left the two landsmen to make the dirigible secure and attend to its engine, and followed their host through the narrow gate that gave entrance to the city.

Beyond the door, they might have stepped into the bottom of a well. The sky above was faultlessly blue, and they could see, far above, the rooftops burning in the sunshine; but down at street level, the cobbles still gleamed after the night's cold dew, and a chill shadow filled the street. The city seemed to be wakening: shutters were flung open as they passed, and curtains drawn; they saw the arms of unseen women reaching out to draw their washing on lines across the street, high above; there was a smell of baking bread that made Yuste at once homesick for Masalyar, and the sound of iron-shod feet clattering on the cobbled streets, though there was no one else in view ahead of them.

It became quickly apparent that the city was like a warren. Ignatius took a turn to the left, and led them through a passageway into a narrower street, where Yuste could reach out to touch the walls on either side. These houses were faced with dun-coloured plaster, but there were the same displays of brightly coloured washing overhead, and quilts had been hung out of windows to let them air. Once or twice, as they passed, someone would call a greeting down to Ignatius, seldom more than *'Bonjour, M'sieur Brunelleschi. Ça va?'* Ignatius would pause to return the salutation, but he seemed intent upon returning to his house.

After they had left the narrow street, he turned right into a ramped stairway that curled to the right. Here, the houses seemed shorter, though in fact the road was merely higher up; when they passed a gap between the buildings, Yuste glimpsed another road crossing below. These dwellings caught more of the sun, and several possessed roof terraces stocked with terracotta pots and a number of succulents, even the occasional palm. Ignatius walked even faster, and they found it hard to keep pace with him. When he realised that they were falling behind, he stopped and waited for them, curling the end of his moustache.

His own house proved to be at the end of the incline, where the street ended in a cul-de-sac. A round tower jutted up from the cobbles, and Ignatius unlocked the front door with a substantial key, flung it open and shouted into the interior, *'Beatrice! On a du monde!'*

He did not go in, but waited for them to join him. During that time, a short, blonde woman wearing a long white apron over her dress came to the door. She had the same fair skin and rosy cheeks as Ignatius, and Yuste wondered what land they hailed from.

'This is my sister, Mademoiselle Brunelleschi,' Ignatius announced as they reached the door. The young woman bobbed a curtsey; her eyes were wide as she looked at Cluny and Planchet – not to mention Yuste – in their tunics and chain-mail.

'You are very welcome, Messieurs et Madame,' she said. 'Has Ignatius invited you to stay for a fortnight, or simply for breakfast?' This might have sounded rude had she not accompanied it with a smile that suggested she was mocking her brother, not his guests.

'We will not impose on you, Mademoiselle,' said Yuste. 'Your brother insisted we accompany him; he would not be denied.'

'Nonsense,' said Beatrice. 'This is a large household, and we are always prepared for visitors. Especially since Ignatius likes to bring so many with him.' She laughed. 'If you would come with me, Madame, I will bring you to a place where you may refresh yourself, while my brother looks to the gentlemen.'

Boris gave Yuste a little pat on the small of her back, and thus fortified, she stepped over the threshold. Inside, a spiral stair led up the inside of the tower, and a wide passageway gave entrance to the body of the house; sunlight washed in from an unshuttered window on the far side. Beatrice began to mount the stair, pausing for Yuste to follow her, and as she climbed, she began to talk.

'You must excuse my brother, Madame; we are islanders, and hospitality does not come naturally to us, but since Ignatius became captain of the *Arabian Bird*, he has taken to bringing home anyone that he picks up on the last run of the day. I take it that being a Wanderer, you will not be eating bacon?'

This sudden question caused Yuste to stop on the stair. 'I should not be wearing these colours,' she said.

Beatrice turned to look down at her. 'Dieulevaut is a free state and not subject to Neustrian law,' she said. 'You need not trouble yourself about the dress-codes while you are here. Though few Wanderers live here, many pass through the city on their way from Neustria into Sklava and back.'

'Wanderers dare to enter Sklava?' said Yuste, leaning against the newel post. She was suddenly concerned that her legs might give way. Beatrice noticed her exhaustion and with tact, slipped down to offer her her hand.

'You must pardon me, Madame,' she said. 'My brother remarks often that I am apt to prattle. I can see that you need to wash, and eat, and rest.'

Yuste smiled into the girl's face. 'You and he are twins?' she said.

Beatrice laughed. 'Not many people realise it, since he is tall and I am not. But we shared the same womb.'

'I too am a twin,' said Yuste, squeezing her arm. 'I have a brother, though we also are not much alike. Except in stature.'

The tallest towers in the town of Zlonice reached no higher than Huldis's waist. There was only one street wide enough for them to enter the city, and once inside they had to tread carefully. Huldis found herself gazing down on sloping slate roofs and flagstaffs from which bright banners flew. Sometimes she began to feel as if she were indeed looking down from a great height on the buildings spread out below. To avoid stumbling, she would have to pause and stare at her own hand, to remind herself that she was not in fact hundreds of feet tall.

Bells were ringing as they walked down the street; Huldis gazed at the pointed steeples and wondered what these people worshipped, and whether their temples looked similar to those of the Doxoi. It was unlikely that she would ever see inside. She could barely make out the people who thronged the street below, pressing back against the walls to stay out of the way of her steps. They reminded her of dolls, or of *fées* from the books of fable she had learned to read from. Their faces were grave, dark-skinned, and they all had dark eyes, the irises so large that only a tiny hint of white showed at the corners. She almost expected them to have pointed ears and wings, but in all other respects they resembled humans. She noticed swiftly that they were slow to smile; indeed, the city itself seemed to her to have a desolate air, though she could not ascribe this impression to anything definite.

Yuda walked ahead of her. Though he was light on his feet, he too was watching the ground to make sure that he did not tread on the people or their beasts. From time to time, he would pass through the middle of a cloud, starting a shower of rain that wet Huldis's gown as she caught up with him. She wondered how large the sun would be; high above in the sky, it looked no different to the orb that gave light to her own world.

The King and his huntsmen led them to a square, broad and open enough for them both to sit down. It was ringed with what looked like plane trees, and as Huldis lowered herself to the ground, she took care not to uproot any of the delicate plants. She and Yuda sat facing each other, at opposite ends of the square, with their feet almost touching. Behind Huldis stood a magnificent classical edifice, like one of the temples of the Kadagoi, with a wide triangular pediment carved from marble set atop a row of columns, above a stair of broad and shallow steps. On her left was a row of tall houses with stepped roofs, their walls faced with saffron-coloured distemper. A fine, castellated hall lay to her right, and she guessed that this was the royal palace; the King reined in outside its splendid gilded gates, and a servant in crimson livery came to take his horse. King Yaroslav mounted the steps of the palace.

He had a handsome face and an athletic figure, but in spite of his yellow hair, he too shared the dark, melancholy eyes of his people. Huldis noticed that none of the men had beards; their faces, though shaped like those of grown men, were smooth as children's. The King carried a hunting crop in his right hand; he wore a scarlet doublet, a short cloak and dark hose, and long, pointed shoes that might have been made of leather. Instead of a crown, he sported a feather bonnet. One by one, his courtiers came to join him, and they were habited in a similar fashion, except for Stanislaus, who wore a longer gown cut below the knee and fringed with ermine.

Huldis reflected that they presented a sight that would have pleased her father, though he might have found the fashion of their garments unfamiliar. The colours were brighter and more varied than those she knew from the court of Ademar; the effect was cheering to the heart. It was a pleasure to see a city whose ruler was young and vigorous, living in the midst of his subjects, not shut away in a brooding castle that never seemed to feel warm.

Huldis noticed that the citizens, though they thronged the edges and corners of the square, made no attempt to approach her or Yuda. In their place, she imagined that curiosity would have overcome her fear. It was strange that there were no children bold enough to break from the crowd and dare to look more closely at the strange giants.

Servants had emerged from the palace, carrying trays of goblets to refresh the hunting party. Huldis was amused and touched when the King himself brought one such goblet and offered it to her with a bow. She would have liked to curtsey, since his rank was higher than hers, but she took the goblet between thumb and finger and raised it to her lips. It was about the size of a large thimble, and filled to the brim with delicious-smelling dark red wine. Huldis drank it in two sips, and was surprised at its strength; she felt a fiery warmth rising from her stomach. The King refilled the cup, and returned to his place on the steps, from where he pledged both her and Yuda. It felt a little absurd to raise the tiny beaker and pledge the King and his companions, but both she and Yuda did the same, though he paused to mutter a few words.

To save the King the trouble of picking up the goblet, Huldis carefully reached out to place it on the top step. After the horror of the attack in the forest, and their strange flight, she was beginning to feel warmed and cheered. She wondered whether their hosts would proceed to feed them. She also hoped that Yuda would soon have a chance to address the subject of their departure from this planet; she was not eager to be reunited with Semyon and her brother, who were all too likely to follow them by the same route.

She rested her head on her knees, feeling pleasantly drowsy. An amusing thought occurred to her, that nowhere in this city would they find a bed or a couch that would be large enough for her to stretch out on. She glanced at Yuda, and saw him yawn. With the clouds scudding overhead, and the sun shining fitfully between them, it was warm in the square. The atmosphere here felt much closer to summer than on her own world; she had already noticed that the trees were in leaf. Idly, she reached out to pluck one from the topmost branches of a tree, and was delighted to discover that it was indeed a plane. She closed her eyes, just for a moment, to listen to the tolling of the bells. It seemed the most delightful sound she had ever heard in her life; a sweet carillon playing a tune she did not recognise, but which stirred in her a nostalgia for her home, and her childhood, when Aude had been alive to keep her company.

Huldis woke with a start. The first thing she saw was a coffered ceiling, painted with gilt and red. In the centre of each coffer was a boss in the shape of a sunflower, painted gold. She was lying stretched out on what felt like a wooden floor, and she had the disagreeable sensation of being wrapped in a cocoon, like a caterpillar. She tried to sit up, but her head was pinned to the floor. Her arms and legs were similarly anchored, with a fine but strong cord that reminded her of spider-web. She wriggled her toes inside her slippers, and flexed her fingers, but that was all she could do; she might as well have been paralysed.

Her mind woke up more slowly than her senses. It took her some minutes to remember the leap into the suitcase, the endless fall, and their arrival on this world. The last thing she recalled was the cups of wine she had tasted; she thought in dismay that it must have been laced with a powerful drug if such a small amount could subdue someone as large as she was. She became aware, little by little, that she was not alone; light-shod feet were moving over her body, and small hands were prodding and pinching her, though never hard enough to cause discomfort.

'What are you doing?' she demanded. There was a pause, a silence, before a woman with a wrinkled face came to stand on her breastbone. The woman was dressed in a robe of damask shot with gold thread, gathered by a belt around her narrow waist. The plunging neckline was edged with ermine, revealing a stomacher embroidered with a pattern of acanthus leaves. Huldis all but gasped at the structure of gauze and wire that flourished from the woman's head, veiling her plaited amber hair.

'*Je suis la Reine-Mère, Demoiselle,*' she said in perfect Franj. Huldis stared into the black eyes, which for the first time seemed to her alarmingly remote in their expression. She tried to struggle in her bonds, but she could not stir a limb. The Queen-Mother continued 'foot *Nous sommes bien curieuses savoir si les femmes géants sont faites comme nous. En toutes particuliers.*'

Huldis shuddered. She wondered what they had been doing while she was unconscious; the Queen-Mother reminded her of those zealous mothers-in-law who wanted to see tangible proof of the bride's virginity, and to examine the sheets on the morning after the nuptials. If there were no bloodstain, the bride was held to be a whore, and cast out or worse.

'*Mais Madame, ce n'est pas gentil de traiter vos invitées er cette façon,*' she protested.

'*Tu n'es pas une invitée,*' the Queen-Mother responded. Huldis noticed that she used the familiar '*tu*', reserved for friends, children and animals, rather than the formal '*vous*'. This was not a good sign. '*Tu es notre prisonnier.*'

'*Où est mon copain? Qu'est-ce que vous avez faite avec lui?*' Suddenly Huldis was seized with fear. This examination by the ladies of the court was harmless enough, though it intruded upon her privacy. But she did not like to think that she had been separated from Yuda. It seemed more ominous than she had reason to believe.

The Queen-Mother gave a small, expressive shrug. She might have been Franj herself. Franj was the *lingua franca* of the courts of Yevropa, and this might have been one of those courts, except for its size. '*J'sais pas, ma petite,*' she said, and the irony was not lost on Huldis. '*D'ailleurs, il est avec mon fils. Ne t'inquiete pas.*' She glanced over her shoulder and said something in her own tongue to her unseen ladies; Huldis heard them tittering.

'Let me go!' she said, struggling to raise her head. '*Laissez moi tranquille!*'

The Queen-Mother shook her head. '*Point ne c'est possible,*' she said. She sat down on one of Huldis's breasts, and spread out her skirts. Then she began to explain to Huldis the history of her people: how, ever since Semyon caught their world, some of them disappeared every time he wrought a spell. No one knew where they went, save that they vanished into the dreadful place known as the Glass Mountain. Last year, her son had lost the Queen, his bride, and had sworn a great oath by the Holy Prism that he would do whatever he must to win her back.

The Queen-Mother sighed. 'You should understand, child, that you and your friend are like a gift from the gods. When the wicked Magus follows you, as he will, we will offer him your lives only if he restores us to our freedom – we and our lost friends.'

Huldis thought of Yuda's powers. Surely, even if he had drunk the drugged wine, he would have been able to break free?

'We are shamans,' she said, trying to sound fierce, though it was difficult when pinned to the floor, with a small queen sitting on her chest. 'We are not like other mortals.'

The Queen-Mother shrugged again. 'We have learnt the weaknesses of shamans,' she said. 'You may be great in size, little one, but your wits are not as sharp as ours. Our best philosophers and doctors have studied this matter for many months, and we have our own magic prepared against such a time as this. You are not the only monstrous creatures to happen upon our world, though you are the only ones human in shape. We have built nets that restrain your powers – and if need be, there are other means to hobble you.'

A cold shiver moved down Huldis's back. She felt tears welling up in her eyes, and though she was filled with rage against these people, she could not keep them in. The Queen-Mother summoned her ladies, and they swarmed over Huldis, standing in a row to stare at her weeping. She was a little comforted to see that

some of them regarded her with pity. One, younger
than the rest, ventured down to her throat and lifted
a tiny kerchief to dab at her eyelid.

'Thank you,' said Huldis.

'Pah,' said the Queen. 'Sentimental nonsense. We
know that these creatures are not sensitive to pain or
the finer feelings, as we are.'

'The giantess is sad, Madame,' said the girl. She
looked at her kerchief, now sopping wet, and tucked
it into her belt. Like the others, her hair was concealed
by a butterfly-wing head-dress of the finest gauze.

'What are you going to do with me?' said Huldis,
fighting back her tears.

'*On doit attendre*,' said the Queen-Mother. 'We must
wait for the Magus. No doubt he will not be long.
Indeed, he has already arrived on our world. Until he
comes, we shall keep you safe. Very safe.'

Annat came back to consciousness in the dark. Someone was holding her, and she struggled and thrashed
about, until she heard Malchik's voice.

'Steady, Natka,' he said. 'It's only me.'

'I can't see anything! I'm blind . . .'

'There is no light in here,' said Malchik, but as he
spoke she felt anew the searing pain in her left eye.
She raised her hand towards it, and touched the blood
on her cheek.

'Malchik, she put out my eye. She blinded me.'

He rocked her as if she were a little child. 'Ssh, ssh.
They've all gone away.'

'But she said they would take our souls. Why does

everyone want our souls? Why do they want to hurt us?'

'I don't understand,' his voice said. 'And I can't even heal you. I'm not much use.'

'Did they hurt you, Malchku? What did they do to you?'

'They didn't touch me.' He sighed. 'I don't know why not. They put us in this rock chamber, and took off our bonds.'

'What are we going to do?'

'I've been thinking. While you were unconscious. This place is riddled with shafts and chimneys. I don't know why the Miners stay here. But there's a shaft leading out of this room, up into the outside world. Too narrow for you or me to climb, but something could come the other way.'

'What do you mean?'

Malchik's long fingers stroked her cheek. 'You never asked what I was doing in the woods,' he said. 'While you were having your adventure with the wolves.'

'Likan,' she said. 'If only I could summon her . . .'

'She couldn't reach us,' he said. 'But Derzu brought me to meet my spirit animal too . . .'

'Derzu! What have they done to him?'

'Well, that's the odd thing.' He paused. 'They man-handled him, pushed him and prodded him – until they discovered that he was lame. Then they left him where he was. Didn't touch him after that. He wanted to come with us, but they wouldn't let him. They fired their arrows until he was forced to turn back. They

The Glass Mountain

are odd creatures; they look human, but there's something empty about them.'

'My eye hurts so badly, Malchku.'

'What you need is a real shaman, not me. But I'm all you've got. I've summoned her, Natka; I've summoned Chovotis . . .'

'What are you talking about?' she said, turning restlessly.

There was the sound of a door opening, and light filled the room. Annat blinked, finding that it hurt her good eye. She had to turn her head to see who was entering the room, and recognised the small figure of the Queen, carrying a lighted torch. The Queen set it in a sconce on the wall, and approached them. Her pale face seemed luminous in the subtle glow; her footsteps were so light that she might have been gliding across the ground.

'How is the child?' she said, in a low voice.

Malchik growled in his chest, like a bear. 'Just stay away from us,' he said. 'I'm not bound now, and I could squash you like a beetle.'

The Queen's impassive face showed no sign of fear. She approached them until she was a few feet away.

'You do not understand, human child,' she said. 'It had to be done. It is the gift of our people to shamans.'

'Gift?' Malchik reached out and seized her with one hand, lifting her off her feet. He held her inches from his face. 'You have blinded my sister. She could lose the sight of both eyes. How is that a gift?'

The Queen steadied herself, resting her tiny hands

on his fist. She was a little breathless when she spoke, but still composed.

'She will not lose her sight. She will gain in inner sight. Look.'

She pointed, and Malchik, in spite of himself, turned to look at Annat. She saw his face change. He set the Queen down on the ground and reached out to touch Annat's face, on her blind side. She was about to flinch away, when she realised that she could see his hand with both eyes. In her right eye, she saw it clothed in flesh and bone, turned golden by the torchlight; but her left eye saw a blue outline, picked out against a background of velvet black: an essence of Malchik's hand. She raised her hand to her face. She could feel the blood dried on her cheek, and clotted on her lashes; but where the ball of her eye should have been, there was an emptiness that burned her fingertips.

'I don't understand,' she said. Malchik put his arm round her shoulders.

'You have come to us by yourself, Queen,' he said. 'You know what we could do to you. Tell us what this means.'

The Queen folded her hands against the skirt of her gown. 'It is the power of the Prism,' she said. 'I have taken her natural sight, but I have given her inner sight. So it is with shamans. We can show them the truth that lies within. But always at a price. In the old times, they would come seeking our knowledge. We did not touch the old man, Derzu; he has the blessing of being lame.'

'You . . . hurt shamans?' said Malchik.

'We take, but we also give.'

Malchik let Annat go, and sat back on his haunches. 'It's not right,' he said, after a pause. 'My sister didn't ask you to maim her.'

'Let her decide when she has learned what she can do; what she will see.'

'It hurts,' said Annat.

'It will hurt until your new eye has had time to grow. Judge me then.'

'But you said you would take our souls.'

'Not take; use. The Prism does not work by force. Your human souls can draw the power from it that ours cannot.'

'And that will send you back to your world?' said Malchik.

For the first time, the Queen lowered her gaze. 'We do not know for certain what it will do,' she said. 'The Prism belongs on our world; it is the source of the power that the Magus has been using. I carry it with me, and so when I was driven into exile, it came too. I do not know how it will work if it is used here. Or whether the Magus has drained so much from it that it will not work at all. But the power of your joined souls will set it aflame, and then we shall see. If you consent.'

'Will you let us go, if it works?'

The Queen sighed. 'I cannot free you from the mountain,' she said. 'I have given you all that is within my power. Your only way to freedom lies above you, in the sky. Do not go any deeper into the roots of stone.'

Just as she finished speaking, the darkness rustled, and seemed to come alive. With a swoop of brown wings, a big shape flew down from the roof of the chamber, to settle on Malchik's wrist.

'Chovotis!' he said. The owl turned her head towards him and glared at him with black eyes that were almost all pupil. Malchik tickled the downy feathers of her neck. Annat glanced at the Queen to see how she would react, but the small woman showed no fear.

'You too are a shaman,' she said to Malchik.

He stood up, rising to his full height, which lifted him beyond the reach of the torchlight. 'You won't be maiming me,' he said. On his wrist, Chovotis ruffled her feathers.

The Queen spoke a few words of a strange language. The owl plopped to the floor and sidled towards her on its clawed feet. They were about the same size. The Queen held out her hand to the bird, which regarded her with its brilliant black eyes.

'I do not need to maim you, boy,' she said. 'Your powers are too weak. But we, the People, have much in common with these birds. In our own world, we spoke the language of birds; and in this world, we hunt with the great owls and are not their prey. It is they who have kept us fed within our prison, just as they would feed their young.'

Malchik sat down once more. Without looking at Annat, he reached out and grasped her wrist. 'Then I will help you,' he said. 'I will light the Prism for you and send you home. But I cannot speak for my sister.'

Annat covered her good eye with her hand and looked at Malchik with the other. She could see his outline quite clearly, and the faint *ðurmat* that marked out his hidden powers. It was a dim blue, almost lilac against the strange blackness that surrounded him. She had not been able to see her brother's signature before; she had not known that he possessed one.

'What is happening to me?' she said, lowering her hand.

The Queen looked up at her. 'I have given you insight,' she said. 'Your new eye will look strange, but it will not be ugly. The People understand that such great power as you possess must not be taken lightly. You are like a little god; but you are a mortal creature.'

Annat wanted to weep; she wished to seize the small figure and shake it like a kitten. Instead, tracing a meaningless shape on the stone with her fingers, she heard herself say, 'I will help my brother. We will both light the Prism for you, if we can.'

Chapter 16

Semyon knew little about the world imprisoned in his suitcase. He had never wished to view it from close quarters, but he had taken a leap of faith, partly because he was worried about Huldis, and partly because he had no wish to remain with Sarl as his only companion. He could not prevent the Heir from following him, however; Sarl had taken a firm grip on the tail of his robe as he jumped into the open valise.

After that had come the plunge through space, and the painful landing. Semyon had only just escaped having Sarl fall upon him. When he got his breath back, he stood up, stretching his limbs and breathing in the milder air of the small planet. If anything, it was a relief to have escaped from the wretched forest, where Sarl's crows had driven off the wolves. Semyon did not like animals, and he could not understand why certain shamans seemed to have a special bond with them. He had worked out that the wolf attack was somehow connected with Yuda; it irked him that Sarl had rescued them with his own aviary. He was not displeased to see the tall man lying winded on his face.

'Come on,' he said, trying not to smirk. 'We don't have much time.'

Sarl rose without a word, dusting off his clothes. In the softer light of this world, he looked even more like a corpse. Semyon noticed that he had put on his gauntlets.

'Why the hurry, Magus?' he said. 'You told me they cannot escape from here without your help.'

'The hurry,' said Semyon, taking his time, 'is needed because the people of this planet, though small in size, are fierce, short-tempered and great bearers of grudges. Especially against me. They have a well-developed science of magic, which they will not scruple to use. I do not know for certain how my use of this world has affected it, but I do know that the effects have been deleterious. If you want to find your sister and our prisoner in one piece, I recommend that you hurry.'

'Then why waste time in words?' said Sarl. 'Bring me to them.'

'I don't know exactly where they are,' said Semyon. His patience was wearing thin. 'I need to do a casting spell to find them.'

'Save your spell,' said Sarl. 'I will find their tracks.'

Semyon waited with folded arms, trying to quell his irritation as he watched Sarl examining the ground closely, turning over the turf with his fingers. He was relieved that the Heir did not take long to find what he was looking for: the prints that Yuda and Huldis had left in the springy grass. The two men began to follow their track, and Sarl pointed out the hoof-marks left by the little horses, and the tiny paw-prints of the hounds. Semyon had to own himself impressed; he would have missed the many, often barely decipherable signs that the riders had left in the soil.

It took about half an hour for them to find the city, spread out amongst its shallow hills like a burgh of many assembled doll's houses. Semyon paused at what he judged was just beyond bow-shot range, inspecting the walls. The great gate of the city was shut, and he could see the helms of armoured men above the crenellations that topped the walls. The city had been made fast against them.

'It seems they are expecting us,' said Sarl.

Semyon rubbed his hands together, wondering how much magic he could summon up without drawing on the energy of this world. He had no idea what effect it would have if he drained it while he was present within the world itself. He did not trouble to answer Sarl's remark. For these purposes, he must behave as if he were alone; he could not trust Sarl to help him if he got into difficulties. But the Heir would not leave him alone.

'What are you planning to do, Magus?' he said.

'I wish I knew,' said Semyon, staring at the walls. He could just make out the glint of weapons and the reed-like shapes of arrows. This was a place where he could neither deserve nor expect a welcome.

Suddenly, a figure rose up in the centre of the town, towering above the rooftops. It was Huldis, her long fair hair trailing loose about her shoulders, and from this distance, she appeared unharmed. Semyon allowed himself to draw breath. If the People had allowed her to remain unscathed, it was possible that they had not damaged either of their prisoners.

Huldis walked towards them. She moved with care, pausing from time to time to watch where she placed her feet. As she came closer, Semyon noticed that she was pale, except for her nose and the rims of her eyes, which showed red from crying. He tightened his hands. Huldis was not the sort of woman who wept easily; it distressed him to see her face so clearly marked with recent tears, and re-awakened his fears.

As she reached the gate, Huldis lifted her skirts to step over the wall. At another time, Semyon would have been pleased to glimpse her slender limbs, but now he could only think of his anxiety for her safety. She stopped close beyond the gate, and did not move any further.

'I bring a message from the King of the People,' she said, in a clear, steady voice. 'He holds myself and the shaman as hostages. He will ransom us to you, Magus, if you set free his world and return to him those of his people who you have abducted by magic and secret practices.'

Sarl took a step forward, and began, 'Tell this King—' but Semyon put out a hand to restrain him. Sarl looked at it with distaste, as if a toad had landed on the front of his tunic.

'Her life hangs by a thread,' said Semyon in a low voice. 'Do you understand?'

'These dwarfs shall not keep me from my sister,' said Sarl.

'Look! On the battlements! Can't you see the archers?'

Semyon heard his voice shaking with anger. He had noticed, as soon as Huldis stopped, that the archers standing on either side of the gate had trained their bows on her.

'I do not yield to threats,' said Sarl, fixing Semyon with his cold stare. But Semyon was learning not to fear him.

'If you don't listen to me, and do exactly as I say, you can bid farewell to your sister, your prisoner and your new life, Mon Seigneur,' he said. He had disliked Sarl before; now, he was beginning to hate him. 'Let me talk to the people. I know a little of their ways. They have not hurt your sister – yet – and that gives me cause to hope. Believe me when I say that if they thought it would help their cause, she would lie dead at our feet.'

Sarl gazed down at him, and frowned. 'Very well, Magus,' he said. 'I put my sister's life in your hands. And you know how precious that is to me.'

Semyon turned his back on Sarl, and faced Huldis. Though she had composed her features, he thought that fresh tears were streaming down her face. He ran his hand back through his hair.

'Tell the noble King,' he began, shaping the words as he spoke, 'that we accede to his requests. We shall restore his people, and set free his world. But only if you and your companion are released to us, free and unharmed.'

Huldis turned back to the barbican in which the gate was set, and Semyon deduced that she was speaking to someone on the roof of the tower. She raised her head and answered, 'The King will have it known that he does not make terms with such as you. Once you have freed his people and his world, then he will send us back.'

Semyon clenched his hand into a fist. If the People had consented to release both Huldis and Vasilyevich, he would have been ready with a spell, however uncertain, to transport them all to the Glass Mountain. But when only Huldis was present, he dared not take the risk, or he might find himself arrived home only to lose his life on the edge of Sarl's knife. He needed time to think, and he could buy time with words.

'Then tell the King we accede to his demands,' he said. 'We will withdraw into a convenient place, where I may prepare the magic to release this world. The matter of returning his people may take some longer time, since I do not know where they have gone.'

He saw her blinking rapidly, as if trying to hold back the tears. 'His Majesty King Yaroslav is content,' she said. 'But you will be watched, to ensure that you do not try any tricks. And His Majesty declares that if you play him false, he will have both of us put to death.'

Semyon could hear the desperation in her final words. He found himself filled with unexpected emotion, and answered her with a nod. When she turned her back on them and began to walk back towards the centre of the city, he all but cried out her name. Instead, he had to turn to Sarl, the enemy on whom he must rely, and say, 'Let us go. Time is short, and I need to think.'

As Huldis turned away from the Magus, her brother and safety, it was all she could do to stop herself from sobbing aloud. She was ashamed of her weakness; women of Ademar did not weep, least of all in the presence of their enemies. She paused to wipe her face on the sleeve of her gown, before beginning once again to traverse the wide boulevard that led to the central square. She was scarcely aware of the staring, expressionless faces of the People. Once again, they lined the streets to watch her pass, but she construed a very different meaning from their silence and their relentless gaze.

She paused on the edge of the square, steadying herself with one hand on each of the rooftops on either side. From where she was standing, she could see Yuda, lying on the ground, curled up on his side. She felt as if her heart tore like a letter, ripped in half by angry hands. The last few paces were difficult. She knelt down near his head and lifted it carefully on to her lap. Aware of her presence, Yuda rolled on to his back.

'What did he say?' he said.

'He agreed to the terms. He said he would go away. He went away. Yuda . . .'

'Courage,' he said. 'This is the time when you need

to hold on. Trust Semyon; he may not be much, but he's all we've got.'

Huldis opened her mouth to speak, but the sob escaped instead, an inchoate noise that sounded like a baby's cry. Yuda opened his eyes and looked up at her. There was a frown between his brows. 'You need to think too,' he said. 'We don't know whether this King keeps his promises.'

'They left us. They went away.'

'That's good,' said Yuda. He closed his eyes, and Huldis knew that he was hurting. She swallowed hard, and reached out a hand to stroke his face, though she was half afraid of touching him. The world, the city around them had contracted to the space the two of them occupied, and the third, invisible presence, Yuda's pain. It reminded her of the narrative of the Son's death, when the Kadagoi broke Him on the Wheel. The People lacked the means and the strength to do the same, and it seemed they had not intended to kill Yuda. They had driven iron spikes through his joints, his wrists, elbows and knees, and worst of all, through his feet. He could not move, because his feet and hands were pinned together; but they had also stuck several of their spears into him, as though they wanted to see how far they could goad him. Yuda's back was arched, and he was taut as a spring, but he did not make a sound, did not complain. He struggled with his suffering like a wild animal he had to overcome, and his fierce and powerful self-denial frightened Huldis.

– *They're not cruel. Just curious. They don't think we're human.*

– *Not cruel?*

– *You were right. They wanted to see how far they could go.* He winced. – *Something else. Don't understand it. Something about maiming shamans. They have to do it.*

– *But why?*

– *Zyon knows. Zyon.* He turned his face against her leg. – *It hurts like fuck.*

– *I wish there was something I could do . . .*

– *You're doing fine.*

In spite of the nets that bound them both, Huldis sensed the core of golden power in him. His courage, his strength, seemed to hold them both up. She laid her hand on his breast, as if she could draw strength from his heart. Yuda covered her hand with his own hands, though they were pinned together.

– *I couldn't . . . without you, Huldis. Not if I were alone.*

Huldis did not know whether he was thinking the words simply to comfort her. All she knew was that, in his place, she would not have cared or thought about anyone else, anything outside of her. There was something rare within him that helped him not only to withstand the pain, but also to care for her distress. She wondered whether this was what the People were seeking when they maimed their shamans; to see whether they could reveal that inner brilliance, the one stone which shone forth amongst the coal. It seemed a terrible way to discover it; and yet, in Yuda, they had uncovered the true greatness of his spirit, something finer than his pride. She kept these thoughts to herself.

– *Your magus is taking his time.*

— He's not my magus. She lifted her hand to caress his head. She felt empowered, not embittered; she wanted her soul to be like his.

— He's damned slow, whoever he belongs to. He shifted his back, and grimaced. Something made Huldis lift her head and look towards the palace. The King was standing there, with his nobles. Suddenly, she thought it obscene that they should stand and watch, as if they were viewing an experiment.

'Go away,' she shouted. 'Leave us in peace!'

'They aren't going to do that,' said Yuda, softly. 'They're waiting to see what we do next.'

Huldis looked down at his face. 'But there is nothing we can do,' she said.

His eyes opened; they were very black, like the eyes of the People. 'They wanted to see what a man is capable of; let them see,' he said. Huldis did not know what he meant at first, until she realised that he was referring to his silence, and the effort it cost him. She touched his cheek with her fingertips.

'I think they do see,' she said. 'But more than that, I see; I am your witness. I will remember what you have done.'

Yuda did not answer. He turned his head away, letting his hair shadow his face. Huldis held him tight. It was the only thing she could do for him; not to let go.

Beatrice brought Yuste to a room with one window that looked west over the valleys below Dieulevaut. The sun cast a pure and slanting light through the window, and there was a scent of hyacinths. The walls had been whitewashed, and the room held only simple furniture: a couch, a washstand and a chair. A plain mirror in a gesso frame hung above the washstand, on which stood a basin and ewer, a folded white towel and the pot of hyacinths that had newly flowered.

'I thought you might refresh yourself here,' said Beatrice. 'Would you like me to see if there are any clothes that would fit you? The ones you are wearing look damaged beyond repair.'

Yuste glanced down at Cluny's tunic. There were burn marks and several tears in the fine fabric; it would not be comfortable or suitable for a further journey.

'That would be kind of you,' she said. 'I need something modest – but practical. Hard-wearing,' and she and Beatrice shared a smile.

'I will see what I can find,' said the young woman. 'In the mean time, I will leave you in peace to wash. There is warm water in the jug.'

She left the room silently and closed the door behind her. At once, Yuste approached the mirror and looked at her face. She was forced to laugh. Her hair was standing on end and her skin was smudged with soot; her clothes smelled like a bonfire. With sudden energy, she stripped off Cluny's tunic and shirt, removed his hose and stood naked on the wooden floor, shivering a little. With quick hands, she lifted the ewer and poured its contents into the basin. There was a bar of olive soap manufactured in Masalyar, and she began to wash herself vigorously, splashing water everywhere. There was a wool drugget on the floor in front of the washstand which absorbed most of the spills.

When she had cleansed herself to her satisfaction, Yuste wrapped herself in the clean towel and went to sit on the bed. It was the first time she had been alone since last night's events, and she found their sounds and images flashing unbidden before her inner eye. It still seemed oddly remote, as if it had happened to someone else. She wondered what had become of Yuda when she lost touch with him, and where he was.

The world cracked like an egg, and Yuste fell to the ground. She lay on the wooden floor beside the couch, doubled up, with the warm sunlight touching her bare shoulder. The pain was like nothing she had experienced, even in the days when she was in hospital, before they removed the cancer. She lay quite still, unable to cry out; she felt as if she had fallen from a great height and broken all her limbs. She spread the fingers of her outstretched left hand, and they looked strange to her, like the points of a starfish.

'What is happening to me?' she said; her voice was choked in her throat. She did not feel any fear, as she might have expected; nothing in the room seemed threatening or out of place. She was safe, but the pain racked her. Yuste shut her eyes.

The dark face of the Mother, looking down from the wall of a Doxan temple, where she was painted sitting in majesty. Since she had seen those eikons, Yuste had been haunted by the faces, Wanderer faces, with their sad eyes. She had not expected to see those figures in the Mother's Temple in Masalyar, Notre-Dame de la Garde. In the few other temples she had visited, the images of the Mother had shown her blonde, fair-skinned, with flowing yellow hair. But in this one basilica, the frescos had been ancient, painted only a few centuries after the events they depicted. The artists who had created them had come from the east, from the great city of Mikalgrad, on the furthermost shore of the Middle Sea. They had painted in the old style, or made mosaics with tiles of azure, lapis lazuli, gold and crystal.

The Mother looked down on Yuste, serene in her heaven. She was not the vengeful matriarch of the Doxan doctrines, pronouncing her curse on the Wanderers because she thought they had betrayed her Son to the Kadagoi. Her face showed the knowledge of one who has seen great sorrow. Her large eyes, rimmed with kohl, had a look of pity and compassion. Yuste lay on the ground at the foot of the eikon, naked as a worm. It was as if she had strayed into the wrong dream, a Doxan dream of salvation, in which she was a trespasser. But the Doxoi did not deny the One; they had banished Him to immanent distance, only to be reached through the intercession of the Mother and her Son.

'What does this mean?' said Yuste aloud in her thought. It seemed to her that she was being vouchsafed an insight, but that it had been offered to her in a riddle. The scent of hyacinths seemed to fill her with their light and refreshing perfume. She lay quite still, staring at her outstretched hand, the pale starfish. If she waited, she might learn the answer to her question . . .

Beatrice was kneeling beside her, touching her shoulder. 'Madame!' she called, in a soft but urgent voice.

'Not yet,' said Yuste, half awake. 'I have to know

the answer,' then she cried out as the pain cracked through her. She was just aware that Beatrice sprang up and fled the room, her light steps pattering down the stairs outside. Yuste tried to sit up, but her body seemed made of lead.

Women in dark robes were hurrying past a white wall, their heads and faces veiled. Spread out on the white distemper was a scarlet handprint, glowing in the sun. It was the only mark on the wall. There had been others, but they were painted over each time the distemper was renewed. The print of a bloody hand. Yuste stared at it, aware of the heat, the cloudless sky, the sun that cast deep shadows. She stood barefoot in the dust, and realised that she was in Zyon, the lost country she prayed for in exile. She approached the wall, and stretched out her hand until it covered the handprint; it fitted exactly.

'Yuste!'

Boris was shaking her, calling her name. Yuste opened her eyes to look up into his troubled face.

'What's the matter, Boris Andreyevich?' she said, drowsily. Her fingers tugged at the edges of the towel, as she wondered whether it covered her body. Then it occurred to her that she would not mind very much if Boris saw her naked; the thought made her smile.

Boris placed her hand under her head and lifted it up. 'Beatrice found you lying on the floor like this,' he said. 'And then you screamed – we heard it down-stairs. Yet I can't find anything amiss with you. Can you tell me what's happening?'

Yuste gazed at his face. 'Dear Boris,' she said. 'You do care for me.'

Boris gripped her shoulder hard with his free hand.

'You've got to tell me what's the matter, Yuste,' he said.

Yuste wondered why he could not understand. 'I need to separate,' she said. 'Two eggs, one womb. Two minds, one soul.'

'Are you talking about Yuda?'

Yuste shut her eyes, his question reverberating in her head. Was she talking about Yuda? In the darkness, she reached out to him, and found him. They were never far apart.

– *You've got to let go, Yuste. If this kills me, it'll kill you.*

– *I can't leave you now.*

– *You must. For your own sake. For my sake.*

– *It was your handprint on the wall . . .*

She was looking down on a pool, blue where it reflected the sky, red with oxidised iron below the surface. There were two faces reflected in the water, her own and her brother's. She could feel the warm, sandy earth underneath her as she lay on the edge of the pool, staring at her reflection. The sun was setting behind them, and overhead the sky had changed to a deeper, richer colour. Her brother's skinny hand gripped hers; they were children.

– *Do you think there are fish?*

– *I don't think so. The water is too rusty.*

Prepared to argue with him, Yuste sat up, and Yuda sat up too, still joined by their hands. They looked into each other's eyes and laughed. Sometimes it was hard to tell who was thinking which thought.

There was blood on her brother's hand. Blood that stained her palm. The light had faded from the sky and they were alone together, in the dark.

– *We have to separate . . .*

– How can I live without you?

It was impossible to tell whose thought was which. They released each other, and stepped apart.

– Goodbye . . .

'Yuda!' she cried. She sat up, balling her fists, tears spurting from her eyes, but he was gone. And the pain had gone too. Boris wrapped his arms round her.

'Hush,' he said. 'Don't cry.'

'He's gone, Boris; I've lost him.'

'What do you mean?'

'He was always there. I could always speak to him. But we've separated; and I don't know if he is alive!'

Boris stroked her head. 'Yuda is one tough little Mother,' he said. 'Don't write him off just yet. You did the right thing; you had to separate. You'll still be able to *sprechen* when you see him; just like you do with me.'

Yuste looked up at him. Her eyes were blurred with tears. 'I feel as if . . . half my soul has been torn away,' she said. Boris took his handkerchief and dabbed at her eyes.

'It's like being born,' he said. 'Babies never seem too pleased about it. The first thing they do is yell.'

Yuste leant her head against his sleeve. He had taken off his trench-coat and was wearing his shirt and trousers, with the gun strapped to his chest.

'The best thing we can do now,' he said, 'is to make for the mountain as fast as possible. I've been talking to Ignatius, and he's willing to take us there and back. If we survive.'

Yuste lifted her head, and wiped her face. 'You're

right, Boris,' she said. 'I can't help Yuda. I don't even know where he is. But I can do something for Annat and Malchik.'

He helped her to her feet. 'Then you'd better get dressed,' he said. 'I'll go down and tell Beatrice that you're alive. You might even want some breakfast.'

When he had gone, Yuste sat down on the edge of the couch, her hands clasped together. Her mind was empty. After a few moments, she stood up, clutching the towel round her, and returned to look into the mirror. Her own face, forty years old, with its lines and marks under the eyes, gazed back at her. She reached out to touch her reflection. It was as if she had never truly known herself. The face reflected in the mirror was so familiar, yet she seemed to be seeing it for the first time. It reminded her of her mother's face. She thought of her mother, still living in Sankt-Eglis, and wished that she had visited her more often since moving to Masalyar. She had been back once in four years; Yuda never visited.

Yuste turned her back on the mirror. She could hear Beatrice coming up the stairs. Soon she would put on fresh clothes, and go downstairs to face the company. Alone. It was a new word, and a new world; she would have to learn how to walk again.

To Annat's altering vision, everything looked just a little different. When she used both eyes, she saw the skin of the world and what lay beneath superimposed upon each other; the effect was dizzying. She was constantly impelled to cover one eye with her hand, in order to see where she was going. With her blind side, she saw a liquid blackness in which shapes had a glowing and luminous life, but when she covered that eye, everything looked as it had before, solid and unambiguous. She was forced to hold on to Malchik's arm as they walked through the winding passages down which the Queen lighted their way. The flickering flames from the torch burned green when she viewed them with her new sight.

Malchik kept his arm about her shoulders, guiding her amongst the chaos of shapes and colours. Her sense of touch kept her from panicking and anchored her in reality. She could feel Malchik's arm through the stuff of his corduroy jacket as a structure of bone and muscle that promised her she had not been cast adrift on the sea of unformed matter. She heard the Queen's soft-shod feet pattering over the stone, a small sound which was amplified by the echoes in the tunnel. All around them was movement and life: the crystals in the walls pulsed, unseen minute creatures burrowed through the rock, and the Miners themselves were busy tunnelling and quarrying, digging up gems from the abundant stores the mountain held.

Annat longed to stop. To lie down, close her eyes and cover her ears so that the clamour and glittering lights were shut out. Her wounded eye hurt, and the whole one throbbed in sympathy. Every neurone in her brain seemed to be on fire, sending branching messages through her nervous system as it struggled with the deluge of sensations. It was as if a full orchestra were playing inside her head, and she could not only hear but see every note. If she had been alone, and sitting still, she might have been able to withstand the onslaught, but the strain of having to move brought her close to breaking.

'Malchik!' She had to shout to hear herself above the storm of sound. Her brother stopped and took her face in his hands. She had to shut her eyes; when she looked at him, she saw both his well-known face and the inner core of blue-green radiance.

'What's the matter, Natka?'

'I can't bear it. Tell her to make it stop, make it go away!'

She felt the heat of the Queen's torch on her face as the small woman held it up to illuminate her.

'It will pass. Once you have offered your soul to the Prism.'

Annat blundered against Malchik, hiding her face in his waistcoat. He hugged her to his chest.

'Come on, Natka,' he said. 'It isn't much further.'

'I want *Tate*! He would make me well . . .'

'But he's not here, Natkeleh. Just the two of us. Come.'

Holding her upper arms in a gentle but firm grip, he lifted her away from him. His face swam in the tears that blurred her good eye, but she could see the frown that marked his concern, and the smile of affection. How things must have changed, when she needed to lean on him! He took a handkerchief from his breast pocket and dabbed at her eye and her cheek.

'Thank you,' she said. Somehow, the tears she had shed cooled the turmoil in her brain. She let him lead

ter down the winding stone corridors, and she kept
her injured eye covered with one hand, to shut out its
changed vision. She realised, as perhaps she had not
done before, that Malchik had other meanings than
the familiar one, as her bumbling, vulnerable brother.
He was a force that anchored her in the world. She
had not known that she might need someone like him
around; she had been so full of confidence and the joy
of her burgeoning powers.

The hall where they had first been brought as prisoners was empty when they returned there, except for
the rustling whispers of sound that seemed to collect
beneath its vaults. The Queen doused her torch, for
here was sufficient daylight from the many shafts that
pierced the walls to make other lights unnecessary. The
Prism remained where she had placed it on her throne,
catching and refracting the sunshine that fell upon it.
She walked across the deserted chamber, moving in
and out of the rays of light, which showed for an instant
a different creature to the pale, colourless form that
inhabited the shadows. When she came to the throne,
she stooped to pick up the Prism, which needed both
her hands. Malchik guided Annat to the dais, and they
paused, gazing at the strange, clear gem in the Queen's
grasp.

'You must both take hold of it,' she said. 'Lift it up
to the light. The rest will follow.'

'You are certain this won't harm us?' said Malchik.

'I can promise nothing.'

He reached out and took the Prism from her, holding
t up where Annat could see it. Quickly, almost

greedily, her hand closed on his and she touched the cold facets of the stone.

'It is very beautiful,' said Malchik, lifting their joined hands so that the Prism caught the light once more.

Annat looked up at it. All she could see was the clear crystal and the rays of rainbow colours that escaped between their fingers. She was glad that she could feel Malchik's hand touching her own. The dark and the glowing hues, red, blue and purple, reminded her of standing in a Doxan temple where the light entered through painted and stained glass. All colours of the spectrum were present, separated and refined. Each one seemed to have a meaning, and Annat recalled when she had been a bodiless soul, drifting amongst the words that formed the universe.

Something rose out of the ground, piercing the Prism, and vanishing straight into the roof above. A fibre-thin line of violet light that seemed to thrum like a string, though she could hear no sound. Annat felt something go out of her, coursing down her fingers into the stone, where it was hurled upwards along the line of light, far into the sky. When she closed her eyes she found herself soaring upwards, drawn out from her body like a thread, but a thread of infinite length. It stretched beyond the earth's atmosphere, deep into space. A single stitch, joining the world where her feet stood to something so distant her thoughts could not encompass it.

There was no sense of stretching or stress, no fear that the fibre would snap. Instead, pulled atom-thin, Annat felt her troubled senses slipping into place. She could still think, even though she found herself drawn across space. Then, with a sudden recoil, the fine filaments drew back, receding so quickly that, when she blinked, no time had passed. The violet line had vanished, but in its place, the Prism glowed with gathered light, though it remained cool to the touch. Annat looked along Malchik's arm until she reached his face. His lenses reflected the pale glow twice. She realised that she was looking at him with both eyes, the new vision superimposed on the old.

'I think we've done it,' he said.

They turned to the hall and saw that they had indeed wrought a change, though it was not the one the Queen had predicted. She had hoped the Prism would send the Miners home; instead, it had brought their people to the mountain. And they were not alone . . .

Chapter 17

The clothes that Beatrice had brought for Yuste were much more suitable, she thought – modest yet practical. There were no stiffened corsets and the skirt, though long, did not trail on the ground. And there was only one petticoat. She studied herself in the mirror and considered that she might almost be mistaken for someone respectable! The colours were neutral, even drab – a tight-fitting jacket and skirt of grey wool and a white blouse. It was a ladies' travelling outfit, and would enable Yuste to blend into the background – though she wondered if, where she was headed, that would matter at all.

She found Boris and the others already eating breakfast. She eyed the bacon on their plates and was thankful to be offered nothing but eggs. Though she felt hungry, she was too nervous to eat much. Her mind was so full that she did not attempt to join in the conversation. She concentrated on saying the Blessings

over her food, gabbling them as she had always told
Annat and Malchik not to do. Cluny watched her with
covert admiration, but did not try to interrupt. Boris
was reading the newspaper. She noticed that Cluny
and Planchet had taken off their chain-mail; they
looked a little less remarkable in their plain homespun
tunics, but their swords were propped against the wall.

When she had given up the struggle with her eggs
and was sipping from a bowl of black *kava*, Cluny
cleared his throat.

'Madame,' he began.

'Oh Zyon, Cluny, please call me Yuste!'

He smiled, lowering his eyes. 'Ignatius thinks we
will come to the mountain by dusk.'

Yuste dabbed at her mouth with a napkin. 'So soon,'
she said. She reached out and laid her hand over
Cluny's. 'I'm worried about my brother,' she said.
'Worried sick. And the *kinder*. I don't know anything.
We broke off the link that bound us. It was as if he
was dying.'

Boris made a noise behind his newspaper. 'What's
the matter, Boris Andreyevich?' said Yuste. He lowered
the paper.

'Listen, *Zhidova*. We've got a mission, right? We're
going to rescue your niece and nephew. If we can. And
we have to stop this magus from making Sarl immortal.
It's all we can do for our city, our people. With all
respect to your feelings, we need to think about that.
Only that.'

'But Boris, I didn't ask him anything. Where he
was, what was happening . . .'

He cut across her. 'That's how the rest of us have to live, Missis. We don't know what's happening to our friends, lovers, brothers, sisters – not even if we are shamans. That's what separation means.' He folded the newspaper, stood up and stretched. 'We're going blind to the mountain. We don't know what we'll find when we get there. Have you got any plans?'

'No . . . I thought it would be a longer journey.'

Ignatius put his head round the door. 'I'm ready when you are,' he said.

'We're ready,' said Boris. Before Yuste could protest, Ignatius was gone. Planchet and Cluny started to put back their chairs and pick up their gear. Yuste was left sitting at the table, the bowl of coffee in her hand.

'I can't do this, Boris Andreyevich. To just rush off into the blue without . . . any preparation.'

Boris walked round the table, and bent over her. He kissed her cheek. 'Listen, Missis,' he said. 'We've prepared all we can. Ignatius has loaded the ship with some provisions. Beyond that, all we need is ourselves and our kit. We have to travel light. We're going on a raid into foreign territory, not an expedition.'

Yuste looked into his face, which was close to hers. She thought of several retorts, but instead she lifted her mouth to his. Boris squeezed her shoulder as they kissed. When they separated, he grinned. 'How's that?' he said.

'I'm frightened, Mister.'

'Yup, me too. Frightened is the right thing to be. What with Sklavan magicians and undead warriors.

They may just blow us out of the sky. Who knows? Remember last night. You just finished off a whole troop of mailed horsemen. Blam!' He spoke so suddenly that Yuste jumped, and he laughed. 'Come on, Missis. Time we were going.'

'I wish I had my handbag . . .' said Yuste.

'You left that behind with the Rom, remember? Nothing to carry, just yourself.'

As soon as Yuste was on her feet, he seized her hand and began dragging her out of the room. But Beatrice was waiting for them on the landing, with a small, leather-wrapped package in her hand. She saw them, and laughed. 'For Madame,' she said, holding out the package.

Boris made a face. 'Not more sandwiches,' he said.

'Madame may find it useful . . .' said Beatrice. After they had exchanged thanks and farewells, Yuste paused on the doorstep to examine the package. It proved to be a small purse on a long strap. She slung it over her shoulder and tucked it under her arm; there would be a chance later to see what it contained.

Ignatius was waiting for them in the street outside, exchanging small talk with Cluny and Planchet. He was wearing a strange woollen hat with earflaps, and looked almost as outlandish as Cluny and Planchet in their chain-mail coats and coifs. Over his thin frame he had draped a long, steel-blue greatcoat, and there was a pair of goggles set back on his head.

'Good morning,' he said. 'Are we all ready?'

'I hope so,' said Yuste. 'How much must we pay you for this journey?'

Ignatius waved her away. 'We can settle accounts upon your return,' he said.

'If we return,' said Boris. 'I think maybe we should pay you a deposit.'

Ignatius beamed at them. 'It's always chancy flying into the territory of the Sklav Empire,' he said. 'We have special insurance to cover the flights.' He began to pull on his leather gauntlets. 'We'll be on the edge of nomad lands, so at least we don't have to worry about archers using us for target practice.'

'What about flying wizards?' said Boris.

'To be honest, it's no good worrying about things like that. One might as well worry about a rain of cows. Not impossible, but very unlikely.'

'This mountain we're aiming for belongs to a wizard.'

'The Glass Mountain. It's quite a landmark. You can't miss it. It – ahem! – looks like glass.'

'There's a surprise,' said Boris.

'Most airmen avoid it like the plague. It's the only wizardly stronghold anywhere near the Lepas Mountains. An anomalous outcrop of rock slap bang in the middle of the *puszta* – the grasslands. I have been wondering for some time what sort of geological formation is involved. The only thing I have been able to identify is a granite batholith, but that doesn't explain its glassy appearance. Fascinating,' and he turned on his heel and set off down the sloping street.

'Imagine,' said Boris. 'A granite batholith. Who'd have thought it?'

'Myself, I would have expected it to be obsidian,'

said Cluny. 'But obsidian is an igneous rock, and I'm not sure about the formation of the *puszta* . . .'

'Perhaps we could discuss the geological formation when we get back?' said Boris.

'I'd love to,' said Cluny, cheerfully. 'Assuming that we make it.'

It seemed to take much less time to find their way back from the Brunelleschis' house to the airship moorings outside the city. They found the promenade crowded with people, some preparing to embark, while others had just returned from an overnight journey. Ignatius strode through the crowd, shouting greetings to other pilots. Boris slipped his arm through Yuste's and they hastened after the captain like a respectable married couple. Yuste wished she were wearing her poke bonnet, for it was unusual to see any married woman with her hair uncovered, but she could tell from inspecting the people that Neustrian law was not so strictly enforced here as it was in Masalyar. Of course, Ignatius had told her that only one Wanderer lived in the city, but she was certain that she identified several amongst the travellers, and not one of them seemed to be wearing the customary black, white or brown, let alone a badge. One young woman was elegant in a costume of burgundy damask, though Yuste could not help observing that her dark ringlets were suitably covered by a straw bonnet.

– *Women*, thought Boris. – *Do you only think about fashion?*

– *It isn't about fashion, Boris. It's about freedom.*

– *I'll allow you that. Don't you envy these folk? Going*

about their business, while we have to fly off Mother knows where.

— *Perhaps she does know*, thought Yuste, recalling her visions.

— *That's a remarkably heretical sentiment for a Wanderer.*

— *I sometimes think all our little religions are just pieces of a much bigger jigsaw. One we can't see.*

— *I'm only too glad not to see it. I find all this wizard stuff too much as it is. But Sklava is full of it. I'd say most of them were charlatans. Unfortunately, we seem to have run into one who isn't.*

The *Arabian Bird* was waiting for them, bobbing against its moorings. Yuste tried to avoid seeing the drop that lay below the platform. Today, a small gate had been opened in the side of the gondola, and a gangplank led from the jetty up to the deck. She was only too glad that Boris led her across; she clung on to his arm and stared hard at the deck. Once they were on board, with Cluny and Planchet, the landsmen folded up the gangplank and closed the gate. Ignatius was already at the tiller, and the engine was busy, puffing and rattling like an overlarge kettle.

'Look's like we've got a good morning for it,' shouted Boris.

'Not too bad,' Ignatius replied. 'I'll have to take her up quite high. The prevailing wind blows south or south-west over the mountains, so we need to get above it. We'll spend the next half-hour rising to the right altitude. You may be cold, and the air is thin up there.'

The four of them crowded round the boiler and the firebox, where there was some warmth to be had.

This morning, Ignatius had set up a row of seats for them to sit on, and they made themselves comfortable with their backs to the engine. There was also a pile of woollen plaid blankets for their use. Yuste snuggled up against Boris. The clothes Beatrice had given her were warm and well made, but she had not forgotten from last night how cold it could be on board the airship.

'It feels as if we are going on a day-trip,' she said.

'It is a pleasant day,' said Cluny.

'May as well make the best of it,' said Boris. 'What bothers me is what we do when we reach the mountain. Has this wizard built some sort of fortress on the outside, or is he all safely tucked up in a mine? I hate magic.'

'I suppose it's possible the wizard won't be there,' said Cluny. 'When you last heard from your brother, Yuste, didn't he say that he'd seen the wizard in Yonar?'

Yuste looked at her gloved hands. 'When we were with the wolves – that time when you had to break camp in a hurry and leave with the Rom – Yuda was with Sarl and the Magus, and they were trying to cross the mountains further north. But when I saw him last night, he didn't say where they were. And this morning . . .' She trailed off.

'Basically, we don't know where the wizard is. Or Sarl. Or Yuda,' said Boris. 'All we know for sure is that Annat and Malchik are at the mountain.'

'But what if we're too late, Boris? What if the Magus has already killed Yuda and taken their souls?'

'You'd know if they were dead, believe me,' said Boris. 'I knew when Stromnak was killed . . .'

'Your partner?' said Yuste.

'And my wife.' He leaned back in his chair, staring up at the ramparts of the city.

'Your *wife*? Zyon, Boris, you never told me!'

'It was a few years ago. I'm not just a funny old bachelor, Missis; I'm a funny old widower. I never could get to like other women . . . until now . . .'

'Tell me about her,' said Yuste.

Boris stood up. 'Not now,' he said. 'We're casting off.'

While Sarl sat on the ground, staring into space, Semyon paced to and fro, struggling to order his thoughts. From time to time, he aimed a kick at a tussock. If he let this world go, he would no longer be able to draw on its power, and without that source, he would not have the means to complete the spell that would restore Sarl to life. But he was not even sure that, while he was inside the suitcase, he would be able to perform the necessary incantation to free the world. He was here, and the enchantments that kept the world of the People imprisoned now held him also.

'Time is not staying for you, Magus,' said Sarl. 'If you are not ready soon, I will go and fetch my sister.'

'I've told you, Mon Seigneur, you will not be able to use your powers against them. They have subtle nets – but enough to stop you.'

'I do not need my powers to subdue such paltry enemies.'

'Face it, my lord, they will kill your sister before you are at the gate. You have no choice but to wait for me. Doubtless they will send word if they are becoming impatient.'

'I am becoming impatient, Magus,' said Sarl. 'I do not think you know how to perform what they require of you.'

Semyon rounded on him. 'No, I don't know!' he shouted. 'The world is inside the suitcase. We're inside the suitcase. To set this world free, I need to be outside! But to get back up there,' he jabbed his finger in the direction of the heavens, 'I will have to draw on the power of this world – and they will know. What do you suggest I should do? I don't want your sister dead any more than you do. And I'm almost fond of the little fellow – at least he doesn't keep threatening to cut out my heart!'

To his surprise, Sarl broke into a slow smile. It was not pleasant to see, but nonetheless it was an ordinary smile, with nothing menacing about it.

'Magus, I believe you're not afraid of me any more,' he said.

Semyon was about to shout at him again, but he let it go. He sat down on the grassy hillock where Sarl had made himself comfortable.

'I'm out of ideas, and out of luck,' he said. 'The only thing I can think of is that I should go and tell the People the truth – that I have to leave the suitcase in order to free them. Do you think they'll let me go? They've got their hostages.'

'I don't think they will believe you. I wouldn't, in their place.'

Semyon looked at his nails. They were all bitten short. 'I suppose I could try a spell to bring your sister and the captive here,' he said. 'But I don't know about these nets the people use. I should have spent more time studying this world, instead of just using it as a power source. Well, I have to do something; I can't think of anything else . . .'

As he finished speaking, something happened. The sun went out, and the sky changed to a thundery black. A rushing wind sprang up, tossing the short grasses from side to side, and the small trees were bent flat. Semyon stood up, to find himself caught in the gale. He shaded his eyes to look towards the town, and saw it grey against the horizon, the hidden sunlight still glittering on its flags and vanes. There was a shower of cold, pinching rain, which soaked his clothes. Semyon saw lightning flashing in the distant clouds, tearing apart the sky. He began to walk slowly towards the city walls, without waiting for Sarl. He could feel the tingling of powerful magic in the air, just as he smelled the wet grass underfoot. It might be nothing more than a spring shower, but he knew in his bones that it was not.

When he came to the city gates, the walls were deserted. He stepped over the gate to find himself in a broad avenue. Everywhere, there were signs of recent occupation. Dogs ran through the street barking and stopping to howl. There were abandoned carts, riderless horses. He walked along the street, pausing often to stoop and peer in at the open windows of the houses on either side. In every place that he looked, there was no one to be seen. He could smell baking bread; he was able to crouch down and peer through the windows of the bakery, where he saw open ovens and tiny loaves made of fresh dough waiting to be baked. But no bakers.

Semyon stood up, and looked back towards the place where he had left Sarl. He saw the tall figure standing outlined against the sky, and beckoned him. Then he walked on into the centre of the city. He saw two things very quickly: the huge central square, deserted, with the banners still flying from the roof of the palace, red and orange and white; and the stains of blood on the ground. Semyon shuddered, hugging himself; his clothes were wet, and the wind that still blew sent a chill through him. When Sarl came to join him, he pointed to the ground.

'They've gone,' he said. 'Every one of them. But what do you think those mean?'

'I cannot tell, Magus,' said Sarl. 'If these people bleed as we do, there is no telling who was wounded. It could even be the blood of beasts.'

'There's no sign of Huldis or the shaman. And they'd be too big to hide. If there were anyone left to hide them.'

'Do you understand what has happened?' said Sarl.

'It is very strange. As if someone cast a spell – a mighty spell – and the last of the People vanished.

Remember what Huldis said? Somehow my magic — each time I drew on the world — made some of them disappear. And now they've all gone.'

'But you do not know where they went.'

'I don't know for certain. I have a suspicion. But I think there is nothing left for us here. We need to return to the Glass Mountain, and swiftly.'

'I should wager the mirrors in this city are a little small for us to step through,' said Sarl. Semyon blinked at him; he was not sure he could remember Sarl making a joke before.

'We won't use the mirrors,' he said. 'There is another way, but I have hesitated to use it because it will require so much power. It may use up all the power left in this world and . . . I've wanted to avoid that.'

'That is very scrupulous of you, Magus.'

Semyon avoided his gaze. He wondered whether Sarl understood the implications for himself. If Semyon drained all the remaining power from the world, the consequences would be much like those of setting it free. Except that the world would die. But there would be nothing left for Semyon to perform the spell that would bring Sarl back to life, even if they were able to bring together all the other . . . ingredients. He turned his back on Sarl, and began to work up a spell. Translocation was well known to be difficult and hazardous. It was not like the travel of shamans, who used gates and passages to pass from one world into another. He would somehow have to wrench himself and Sarl from this reality into their own, causing them to travel in time and space.

And the world would die. Sarl had been right, despite his irony; Semyon did scruple to destroy this planet, and its strange inhabitants, just because he needed a short cut to bring him home. The words of the spell, and its complex formulae, arranged themselves in his mind. He stretched out his arms and began to chant, remembering to invoke the god Tchernobog before he started. He found his thoughts straying to Kaschai, who undoubtedly daily drained the power from many small worlds as if they were of no significance. Semyon made himself close his eyes and concentrate on the spell. Like all such incantations, it was not only effective, but well designed. It drew on the alignment of the planets, and the juxtaposition of the worlds. It steered a way between these multitude of complex conjunctions, finding a way that would send him exactly where he wanted to be. But it was wasteful, a fat spell that demanded luscious dollops of expensive power to make it work. Any shaman who tried to perform it without a separate source of energy would die.

Semyon could see the spell unfolding in the air before him like a scroll with writing on it. The closing words were always the most dangerous; they were the phrases that would trigger the spell and set it working, when so many small things could go wrong and bring disaster. It was these words that would link the magic to its source of power, to make it work.

The last phrase left his mouth dry. He shut his eyes, waiting for tremendous forces to wrench him apart. There was a brief silence, and then he was flung through the air. He seized hold of his bonnet and pulled it down over his ears. It must feel like this to be torn from your feet by a whirlwind, he thought. He had no idea what had happened to Sarl. He opened his eyes for an instant, and saw the ground rushing beneath him at frightening speed. It looked like the earth, and it was far below. If the spell let him go, he would plunge through the air and become nothing more than broken bones and flesh in those distant fields.

Semyon closed his eyes once more, but he could not stop his ears against the rushing sounds and the keening of the wind. He opened his mouth and yelled, not caring who could hear him. At that moment, he began to fall. His clothes flapped about his body, and he felt himself tumbling, head over heels, towards the ground.

The People were looking about them, gazing up into the sudden darkness; they seemed dazed. As she saw them, the Queen gave a little cry and ran towards them, snatching up her skirts to spring on to the low dais where they had appeared.

'What has happened?' said Annat.

'Look,' said Malchik, and they followed the Queen, clearing with a single step the projection she had been forced to climb. Yuda and Huldis were there, the man lying with his head in the girl's lap. Annat dropped on her knees beside him and passed her hands over his body, feeling with a shock echoes of the pain she no longer shared.

'Yuste?' said Yuda, without opening his eyes.

'No, *Tate*, it's me,' said Annat. She realised she was crying when one of her tears splashed on his skin, and he looked up at her. Malchik swore.

'What happened to you?' she said, looking from her father to Huldis, who was holding his head between her hands.

'What happened to *you*, *meine kind*?' Yuda said in a whisper. She could tell that it took all his power not to cry out. She let her hands hover above him, passing from his head to his feet, to draw out the pain. She saw the tautened muscles relax, and the lines of stress and anguish fade from his face. His clothes were torn to pieces and stained with blood; wherever she looked, there seemed to be an iron spike or a wooden-hafted spear protruding from his flesh. '*Mein Gott*,' she said. Malchik was in tears, but his face was flushed with anger, too.

'Good girl,' said Yuda. He was wrapped in the golden aegis of his power; he shone like a piece of pure amber, freshly shaped in the depths of a mine.

'They separated us,' said Huldis. Her voice cracked. 'When they brought us together, they had done this to him. We meant them no harm. Why did they do it?'

'I think I know why,' said Annat. She reached out to caress Yuda's forehead, brushing the damp hair back from his face. 'What did they say to you, Yuda?'

Yuda gazed at her. 'Perhaps for the same reason they put out your eye,' he said.

'The Queen told me,' said Annat. 'They hurt shamans. They believe it will bring us understanding. But what did they do to you, Huldis?'

411

She looked at the face of her mother's friend. The young woman's mouth trembled as she tried to answer. 'Nothing,' she said, 'except to see . . . to witness . . .'

Annat screwed up her face. 'I'm afraid that might be part of it,' she said.

'I'd be grateful if you got the damn things out, Natka,' said Yuda.

Annat nodded. She looked across at Malchik. 'Can you do it, Malchku?' she said. 'I don't think I have the strength. I will work to ward off the pain.'

Malchik nodded. Once, not so long ago, he would have cried out in protest. He bent over Yuda and gave him a gentle smile.

'How shall I do it, Mister?'

'Quickly,' said Yuda.

Malchik looked into Huldis's face. 'You hold him,' he said. 'Trust Annat; she'll make sure it doesn't hurt.'

It took about ten minutes to remove all the spikes and spears that the People had stuck into Yuda. The wounds bled freely, but Annat did not try to close them at first, in order to cleanse them. She was impressed to see how swift and sure Malchik was, and she worked to lay the balm of healing across Yuda's suffering; but it still hurt her when they finished and she saw his face. She could sense his exhaustion; he had stretched every nerve to its limit. Malchik sat back on his heels, wiping his bloodstained hands on his trousers.

'By the Mother, I trust I never have to do anything like that again,' he said.

' "By the Mother"?' Yuda echoed his words. Annat could not imagine a worse time to tell him that Malchik was an apostate. But there would never be a good time.

'I'm a . . .'

'Malchik's become a . . .'

They spoke together, but neither finished their sentence. Yuda looked from one to the other; Annat knew he understood what they had been trying to say.

'I can't think about that now,' he said. 'Malchik is a man. He must do what he wants.' He stopped; speaking was an effort for him. Annat took one of his hands and turned it over between her own. The palm was undamaged, but there was the mark on his wrist where the spike had gone through. Yuda closed his fingers over hers. His grip was still strong. 'Heal me now, Natka,' he said.

For a moment, Annat wondered if he knew how badly he had been hurt. It was clear to her that, though she could close the wounds, she would not be able to fix the damage to his joints, where the iron had pierced through bone and cartilage. They would need time to recover; she could only trigger his body's natural healing.

'I know,' he said. 'They've crippled me. Just do what you can.'

Annat touched the ring that he still wore on his right hand. 'What about this?' she said.

'It's done its work in me. You can't use it for that again. And I'm not dying.'

Annat set to work. She began with the smaller wounds; it was easy to mend skin and muscle. But when she came to the holes the spikes had made in

his joints, there was much less that she could do. Yuda
lay quite still, except to prompt her from time to time.
She had not yet finished when she raised her head to
see the Queen of the Miners standing opposite, with
her consort beside her. Annat's heart beat faster, with
both anger and fear. Malchik noticed the change in
her gaze, glanced behind him and sprang to his feet.
He must seem tall as a steeple.

'No,' he said. His voice was a roar; something else
that was new about him. 'You've hurt him enough. Go.'

'Malchik,' said Yuda. He spoke quietly, but there
was that in his voice not to be disobeyed. 'Let them
come.'

'Very well,' said Malchik. He knelt down once more,
turning his back on the royal pair. Annat paused in
her healing, watching as the Queen approached, until
she was standing close to Yuda's head. Her face looked
sad, even troubled. Yuda gazed back at her, a frown
showing dark between his brows. Annat thought that
despite the difference in their stature, there was little
separation between them in fierce pride and strength
of will.

'Give me the Prism,' said the Queen. As Annat wondered what had happened to it, she saw Malchik reach
into his jacket pocket and produce it, clear and lifeless, a lump of stone. He held it out to the Queen, his
hand shaking, and she took it from him. She stared at
it, as if hoping to see an image in its depths. 'We called
on the Prism, but it did not restore us to our world,'
she said. 'It worked backwards. Now we are all cast
into the mountain, and slaves of the Magus.' She

reached out and placed the Prism on Yuda's breast, above his heart. Slowly, it changed colour, until it had turned a cloudy red, as if it was full of blood. The Queen nodded, as if she had been expecting this. 'The Prism worked for you, not for us,' she said. 'It brought you here, to be healed.'

Yuda picked up the stone and held it up; almost immediately, the colour faded. Where the Queen had laid it, there was now a star-shaped scarlet mark, like a brand. He touched it with his hand.

'What does it mean?' he said, offering the stone to her.

'Shaman, your blood has stained the Prism; never again will it show pure and clear,' she said. She held out her small hands, and Yuda gave her the stone; when she held it up to catch the light, it seemed to retain a pinkish tinge. The Queen inspected it closely, like a watchmaker, though it was bigger than both her fists. 'It does not speak to me,' she said. 'It is like a clouded mirror, in which I see nothing – ah!' She gave a little choking cry, and fell to the ground, like a moth that has broken its wing. Behind her, the King crumpled in the same moment; when Annat looked round, all the People were falling, with a rustle like the dropping of dead leaves.

'What is it?' she said. 'Why are they dying?'

Yuda picked up the Prism, where it had fallen from the Queen's grasp. 'It's the Magus,' he said. 'He has made a spell to bring him and Sarl back to the mountain. And he has drawn the last energy from the crystal. That was why she could not read it.'

Annat looked at him. 'If Sarl and the Magus have returned, why aren't they here?' she said.

'I don't know. This is not a good time to face them when I am spent.'

'But do they know where we are?' said Malchik.

'They will have gone to the chamber beneath th summit, where Semyon keeps his mirror,' said Huldis 'When he looks into it, he will find us.'

'Then we should be on the move,' said Yuda. H tried to sit up, but was defeated by the damage to hi joints, which had weakened his arms.

'I'll help you,' said Malchik.

'Wait,' said Huldis. 'If Semyon has drained all th power from the Prism, what will he use to give life t Sarl? Even if he recaptures you, he can't do it.'

Yuda made a second attempt to sit up, and suc ceeded. He looked at the Queen's crumpled body, the picked it up and laid it across his knees. 'Poor littl sods,' he said. 'No wonder they hated humans. But sh was different . . .'

'She pierced Annat's eye,' said Malchik.

'How is it, Missis?' said Yuda, as Annat touche her face with trembling fingers.

'It doesn't hurt any more. But I wish I knew wha it looked like.' She felt ashamed, admitting to this van ity when her father had been crippled. He studied he face with his unwavering gaze, and said, 'It is beaut ful. Strange, but beautiful. Like a living marble.' H glanced down at the Queen's still form. 'We can't le them die.'

'I think we should,' said Malchik. He held up on

of the bloodstained spikes that he had taken from
Yuda's body. 'They have no humane feelings. They
would do it again.'

Yuda turned his head back towards Huldis. 'What
do you say, Missis? Would you let them die?'

Huldis touched his cheek. 'I will do whatever you
say, Yuda. I hate what they did to you; but there are
so many of them, they cannot all be cruel. And it's not
our place to decide their fate. I am sure not even the
Magus would wish them this harm.'

'Good,' he said. 'Come now, boy; you can help me
up.'

With some muttering, Malchik assisted Yuda in getting to his feet. Because of the wounds, he could not
place his full weight on them and leant against his son
for support. The Queen's lifeless form dangled from
his hand like a dead bird.

'Zyon,' said Yuda through his teeth. 'This is . . . the
pits.'

'You haven't changed your mind, Mister?'

Yuda snarled at him like a wolf. 'You wouldn't talk
so clever if you had my feet,' he said. As he spoke, the
owl Chovotis flew out of the dark, a striated pattern
of shadowy wings, and landed on Malchik's shoulder.
'What's that?' said Yuda. Malchik reached up to stroke
the feathers under her chin.

'She chose me,' he said. 'Just as the wolf chose you.'

As he spoke, the old shaman Derzu came limping
out of one of the tunnels, following the owl. About his
feet, the People lay scattered like dead leaves. As he
picked his way amongst the bodies, Annat could see

from the way he walked that his feet must have suffered injuries like those done to Yuda. When Derzu reached them, he paused to gaze from one to another. The two men leaned together, and the top of Yuda's head was just below Malchik's chin. Though one was very dark and the other fair, the similarity in their looks was clear when they stood so close. Malchik was supporting his father with his left arm, while Chovotis nibbled at his right hand with her beak. And though Malchik was untidy and unwashed, and Yuda looked like a scarecrow whose clothes were stained with blood, there was no mistaking the utter trust with which he leant on his son, or how proudly he bore the mark of the Prism. The People might have broken his body, but they had done nothing to humble his spirit. Derzu turned from them to Annat and Huldis.

'Four shamans,' said the old man. 'Five. That's a lot for one mountain.'

'Hallo,' said Malchik. 'This is my father.'

The old man approached him and Yuda, but it was the latter he spoke to.

'It is very hard,' he said, 'when they first make you lame. But if you cannot walk, still you can fly, wolf man.'

Yuda lifted up the Queen's limp body. 'We have to help them,' he said.

'You have the Prism?' said Derzu. Yuda reached into his trouser pocket and brought it out.

'Even if we can somehow restore its energy, Derzu, the Magus will draw on it for his spells. And he has one in mind.'

Derzu touched the mark on Yuda's chest. 'Your soul is stronger than his,' he said. 'Much stronger now. I am not speaking of power. If you heal the Prism, he cannot use it.'

'My soul?' said Yuda.

'I see you with the eyes of a shaman. The People hurt you, but they also gave you a gift. Heal the stone,' said Derzu, stabbing at the crystal with his finger, 'and you'll see.'

'I'm too tired to heal anything, old man,' said Yuda. 'I feel like an empty cup.'

Annat rose up from where she had been sitting, and approached them. She was shy of her father's black gaze.

'He's right, Yuda,' she said, lowering her eyes. 'I can see you. I can see into your *durmat*, and it's changed.'

'My *durmat*?'

'It's the signature of your powers. The one we all have, even Malchik. Mine is silver-blue.'

'Mine used to be that colour,' Yuda said. He laid the Queen's body in the crook of his arm, as if she were a baby. Annat felt a lump in her throat. It was partly the touching absurdity of the way he cradled the small figure, and partly the compassion she saw in his face. She dared to go nearer and touch his arm. 'No,' she said. 'It's not that. It hasn't changed colour again. But there's a mark on it, like the one on your chest.'

Yuda looked up at Derzu. 'You're saying this means I can heal the Prism?'

'Only you,' said the old shaman. Yuda offered him the Queen's body, and Derzu took it. Yuda held the Prism up before his face, studying it. 'What would you do, Natka, to heal a crystal?' he said. Annat bent over to study the stone in his palm. It looked like nothing more than a lump of rock. But if she shut her good eye . . .

'Oh!' she said, clutching his arm. 'It looks like a small heart, all tubes and valves!'

'I'm glad I can't see that,' he said. He paused. 'Maybe it needs blood. The Queen said mine had stained it . . .' and he clasped the stone to the mark on his chest. Under his hand, the crystal changed colour; at first a thin pink, then ruby red, then a much darker shade like wine. Yuda bent his head so the black hair hid his face. Then he caught his breath, and said, 'Hold me tight, Malchku.'

Annat touched his arm. 'You must stop. It's hurting you,' she said.

'No,' he said.

He opened his hand, and the crystal lay on his palm, burning clear and brilliant; there was no trace of red in it. 'Zyon,' he said, softly, and dropped it. Where it had lain against his heart, the mark burned scarlet. He sank back against Malchik, who had to support his whole weight.

'How is it with you, Mister?' he said.

Yuda gripped Malchik's arm where it held him. '*Mein Gott*,' he said. 'That was the sweetest – and the most bitter – thing.' He covered the mark with his hand.

The Glass Mountain

Annat picked up the Prism from the ground where it had fallen, finding it cool to the touch, and turned to Derzu. Lying across his knees, the little Queen had opened her black, blank eyes.

Chapter 18

The *Arabian Bird* rose, borne up on a thermal. The city of Dieulevaut dwindled beneath it, becoming more ethereal under the haze. Due east stood the bulk of the Lepas Mountains, their tops white with snow which had such brilliance in the sunlight that the shadows cast by the trees lower down showed a deep, smoky blue.

When they cleared the peaks, the wind smote them, buffeting the dirigible and trying to push it westwards. The engine laboured as Ignatius aimed the craft head-on into the gusts, and still they climbed. From time to time there would be a dragonish roar as he fired the burners, heating the air in the envelope to make the balloon rise. Yuste and Boris leaned together, wrapped in their blankets, while Cluny and Planchet squatted on the deck. It was too cold to think, and the air was growing thin; all they could do was to gasp for breath and watch the luminous landscape spreading out beneath.

Cluny seemed to know the names of all the peaks. He suffered least from the effects of lack of oxygen, and was eager to point out the mountains and passes below. Yuste, her hands tucked under her armpits to keep them warm, wished she could share his enthusiasm. The cold seemed to have reawakened her anxiety, and she kept thinking about Yuda, Annat and Malchik. There was an ache, an emptiness in her mind where once she had been able to reach out and touch her brother, just as if he were standing beside her. She wondered how she would ever become used to her loss.

Boris seemed to understand. He did not try to talk to her, or send his thoughts into her mind, but his big arm stayed wrapped round her shoulders, and she took comfort from his presence. He used his powers just a little to give them both a share of warmth, and Yuste realised that there was true value in someone who could control small and delicate quantities of power; she could not have managed anything so subtle.

At last, they rose above the wind. Ignatius no longer tried to make his craft climb, and the ship began to travel eastwards. Its pinned-down sails thrummed in the breeze. Sometimes, the *Arabian Bird* would find itself in the midst of cloud, and they passed through a thick, grey mist that shrugged past them like showers of rain. When Yuste looked back, she could still see the mountains, their peaks on fire beneath the sunrise. Her heart beat strangely in her chest as she realised that they had left Franj, and were crossing into the lands of the Staryetz and his great empire, which stretched for hundreds of miles, into an east she could not imagine.

They were sailing due east of the Lepas Mountains, over the many small states and principalities that lay in the centre of Yevropa. As they got underway, and the dirigible descended, it became possible to see something of the lands below. They were hilly landscapes, almost mountainous, and Yuste glimpsed slate roofs and the steeples of Doxan temples, spires that thrust above domes shaped like tulip bulbs. Some of the villages held little more than a temple and a few ramshackle huts, with sheep scattered over the hillside like pale beads. Others were burghs made up of stone houses, overhanging the valleys as if they had grown out of the rock. They were not like the towns of Franj; darker, more shadowy, they seemed to huddle amidst their high walls.

And then there were the castles. One or two perched crookedly atop a rocky summit; others, like the towns, clung to the sides of cliffs or overlooked green, open valleys. Some were ruins, jagged shapes of stone in which eagles nested; others had been patched with new stone, and she could just make out the sentries on the walls. Flags flew from the towers, a cluster of bright colours that defied the chill morning.

'What country is this, Boris?' she said.

'Ostria. It used to be part of a great empire, like the Neustrian Empire. But it fell to the Staryetz long ago. And west of Ostria, we will come to the *puszta*, the great Angrian plain.'

The names jostled in Yuste's mind. She had seen

them drawn on maps when she taught geography to the children of Sankt-Eglis, but they had never seemed to her like real places. The children had been obliged to learn by rote the names of all the capital cities. But it no longer seemed to matter since the Staryetz had conquered all the lands east of the Lepas Mountains. All those kingdoms, principalities, bishoprics and city-states, all had to pay him tribute. She wondered whether the Doyen knew that he would restore the old kingdom of Franj and the Neustrian Empire only for them to fall subject to the Staryetz's imperial greed.

'Does it feel like home, Boris?'

'Not to me, Yuste. I'm from Sklava, not these odd places. But it's more than twenty years since I left Kiyev.'

Midday seemed to come too soon. They shared out the rations that Beatrice had provided, brown bread and cheese and a flask of wine. Yuste declined the wine and Boris contented himself with a swig of slivovitz from his flask. It was odd to be eating sitting in a rocking boat that floated not on the surface of the sea but in the air. While they ate, Ignatius chatted to them. His sister had prepared a special repast for him, of sliced chicken placed between two pieces of bread that she had smeared with butter. Yuste thought it very odd.

'What are you planning to do when you get to the mountain?' said Ignatius.

'A lot depends on what it's like,' said Boris. 'But I'd vote that you lower us down to the summit so we can have a look around.'

'If it is a granite batholith, it will probably be a rounded rather than a jagged formation,' said Ignatius.

'I was wondering if the glass effect might be due to the presence of obsidian,' said Cluny.

'Or magic,' said Boris.

They were speeding over the landscape now. Ignatius had adjusted the rudder to set a course to the south-east, which he swore was where the mountain was reported to lie. They had left behind the rocky gorges and valleys of Ostria and were flying over rolling hills where villages small and rounded as loaves of bread sat amongst the slopes. There were many trees, but no forests. The trees seemed to be deciduous, and not all were in leaf, though Yuste noticed one or two that had faint clouds of pale blossom.

It was a fine day, but cold. They had escaped the clouds, and the sky was clear above and below. Yuste could see their shadow travelling over the ground. She studied the long grasses of the pasture that waved in the wind, making rolling and rippling patterns. She had become accustomed to the altitude, and it no longer troubled her to stand at the side of the gondola, gazing over the edge at the earth rushing past. She had managed to locate a scarf and gloves that Beatrice must have packed for her use along with the food and other necessaries. They reminded her of the leather purse that Ignatius's sister had given her; she opened it and took out the contents, a small, hard object wrapped in a handkerchief. When she unwrapped it, she found it to be a revolver, not unlike the one that Boris carried. She brought it to show him.

'A gun,' said Boris. He flipped open the magazine to show her that it was loaded with six bullets. The safety catch had been left on, and he showed her how to disengage it. 'You may find this useful, where we're going,' he said.

'I have my powers.'

'And look what happened last time you used those. You won't have your brother to help you now.'

He stopped and she saw the look of shame in his face. 'It doesn't matter, Boris,' she said. 'You're right. Yuda couldn't nanny me for ever. I wouldn't want him to.' She sat down beside him and laid her hand over his. 'But I'd be grateful for any advice and guidance you could offer me.'

'You're very powerful,' said Boris. 'More powerful than me. But I think, without training, you'd be unwise to use your powers. We'll have to see. This gun may be useful.'

'Land ho!' called Ignatius.

The four of them rushed to the bows, and saw what he was referring to. On the eastern horizon, rising straight out of the plain, was a massive outcrop of rock. It did look much like a child's sketch of a mountain, except that the top seemed to be rounded. It caught the sunlight and glinted like a sheet of burnished metal.

'Well, there it is,' said Boris.

'What are we going to do when we get there?' said Cluny.

'I vote we ask Ignatius to hover over it, while we shin down a rope and take a look around.'

'It's difficult to tell how high it is from here,' said Cluny.

'I can lend you a spyglass if you want a closer look,' called Ignatius.

While Cluny hurried back to collect the telescope from him, Yuste, Boris and Planchet leaned on the side of the ship, gazing at their destination. It was the only tall formation for miles around; into the distance on every side stretched the soft, stirring grasses of the *puszta*. When Cluny returned with the spyglass, he offered it to Boris, who in turn passed it to Yuste. She lifted it to her eye, and adjusted the focus. The mountain sprang into view. Its walls were sheer, great planes of dark, sullen stone that shone like crystal, reflecting the light. There was no sign of any fortress on this side; but she could make out a small, steel-blue lake and a cluster of nearby trees. In every respect, it resembled the painting that Cluny had made after Malchik's dream.

She handed the telescope to Boris, and he trained it on the mountain as she had done.

'It is the one, isn't it?' said Cluny. Yuste found it hard to wrench her gaze away from their objective.

'It must be, Cluny,' she said. 'But I can see no openings or caves, not even a handhold. It looks smooth . . . as glass.'

Boris lowered the spyglass and offered it to Cluny. 'We'll have to land on the top,' he said. 'There's no way we could climb that. Though I suppose we should take a look at the other side before we make up our minds.'

Yuste squeezed her hands together, inside their gloves. 'Do you think we should scan it, Boris Andreyevich?' she said.

'We could . . . so long as we don't alert the occupants. On the other hand, if they're keeping a lookout, they will have seen us by now.'

'It must be a granite batholith,' said Cluny. 'But I cannot believe that the walls could be so sheer. They look as if they have been finished by human hands.'

'Or magic,' said Boris again.

'I don't like it,' said Yuste, as Planchet in his turn took a sighting on the mountain.

'It would benefit from a coat of paint. Something more cheerful than grey,' said Boris. She could tell from his humour that he was as nervous as she. Cluny drew his sword a short way out of its sheath, and slapped it back in.

'Though I spent many years living with dark magic about me, I have never faced a warlock before,' he said.

'There is one thing,' said Boris. 'Surprise. He may not be expecting an attack from the air. I think it's time Yuste and I made that scan, to see what this mountain is made of . . .'

The top of the mountain seemed to open a black maw, and it swallowed Semyon in one gulp. He hit the ground much more softly than he had reason to expect, and lay gasping on his back. Above him, the roof of the Crystal Chamber seemed comfortingly familiar; he had fallen neatly through the air-hole in the roof, through which he could see the sky. He could scarcely believe that he had performed such a dangerous spell without blowing himself to smithereens. He closed his eyes and waited for the thud as Sarl arrived. It was too much to hope that the magic might have brought Semyon home while sending his master away. He allowed himself a few more moments' peace, lying still on the hard floor while his body readjusted to its new circumstances.

Sarl arrived after a short interval. Semyon sat up and opened his eyes, disappointed but not surprised to see that the Heir had been conveyed in one piece. Though he lay very still, Semyon knew that it would not be long before he rose suddenly and stiffly, like a corpse arising from the grave. Semyon began picking himself up, dusting off his robes and straightening his hat, unwilling to be deprived of his advantage, however small.

The cave looked much as he had left it. There was the table and chairs, with the plates of uneaten and now rancid food. The passageway that led to the mirror. The open door in the wall . . . Semyon swore, pulling his hat down over his eyes. The cave was empty and the prisoners gone. They must have found the elevator and used it to escape into the interior of the mountain. Though 'escape' was not the word that he would use. It was likely that they were already dead, having been finished off by one of the mountain's other inhabitants. Whether or not that was the case, he faced the tiresome task of finding them, as well as securing a fresh power source and retrieving Huldis and the shaman.

Readjusting his hat, Semyon staggered to a chair. He muttered a small charm, and the plates were swept clean. Fresh wine sparkled in the goblets, fresh fruit in the central bowl, and a basin and ewer of warm water were ready to his hand. He bathed his face and dabbed it dry with the clean towel that his unseen servants had provided, noticing how his untrimmed beard had grown straggly once more. When he had finished his ablutions, he found Sarl on his feet, staring about the cave with the unblinking gaze of an eagle.

'Where are the prisoners?' he demanded.

'Gone,' said Semyon.

Sarl strode across to confront him over the table. 'What do you mean, "gone", Magus?' he said. 'Are you telling me that you have lost not only the shaman but also his children?'

Semyon picked up a large unseasonable green apple and bit into it loudly. 'I have lost the lot, Mon Seigneur,' he said. 'Even if you butcher me and cut out my heart, it won't do you any good. There are no living souls within a hundred miles.' He thought it prudent not to mention that he lacked the power to perform the spell; better to keep that knowledge in reserve.

Sarl stepped back a pace as if he had been slapped. Semyon enjoyed the look on his face. 'That's right, Mon Seigneur,' he said. 'You are going to decay and die once more. Your life is in my hands. I wonder how that feels?'

Sarl did not answer. He pulled out a chair and slumped on it, his face averted from Semyon, who took several more loud bites from the apple. It was the best food he had tasted in days.

'You have your orders from the Staryetz,' said Sarl at length, in a toneless voice. 'If you do not obey him, he will destroy you.'

Crunch! 'Maybe,' said Semyon. 'I don't know what he was planning. Maybe he intended me to fail, and your father to be defeated. All I know is that I am the master now. You can threaten me as much as you wish. You need my help.'

'If you expect me to plead with you, Magus, you will be disappointed,' said Sarl.

'Why should I want you to plead? I've got you where I want you. And now we shall do things my way, in my time. You can rot a little longer. It's just your hand now, but what happens when it spreads to your face?'

The apple had become a denuded core. Semyon set it down on the table, picked up a goblet of wine and drank. He knew he must not goad Sarl for too long. It was quite possible that the Heir would simply kill him, even though he was Sarl's only hope of recovery.

'What are you going to do?' said Sarl, his voice hoarse.

Semyon smacked his lips on the rich wine. 'First, I'm going to take a look in the mirror, to see if I can find out what has happened to the prisoners. You can do as you please. Eat, drink – be merry!' He choked off a laugh. 'As far as I'm concerned, my main purpose is to find Huldis and the little shaman. I almost care for them, Mon Seigneur, as I don't much care for you.'

He stood up and set the empty goblet on the table. He felt good, even happy, for the first time in days. He did want to rescue Huldis, if he could manage it. As for the shaman, Semyon would not be too troubled if he had escaped. They could look for other, more convenient victims if they needed them. He left Sarl sitting at the table, motionless, not looking at him, and hastened down the passage that led to the chamber where his mirror stood.

Mirrors were not essentially magical, but Semyon knew how to put them to a variety of magic uses, not confined to travel. He stood in front of the tall glass, confronting his own unlovely reflection. His beard was unkempt, his face flushed with wine and unpleasant emotions. He cast off his robe and bonnet and stood before the mirror bare-headed in his shirt. The figure that presented itself to him was more likeable: a man with a sallow complexion and a thick mat of brown hair. He rolled up his sleeves and began to conjure the mirror. He wanted it to show him his prisoners. He decided to focus on Huldis, and spoke her name to the glass, almost tenderly.

'Show me Huldis.'

The surface of the glass clouded, as it gave up its usual reflection. Semyon watched his image dissolve. He hunkered down, staring as close to the surface as he dared. The mirror seemed to be hunting; it showed various pictures, too flickering for him to make out. Then at last, it showed him the face of Huldis. She looked much as he had last seen her, with her uncovered blonde hair wild and dishevelled, and her eyes and nose and mouth reddened with weeping. Without realising what he was doing, Semyon reached out to touch her face, and the surface of the mirror shivered like water. He quickly withdrew his hand, and the mirror drew back, showing him where Huldis was.

Semyon sat down hard on the stone floor. He stared at the picture before him in the mirror for a few moments, letting its implications wash over him. Then he struggled to his feet and called out, 'Mon Seigneur! Come and see this!'

There was a pause before Sarl's heavy tread sounded in the passageway. Semyon turned back to the scene before him in the mirror, trying to work out how it had transpired. The mirror kept showing him the Prism, as if it were trying to tell him something. He heard Sarl stop just behind him.

'What is it, Magus?'

'I've found the prisoners. All of them,' said Semyon. Sarl stooped to peer at the small image on the surface of the glass, and then exclaimed.

'What are those . . . things?'

'Those, Mon Seigneur, are the People. It seems they have been transported to the mountain.'

Sarl crouched down beside him, fascinated. 'They are all there,' he said.

'Indeed they are, Mon Seigneur,' said Semyon. 'They are there and we are here.'

'Then we must bring them here,' said Sarl, hungrily. Semyon shuddered.

'You are saying, Mon Seigneur, that I should bring here at least two powerful and angry shamans?'

'Vasilyevich doesn't look like much of a threat in that condition. Or are you afraid of him, Magus?'

Semyon stood up. He must not lose his advantage. 'Very well,' he said. 'I will cast a spell that summons them here. Then we shall see.' He hurried back to the Crystal Chamber without waiting for Sarl, leaving his outer garments scattered on the ground. He had been such a fool! It no longer mattered whether he summoned his former prisoners, or they came here of their own accord. Now Sarl would expect him to perform the spell, when he lacked the power that would make it work. He must think quickly. To mislead the Heir, he might have to go a long way in his pretence; he did not like to think how far, though he meant to save his own skin. He turned and grinned at Sarl, hoping his face did not reveal the turmoil of his thoughts.

'We will be ready soon,' he said. 'Now I need only to harvest one heart and two souls.'

A rustling like the stirring of leaves filled the darkness of the hall at the foot of the mountain, as the bodies of the People strewn across the stony floor wakened from their deathly slumber. The ground seemed to come to life as, in ones and twos, they sat up, stretched, or turned over like sleepers unwilling to wake from their dreams.

Annat held the Prism up before her face. With her good eye, she saw a lump of colourless crystal, clear and faultless, but with her altered eye . . . She lowered her hand and focused on the Queen, who was sitting up on Derzu's knee, her face buried in her hands. Annat took a pace and knelt down beside the old shaman, holding up the stone. When the Queen lowered her hands, it was the first thing she saw, burning in the light like polished glass. She stretched out her arms and Annat placed the Prism between her palms, wondering if the Queen too could see its many hidden forms. She watched the Queen staring into the depths of the stone and reading it like a book. At last, the small woman looked up at her. The Queen's face was neither young nor old; without blemish, her skin looked pale and fragile, so that the blood vessels shone through like streaks in marble.

'Take me to him, child,' said the Queen. Annat smiled. Her wounded eye still throbbed from time to time, but she knew its metamorphosis was almost complete. She had ceased to hate the woman who had injured her. She grasped the Queen round the waist and lifted her lightly, rising to her feet. The woman was no heavier than a porcelain doll, and Annat wondered if she had hollow bones, like a bird. She brought the small figure round and held it up so that the Queen was face to face with Yuda. He looked tired, but Annat could see he was already recovering. He reached out his hand as if to touch the little Queen, but withdrew it.

'I am glad to see Your Majesty restored to health,' he said.

'Shaman, we are in your debt,' said the Queen. 'How can we repay you when you have given life to the Prism, our only hope?'

Yuda looked down, and smiled. 'The stone has rewarded me,' he said. 'It has taken away my pain and replenished my strength, though it could not mend my limbs. But I only let the stone feed off the power that flows through me – power much greater than I am, and more than I understand.'

'My King saw that power, which is why he used you so harshly,' said the Queen. 'I am sorry for it, since it seems all we did was to hurt you. But we maim your kind only to make you wise.'

Yuda looked at her from under his dark brows. 'Some things don't heal so well, Majesty,' he said. 'I don't mean what was done to me. You saw the girl, Huldis. They didn't touch her; they only made her watch . . . That seems as cruel as anything mortals could do. I healed the stone for you because you looked at us with pity, and not as if we were strange, unfeeling beasts. That is what hurts, not spikes and spears . . .'

The Queen stretched out her arms, holding the Prism. 'Take it,' she said, 'take the stone. Keep it safe for me. We will go back to our planet and our world, and this will stay with you. Only you can guard it from the Magus, and others like him.'

Yuda took the crystal from her and held it up. 'The Magus needs to kill me,' he said. 'It may be against his wishes, but that's what he was engaged to do. And then what will become of the stone?'

'The Magus may understand the lore of stones, but he does not know their hearts,' said the Queen. 'It is part of you, and you have a share in it. The Magus would not value a rock of little worth – for what is it but a lump of quartz, a common stone, unlike the gems we mine?'

Yuda closed his fist on the Prism. 'I will keep it, Majesty, and guard it for you,' he said. 'Though I'm not much use when I cannot stand without my son to hold me. The Magus and his lord will find us easy prey.'

'Do not mock me, shaman,' said the Queen. 'Your limbs may be shattered, but the stone hardly touched your power. Without our nets to bind you, you are a creature to be reckoned with. My eyes can see the threads that weave you together, you and your children and the maiden you call Huldis. Go to the Magus and tell him I sent you. Let him think on. He too has mighty powers, but he is not wise. When we are gone, the stone will carry you there.'

'We have no other way to travel,' said Yuda. 'Thank you, Majesty, for your strange gift.'

The Queen inclined her head in a haughty bow. She motioned Annat to set her down, and walked to the edge of the dais to address her people. The King stepped forward to take her hand. As she began to speak, Huldis slowly stood up. Her fair hair was wild, full of elf-knots and tangles, and her eyelids and nose were red with weeping. She joined them, but she was hardly looking at Annat or Malchik; her eyes were shining as she came to Yuda. As they gazed at each other, Annat realised with a little shock that they were using *sprechen* – and she could not hear what they were saying! Then Yuda spoke aloud.

'Nah,' he said. 'We want to escape – but we have

to stop Sarl. If the Magus can find a way to make him whole, he will return to conquer Masalyar – and rule. He won't finish there. The Doyen might be a harsh ruler, but your brother . . .' He stopped, gave a shrug, and winced. 'I promised the ambassador,' he said. 'I want this ended. The city may hold back the Doyen's army, but if Sarl comes, they will be overthrown. I'm sorry, Missis.'

'There is only one way out, and that lies through the Crystal Chamber,' said Derzu.

Annat focused on the People. Caught between the rays of light and shadow, they seemed more ethereal than ever. She almost felt that she did not want them to go. Their small lives had cut across hers, and changed it for ever. She glanced at the Prism, and saw it glowing in Yuda's fist. It was a stone, but also a living thing that fed on blood; and it was a tiny clockwork motor, running on a perpetual spring. Now, as she watched, it sent the People home. Their outlines became silvery and indistinct; then, with a rush of light, they vanished, and the sunlight from the vents in the walls played on emptiness.

Yuda held up the crystal. 'They've gone, and it's time for us to go,' he said. 'Are you coming with us, Derzu?'

The old shaman shook his head. 'I will stay here,' he said. 'The stone of my prison has grown under my skin. But I can still travel where I want.'

'I'd like to stay, and talk long with you,' said Yuda. He shook his head. 'But I have business to attend to. Unfinished business.' He glanced from Annat to

Huldis and back. 'I guess we all do,' he said. Then he held the stone high, and light poured from it, enveloping them in brightness. Annat caught her breath she knew that, very soon, they would be swept up and borne into the presence of the Magus – and Sarl.

Chapter 19

The dirigible hovered over the summit like a float bobbing on the surface of a pond. Boris and Yuste had made their scan, but they had divined little beyond the fact that the mountain was hollow and inhabited. While Ignatius held his craft steady, the four of them leaned over the side. They were about a hundred feet shy of the top and they could see what looked like a hole or small crater in its surface. They had no other plan than to climb down and examine the mountain from close to, to see if they could find an entrance or weak spot. Boris insisted that he should be the first to descend, so Yuste watched as the others lowered a rope over the side and he shinned down it. Though Ignatius was trying to keep the ship still, it juddered and shifted in the breeze, and the rope swung and swirled, so that there were times when Boris dangled not over the narrow plateau but above the drop to the plain hundreds of feet below.

Yuste only realised she had been holding her breath when she saw him set his feet on the dull, glistening rock. She gasped, and Cluny put a steadying hand on her arm.

'I must go next,' she said.

'Are you sure?'

In answer, Yuste started to take off the skirt Beatrice had lent her. This was no time to worry about modesty; at least she was wearing a sturdy pair of cotton pantalets. Hitching up her petticoat, she climbed over the side of the gondola. The distance beneath her feet seemed to gape but she ignored it and took a firm grip on the rope. There was a moment when she hung in mid-air, suspended only by her hands as she tried to catch the hawser between her soft shoes. However, once she had caught it and begun to lower herself hand over hand, she fixed her gaze on the worried faces of the men above and not to the place where Boris stood below, anchoring the tail of the rope.

At last, his hands caught her about the waist and lifted her the last few feet. Breathless, Yuste turned to face him. Wisps of hair had escaped from their chignon and she brushed them back from her face. She had expected the stone to be slippery underfoot but its crystalline surface was rough-edged and granular.

'Here we are,' said Boris, keeping hold of her for longer than was necessary. Yuste smiled up at him. She would have liked to reach up to kiss his mouth but instead they shared a smile.

While Boris held the rope steady for Cluny and Planchet to descend, Yuste picked her way over the strange, pitted skin of the summit until she found the crater they had noticed from above. Crouching down beside it, she saw at once that it was a vent cut into the rock from which she could glimpse a chamber below. Taking care not to let her head obstruct the light, she lay down on her belly so that she could peep through the opening.

She could not see much while her eyes were becoming accustomed to the dim light of the cave. Little by little, she made out the edge of a table, several chairs – and then someone walked across her field of view. Yuste shrank back, having glimpsed a head of brown hair.

The others came to squat beside her; they too were careful not to let the sun cast their shadows across the opening.

'What did you see?' said Cluny in a low voice.

'There's someone down there. I think it was a man.'

One by one, they all did as Yuste had done, stretching out on the ground in order to peer into the hole. It was Boris who, as he was kneeling down to take his turn, uttered a soft exclamation.

'What is it?' Yuste mouthed.

'We don't need a spy-hole. The roof is transparent.'

The four of them stood up to stare at the grey crystal beneath their feet. It was like standing on a sheet of ice and studying the dark water below. They began to make out the shapes of the room underneath: the two men, one tall and light-haired, the other stocky and dark; and the tables, chairs and coffers, all seen dimly as if through a thick layer of mist.

'Bloody hell,' said Boris.

'That is Sarl. My brother,' said Cluny. Planchet nodded.

'But surely they will see us?' said Yuste.

'Not if they don't look up,' said Boris. He grinned at her. 'Maybe it only works one way. Like a spy mirror.'

'We could drop in through the hole . . .' said Cluny.

'They'd pick us off one at a time,' said Boris. He bent down and touched the stone. 'This stuff can't be that thick. I reckon we could blast our way through. What do you say, Yuste?'

She folded her arms. 'I'm sure you're right, Boris Andreyevich. But Sarl and the Magus are by themselves. No sign of our people.'

'That's good. If we act now, we can kill Sarl or the Magus before they can enact the ritual. They need your people for that.'

Yuste looked at Cluny and Planchet. 'Could you do that? If it meant killing Sarl?'

'I came to save Annat,' said Cluny. He hesitated. 'I'd kill Sarl if it was the only way to save her. But . . .'

'But what?' Boris stood up, squaring his shoulders inside his trench coat. 'This isn't a good time to change your mind. Stop this Sarl and we end the power of Ademar. The Doyen's plans will collapse. If we rescue our friends and make our escape, what happens then? The Magus will find some other victims to make Sarl immortal. Then he'll join his dad and get down to business. Masalyar is just the start, remember.'

'He is my brother,' said Cluny.

Yuste found herself looking at Planchet. The old soldier's face was set as stone.

'I have been a loyal servant of Ademar all my life,' he said. 'But I chose to serve Seigneur Cluny. His ways are my ways. I will do what he commands.'

Boris covered his face with his hands. 'Holy Mother, I can't believe this. We've come all this way, we could take them now, and instead we're arguing about niceties. Niceties? If we don't kill them then Yuste and I won't have a home to return to. There won't be a safe place where we can go. Anywhere.'

Yuste did not hear his last words. She had dropped down on her hands and knees; she might as well have fallen. Through the cloudy lens of the roof, she had seen a movement, a flicker of shadow. Sarl and the Magus were no longer the only ones in the cave . . .

In the Crystal Chamber at the summit of the mountain, everything had been made ready. On a tripod stood a metal dish filled with glowing charcoal, intended to reduce what was placed upon it to ashes. On a purple velvet cloth, the instruments of divination and butchery were laid out: a knife carved from obsidian, a pewter goblet filled with wine, a jar of mixed powders and two long-handled hooks. Close by, Semyon sat at his table, writing on a piece of parchment. He was doing everything needed to perform the magic; what he did not know yet was how far he must proceed with the charade, and what he must do to save himself from Sarl's anger when the Heir discovered that he had been duped.

'What's that?' said Sarl, starting to his feet; he seemed nervous, flinching at every small sound or movement. Irritated to have his concentration disturbed, Semyon looked up from his thoughts to see an owl winging across the chamber, to land on the back of an empty chair, whence it regarded him with its round-eyed stare.

'It looks to me like an owl,' he said. He was copying out the formula for the spell with which he had planned to make Sarl a living – and perhaps immortal – man. He scratched out a mistake with his quill. It made him uneasy to write down even the words which made up the incantation and he was trying to use runes and shorthand to denote its meaning. He was half afraid that, if he set the spell down in full, it would come to life despite the fact that he lacked the power to perform it. Even without his furred robe and hat, he was perspiring, though the air in the cave was cool.

He heard Sarl's intake of breath, and the silence of the chamber changed subtly, as if its echo had altered. Semyon put down his pen, wondering if the mere act of writing had summoned some horror from one of the thousand worlds. He looked up from the page, and sprang up, knocking over his chair.

'Tchernobog,' he shouted, unable to dissemble his surprise. Though he had not summoned them, they had come to him just the same: the small, dark-eyed girl – but one of her eyes had gone, and in its place a whorl of colour seemed to spiral and change ceaselessly; the tall, thin young man, scowling with a look that reminded Semyon of the owl perched close by, and leaning against him the little shaman, his face pale as the parchment and his clothes torn and dabbled with blood. His black eyes watched Semyon, and the Magus could almost smell his power, like burning tar. Beside him stood Huldis, tall and slender as a birch tree in her green dress; but her hair was dishevelled and the green cloth was marked with ugly stains.

Sarl took a step forward. 'Huldis,' he said. 'How is it with you?'

Semyon ran his fingers back through his hair so that it stood on end. If he used *sprechen* now when Sarl was standing so close, the Heir might catch his thoughts. He needed to prolong the deceit, but he also needed to know what they were thinking – above all Huldis and the little man. If they had come to oppose him, he might have to use his own powers against them – was he not a thrice-powerful shaman? – but he was not sure if that was what he wanted to do. Whatever he decided, he needed Sarl to believe that the spell would proceed as planned.

Huldis looked at her brother in an odd way, as if she had no idea who he was. It was as if the events that had passed since she left him had erased her memory. She tugged at a lock of her blonde hair.

'Zhan Sarl,' she said. 'It is so . . . strange to see you.'

Sarl went nearer to her, ignoring the others. 'You are no longer a prisoner,' he said. 'Once this is finished, we will return at once to Ademar.'

Huldis gazed at him a long time. 'Once this is finished,' she repeated. She lowered her eyes. 'I wish I could do what you want, Zhan. I shall be sorry to grieve you. But my place is not with you now. It is here, where I am standing now.' She put out her hand to touch Yuda's shoulder. 'These are my friends. And if you are going to kill my friends, then you must kill me too.'

Semyon stared at Sarl's face with fascinated horror. He could not see the movement of any expression, but inside, under the surface, it was as if the skull had pushed forward beneath the skin.

'Huldis,' the Heir said, 'I do not understand. These are not your friends; these are our enemies. They must die for me to gain new life.'

'Then I have gone over to the enemy,' said Huldis. 'If such is the price of your life, you are the one who must die. I have watched you, Zhan Sarl, and seen what you are. Though you were my brother, I cannot help you to complete this spell. I do not want to see you ruler over Neustria, immortal – and a monster. If nothing else, I am in debt to these people many times over. Should I repay that by standing by while they are butchered?'

Semyon had to stop himself throwing up his arms and cheering. He was glad that all Sarl's attention was centred on his sister. But the little shaman was more perceptive; he caught Semyon's eye and Semyon wondered if – for a moment – he saw understanding in the other man's face. He dared not permit himself to send the thoughts that would confirm his surmise; instead, he stepped forward and laid his hand on Sarl's sleeve.

'Let it be, Mon Seigneur,' he said. 'Your sister is not

herself. She will doubtless see wisdom when all is finished. It is time to begin the spell.'

'You have them in your power?' said Sarl. He was still watching Huldis.

Semyon wondered what would happen if he said yes. Any or all of them might speak up to contradict him. They had come here of their own accord, and he did not see how he could make them submit to even the beginnings of his ritual. But if he told Sarl the truth, the Heir would realise that Semyon had not summoned them, and might begin to question whether he had the power to complete the spell. Once more, he found himself looking at Vasilyevich, and he thought he saw the man give a slight, barely perceptible nod.

'Mon Seigneur,' he said. 'This is a perilous magic. Before I begin – before I can think of beginning – I must make sure that you are well protected.'

Sarl turned his head. His eyes looked dry and hard in their sockets. 'I want to see them die first,' he said. 'To know that it is finished.'

Semyon checked his own powers, just as a man might touch his balls for luck. If Sarl insisted that he kill the prisoners, he would have to fight them first.

'The heart and the souls must be taken at special points in the ritual, or all will be lost,' he said. 'But you will see everything that is done.'

The boy spoke, and said what Semyon had been dreading he would hear. 'If you want our souls, Magus, you'll have to take them. Let's see if you can.'

'What does he mean?' said Sarl. 'You summoned them here. You told me they were at your command.'

Though Semyon had said no such thing, he guessed that Sarl had heard what he wanted to hear. He drew Sarl away from the others, and muttered, 'I have been very careful, Mon Seigneur. They do not know that they are bound with magic. But they will learn if they try to resist.' He wondered as he spoke whether he had indeed seen Vasilyevich nod at him. If the little man had understood – and he was quick-witted enough – he might have been able to communicate his thought to Huldis and the girl. But not to the boy, who was barely a shaman. The boy might not know what the others shared. Semyon wished he could look at them, but he dared not move his head.

'Mon Seigneur,' he said, 'I am ready to begin. You must come to stand in the place where I show you.'

And Sarl obeyed. Semyon made him stand in the centre of the chamber, a little way from the circle of light that fell from the air-hole in the roof. Here in the shadow, he began to draw a chalk circle round the Heir of Ademar. This would be magic enough for today. He could see with his inner sight pale blue flames beginning to flicker along the inner edge of the ring. He muttered a few words, and the circle was complete. Sarl stood at its centre with his arms folded.

'Mon Seigneur, listen to me. At no time must you leave the chalk circle. Whatever happens, whatever you hear or see. If you try to step over the edge, your new life will be in peril and you may be utterly consumed.'

'I hear you, Magus. I must stay within the circle.'

Semyon turned to pick up the obsidian knife. He

could not be certain that Sarl would not break out of the circle, despite the magic Semyon had woven into it to keep him there. If Sarl were after revenge, he might not care how much the blue flames seared him; he doubtless had little sensation in his moribund limbs. Semyon tested the tip of the glass knife with his finger, and saw it draw blood. It was so sharp, he felt no pain as the bead of crimson welled on his fingertip. His gaze moved beyond Sarl and the knife to the group at the other end of the cave. The time for illusion had passed; what he needed now was true magic, drawing on his innate power, since that was all he had left. He had gained a clue as to what was needed from Sarl's hatred of Vasilyevich. Hatred and fear. Something bound the two men together, as if neither could be at peace while the other lived.

Semyon took a deep, shuddering breath. He looked at Sarl, feeling cold beneath the skin. Swinging round, he raised the glass blade high, and bore down on the cluster of shamans. He could feel his arm trembling and he hoped the tremor was not too obvious. He saw the boy's eyes widen with fright and shock, their pupils large and blank. But the girls, though they put their arms across Yuda to shield him, were watching Semyon intently. He strode past Sarl and seized Vasilyevich by the shoulder. His thought was quick and as quiet as he could make it; he used their shared language.

— I don't want to kill you. But this has to look . . . right.

In response, Vasilyevich pressed something into his free hand. To the touch, it felt like a lump of crystal, cold and smooth. Semyon was perplexed until, as he lifted the knife, he saw that the crystal looked like a human heart. Vasilyevich smiled before Semyon brought the knife down.

When he had finished, he placed the stone heart in a silver chalice he had selected for the purpose. He could not believe that he had been preparing all this time for such a bloody act. The heart looked horribly convincing, and the cries and wails of the stricken girls chilled him through; their voices were like the keening of wolves. Now Semyon had a slick of the shaman's blood on the blade of his knife. Every drop of that blood, every cell, would be poison to Sarl. Taking the knife in his right hand, he swept it in an arc and began to chant. The words came from a language much older than the Sklavan he spoke today; from a time before the missionaries of Doxa brought the sacred Chrism to the holy city of Kiyev. It was an incantation that a village shaman such as Derzu might have recognised, or the sorcerers who dwelt in the tents of the Halekkai, men like the Staryetz, his master. Semyon drew a line in the air, leaving a mark that only he could see, and intoned the words of binding and separation.

As Yuste lunged for the opening, Boris grabbed her and covered her mouth with his hand before she could cry out. She struggled against him, but his thought intruded into her mind.

— *Keep quiet, or you'll ruin everything. Yuda isn't dead.*
— *But the Magus cut out his heart!*

The Glass Mountain

– *It's a trick. You should know he's alive; trust all your senses, not just your eyes.*

– *A trick – but why?*

– *I don't know. It's curious. Why should the Magus do that? I thought he was planning to make Sarl live.*

– *Let me go.*

Yuda was lying on the ground, and the girls had flung themselves across his body, screaming and crying; Malchik had dropped to his knees. And the Magus held up a bloody human heart, showing it to Sarl. How could this be a trick?

– *We have to go in now, Boris.*

The golden power rose up in her like a fountain welling from an underground spring. Raising her arms, she blasted the area round the vent, and the stone wrinkled and cracked in the heat. Like breaking ice, it shattered, and as the fragments fell into the chamber below, Yuste found herself standing on the lip of a wider hole, a fissure in the glass. Boris snatched at her, but she slipped through his grasp and leapt into the gap, plunging down from daylight into gloom. She landed lightly on her feet, and her hands were already scrabbling at the purse Beatrice had given her.

The cave was full of smoke and dust. About her feet lay fragments of the shattered roof, but no one had been standing beneath when she broke through. She made out dim shapes, the stocky magus and the tall Sarl, turned in amazement towards the place where she stood. Beyond them, only Malchik looked up to see her, and staggered to his feet.

The Magus raised his hands like a shaman preparing

to fight. The dust was settling, powdering his face and hair with silver grains.

'Who in Tchernobog's name are you?' he shouted. A few more shards of crystal dropped from the roof, and Yuste sprang out of their way. She felt no fear, only a mad, boiling rage that was like nothing she had ever known. She pointed her hand at him; she was holding the gun.

'You killed my brother,' she said.

A light thud behind her told her that Boris had arrived.

'Devils and demons! There are more of them,' said Sarl. But he was smiling; smiling because her brother was dead, and he saw only a small woman and a little man.

Boris came to stand at her side. He too had drawn his gun, but he held it casually in his right hand, as if he had not noticed it was there.

'Give us the prisoners,' he said.

Yuste ignored him. She advanced on the two men, Sarl and the Magus. She had begun to see their faces clearly. More than their faces . . . The Magus was holding a black knife in one hand, and in the other . . Yuste reeled. For a moment the air went dark, and she tasted salt on her tongue. She raised the gun. She took aim, sighting on the front of the skull between the wizard's eyes. She knew what would happen; the bullet would shatter his face and blow out his brain, in a mess of blood and dark mush. All it needed was for her to squeeze the trigger . . .

She heard Cluny and Planchet jump down behind

her. And in that small moment of distraction, the gun was plucked from her hand and flung across the cave by an invisible force. She stood alone, her three companions at her back, and heard her own, crazy laughter; why had she tried to use a weapon when she had powers that could burn up a living man and kindle the ground? She lifted her hands, and Sarl spoke.

'Messire Cluny. Planchet. What are you doing with these renegades?'

'Zhan Sarl,' said Cluny. 'I would be obliged if you could hand over your captives. All your captives.'

Sarl took a pace forwards. He took no notice of Boris or Yuste, as if they were of no significance. 'You do not understand, Cluny,' he said. 'The great spell is already under way. The spell that will restore my life. The Magus holds the shaman's heart in his hand. In a little while, I shall be made immortal. And our house will rise to restore Neustria to its former glory. You are my father's son, and our cause is your own. No matter that you have been suborned; now you are here, you will bear witness to our triumph.'

Cluny moved towards Sarl, drawn sword in his hand. 'No triumph,' he said; his voice shook though his hand was steady. 'I cannot let you stain the honour of our name with foul magic. A man has been butchered, and I know what ill deeds you have planned. I challenge you, Zhan Sarl; fight me like an honest man, if you are not afraid.'

'Afraid?' Sarl laughed. 'You could not kill me. I bear a charmed life until my ninety days are done.'

'It is too late,' said the Magus. 'The spell has

begun; it cannot be stopped. You are . . . too late.'

In the midst of her grief, Yuste could not help noticing something strange about the demeanour of the Magus. He licked his lips nervously; his eyes kept flickering towards the place where her brother lay, and the weeping girls. Was it indeed possible that the whole act had been an illusion? But why should their enemy act so much against his own interests? He had been engaged to help the Doyen and raise Sarl up; there was no reason that he should subvert the magic he had already performed.

A movement caught her eye. The two girls, Annat and Huldis, were sitting up, sweeping the hair back from their faces. Yuste saw them gazing at each other with a kind of complicity, and she saw no tears or marks of grief on their faces. Then Yuda moved, not with a twitching spasm of death; he lifted himself on to his elbow and looked at her, stared straight at her. There was no wound on his chest, not even a scratch, but only a red mark like a brand over his heart. Annat too was gazing at her, and she was marked and changed also; one of her eyes looked like a rainbow, trapped in the socket.

Yuste dropped to her knees. She hid her face in her hands and began to sob. She had watched her brother die, and now he was alive; what she had witnessed was indeed an illusion, a trick. In her confused mind, it seemed like a cruel hoax, intended to bring her here and betray her. The Magus had put down the false heart and was chanting once more, with hands outstretched and eyes rolled up so that only the whites showed. The knife in his hand dripped blood, and each drop seemed drawn as it fell to the rim of the circle where Sarl stood. Boris Grebenshikov's hand closed on Yuste's shoulder.

'There'll be no more magic,' he said. 'This thing stops here.'

And Yuda spoke. 'You'd better listen to the man, Magus; he's come a long way to see you fail.'

As Sarl swung round at the sound of the shaman's voice, Semyon fell back against the table; he dropped the knife, which shattered into pieces on the ground. That did not matter; with the instrument of the magic broken, no one would be able to undo the spell.

'Devils and demons!' said Sarl. 'I saw you die. He cut out your heart.' He lunged towards the edge of the circle, but the spell spun out and coiled round him, encircling him with blue flame. It moved from the top of his head down to his feet, so that he stood at the centre of a ring of fire. Semyon drew a symbol in the air, muttering charms of warding and protection. The magic had broken out of his control, and he did not know what it was going to do. It might serve merely to pin Sarl within the circle, or it might have other, unexpected consequences. He had released the ancient force that dwelt in blood.

'What is this?' shouted Sarl. 'What have you done? This is not the spell you promised me.'

The blue flames yawed and rippled as he tried to break through. Though he staggered back, the power that had raised him from the dead still animated him, and it was stronger than anything Semyon could muster. The Magus picked himself up.

'That, Mon Seigneur, is a spell of binding,' he said. 'Not a great spell, or one that requires much power. But I would advise you not to cross the circle.'

'You have cheated me!' roared Sarl. 'I will take your heart and burn it before your face.'

He lunged once more at the edge of the circle, and the spell of binding strained and bulged. Semyon saw the white smoke seeping round the edges of the bulge, trying to get in at Sarl. The Heir recoiled, throwing up his hands to shield his face.

'Curse you, Magus,' he said. 'What have you done?'

'It is not what I have done,' said the Magus. 'I bound the circle with the shaman's blood. It has brought forth forces which are – inimical to you. But they cannot enter the circle. Inside it, you are safe.'

'I cannot stand within the circle for ever . . .'

Semyon found himself looking at the little shaman. Vasilyevich had come, leaning on his son and daughter; whatever the People had done to him, he could not walk unaided.

'You used my blood to make this spell?' he said.

Semyon nodded. 'I did,' he said. 'And I think we would be wise to leave. Blood, like iron, is an ancient and unstable magic.'

The balding man interrupted him. 'Wait,' he said. 'What's with the we? We shall be going, and the prisoners – but you'll be staying here, Mister Wizard. You can find your own way home.'

Before Semyon could reply, Sarl cried out like a

wounded animal. 'You cannot leave me here to wither away, and die . . .'

Planchet stepped forward. 'I shall stay here with you, Mon Seigneur. You will not be alone.'

'Planchet!' said Cluny. 'That would be madness. You cannot free my brother from the circle; if you stay here, you will starve.'

'Messire Cluny,' said Planchet, 'I have served you long, and it has been good service. But I am a servant of the House of Ademar. I could not walk on this earth knowing that I had left its last son to die like a dog. That's a terrible fate, for a man to die alone; almost as bad as cutting out his heart.'

'Then I shall stay with you,' Cluny began, but Malchik stopped him.

'Not you, Cluny,' he said. 'Let Planchet do as he wants. You always swore he was more of a friend than a servant. Set him free.'

Semyon started. He found that Sarl had moved round the inside of the circle and was standing very close to him. 'Magus, I beg you,' he said in a low voice. 'Forgive my threats. If you let me go, I will see you handsomely rewarded. The Staryetz himself could not offer you such wealth.'

Semyon looked at him through the thin and insubstantial-seeming veil of flame. 'There is nothing I can do,' he said. 'And even if I could set you free, you would still be fated to die. I lack the power that would raise you up and make you an immortal. I drained all the power from my captive world when I made the spell to bring us back here.'

'What do you mean?' said Sarl.

'The Magus is right, Zhan Sarl,' said Vasilyevich. 'He drained the last of its power from that world – and its people. He did his best for you – or his worst. As I know to my cost.' He stretched out his hand. 'Give me the crystal, Semyon Magus.'

Semyon had laid the false heart in a silver chalice on the table. As he glanced towards it, he saw that it had resumed its true shape, a lump of clear and flawless stone. He picked it up and handed it to the little shaman, who weighed it in his palm. 'The heart of a whole world,' he said. 'Did you ever wonder, Magus, what would happen when you used it for your magic?' He looked at Sarl and held up the crystal where he could see it. 'Nothing but a lump of rock,' he said. 'I could pity you, Zhan Sarl, until I think what you were planning to do. Not just my life, and the souls of my *kinder*, but thousands of lives – all to be used up in your service. When you die, that will be the end of it. The end of your father's great plan, the limit of the darkness.' He lowered his hand. 'You could do worse than return to your hell.'

'I beg you, take me with you,' Semyon said to him. 'Wherever you are going, whatever demands you make. There is nothing left for me here.'

The shaman weighed the crystal in his palm. 'I thought this was your mountain, Magus,' he said.

Sarl laughed. 'He fears me still,' he said. 'Even when he has bound me to a living death.'

The small woman who had threatened Semyon slipped between him and the bald man. She touched the shaman's arm, and they smiled at each other. Only when they stood so close did Semyon see the likeness between them.

'We must let the Magus come, Yuda,' she said. 'He saved your life. And maybe other lives as well.'

As she spoke, an oily smoke began to brew up from the edge of the chalk circle. Sarl shrank back as it swirled up to the ceiling, its darkness shot with sparks.

'No more talk,' said Semyon. 'I have unleashed something I cannot curb. If you are going, leave now, and take me with you.'

It was as if Sarl were standing in a glass beaker, within which an alchemical reaction was beginning. Already, he was almost hidden behind the dirty smoke; Semyon could see him writhing and struggling as it coiled around him.

'Planchet,' said Cluny, 'for the last time; I ask you as a friend not a master, do not stay here to die. I think my brother is beyond your help.'

An inhuman scream echoed his words. Semyon ran for the opening, and the others followed him. The boy, who was the tallest, reached up and swung himself up through the gap. The bald man lifted the little woman by the waist and passed her up to him; it was Semyon himself who helped Huldis to raise Vasilyevich high enough for the others to catch hold of him. Her smile was enough reward for the Magus. In spite of his fear, he made himself wait, letting the dark girl clamber up him as if he were a ladder. Huldis sprang up, light and lithe, and caught the edge of the sharp rock. She turned and offered him her hand, her fair hair falling about her face.

'Are you coming?' said Semyon to the other men, and Sarl screamed again. There was nothing to be seen but a column of glistening black, veined with lightning. Suddenly, the two men were running towards them. He was much relieved that the old man-at-arms made him take the next turn, and hefted him on his shoulders so that he could clamber out on to the summit of the mountain.

It took him a few seconds to work out how they were planning to escape. He saw the ropes dangling from the sky, and glanced up to see a strange craft that puffed steam like a dragon hovering above. Those who were fit enough could climb; the others wound the ropes about them and were hauled up like bundles of wool. The bald man and the small woman shared a rope; Huldis and Semyon managed to secure Vasilyevich to another, and the rest made good their escape as best they could. One by one, they rose into the sky, and Semyon was never more glad to lift his feet from solid ground. He spun dizzyingly, hauling himself up hand over hand towards the flying ship Beneath him, he could hear the mountain itself creaking like a floe of ice; smoke was pouring from the hole in the roof.

He clambered over the side and flung himself down on the deck. He was alone; the others were helping those who remained. Semyon took a few gasps of breath, and made himself stagger back to the side. As soon as everyone was aboard, the captain made haste to sail away, and with a roar of grinding iron, the craft began to forge its way westwards, drawing away from the summit of the mountain. As Semyon watched, the smoke grew to a plume like the flow from the mouth of a volcano; and a few moments later, the top of the mountain blew apart. He saw the shards of glassy stone flying outwards, enveloped in dust and smoke; but as the sound of the explosion reached him, the fragments imploded, rushing back into a void that had appeared where the summit had been. There was a light like the sun, blinding white and close, and the mountain's head vanished, leaving only a stump of broken stone that mouldered, sending up a haze into the sky. And he could hear the silence.

Epilogue

The *Arabian Bird* flew westwards, dawdling toward
the sunset. Annat stood in the prow, letting th
wind blow back her hair. Letting it blow the darknes
and confinement from her thoughts. She could no
believe it was over; Sarl was gone, and with his passing
she knew that the Doyen and his army would fall bac
from their triumph, retreating into the forest from
which they had emerged.

She was not the only one taking her ease. Yuste an
Boris Grebenshikov were sitting huddled together wit
their backs to the engine, lost in the outward silenc
of *sprechen*. Yuda was lying on the deck, where the
had managed to spread blankets and cushions to mak
him comfortable, but Huldis had insisted that h
should rest his head on her lap. The Magus was dee
in talk with the captain of the dirigible, who seeme
to be enjoying the curiosity of his new acquaintanc
And she had left Malchik with Cluny, who was tryin

to console Planchet; the old soldier showed a silent, stoical grief, but he was the only one.

Annat turned to watch them. It was growing cold as the sun set – wonderful cold! With sudden energy, she strode across the deck and squatted down beside her father. He looked up at her; the blanket was drawn up to his chin and his long nose jutted above it.

'What a hell of a way to die,' he said suddenly, and they both laughed. When Annat looked up, she found her aunt standing beside her.

'What are you laughing at?' said Yuste.

'Nah. Nothing,' said Yuda. He grinned at his sister. 'I hope you're planning to spend the summer pushing me round Masalyar in a bath chair.'

'No, Yuda, I am planning to be married,' she said, tartly. 'Boris Andreyevich has offered to make me a partner in his firm. And his wife.'

'*Mazel Tov!*' said Yuda. 'I'll have to find another victim.'

Yuste sat down beside him, and he reached out to take her hand.

'I don't see you in a bath chair,' she said. 'You'll be walking before the summer's out.'

'I'll be walking on crutches,' he said. 'But it could have been worse.'

The four of them sat without speaking for a while, though their thoughts nudged together like boats moored in a harbour. Then Annat said suddenly, 'Do you think Madame Mireille will take me back, *Tante*?'

'Zyon, child! How should I know? My head is still spinning, what with Malchik babbling about apostasy

and countesses. I should think you will return to find
yourself a hero. Or a heroine. Thanks to you, Masalya
has escaped an unspeakable fate. Let Madame Mireill
sing for her supper!'

'Where shall I go?' said Huldis.

Yuste looked up at her, and smiled. 'You will b
welcome in at least two homes,' she said. 'Until Bori
and I have set up our establishment, you can stay with
Annat and myself at the *Shkola*. And you can stud
where she studies, though quite what school will accep
her is uncertain. I suppose Malchik will want to retur
to his university – and his countess – but Yuda wil
be spending the summer in Masalyar for once. N
doubt he will be only too happy should you wish t
push his bath chair!'

Poor Huldis blushed, and Annat gave her aunt
little shove. 'What?' said Yuste.

Yuda said nothing, but he reached up with his fre
hand, and Huldis took it.

'This is the life,' he said. 'Surrounded by adorin
women. I think I might retire. Live by the sea an
write my memoirs.' He grimaced. 'Zyon, what a ho
rible thought!'

'Don't flatter yourself, Yudeleh,' said Yuste. 'Th
Railway will find something for you to do. Take it eas
while you can. One can only enjoy being an invali
for so long. I know I was bored long before I was we
enough to do as I pleased.'

'I'll bet you were bored two minutes after you cam
round from the operation,' said Yuda. 'Well, you ca
make up for that now. Do all the things I can

"Grebenshikov and Vasilyevich." He'll have to widen the door to fit you both on.'

Somebody cleared his throat. Everyone looked up to see Cluny standing nearby, his hands behind his back. He looked very formal and awkward. Annat stood up before anyone could say anything. He returned her smile with a worried look.

'Go, go,' said Yuste, waving her hand. 'We have lots of time. Hours before we reach Dieulevaut.'

Side by side, Cluny and Annat wandered back towards the prow of the ship. The sun had set, but the western sky still showed a glow of orange, shading upwards into lemon and watery green. They leaned on the side and stared ahead, not looking at each other.

'Malchik seems much happier now he's confessed,' said Cluny after a while.

'Perhaps he is lucky. He chose the right time.'

'How do you feel – about that?'

Annat looked at him sidelong. 'I could never do it,' she said. 'I am a Wanderer. But mother was a Doxan. I think Malchik . . . I just hope he is happy. With his countess.' She giggled.

Cluny reached out to stroke her hair away from the nape of her neck. 'There's no one left,' he said. 'I'm illegitimate, and my father will die without an heir. Casildis will become Lady of Ademar, but that is the end of our line.'

'Are you sorry?' said Annat, turning to look at him.

'I don't know. Planchet . . . Planchet is heartbroken. Ademar was his life. But he knows as well as I do what Sarl was.'

'Don't let's talk about Sarl,' said Annat. 'He's gone. Finished.'

'I'm glad it was over quickly,' said Cluny, lowering his head.

'Will you go back to college?'

'Oh yes! I'm not returning to the chateau. Not ever. I couldn't, after my father massacred those Roma. So I expect I'll be coming to Masalyar during the vacation.'

'I hope you will come to see me,' said Annat in a rush.

'I should like that,' said Cluny. 'We won't have much time together once we reach Dieulevaut. I mean alone together.' He gave a rueful smile. 'We're not really alone now. I'm sure I can feel Yuste's eyes boring into my back.'

Annat laughed. 'She looks out for me,' she said. 'It's like that with shamans, especially kin. We look out for each other.'

Cluny turned, leaning his back against the prow. 'I'll always be envious of that,' he said. 'The way you can talk to each other without saying a word.'

Annat nodded. 'It's good,' she said. 'But Yuda never has shaman lovers. Unless Huldis . . .'

'That's a remarkable possibility,' said Cluny, raising his eyebrows. 'Though it's plain that she adores him. But what about you?'

'Me?'

'Would you avoid shaman . . . lovers?'

Annat shook her head. 'I don't know,' she said. 'Maybe. It's too soon to lay down rules.' She thought of Eugenie and sighed. She was beginning to see why her father's life had become . . . complicated. Cluny put his hand on her shoulder.

'You're right,' he said. 'We can talk about it later.'

As he bent his head to kiss her, they did not see a solitary bird flying across the vivid, fading sky. It might have been a crow.

WANDERERS AND ISLANDERS
Legends of the Land: Book 1

Steve Cockayne

In the secluded house, an invisible presence watches over Victor Lazarus as he carries out the instructions of an unknown benefactor . . .

In the village, Rusty Brown encounters a strange girl who tells him a secret that will haunt his dreams and lure him to the dark underworld of the city . . .

In the city, Leonardo Pegasus tinkers with the Multiple Empathy Engine – a bizarre contraption of his own invention that enables the user to see the whole world without going anywhere . . .

An old man, a young boy and a magician. Three tales beautifully interwine to create a wonderfully original novel of magic and mystery, of secret pasts and forbidden futures – of wanderers and islanders.

Wanderers and Islanders marks the arrival of a major new British fantasy writer.

'Startlingly original' *Starburst*

'A compelling read' *SFX*

'Intricate, important and moving' China Mieville

SHADOW

Book One of The Scavenger Trilogy

K.J. Parker

A man wakes in the wilderness, amid scattered corpses and inquisitive crows. He has no memory of who he is or how he came to be there. The only clues to his former existence lie in his apparent skill with a sword and the fragmented dreams that permeate his sleep.

Alone in a hostile world he moves from village to village, masquerading as a god to obtain food and shelter. But the shadow of his past pursues him relentlessly. It whispers to him a riddle far more complex than he could ever have imagined – and a truth he may not wish to believe.

Praise for K.J. Parker

'Assured, intelligent, compelling . . . This is exactly what the fantasy genre needs' *SFX*

'Action-packed adventure . . . An intriguing tale of magic, manipulation and revenge' *Starburst*

Orbit titles available by post:

☐ Children of the Shaman	Jessica Rydill	£7.99
☐ The Glass Mountain	Jessica Rydill	£6.99
☐ Wanderers and Islanders	Steve Cockayne	£9.99
☐ Shadow	K.J. Parker	£6.99
☐ Pattern	K.J. Parker	£10.99

The prices shown above are correct at time of going to press. However the publishers reserve the right to increase prices on covers from these previously advertised, without further notice.

ORBIT BOOKS

Cash Sales Department, P.O. Box 11, Falmouth, Cornwall, TR10 9EN
Tel: +44 (0) 1326 569777, Fax: +44 (0) 1326 569555
Email: books@barni.avel.co.uk.

POST AND PACKING:

Payments can be made as follows: cheque, postal order (payable to Orbit Books) or by credit cards. Do not send cash or currency.

U.K. Orders under £10   £1.50
U.K. Orders over £10   **FREE OF CHARGE**
E.E.C. & Overseas   25% of order value

Name (Block Letters) _____

Address _____

_____

Post/zip code:_____

☐ Please keep me in touch with future Orbit publications

☐ I enclose my remittance £_____

☐ I wish to pay Visa/Access/Mastercard/Eurocard

Card Expiry Da

| | | | | | | | | | | | | | | | | |

| | | | |